BLOOD AND SAND

First published by Rogue Sonobe May 2025

Book design by Rhys Cutts

ISBN 978-1-7635317-2-7

1 – Ender

Here I was, once again floating through space in a ship cobbled together from parts from all over the multiverse. I remembered the day fifteen years ago when I hailed the U.E.S. Cronus. The disbelief in the comms officer's voice made me laugh, especially when Colonel Summanus joined the connection. His voice betrayed bewilderment, but just barely. It was the first time I had heard any emotion sneak through his stone demeanour.

The entourage in the docking bay was enormous, larger than I was expecting, with Erwin and Colonel Summanus standing at the forefront, both of their eyes fixed on the baby in my arms the moment I appeared, as was everyone else's as soon as she opened her eyes and peeked her head around, her purple orbs drawing everyone in.

The days that followed were strange, full of secrecy and agreements and the inherent problems of trying to take care of a newborn on a military vessel without her mother. How I missed her mother. Every cry and every sleepless night reminded me of Nadira's absence, a void that could never be filled. I often found myself staring at Alira, wondering how different life would have been if Nadira were still with us.

Luckily, Alira was born stronger than most babies, especially for being technically four months premature. It let me believe that Nadira was still here protecting her even now, if not with her hands, then with her lifeforce, allowing Alira to survive on the sub-par baby formula cooked up in a collaboration between the chefs and one of the chemical engineers. They were certainly interesting times.

Eventually, we made it back to Earth on the condition that I surrender my ship for study, to be returned once it had been properly examined and replicated to the best of the military scientists' abilities. I would be compensated, of course. It was all pretty quiet once we were on our way back to Earth until I ended up on my parents' doorstep, where I found them staring at me in shock, watching my military escort drive away. Hailey instead burst right out of the door and scooped Alira up out of my arms. Alira immediately giggled, further shocking my parents as they refixed their gaze on her while Hailey spun her around in the air.

Our conversation that evening lasted well into the night, with me trying to explain everything as best I could. My parents didn't seem to believe me, wondering if I'd even gone to space at all. The only possible reason that they could think of for me having a child already was that I'd secretly stayed on Earth and managed to get a girl pregnant. Hailey, on the other hand, excitedly listened to everything I said, her eyes flicking back to Alira every time she stirred as she slept.

Eventually, with the help of the military and a decent payout from being lost in space for five months, I managed to buy a place out in the countryside. It wasn't massive, just a few acres, but it was large and isolated enough to live a nice quiet life. I hadn't imagined myself settling down so soon. I was only twenty, after all. But I guess fatherhood changes your priorities, no matter what stage of life you're at.

Hailey came with us to the countryside, having grown quite attached to Alira during our stay with our parents and not being able to afford to move out yet. She was in many ways like a mother to Alira, at least for a little bit. Soon enough she found a nice man in town near our new place, and only a few years later, she moved out down the road and had her own children. Her capacity to love all of them, as well as Alira whenever she could get her hands on her, was what I most admired about her.

Raising a child in the countryside was nice, especially after living in the city for most of my life, then in space, and then at the edge of an alien desert that vibrated too much. But even with the trees, the nearby creek, and the giggles that burst from Alira whenever the neighbour's goats escaped from their yard and chased her around ours, it was rather lonely at times, and no one on Earth could relate to what we'd been through. I tried my best to always seem happy for Alira's sake, but I knew she could always tell something was missing, or that she could tell I knew there was something missing. It was hard to tell if she really knew what to feel, having never met Nadira, her mother, or experienced what life was like in her universe.

As Alira grew older, I could see the restlessness building in her. Her innocent questions transformed into complex ones that I often struggled to answer. Sometimes, she would say something with a tone and cadence too similar to Nadira's, and the look in my eyes would betray me. She would storm away, leaving me uncertain whether her anger was directed at me or the mother she never got to meet. If it weren't for the heterogeneous alien ship parked in our barn, I don't think she would have believed a word of it. Sometimes, I think she still didn't.

Fourteen years after our return to Earth, I received a call from a number with twenty-three digits. I didn't know what to think at first—it seemed impossible. But as I stared at the number on my epicode, hope and curiosity got the better of me. I picked up, expecting nothing, but hoping for everything. The voice on the other end was crackly, but I could tell it was female. The call ended abruptly, taking my hope with it, but I couldn't stop thinking about that call.

A week later, driven by curiosity, I taught myself how to trace a call. It took much longer than I expected, especially with such a long number, but I managed to get a signal. It traced back to the cobbled-together alien ship. That was enough. It had to have been Cybele.

A month later, I received another call. This time the audio was clearer—not perfect, but enough for me to confirm it was Cybele. She sounded older, but then again, so was I. She hadn't said much, only that the connection was unstable, being across universes and all, but she left me with a plea for help and a date and time. All I had to do was be inside the ship and in space at the right moment, and it would return. I didn't get a reason from her for why this was happening now, after all this time, but I knew it was serious. The call might have been somewhat vague and crackly, but the fear in Cybele voice was unmistakable. That she had made to the effort to call me fifteen years after we had last spoken and from an entirely different universe was also not a good sign. There was no doubt that she and many others had tried everything before deciding to contact me. I was likely a last-ditch attempt to solve a problem that was far beyond me.

That afternoon, I had a lot to think about. Alira came home from school to find me staring absently from my armchair, recognising my mood and retreating to her room. Would going back even solve anything? Life here was rough and lonely, but it was safe and peaceful. We had no idea what we would be walking into if we returned to that place. I took a deep breath, filling my lungs with the cool breeze drifting in through the window, carrying the scents of the countryside. I felt a sudden wave of nostalgia for the planet where pockets of atmosphere hung in the air, each with its own distinct smell and feel, some more dangerous than others. I sighed. As much as I knew the dangers of that place, the memories I had made there were more vivid than many from the last fourteen years spent hiding in our little corner of the Earth. Those memories, though filled with peril, were also filled with a sense of purpose and connection that I had longed for ever since. The thought of returning to that place, of giving Alira the chance to experience it, filled me with a mix of excitement and trepidation. It would be a mistake to deprive Alira of that part of her heritage—of the life her mother had lived, of the place where she was born, of the magic that had made her possible. Maybe we would go. Both of us. Maybe it would be what we both needed. And who knows, maybe in the process, we'd save the city again.

Cybele didn't have time to explain what was happening, but she sounded tired, and it was clearly beyond her capabilities to fix. Yes, we would go. Alira and I in a ship on our way back to the place where she was born, the planet that vibrated, full of magic. It was then I realised I had never told Alira about her alexandrite magic. I knew she had it—she had used it as a baby when Cybele and I were sneaking to the command room of the world-ship—but magic didn't work on Earth, so I had never felt it important to mention it to her, especially if there was no chance she would ever get to use it. But now there was a chance, and it was approaching quickly. I had just a few months left before the date Cybele had given me. Just enough time to break the news to Alira, to tell Hailey, to figure out how to get fuel for the ship to make it into space, and to buy equipment, clothes, maybe weapons. There was so much I was unsure about. How much had changed in the city since I had left? Was it still as dangerous as before? Would I have to train Alira in some weapons combat, just in case? There was so much unknown about this trip, but at least I had time to prepare properly, and all of it just in time for Alira's fifteenth birthday.

2 – Alira

This was ridiculous. I had wanted a new phone for my birthday, not a trip to space chasing an imaginary planet that my mother was supposedly from. Dad always talked about this place, but it wasn't on any of the maps of the galaxy. He couldn't even be bothered to come up with a name for the planet, or the solar system, or the city, even. He was a lazy liar, and this was a new low. I was starting to think he was losing it a bit, spending the last few months thinking too hard, daydreaming a little too much. He had even started teaching me to fight. I protested at first, but after dislocating the knee of a boy at school who was making fun of my eyes, I started enjoying our lessons, liking the feeling of being able to stop people from talking crap for once. Dad had had stern words with me about that incident, saying that wasn't why he was teaching me, and that it was only to be used for self-defence. I was defending myself though. I just defended myself from a verbal assault with a physical reaction. He hadn't liked that rebuttal, but he had continued teaching me anyway, saying that I might need it someday. I was happy to play into his delusions if it meant I got to get home from school, pick up a long stick, and try to whack him with it for a few hours. It was cathartic. Even more so when I started landing hits on him too. But that's all besides the point. I wanted a new phone, and instead, I was being dragged to space for no reason.

"Dad, do you really expect to find anything up here? You didn't even pack enough supplies for us to make it as far as Mars. What makes you think we're going to 'cross the multiverse' in a few minutes?" I said, sarcastically motioning air quotes. Dad just sighed.

"I know you don't believe me, but it's all true, and we'll be there any minute now. If you could stop whining about it until then, that would be great."

I rolled my eyes at him and crossed my arms, staring out the window, watching the moon ahead of us get larger as we sped away from the last layer of the Earth's atmosphere. My gaze wandered along the frame of the cockpit window and around to the walls of the ship. I suppose this ship was pretty alien. Even HITNE, the ridiculously named 'Hypernova Inter-Terrestrial Navy of Earth' couldn't figure out this ship. And then there were my eyes. They certainly weren't very natural, at least not on Earth. But I was otherwise completely human.

They were bright, sure, but that didn't mean my mother was an alien or something. Especially not one from a whole other universe. A voice crackled through the ship's audio systems—a woman's voice, "Ender….I..ready…time delay…thirty minu….now.."

Dad went to say something back, reaching for the comms system, but the edge of the ship started to glow a soft golden colour. He froze, as did I, and leant back in his seat.

"Buckle up, kiddo. Universe hopping isn't the smoothest way to travel."

I watched Dad close his eyes and lean back into his seat, gripping his armrest, his expression unreadable. I didn't know what to think now. Was this seriously happening? The gold was growing brighter now, the edges of the ship seemingly on fire, but the gold flames looked more like the sun's corona during a solar eclipse than typical flames. What was going on? My breath quickened, and I found myself gripping the straps that were holding me in my seat. Dad's words as we sailed through the sky on our way out of Earth's atmosphere floated through my mind then, reminding me to relax, and I did for a brief moment, but that was before the gold flames burst out into full-on celestial kraken tentacles and whipped themselves through the space around us so fast I couldn't keep track of them.

I could hear my heartbeat in my ears now, the thudding not doing much to calm me as we got swallowed by a celestial beast made of solar fire and some sort of semi-transparent mirrors? What were those? I thought for a moment I saw my own reflection in one of them as it hovered outside the window, a version of myself staring at me with equal horror through the cockpit windows, but the violent rattle of the ship and the sudden collapsing of the long tendrils around us blurred my vision, and I soon passed out.

When I woke, the first thing I saw was Dad crouching in front of my seat, searching me worriedly for injuries.

"Dad? Where… What happened?"

He smiled, seeing that I was okay and awake. Before he spoke, I felt a pain in both my palms, drawing in a sharp breath through my teeth. I raised my hands to look at my palms, finding two red lines cut across them, presumably from the straps that had held me to my seat. The straps now had red stains on them, right where my hands had been as I gripped them while we hopped universes. Holy crap. Were we here? I suddenly forgot about my hands and looked around, not seeing much but the ship, or at least the remains of it. It appeared that we didn't have a particularly soft landing.

"Did we crash?" I asked, my voice shaky.

"Not exactly a crash, more of a rough landing," Dad said, trying to sound reassuring. Beyond the shattered cockpit window, all I could see was sand and dirt—a strange landscape given how they were put together. The two refused to mix, and instead blotched the landscape with their hard borders and randomized patterns.

A woman stood just outside the ship, her arms crossed, watching us through a cracked window. I looked back to Dad, who was smiling now as he undid the straps of my seat and helped me up.

"Are we… are we really there… at that place you described?" His smile widened as he helped me up.

"We sure are."

He turned his focus to the woman outside and guided me towards the door of the ship, which miraculously still opened. After a couple of steps, I shrugged him off, content to walk on my own. I reached the door first, my attention drawn to the sky the moment I stepped out. It was like a canvas—a beautiful collection of watercolour-like blotches filling the sky, slowly shifting like clouds would, but they hardly looked like clouds. I squinted harder, wondering what made the sky look like it was wriggling.

"Whoa, this is so weird," I muttered under my breath.

A voice rang out, snapping my attention back to the woman before us. Her curly red hair and the red gemstone around her neck seemed to glow somehow.

"Ender! You wrecked my ship! After everything I've done for you."

Dad responded to the woman, "Cybele, I'm pretty sure you were the one driving, or at the very least, I wasn't."

"Exactly. My job was just to get you here. You could have at least tried to land it in one piece." She glanced back to the ship behind us. "Or maybe just fewer pieces."

Dad grinned at her, and the woman grinned back. Her attention then turned to me.

"Alira, this is Cybele. She's the one who built this ship that got us home." Dad said in a way that made me unsure whether he was talking about when he escaped this planet the first time or returning to it now.

"Ah, Alira. I had always wondered what your name would be. Alira. Yes, I think it suits you, and it honours you mother."

Dad smiled softly at her mention of my mother. I watched him closely, not sure what to think of this woman. I had heard plenty about her from Dad's stories, but not as the kind of woman that made Dad smile like this. This was weird, but I guess this stranger really did know my mother at least. We really were in another universe. On the planet where I was born.

Dad nudged me then, and I found him looking at me with a smirk, realising that I had been staring at a patch of sand, lost in thought, much like he had been often for the last few months. I looked back up at the woman. Her outfit was cute, a similar design to a brown suit, but with something akin to lace replacing the tie and parts of the vest. Her shoes, however, were thick and clunky and sand-coloured, not at all matching the rest of her outfit. It was then that I remembered what Dad had said about the desert here—that it vibrated—and I realised I could feel my teeth chattering. I looked back at Dad with a concerned look on my face, but Cybele spoke before he could open his mouth.

"Right then. We should get back to the city. The vibrations might be getting weaker, but without pearl water you'll still need a nice long rest to recover if we stay out here too long. Come on."

She waved us after her, turning to walk up a dune. I saw Dad frowning after her, confused by something Cybele had said, but his expression softened as he turned back to me. His eyes caught on my cut hands again, and the frown returned, but softer.

"Just a moment, Cybele," he called out after her. She stopped, but said nothing, waiting patiently halfway up the sand dune. Dad smiled back at me and pulled out a roll of gauze from his coat.

"There's no way you just had that on you. You've never just carried gauze around. No one does. Except maybe some doctors."

He smiled. "You're right, but this planet is dangerous and I wanted to be prepared. And believe it or not, I did the exact same thing when I first crashed here, cutting my hands open like you did. Luckily, yours aren't as bad."

His soft smile turned once again into a frown. "And I also healed them straight away with pearl water, but it sounds like that might not be an option anymore."

Dad stood there lost in thought, his brow furrowed as he wrapped my hands. I turned my attention back to the desert and its patchwork of earthy tones. It almost looked like the fur of our neighbour's calico cat, but with dull greys and the occasional deep earthy red thrown in. What a strange place this was. And that was before Dad finished wrapping my hands and we made our way to the top of the dune with Cybele, providing me with a view of the fabled city Dad talked so much about.

3 – Ender

What did Cybele mean when she said she didn't have pearl water? Was it harder to get now? Or was it gone altogether? A horrible thought crossed my mind then, and I wondered if Cybele's machine, the one Jezebel had used for the genocide of multiple gems, had somehow been rebuilt or reactivated and been used to wipe out the pearls. No, surely not. That would either mean Cybele had let its existence be known to the wrong kind of people, or she hadn't destroyed it at all, but kept it, and someone had found it. No, I trusted Cybele to destroy it, and I would continue to believe she had until I was proven otherwise. Something else must have been going on, maybe something connected to the dune's vibrations getting weaker? I didn't think that was possible, but this world always had a way of surprising me.

I watched Alira walking ahead of me towards the city, staring in awe at the sands and the sky and the city ahead. Maybe it was a mistake to bring her. Was she ready for the dangers ahead of us? Was I ready to face them again, this time with my daughter by my side? The weight of my decision pressed heavily on my shoulders as I followed her, my mind racing with questions and doubts. Without healing magic, this place was so much more dangerous than I had previously thought, and I didn't even know what the real danger was—the reason Cybele had brought us here, what she was so afraid of that, after fifteen years, she had potentially risked her life, sneaking down to the command room and somehow gotten us back here. How she managed it without the tail-key, I wasn't sure, but she must've found a way, and there must be a reason. She had a lot of explaining to do. For now, however, I just had to get Alira to the relative safety of the city.

She looked back at me then, her eyes wide and beaming brighter than they ever had on Earth, and I couldn't help but smile. No, it wasn't a mistake to bring her. She needed to see this place; part of her only made sense here, and we both knew it, even if she didn't believe me until she was standing here staring out across the dunes herself. I wouldn't have believed me either. I'm surprised Hailey ever did.

We continued towards the city, Alira occasionally asking Cybele questions—most of which were things I had already told her about the city and magic—but I suppose it made sense she'd want to hear it from someone who was from here. All her life, all she'd known about this place were things I had told her, and she hadn't believed most of it until a few minutes ago. At least not for the last few years. When she was little, she believed all my stories, and we would reenact some of my adventures here, her favourite being when Nadira and I defeated the evil diamond witch, though our play version always had a happier ending. Alira knew the truth of it now, and I was beginning to wonder when her questions to Cybele would turn to Nadira, but to my surprise, they didn't. At least not before we reached the edge of the city and she stopped asking questions altogether.

We both looked up at the sandstone buildings lining the streets, many of which sparkled subtly in different colours, their bricks a mixture of sand and metal—some sparkling a dull copper colour, others silver, and a surprising number of gold, which upon closer inspection, must have been brass.

"What part of the city are we in? I don't remember so many of the buildings having different metal aggregates," I asked of Cybele.

"We're on the south side of West-Tail, heading east towards the museum," she responded. She looked back at me and smirked, but faltered just enough for it to appear almost apologetic as she continued, "Which I'm sure you're familiar with at least."

"All too familiar," I replied, understanding her expression then as the image of her scalpel hovering millimetres away from my eye flashed through my mind. The memory sent a shiver down my spine, but I quickly pushed it aside. This place was brimming with magic and adventure, but also peril and death. I needed to stay focused for Alira's sake.

It was strange that Cybele and I were almost friends now. How that happened, I had no idea. We continued winding our way through the collection of sparkly buildings, getting taller the closer we got to the inner city. Alira and I both absently followed Cybele, our eyes washing over the buildings as they rose higher. We turned right once we had gotten close enough to the inner city to see the wall that surrounded it. The archway through the wall caught my attention, and I stopped, squinting at the six guards standing in the middle of the archway, blocking the entrance. It was then, when I saw the guards, that I realised how empty the streets had been on our way through the city. I knew the city probably hadn't recovered from Jezebel yet—the population devastation would take time—but the streets were even quieter than that. There were even fewer people here, or they were all hiding indoors for some reason. But why? What was everyone afraid of? And why was the inner city being guarded? Cybele had called me here for a reason, and I was starting to worry that whatever it was, it was worse than I thought. It didn't seem like the best time to bring it up, though, and the look Cybele gave me as she turned around to see me stopped, looking at the guards, told me all I needed to know.

I continued following her without a word, Alira noticing the strange interaction and frowning at us. She didn't move once I started following them again.

"What was that all about? Why are you two being weird?"

"It's nothing, Ali. A lot has changed since I was here last. Just keep following Cybele. You're gonna love her museum." I smiled back at her, but she didn't seem convinced, raising her eyebrows at me.

"Uh huh, sure."

She spun back around and continued the way we were going. I caught a hint of a smile on Cybele's face as she quickly turned back and continued towards the museum. I sighed as I followed them. Everything here was weird now, but maybe that was just me. Maybe it all just felt weird without Nadira, or even Araysh and Ava. Now I was back here years later with my daughter and Cybele of all people. Of course it was going to be weird. I chuckled to myself as we went. I had the feeling this whole trip was about to get even stranger.

The buildings started getting smaller as we moved away from the inner city, and it wasn't long before we found ourselves in a square, the museum taking up almost all of the northern side on our left. It looked exactly how it had before, completely unchanged from my memories. Except for the guards on the front steps. And not inner city guards or cathedral guards, but regular-looking people with simple armour and bladed poles. I frowned, Cybele's face a mix of pain and excitement, reflecting my concerned look and Alira's awe.

"Whoa, that's the museum? Why does it look so normal? It's like a regular looking Earth building but with gold dragons climbing up it." Alira squinted at the museum façade. "Wait, no. What are those things?"

Upon hearing the question, Cybele's face immediately lit up.

"Well, my dear, those are Chryacal. Ancient creatures that are believed to be the first inhabitants of this world. Deadly things with scales, claws, horns, and an exceptionally dangerous bladed tail. But they've been gone for thousands of years, so I wouldn't worry about running into one."

Alira stared at the golden creatures in thought, muttering, "Bladed tail…" She spun around and locked eyes with me briefly, before they moved to the long scar across my scalp where my hair now parted.

"No way, that's the thing that gave you that scar on your head?" She turned back to Cybele. "Didn't you say they were all dead though?"

Alira remained staring at Cybele, looking to her for answers. I absently ran my hand over the scar, having almost forgotten the encounter. Of all the scars I had accumulated here, that was the one that stuck around, having permanently disrupted my hairline. The three across my face from Jezebel had faded eventually after a decade or so. They could probably still be seen if you looked close enough, but I wasn't one to stare at myself too closely in the mirror. Cybele looked at me for a moment, having not known how I had my hair violently parted. I smiled back awkwardly, and it clicked in her mind, understanding before I could offer an explanation.

"Ah yes, they are my dear, but as I'm sure you're aware, there are many different kinds of magic here. Why don't I show you mine? I think it might explain what happened to your father, although, you'll have to ask him for the details."

Alira stared at Cybele admiringly, her eyes widening when Cybele closed her eyes for a moment and the red beryl around her neck pulsed, glowing brighter for a moment. When Cybele opened her eyes again, we all turned to watch the commotion now unfolding at the entrance to the museum as one of the golden chryacal began to move, pulling its claws out of the stone and leaping down from the column it had been previously forced to climb indefinitely. It landed much like a cat, its golden body slowly taking on colour, the red sheen of its scales the first to be visible as it started sprinting towards us. Alira stared at it, paralysed, it having locked eyes with her, its bladed tail hovering above it like a scorpion's, the blade pointed directly at her. Instinctually, I dove in front of Alira and raised my arms to shield myself from the beast, paternal instincts fighting the trauma from the last time I fought one of these. As the beast bounded forward, I wondered if this was the end, if Cybele would kill me after all. It wasn't the first time she'd tried. Maybe she blamed me for whatever was happening to this city, and this was her revenge. Of course she blamed me for the destruction of the city. It wasn't the first time she had, and she was right both times. That's if whatever was going on had something to do with the world ship and the regenerative anti-matter engine that we'd stopped from regenerating.

The closer the Chryacal got, the less room I had for any thoughts other than its teeth and claws. Staring down the point of its tail, I found my knees weak, but that didn't matter when I was kneeling, Alira crouching behind me horrified. Suddenly, the beast slammed its hind legs into the ground, sliding across the dirt towards us. Cybele's laughter became audible as the sound of heavy metal sliding across hard dirt died down and the creature came to a stop, sitting down now, its tail waving about lazily like a cat's. Cybele continued laughing,

"I'm sorry, I didn't mean to scare you that badly. I thought you knew how my magic worked, Ender. It's still just a statue, and it's under my control."

I stared daggers back at her, more upset that she seemed to be forgetting that Alira didn't know how real or not it was than the fact she'd played a cruel trick on me. If it was just me, I might've even been amused. But it wasn't, and Alira was huddled behind me, terrified, staring at the Chryacal's tail as it waved a deadly weapon casually through the air. Cybele noticed my hard stare and then Alira's expression, guilt finally crossing her face.

"I'm truly sorry. I didn't think how it might affect her. I'm just a stranger to her, and this probably wasn't a great way to earn her trust." She paused, pensively. "Either of your trusts."

Alira stood up then, still watching the Chryacal, terror giving way to a growing fascination that eventually led her to approach the creature. I stared at her in shock, Cybele eyeing me with a smirk as Alira quickly became almost comfortable around the creature.

"I guess she's stronger than you thought," Cybele posited, watching my reaction to Alira and the Chryacal.

"That doesn't give you the right to test that strength," I replied angrily, not looking at her, but I could see her smirk pull back into a hard line. Alira, not paying any attention to us, spoke up, "It's still made of metal. It's all shiny still, but it's moving."
Cybele sighed. "Yes, since the magic started getting weaker, my magic isn't as realistic. I used to be able to bring those statues to life with perfect realism. But now, not so much. They move fine, but the base materials always seem to show through. When I make smaller objects look bigger, they almost look like ghosts now."

Cybele sighed again, and I turned away from Alira towards Cybele, seeing now the sweat on her forehead and the deeper breaths she was taking. The energy it had taken to bring that thing to life was immense, and it had taken its toll on her. It was much more energy than I would've been able to use with my borrowed magic; I knew that much.

My magic. It had been so long I had almost forgotten I had it. Even after I packed and wore the strap with the hidden compartment containing a few gemstones that I could use the magic of. It was close to empty now, but I still had the obsidian necklace and had remembered to wear it today. I cursed myself under my breath. I was out of practice. I had tried to shield Alira from the Chryacal with my own fleshy arms, rather than remembering to tap into knife magic with my epicode. Cybele waved her hand and the Chryacal stood up, startling Alira who stepped back cautiously but then walked alongside the beast as we made our way to the museum's entrance. The two guards there were a little on edge but appeared much more accustomed to Cybele's displays of magic than the other few people hanging around the entrance, one of whom was passed out face-down in the dirt.

As soon as we were close enough, Cybele called out to the guards, "Can one of you please go get Cordelia? We've got visitors, and you've both just left this woman here passed out on the ground for the last five minutes. What do you think you're doing just leaving her there like that?"

She spoke sternly towards the guards, who seemed uncertain about their priorities. One of them spoke quickly, eager to escape Cybele's judgment, "I'll go get Cordelia, Ma'am."

As he hurried off, the other guard watched him slip inside, shooting him a look of betrayal before turning back to Cybele, who stared him down, waiting for an answer.

"We, um. You said to guard the entrance, and not to move for any reason… Ma'am."

"Yes, to protect those that live inside. Does this look like protecting people to you?" Cybele responded impatiently as she pointed to the woman still on the ground, missing the irony as she also failed to help the woman. Alira was quick to act, rolling the woman over and brushing the dirt from her face. I froze when Alira looked up at me from beside the woman. Her bright green eyes, filled with compassion and concern, reminded me so much of Nadira. She was so much like her mother, and sometimes the reminder was painful. Yet, the pain was worth every moment, seeing the incredible woman she was becoming.

A few moments later, a woman emerged with the guard that had gone to get Cordelia. Cordelia was an older woman, perhaps in her late fifties or early sixties, and wore a surprisingly fancy dress, for this part of the city at least, adorned with a collection of vibrant yellow stones. Seeing her made me suddenly wonder how old Cybele was. She was definitely older than me, but she didn't look a day older than the last time I saw her fifteen years ago. I suppose her magic did lend itself perfectly to looking however you like.

As Cordelia emerged from the museum, Alira looked over to her, catching her gaze and holding it. Alira frowned, and Cordelia stared back at her in surprise. Neither I nor Alira seemed to understand why, but the smirk Cybele was failing to hide told me that she certainly did. Cordelia seemed to mutter something under her breath before glancing at Cybele. Her face became unreadable as she composed herself.

"You must be Nadira's daughter. My name is Cordelia." She held out her hand to Alira, having composed herself, but her eyes betrayed the intensity with which she still regarded Alira. Alira stood up and shook her hand, frowning slightly and glancing at Cybele as she did so.

"Nice to meet you. I... didn't think anyone here would know me, let alone recognise me. Do I really look that much like her?"

Cordelia smiled warmly. "You have my daughter's eyes, and from what Cybele tells me, you have her magic too."

I froze, staring at the pair of them. Alira's eyes went wide as she saw Cordelia with new eyes. I had wondered about Nadira's mother in the months leading up to our journey here, but I figured finding her would be near impossible; I didn't even know anything about her. Yet here she was with Cybele, apparently. Alira stuttered,

"You're my… grandmother."

"Yes, I'm Nadira's mother, your grandmother." Cordelia glanced down slightly at Alira's neck, squinting. Her smile widened slightly.

"I see you've inherited her necklace as well as her eyes. I'm glad it found its way to you."

Alira reached up to the collar of her shirt and pulled out the silver necklace from underneath it, exposing the dark green princess-cut gemstone with deep purple corners and the silver four-pointed stars that were dispersed along the chain. She looked down at it pensively.

"Yeah, my dad gave it to me for my birthday one year. He said it was my mum's, and that it was super important."

"It is, It's one of a kind. Just like you."

Alira beamed up at Cordelia, her eyes going glassy, a little overwhelmed.

"May I ask when your father gave it to you?" Cordelia asked.

"I think it was my eleventh birthday."

Cordelia looked over at me then, finally acknowledging my presence. She spoke to Alira, still looking at me, "He has some good qualities then, if he remembered to do that much."

Alira looked at us both with a puzzled expression. I was confused at the subtle hostility towards me for a moment as well, but then I remembered why. Even though I had never met Cordelia, I had impacted her life in so many ways. I heard Alira whisper a soft, "Oh," as she looked away from us, back down at the woman on the ground. I had told Alira everything, incrementally of course. Telling your daughter you were forced to kill her grandfather wasn't exactly part of the first iteration of that story, but eventually, I told her. Cordelia seemed to know as well, although how that was possible I wasn't sure. My guess was that Cybele had put it together, seeing the portraits in the halls of the world-ship.

Startling everyone, the massive golden Chryacal leapt up into the air, sinking its claws back into the divots in the marble. The red sheen of its scales disappeared, and its tail slowed until it was once again just a decorative weapon adorning the museum's façade. Everyone turned to Cybele, whose face was red from the effort, and she looked particularly on edge.

"As much as I hate to interrupt the family reunion, we really should get inside, and help that poor woman up."

Alira immediately directed her attention to the woman again, bending down and sliding her arms under her top half. To my surprise, Cordelia knelt down and picked up the woman's legs with ease. She was stronger than I expected. As she knelt, I noticed the little tears in her dress, the sturdy boots she wore, and the leather pants beneath, with multiple knives strapped to them. The dress was clearly nothing more than a formal relic of a lifestyle that was no longer viable for her. Whatever was happening in this city was forcing even the upper gems to live like rebels, needing to protect themselves from whatever the danger was. I could no longer avoid asking about it. If it could scare the wife of a parliamentarian—a gem presumably right up there with her husband's sapphire—into living in a museum carrying multiple hidden knives, then it had to be bad. The more I saw, the more afraid I became. I had to know. I couldn't let my mind wander anymore about it. I knew the cruel things this city was capable of, and this was clearly much worse than any of them. As we stepped inside and the guards closed the door behind us, my flood of questions finally burst out,

"Okay Cybele, what's going on? Why did you go to all the effort of contacting me from across the multiverse? I can't imagine the danger you must have put yourself in to get back down to the command room, especially after what we did the last time we were there. The more I see, the more worried I become. Magic is getting weaker, the inner city is blocked off, there's no one on the streets, and a grandmother from the inner city has to carry hidden knives around with her. Just what is going on?"

Everyone was staring at me now. Cybele took a deep breath, and Cordelia uncomfortably adjusted her dress, not enjoying me having seen her knife collection. Cybele, with a sorrowful look, began her story.

"Well, nothing happened overnight, of course. But since the day you left, and we turned off the planet's ability to regenerate its energy, it's slowly been running out. The ambient energy from the anti-matter engine manifests as magic, so as the energy runs down, the magic gets weaker. That much I'm sure you'd figured out."

She took another deep breath. "Furthermore, the... mass murder of a few select gem types completely eradicated their magics all at once, for the most part. Shadow magic seems to have re-established itself somehow. Regardless, this eradication pushed everything out of balance. I've been trying to properly understand it, but it's more complex than I anticipated. Put simply, however, when some magics were eradicated, other new magics appeared, like the energy moved from one to the other. It wasn't that straightforward, though. There was a bit more shuffling about, which is why there's no more pearl magic. It just disappeared when the magic rearranged itself. The new magics that manifested, however, turned out to be useful in their own ways. Most of them, anyway. This, of course, started changing the way the city worked. Suddenly, those who lost their magic couldn't make a living, and others suddenly had abilities they didn't know what to do with. Many turned to the church for guidance, but after the death of two high priestesses within days of each other, the new high priestess, Brigitte, took it as a sign from Varanasi that the high priestesses shouldn't have so much power anymore. When she found the broken pieces of the tail-key, she decided to give them to the city instead, making a speech about how the world was changing and that we had been blessed with new magic. She presented these pieces to the public, and three people stepped forward to accept them, each with new magic, and each restless to reforge their life with its potential. These three were: Teth, an indicolite who now had air magic; Navoi, a tiger's eye who now had sand magic; and Akeldama, a painite who now had blood magic—"

For some reason, a little bell rang in the back of my mind. Somehow, I knew Cybele was going to say blood magic the moment she mentioned painite, like the two already had a connection in my mind. But why?

"—These three each took a piece and left the city, travelling out into the dunes along the still ridges. Each of them built a settlement of their own and have been growing them ever since. This, however, meant that even more people were leaving the city, to go live in these new settlements. Since most of these people were lower gems, or those with new magic, the majority of the working class left the city, leaving the rest of the city with very few resources, very few workers, and a broken leadership. And that was all before Akeldama returned to the city."

Holy shit. It really was much worse than I imagined. Every one of the city's problems was my fault. The fracturing of the church because I killed Jezebel, the lack of resources because I stopped the ships from crashing here, and the problematic redistribution of magic because I gave Cybele the idea for her genocide machine. I sighed; but that was all bound to happen. This was an old argument I had had with myself for years. This city was fragile when I arrived, and Cybele was threatening my life when I innocently gave her a synopsis of how I used magic. That was all. I could see now just how small my role was in the desolation of this city. I still couldn't help but feel terrible for that role, but it was clear that Cybele felt worse about it. She was the one who built the machine after all. Why she did in the first place I still didn't understand. I don't think I ever could. But here she was, still trying to make up for it, and she needed my help.

4 – Alira

I couldn't believe my grandmother was here. I knew she had to be on this planet somewhere, but she was right here in front of me, and she was beautiful. I hadn't met a single person from my mother's side of the family, not even my mother. I really wanted to ask her what her gem was. I recognised Cybele's red beryl, but Dad hadn't shown me any like what Cordelia was wearing. When I was younger, he'd taken me around to jewellery stores and rock shops and told me all about the different magics that were connected to which stones. He had shown me the topaz that he kept in that little compartment within the strap that he wore, but Cordelia's stones were much brighter and more elegant. I looked down at my own gemstone, the alexandrite in the silver necklace, my mum's necklace. I smiled. Cordelia had recognised it. It really was my mother's, and it was all I thought I had left of her. I looked up at Cordelia, who caught my eye and smiled briefly before turning back to Cybele as she spoke. Cybele was explaining everything that had changed in the last fifteen years, but since I didn't know what it was like before, I didn't really feel the need to listen too hard. When I looked over and saw the guilty expression on Dad's face, however, it made me wonder why, and I started listening more closely to her story.

It sounded like there wasn't just one city anymore but four. This city was kind of cool, but it was pretty empty aside from the museum. I wondered what these new cities would look like. I tried to imagine what a city made using only air magic would look like, but you couldn't really build with air, so instead, I found myself thinking about the girls' trip that Auntie Hailey and I went on to Chicago that one time, to the 'Windy City.' I stopped trying to imagine the different cities once I tried to imagine what the one founded by blood magic users would look like and freaked myself out. I didn't know what it would really look like, but it wasn't on my list to find out. Whatever blood magic entailed, it sounded freaky.

Cybele finished speaking, snapping me out of my daydreams, and I saw Dad then, staring into space, as white as a ghost. I wasn't sure what he was thinking about, but clearly, Cybele's description of events wasn't sitting well with him. I walked over, watching him carefully, raising my hand up slowly to hold his, "Dad?"

He snapped out of it, looking down at me with a smile,

"I'm okay Ali, a lot has changed is all."

Cordelia jumped in unexpectedly then, seeing the gauze wrapped around my palm as I reached for Dad's hand.

"Oh, my dear, why didn't you tell me you were injured? I can fix that right up for you."

Cordelia gently but firmly took my wrist and unwrapped the gauze, before drawing my palm closer to her face to inspect.

"Um, I thought only pearls had healing magic, and didn't Cybele just say they couldn't use their magic anymore?"

Cordelia smiled knowingly, "There's a lot more to this world than your father knows. He was only here for a few months. I'm not explicitly a healer, more like a surgeon. Do you know how the abilities of sapphires work?"

"Yeah, that's the one that lets people see the inner workings of machines, and sometimes change them, making them work differently or something."

"Yes, something like that. Well I, my dear Alira, am a yellow sapphire. My magic is very similar but instead of being able to see inside machines, I can see inside people."

I raised my eyebrows at her, "That kind of sounds a bit creepy. Can you like, read my mind?"

Cordelia laughed. "Goodness no. The mind is much too complex, but the rest of the body, let's just say I can see broken ribs, and can help your blood to flow to where it needs to go. Here, let me show you."

She looked closer at my palm, drawing it closer to her face. She pressed her forefinger into one side of my palm, and her thumb into the other half, the cut on my palm between her fingers. For a moment, nothing happened, but slowly I noticed little pink lines starting to bridge the gap from one side of the cut on my palm to the other. When she let my hand go, I examined the pink lines, seeing that they were skin—my skin—acting like natural sutures across the cut. My hand was still cut, but at least it was less likely to split open and bleed more now.

"Now that I've drawn more platelets to your palm, it should heal faster now too." She was amazing.

"Thank you so much."

"Of course, dear."

I unbound and flipped over my other palm. "Could you maybe…"

Cordelia chuckled, seeing the identical cut across my other palm. "Of course I can."

After that was all done, I looked back up to Dad, who looked like he was mentally preparing himself for the answers to more questions he knew he had to ask. I stayed standing by him, taking his hand and nodding to him. He smiled at me graciously in the way that he does that makes me slightly uncomfortable. Not uncomfortable per se, but he looked at me like I was his whole world, and that was a lot of pressure. I was just a girl.
But I stayed holding his hand and looked back at Cybele, wondering what devastating answers Dad was preparing to hear.

"So this Akeldama," He started, "He's come back to the city from the blood magic settlement he went out to form with his piece of the tail-key, and now he's a problem?"

"Yes, he returned right before I made contact with you. I had started tinkering with the technology to do so years beforehand, but his return really made me put my head down and make it work. Ever since then, he's been going back and forth, making appearances in the city of various natures, none of them good."

"Like what?"

Cybele and Cordelia glanced at one another, Cordelia seeming to sense what Cybele was thinking and wasn't too happy about it.

These two had a funny relationship. I couldn't quite figure it out, but it was intriguing. Cybele unexpectedly walked over to a spot on the floor, further into the museum. Now that we had moved out of the doorway, I noticed the museum was pretty empty for somewhere that was supposed to have lots of things on display. Most of the main room was full of small beds and some tables with people all milling about. More like a shelter than a museum.

Cybele had moved to stand in a circle on the design of the flooring and turned to face the entryway, looking up above the doors at the string of various gemstones embedded in the stone there. The sun was shining through the red one slightly to the right of the centre, lighting Cybele's face up, her face now matching her curly red hair and glowing gemstones. She turned back to us.

"Perfect timing. For us at least, less so for Akeldama's soon-to-be victims. If we leave now, we'll get there right on time."

"Where are we going? Do I need to be prepared to fight this guy?" Ender asked.

"No, we're just going to go see his latest…performance. I believe you're familiar with how the arenas work here, Ender?"

"He's fighting in the arena? I thought that thing wasn't used anymore. Why the hell is it back in business? Was this his doing?"

"No, no, it's not the same arena that you visited. It's the newer one. Arena events were still being held every month while you were here, but with the city close to ruin and a growing number of people both starving and starving for entertainment, the arena fights have become much more frequent and outlandish. Akeldama likes to show off his power in the arena to try and convince people to join him, preaching his nonsense while murdering people left and right.

The way he uses magic is…hard to explain. It's why I think you need to see it for yourself."

"I see. Well, sounds like we should go then."

It was hard to know what Dad was thinking when he was overwhelmed. His emotions just seemed to bypass him when there were too many to feel. He was clearly afraid for what this all meant, and I was too, less so because of what Cybele had said, but because Dad wasn't easy to scare, and the fact that he was so thoroughly concerned now was terrifying. I squeezed his hand, and he looked down at me, smiling, but I could tell his mind was elsewhere, his eyes still blank and faraway.

Cybele led the way out of the museum, immediately turning left and travelling east. Halfway through our journey, we passed by a bridge over a river on our right, and I saw Dad smile. He started telling me a story about Mum and him when they first met, and the arena they had gone to to try out different kinds of magic. He seemed hesitant to finish the story, and I had heard it before, so I knew why, especially with Cybele walking right in front of us. But the story had reminded me of something I had been meaning to ask him about since Cybele brought the Chryacal to life.

"Hey Dad?"

"Yeah, Ali?"

"You've always said you had magic here, but I haven't seen you use it yet. And it seems like people only get to use one type of magic. Are you sure you can really use multiple?"

He didn't reply but smiled, before his eyes started moving unpredictably, indicating that he was looking at something on his epicode. I was kind of jealous that I didn't have an epicode. They were so much more convenient than all the other kinds of wearable devices available that kids had to use before they were eighteen when they could legally start getting implants.

Dad's epicode was a military installation though, so it had tons more features than the regular ones. All I had was my old phone, which was basically just a fancy bracelet and an earpiece that was technically removable, but you didn't have to take it out, so no one ever did. Dad could see whatever he wanted right in his eye. I had to hold my arm up and poke at the screen my bracelet projected. It was so much more work. Honestly, though, this trip was already way cooler than a new phone. When Dad was done, he looked at me again, but nothing seemed different.

"How's this?" he asked before he held up his fist, then quickly opened it. His whole hand was on fire! I jumped back, letting go of his other hand and staring at the flames.

"How are you…you're okay? That doesn't burn you?"

"Not as long as I have my garnet activated," he said with a smirk. I let out a big sigh, feeling my heartbeat slow down again. Why was everyone so into scaring me with their magic today? Except for Cordelia, of course; her magic had been a nice surprise.

"So what else can you do?"

"Pretty much any kind of magic that's connected to a strong enough gem. Although some are harder to master than others. Fire magic is pretty straight forward, but things like dream magic and what Cybele does, are much harder to figure out."

"Do you think other people could do it too if they had your tech?"

"I mean, it's possible, but when I was fused with your mother, it seemed to make her nauseous whenever I used different kinds of magic. But then again, that could've just been you making her sick."

"Hey, I wasn't even a full baby yet."

He smiled playfully. "I know. My working theory, though, is that it's harder for your body to adapt to different magics if you're born connected to the same kind of magic continuously. Because I hadn't used any kind of magic, it let me use a little bit of all of them, instead of a lot of one kind."

"So you'd get sick if you tried to use too much of one magic?"

"Well, no. I can only use as much magic as the gemstone connected to it is strong, so when I use too much magic, the gemstone explodes. That's why I have to be careful how far I push when I'm wearing the gemstone I'm connected to, so I don't blow myself up."

I pulled back from him again, remembering roughly how many different stones he had on him. He chuckled. "Don't worry, I know my limits, and I have enough experience now to know when a new gem might be reaching its limit."

He gave me a look then, thinking, and I frowned back at him, wondering what he was thinking about.

"It's entirely possible you'd be able to do the same. Your body hasn't been aligned fully to only one magic yet, so you could probably handle the energy. We'd just have to ask Cybele to sort out the technology."

My eyes lit up. "So I'm getting an epicode like you?"

He laughed at me. "No, Ali, you won't need one. Your bracelet should have close to the right specs; it just might need some tinkering done."

I smirked at him. "So I am getting a new phone after all."

He scoffed, a smile betraying him, his eyes wandering casually until he saw the massive wall ahead of us, his stare drawing my attention to the wall too. The wall ahead of us was twice as tall as the one that separated the inner and outer city, the very wall which stopped halfway up the side of the massive building.

"So uh what's that all about?" Dad asked, looking to Cybele for answers.

"The arena was built on the wall so that both sides could participate, which used to mean the upper gems spectated and the lower gems competed, but today it's a bit less divided. I've even seen a few sapphires from parliament enter just for the thrill of it, but even they avoid going up against Akeldama."

"I see," Dad responded absently. He sighed, and we entered under the series of archways at the base of the outer wall. Beyond it was an inner wall and a staircase wedged between the two that led up towards the stands, following the slight curve of the two walls as it ascended.

We soon saw over the top of the inner wall, the crowds packing the stands, the noise suddenly roaring to life unexpectedly. Either this place had impossibly precise acoustics or some sort of magic sound bubble enveloped the arena. Maybe if they took the bubble down, the rest of the city wouldn't sound so abandoned.

We continued up the stone steps to the second landing, where it was a bit quieter. Cybele led the way out into the stands, our party getting a few strange stares, particularly myself. Dad had told me not to wear my running shoes, that the neon pink and yellow would stand out too much, but all the shoes he suggested were ugly boots and only ever in boring colours like brown or beige. Now I was starting to think I should've listened. Plus, if we were going to be doing this much walking every day, these shoes would wear out in no time, and I got the feeling there wasn't any equivalent to cars here.

5 – Ender

Even if we were all here to watch a bloodbath for whatever sick reason people enjoyed those sorts of things, it was nice to know the city wasn't completely empty. Everyone would just rather be watching people murder each other. I'm so glad I risked my life and got Nadira killed to end the instant genocides, just so the city could take matters into their own hands and start killing each other anyway. I tried to stay calm, but this place was making it hard. I can't believe I ever blamed myself for this. Clearly, mass murder wasn't a problem here, just a bit of entertainment or 'purification' or whatever.

There was currently a team of three on the arena floor, up against another team of three. One team had two with strength magic, and their third was an obsidian. I peered closer. Maybe this would at least be an opportunity to learn some techniques. Maybe there were things I hadn't figured out yet just from my own experimentation with magic. Alira seemed to be frowning at me, raising her eyebrows as she saw how intensely I was watching the fighters. I smiled at her. "Trust me, I'm far from enjoying myself. I'm just watching their technique. You should too; it might help you." She looked skeptical, but I think she was faking it. It was hard to tell with teenagers.

She shrugged. "If you say so."

The fight was over no more than five minutes later, with two of the three fighters still standing and the third lying on the ground with severe burns. Between the duo of garnets attacking him and the surprise flame trap hidden in one of the arena tiles, I couldn't tell what had got him. Before the two remaining gladiators had finished dragging their fallen teammate from the arena floor, a figure emerged from the far end of the arena, the crowd roaring the moment he raised both his arms to them.

I stared around wide-eyed at the crowd, still unbelieving, before focusing on the man at the centre of their attention. He was muscular, I could see that much from this distance, his sleeveless tunic chosen likely for the sole reason of showing off his arms. The details of his face were hard to see from this distance, but he had long black hair, tied back in a bun, and a matching black beard. He looked battle-hardened, but his tunic was loose and flowy around the legs, like he merely wished to show off his muscles but wasn't about to use them. He was too comfortable for a man who had just entered a deathmatch.

I looked to Cybele to gauge her reaction to his entrance, but she appeared more resigned than anything else, and Cordelia simply looked at him with disdain.

Soon enough the fighters started pouring in, four of them in total, each with a different gem type. There was a topaz, an onyx, an aquamarine, and a blue gem that I couldn't recognise from this distance, even with my epicode's zoom.

The topaz attacked first, rushing towards Akeldama with impressive speed. He avoided all three obstacles that were sprung upon him by the arena from the tiles he activated as he sprinted over them. One of the obstacles looked like a little hot spring, which seemed to prompt both the aquamarine and the onyx to move.

The water in the hot spring started to rise, to float, freezing rapidly as it did so. But the topaz had reached Akeldama before the water had taken shape, Akeldama dodging his blow easily, but unexpectedly hopping up onto the man's back as his momentum kept him going. He slowed down just enough as he realised that he had missed to get caught in the next obstacle, stone walls rising out of the ground instantly, just barely blocking a spread of three icicles that had been launched in their direction by the aquamarine.

The onyx was standing at the edge of the hot spring now, using the rippling shadows that his person cast on the water to create some sort of twisted mess of darkness. I hadn't seen shadow magic used before, but it didn't look easy to master.

The aquamarine went to prepare another strike, drawing more water out of the hot spring, but Akeldama emerged from the stone box then, hopping over it as easily as one would skip down the street. Was this blood magic? It looked extraordinarily similar to strength magic. Wait. The icicles flew again, Akeldama ducking like he was spring-loaded and bouncing right back up and towards the aquamarine.

The remains of the hot spring smashed into both Akeldama and the aquamarine as he tried to defend himself with the water magic, being a little too slow for Akeldama as the next moment he was hanging by his ankle from Akeldama's wrist. They were right by the hot spring now, close enough for the shadow magic to reach them. The shadows lashed out in quick flicks as they receded from the exposure to sunlight.

Akeldama then threw the pale-looking aquamarine by the ankle right at the onyx, hitting him square in the chest, grinning as he flexed his fingers, his hand purple now, chunks of ice rolling around on the arena floor loosely matching the way he moved his fingers. What! That's impossible. Surely he can't.

The fourth opponent finally decided to make her move, launching herself into the air, spreading her arms wide to reveal light blue fabric stretched between her arms and her torso, reminding me a little of a wingsuit. She stuck her arms right back to her sides a moment later, going stiff as she dove back towards the ground straight at Akeldama, the air seeming to swirl around her as she did so.

I couldn't tell if it was purposeful or not, but at the very last second before she reached the man staring straight up at her, she bailed off to the side, spinning rapidly but somehow managing to land gracefully. Now this was some magic I was keen to learn. This must be the air magic that Cybele was talking about, meaning that her blue gem must be indicolite.

The spinning air that was twisting around the woman as she dove didn't bail like she did. The air had picked up enough speed to hit Akeldama much like a miniature tornado, lifting him off the ground and sending him flying, his abnormal strength unable to help him while sailing through the air. He landed hard on a tile much closer to where we were sitting, letting me have a closer look at him. This man would not stop grinning, no matter how hard he was thrown. The look on his face was anything but a sane one.

The tile activated as Akeldama rose from the ground, not a scratch on him, both of his hands curiously purple. The tile, it turned out, summoned a large creature the size of a horse. Despite its overall shape, the alien creature was far from a horse, with much tougher-looking skin that stretched over its bones like canvas. The creature's face was almost hollow, its sunken eyes invisible, making them look like shadowy pits embedded in its skull. It did, however, still have four legs, making its shape remain somewhat horse-like, even though what should have been a tail was instead a fifth leg that wobbled as if it couldn't decide which side of its body to stand on.

Regardless, the creature was relatively tame, appearing like it was supposed to be beneficial to whoever activated it, like a horse would be for a knight. Instead of attempting to ride the creature, Akeldama simply raised his hand to its thick neck as if to pet it. But at his touch, the creature withered, its legs crumpling to the ground and every soft part of it shrinking until only a layer of hide stretched over its bones remained.

I stared at them in horror as the water inside the creature left it through its mouth, the stream slowly crystallising into a long-handled battle-axe. I was starting to understand why Cybele was so afraid of this man. He could steal magic and turn creatures, and presumably people, into corpses, taking only what he needed from them to use as his own weapons.

The air magic woman now looked terrified, frantically stepping on an adjacent tile in the hope of finding something useful. Instead, a spike shot up, impaling her foot. Akeldama walked over to her slowly, enjoying his victory before he had even won. Most of the tiles were empty as he strode towards her, but the ones that weren't he just swatted away with his oversized ice axe, never taking his eyes off the indicolite woman bleeding out on the ground.

Thunder rumbled then, and I suddenly remembered that we were in the desert and that thunder was out of place here. I glanced upward, finding a single large cloud growing darker, hovering directly above the arena. I didn't have time to question it, however, as a booming voice rang out, sounding just like thunder but in what I was hearing as English, "Stop this madness! I can no longer sit idly by and watch these massacres take place. The Fovan Church may be weaker now, but us diamonds are not!"

The cloud grew heavier, dark enough for the lightning crackling within it to illuminate it in stark contrast. A bolt of lightning shot down at the ground, gone in the next second, but leaving behind a figure draped in all white, and a series of black scorch marks seared into the tiles all around her. Akeldama remained unfazed. He held out his ice axe in one hand, pointing it at her lazily. "So, a diamond has finally come to play, finally come down from her pedestal to try and stop me. Too bad you won't have any luck."

He grinned wickedly at the diamond now glaring at him from across the arena floor. She stared daggers back at him, furious. "You will die today."

He chuckled and adopted a fighting stance. The diamond lit up suddenly, a flash of lightning striking her position once again.

This time, when my eyes re-adjusted, I found her flying through the air towards Akeldama, palms outstretched and crackling with electrical energy. For once, Akeldama had a challenge on his hands;

his reflexes were fast, but not faster than lightning. He managed to redirect a few blows with his axe, which slowly melted the more it got hit, and he took a few direct hits himself, his apparent strength magic keeping him upright.

How his body was able to channel two different magics and withstand so much lightning was beyond me. Unfortunately for the diamond priestess, Akeldama was cunning, and rather than counter-attacking, he bided his time, waiting for an opening while she unleashed bolt after bolt at him with blind fury.

Eventually, he found it. The cloud overhead had shrunk considerably, and the white, billowy fabric of the priestess was drenched in sweat and condensation, her clothes now weighing her down rather than billowing around her. Akeldama threw the remains of his ice axe, now melted down into a short spear, just slightly to the left of the priestess's head.

She dodged to the right, as he expected, stepping just close enough to the stone walls that held the body of the topaz. By now, it was evening, and the sun had set low enough to hide just behind the edge of the arena, casting its shadow over most of the arena floor.

What happened next was difficult to determine. The shadows cast over the priestess and Akeldama seemed to darken, disguising them from view. It wasn't so dark, however, that I didn't notice the separate shadow that the stone box cast, seeming to solidify and bend up off the ground, sweeping the diamond up into a blocky cage with no discernible shape.

Then all went dark. Flashes of lightning arced out wildly, showing only glimpses of the struggle below, too fast to see anything but the outlines of the two figures left behind by the flashes of light. What was more revealing of the struggle was the desperate and unfocused nature of the electrical charges being fired, before they stopped altogether.

In the strange quiet of the arena, when no one made a noise and the frantic lightning had stopped, I slowly turned my head towards Alira. She stared back at me with a look of terror not dissimilar to my own. There were no words to say to her, and the whole arena seemed to feel the same way.

Lightning then, focused and strong, shot out from the ground up, continuous electrical energy pouring from the man hovering in the air at the centre of the arena, dancing strings of light the only things connecting him to the ground. His voice rang out like thunder. "This is our destiny. The time of the diamonds reigning over us is through. They have no power over us anymore. We have their power. I have their power. And when you join me, it can be yours too. We are the future. This decrepit city has kept us stagnant in our ways for too long. We have been blessed with new magic, and this is what it's for." He held up the limp body of the diamond priestess, still breathing, but shallowly, without the energy to lift her head. The next moment the light cut out, and they were gone, the cloud overhead slowly dissipating.

Some part of the crowd cheered, quite fervently. But the majority remained quiet, stunned. I frowned at the silence, understanding it initially, but the lingering of it felt different. I turned slowly to Cybele, revealing my frown to her, a shocked expression on her face, telling me this outing was much more than she had bargained for. She didn't look at me but knew I was staring, and she whispered so quietly I almost missed it,

"No one has ever killed a diamond before."

I frowned even deeper, knowing for a fact that that wasn't true. She looked at me then, realising who she was talking to and breaking out of the trance a little bit, "Well, not publicly, and not quite so spectacularly. I mean, killing Jezebel broke the church and started all this mess. I'd hate to see the change a diamond's death so public and so clearly a call to arms would bring. Akeldama just might finally get the support he's been vying for."

Cordelia rose suddenly then, and to my surprise, Alira copied her instantly. She spoke softly but sternly,

"We should go. I have the feeling we'll be needed sorely after this."

Cybele nodded absently, leading the way out of the stands.

The walk home was silent and dark, everyone on edge in the empty streets, especially after seeing shadow magic take down a diamond. How he managed it, I couldn't tell. I thought my use of multiple magics was cool. But this guy was something else. All he had to do was touch a person, and he could use their magic. Or maybe he had to kill them too? It was hard to tell. But what was crystal clear was that Akeldama was the biggest threat to this world, bigger than I'd imagined, and I didn't know what Cybele had planned, or why she'd brought me here, but there was no way in hell I was going to fight that guy. No fucking way.

6 – Alira

This place was not at all how Dad said it would be. He said it would be dangerous, but that guy? That guy was crazy. And that lightning magic was insanely powerful. When Dad described it, there were no clouds or flying or anything like that. After seeing that, I was starting to doubt Dad had actually killed a diamond like he said. I mean, that Akeldama guy had buttloads of lightning afterwards, and Dad said he couldn't even use lightning magic at all for whatever reason.

I had no idea what was going on, but the silent walk back to the museum totally freaked me out. Everyone was acting so weird now. No one said anything until we were back inside the museum, standing around awkwardly just inside the door again. Cordelia spoke first,

"I think we might have to change tactics soon. Defending this place might not be an option much longer. Perhaps moving away from the city is our best option, to one of the other settlements. The indicolite and tiger's eye camps."

Cybele sighed, her response almost a whisper, "Perhaps." She was looking pensively around the museum now, clearly not wanting to leave it.

Cordelia continued, "I know you don't want to leave this place, Cybele. The museum is here, and all of your research into the world ship, but it's not safe. This city wasn't designed for defence, and the enemy is already here."

Cybele sighed again, but Dad spoke up instead,

"I don't know much about these new settlements, but if they know the threat that Akeldama poses, then it's likely that has influenced how they went about designing their settlements, perhaps even caused them to form an alliance. I think Cordelia is right, this city certainly isn't prepared for a fight, but the others just might be."

"I know." Cybele responded quietly. But a thought popped into her head and she glanced at Dad's wrist, the one with the dark blue and purple tattoo around it. "Although you're wrong about one thing, Dels. I won't lose my research on the world-ship as long as Ender is here. In fact, I'll actually be able to go back much more easily."

Cordelia blushed slightly at the use of her nickname, and Dad frowned, before remembering his tattoo and holding it up to look at it like he was surprised to find it there.

"Oh yeah, I had almost forgotten this thing had a functional purpose. Although…I don't think I remember the gesture to activate it."

"That's alright. If I can get a closer look at it, I'll hopefully be able to replicate the teleporter signal it sends out."

Dad nodded in response, looking impressed. Thunder roared outside then, and a flash lit up the room through the windows. The terrified voice of one of the guards was audible through the door.

"H-halt. W-what's your business here... Ma'am?"

"I am here to see Cybele and Cordelia about the spectacle in the arena," her voice boomed. No wonder diamonds were in charge here—or at least used to be. It seemed like that was slowly changing.

Cordelia and Cybele both raised their eyebrows at one another, a smirk crossing Cybele's face as she quickly turned to open the door. She swung both large doors open at once, standing in the middle of them, directly across from the angry diamond crackling with energy outside.

"Hey Brigitte, long time no see." Cybele smiled across at the diamond crackling in the square. Brigitte's face softened when she saw us, her lightning dying down.

"May I come in?" she said, with no thunder this time. Cybele stepped backwards, swinging the door open a little wider. Brigitte silently entered.

"What do you know of the battle in the arena this afternoon?" she asked Cybele once the door had been closed.

"We were there." Cybele responded simply, matching Brigitte's sombre tone.

"Then you know what that vampire has done," she spat, looking angry again. She continued more calmly, "Except the diamond that he attacked isn't dead. She's alive, but weak, and kidnapped by Akeldama. I don't know what he wants with her, but I managed to track him leaving the city. I believe he's taking her back to Poenari. Please. Help me get her back. You're the only ones I trust to be able to pull this off."

Cordelia remained stoic through this encounter, but Cybele was uncharacteristically warm, promising Brigitte that they would get her back, especially now that Ender was here.

"So—" Brigitte started, "—You're the famous Ender I've heard so much about. You've caused me a great deal of trouble these past few years. I hope Cybele's faith in you isn't misplaced." She stared at him sternly. Dad seemed lost for words. She lifted her hand out elegantly to greet him, "I am Brigitte Tahtinen, High Priestess of the Fovan Church."

Dad's eyes went wide, but he still took her hand. "I'm Ender, and this is Alira, my daughter."

He gestured to me, making me blush as the beautiful High Priestess locked eyes with me, her countless diamonds gleaming brilliantly in the low light.

"Nice to meet you both," she said before turning her gaze away, back to Cybele. "The one Akeldama took was Mellory. She was my sister. So what's the plan?"

Wow, straight to business. The way this diamond changed emotions was impressive. As fast as lightning, one might say. Cybele thought for a moment.

"I have a rough idea, but without seeing where he's keeping her, there's only so much I can do. We'll have to improvise once we get there. But aside from that, I'm sick of standing around in the lobby. If you'll follow me, we can plan properly. I also have a gift for Ender that's somewhat crucial to my current plan."

Dad raised his eyebrows at this but said nothing.

Cybele led us to the back of the museum, turning left towards a small office built into the wall. Like the rest of the museum, it was elaborately furnished, but I could tell it wasn't what it once was. The corners of the room were piled with various items—mostly rations and clothes.

Cybele approached the bookshelf and reached for one of the books on it, pushing the spine further into the bookcase. The shelf clicked as she did this, a doorway-sized section of the bookcase suddenly going translucent. I stared at the semi-transparent books for a moment, still amazed by even the smallest acts of magic. I chuckled. Even if it was magic, how cliché it was to hide a room behind a bookshelf like this. Dad saw me smiling and chuckled himself.

"Don't worry, it's just as cliché here as it is on Earth. When your mother came looking for me here, she went straight to the bookshelf and started trying all the books to find the switch. It didn't take her very long."

I always loved hearing Dad talk about Mum. It never failed to make him happy, and I felt closer to her with every new story I heard.

We continued through the bookcase—it was solid again when I turned around to look at it after passing through. Dad had described this place like it was a dungeon, all dark and full of scrap metal and such, but it was actually quite nice. There were electric lights all along the walls and down the stairs, and even a nice big round wooden table and chairs in the room that Cybele led us into. Dad still looked unimpressed despite the renovations.

Everyone started taking seats at the table, starting with Cordelia. Cybele remained standing, walking over instead to a large cabinet-like toolbox and opening one of the smaller drawers. She pulled out a blue gemstone, lighter than a sapphire but not by too much.

"Here, Ender, it's an indicolite. It should be plenty strong enough for you to use."

Dad picked up the gemstone from the table, admiring it curiously. "Thanks." He frowned back at her then. "And how is this part of your plan?"

Cybele grinned. "Well, I'm sure you saw the indicolite woman in the arena. All we need now is to stitch some sails onto you, and you can glide right on over and scout out wherever Akeldama is hiding. Of course, getting the rest of us there will be a little more difficult, but I was thinking, if I managed to reverse-engineer the teleporter signal embedded in your parliamentarian tattoo, we might be able to teleport to you. Although that part is completely theoretical at this point."

Everyone considered this but didn't respond, not qualified to completely comprehend what Cybele was saying. Dad seemed to be considering it, being close to the only one who really understood his magic, and perhaps his magic tattoo.

"If it helps," Dad began, "I think it might be possible for Alira to harness magic in a similar way that I do. She doesn't have an epicode, but her bracelet uses similar, and more advanced, technology. Plus, it's connected to a little speaker stuck to the inside of her ear, which will help her to hear the frequencies of the stones. I thought you might be able to take a look, Cybele, and make some adjustments."

"Interesting. I think you may be right. Although, given the circumstances of Alira's birth, it's entirely likely that she'll be much more powerful than you even." She considered the possibilities some more. "Perhaps between the two of you, you might even be strong enough to transport the five of us there on the wind."

Brigitte cleared her throat. "I apologise, but I will not be joining you on this adventure. My position as High Priestess prevents me from taking such a risk, and leaving the city now would be a huge mistake on my part, much as I might want to go with you. I will assist as much as I can in any other way possible."

"The four of us, then. Even easier." The room fell silent, but Cybele carried on as if she didn't notice. "Well, it's not much of a plan, but it's a start until we know what we are dealing with. Cordelia, if you could show Ender somewhere where he can practise with air magic, I'll show Brigitte out through the teleporter; I'll have to unlock the access to the cathedral for her. Alira, when I'm back I'll take a look at your bracelet." Her eyes flashed with intense curiosity. "I look forward to seeing how far Earth's technology has advanced in the last few years."

And with that, the meeting was apparently over, and despite all the tragedy and fear going around, I was ecstatic. I might be able to use air magic. That stuff was crazy. Everyone dreams of being able to fly, and soon I might just be able to. I heard what Cybele said. I mean, Dad's epicode is old, and my phone might not be a military-grade internal device, but it has all the bells and whistles of the base model at least. Dad wouldn't buy me the brand new model. But that didn't matter now; I was about to go flying.

I followed Dad and Cordelia further down the hall, entering a much larger room that didn't have the electric lighting like the rest of the compound did.

"Why doesn't this room have lights?" I asked Cordelia.

"Because, my dear, it's the training room, and things often get broken here with all the magic and spears flying around. We've had to move this room to a separate circuit after training exercises kept causing blackouts for the whole museum. It's broken at the moment, but I believe Ender should be able to fix it, if he remembers how to use the sapphire's magic, that is," Cordelia replied while looking expectantly at Dad.

"I suppose I do, but I don't have any, and yours are yellow, which are slightly different from what you've told me."

"While that's true, from what Cybele has explained to me—most of which goes over my head, especially at the speed she talks sometimes—you should still be able to connect to blue sapphire magic with a yellow sapphire if you make the right adjustments."

"What kind of adjustments?"

"Well, in terms of natural resonance, the sapphires are fundamentally the same. The nuance is in the harmonics, I believe. You'll find my sapphires if you start from the same note, but you'll have to shift the harmonies if you want to instead channel blue sapphire magic. Cybele did some maths to explain the exact sequences once, but I don't believe you'll need it—not that I understood that part anyway."

Dad frowned, determined, his eyes going blank and moving unexpectedly, indicating that he was doing something on his epicode. Cordelia and I both watched him in silence—her stoically and expectantly, and me trying to imitate her—but I was too excited and couldn't help but fiddle with the edge of my shirt, switching frequently from watching Dad to staring into the darkness of the training room, looking for its secrets.

After a few moments, Dad grinned, and the lights flicked on in the training room. I felt like I should be impressed with Dad then, but the training room was much more impressive. Besides, we had a few smart devices back at home, and Dad had his epicode connected to all of them, so it wasn't like him turning the lights on with his mind was anything new. I guess advanced technology really was indistinguishable from magic sometimes.

At least, that's what I thought before Dad turned the training room into a bizarre weather event, sending everything in the room spinning out of control and into the walls—including myself. This was not what I meant when I said I was excited to go flying. The second I let out a scream, the wind stopped, and I was falling to the floor rather than speeding toward the wall. Before I hit the ground, however, I was punched in the face by another gust of wind, sending me right back the way I came, still screaming as I hurtled through the air and crashed right into Dad. We both fell to the floor.

I was stunned for a moment but got up off Dad quickly and stared him down while he was still on the floor.

"What was that? You couldn't start with, like, a light breeze or something?" I glared at him, waiting for an answer, trying not to feel bad seeing the guilt and horror on his face. He seemed even more startled than I was. And I was the one screaming and being hurled through the air.

"I'm so sorry, Ali. I had no idea the magic would react like that. All magics are different, and this one works almost the opposite of the other elemental kinds of magic I've tried. It's like you have to put energy into restraining the wind rather than putting your energy into conjuring it. It's bizarre. Like as soon as you want wind, it's there all at once, and you have to focus on slowing it down rather than speeding it up. This one might take some practice."

I was still mad at him for throwing me at the wall, but he was still sitting on the ground, eyes wide is shock. I sighed.

"I'll owe you one, then. Once I get my magic, I'm going to blow you all the way across the desert to Poenari, just you watch."

He smiled, starting to stand. "I'd like to see you try."

Cybele emerged in the doorway then. "I see you got the lights working again. You figured out how to manipulate the harmonics to channel the different colour variations of gemstones then, I gather?"

"Something like that," Dad replied.

Cybele turned to me next. "Alira, are you ready for me to take a look at that bracelet of yours?"

"Oh, I am so ready," I replied eagerly, grinning so widely that the others couldn't help but smile alongside me.

7 – Ender

While Alira was with Cybele, I continued practising with air magic. The unusual feeling of it constantly threw me off, causing the items I picked up to inevitably be smashed against the wall. Despite my better judgment, after managing to just barely float a few objects in a small tornado and set them down again without breaking them, I tried using the air to float myself. It was risky, I know, but this mission was time-sensitive and depended on me, and maybe Alira, being able to fly across the desert. If I could at least figure out some sort of technique, it would make it easier and safer to teach Alira too.

My first attempt almost ended in a concussion. I had previously lifted smaller objects straight from the ground, but I was larger and more awkwardly shaped than them. When I applied the same technique, I managed to swipe my feet out from under myself, and instantly lost control. The wind went crazy and slammed me into the ground before dissipating. And I thought fire magic was dangerous, but at least with that, you had the benefit of being flame-proof. Being wind-proof wasn't really a thing, unfortunately. It had been two hours of me trying and failing to pick myself up and fly around the room with air magic when Cybele came to the door. I had to keep stopping when I felt the indicolite getting too hot in its storage spot across my chest, but it only took a minute to cool down. By the time Cybele came back, I had managed to hover for a few minutes, but moving in any direction always made me trip and lose control again.

"I've taken a look at Alira's bracelet, and you were right. With some software upgrades, it should easily be able to manipulate magic much like you do. I have most of the program ready to go, but I just have a few adjustments to make. It should be ready by the morning. I've set Alira up on a mattress in my office. You should get some rest too. I can set you up next to her, but it might be a squeeze. If not, there's a little bit of room just outside the office."

"Thanks, yeah, I should. This air magic has worn me out. And just outside the door should be fine. Alira might need her privacy. Who knows what she thinks about this place after seeing what we've seen today."

"It can't have been easy choosing to bring her here, knowing it was dangerous but not knowing yet what the danger was."

"Yes and no. I don't think it was ever an option that I would return here without her. I was afraid, sure, and rightfully so, but this place is half of Alira, half of her family, and she would never forgive me if I left her behind."

Cybele smiled. "You're probably right about that. Besides, Cordelia seems to like her. You, not so much."

I chuckled softly. "Can you blame her?"

"No, but she came around to trusting me of all people. I think you'll grow on her in time. I think she's already starting to see how good of a job you've done with Alira. How'd you manage that, by the way? Was there another woman perhaps? Or do heroics translate into parenting skills somehow?"

"Honestly, I don't know how she turned out so well. It was rough at times, but she's just so much like her mother that understanding her was easy enough most of the time. My sister was around a lot too—her auntie Hailey, who I'm sure had a huge impact. But no, there was no other woman. It's hard to see anyone else in that way when you've found and lost a soulmate who you've fused with. That feeling is impossible to find anywhere else."

Cybele nodded absently, and then I remembered something I had been meaning to ask her. "So, how did you and Cordelia meet? It can't have been a coincidence, surely."

She smiled, reminiscing. "No, not at all. I felt responsible for the events that went down with Jezebel, and I knew that I was the only one left who knew of Nadira's demise. So, I sought out her family to try and break the news to them. It wasn't too hard in the right circles, her being the only alexandrite around—or at least before you showed up. Eventually, I just knocked on her door and told her everything, half expecting her to have me imprisoned as I confessed all of my mistakes to her. But she was understanding. She didn't quite understand the machine or your part in its creation, but she knew her daughter well enough and saw something in me that I didn't see in myself at the time. After that, we became friends, and when the city started falling apart, we became even closer, working as a team to protect some of the people who stayed behind."

I smiled, noticing the way Cybele talked about Cordelia, raising my eyebrows at the flush in her cheeks. It was an unexpected attribute.

"I didn't realise you were close in that kind of way."

She shrugged. "I didn't either at first. We're not soulmates or anything, but I do love her." She looked like she was going to say more but decided not to. It was nice seeing Cybele this way. Strange, but nice.

"Right, well, I think I'm off to bed then. Where can I find myself a mattress?"

The next morning, I woke up on my thin mattress just outside of Cybele's office. I was starving. I had grabbed some rations before I found a mattress and set down for the night, but other than that, I hadn't eaten since I got here, and training yesterday was exhausting. I wearily sat up, blinking around the room. The hushed chatter of all the people camped out in the museum was a strange noise to wake up to after living in the countryside for so long.

My eyes easily found Cordelia in the crowd, her yellow sapphires sparkling in the morning sunlight, and Alira was sitting right across from her at a table, asking questions and shoveling down mouthfuls of bread as she listened to her answers. I got up slowly and walked over to the table where they sat. Alira said good morning through a mouthful of bread as I sat down. Cordelia turned to me,

"Would you like some tea? There is breakfast on the long table set up near the back of the museum as well."

She gestured to the silver teapot sitting by her on the table, the ornate object looking out of place amongst the earthenware and cobbled-together furnishings.

"Yes, please. I'm starving."

Cordelia nodded and started pouring me a cup. Alira finished her mouthful,

"I'm going to get seconds anyway. I'll grab you something, Dad."

"Okay, thanks, Ali."

Alira got up and made her way towards the back of the room. Cordelia pushed a cup of tea over to me. It was kind of awkward now that it was just the two of us. I took a sip of the tea, the flavour instantly recognisable. I grinned, which raised an eyebrow from Cordelia.

"I haven't had this kind of tea since the last time I was here. There's nothing like it on Earth. It's so strange but so good."

Cordelia nodded knowingly. "It's quite the staple in the limbs. Upper society likes to pretend it's beneath them, but all their best teas are just the same flavour with hints of various other things."

"What exactly is it? I've always wondered."

"It's a combination of catacomb-beetle honey and the kind of mushroom that they pollinate and make their honey from."

"Wait, hold on. Beetles make honey here? And they pollinate mushrooms? And why are they called catacomb-beetles? It doesn't sound like the kind of creatures whose honey I want to be drinking."

Cordelia chuckled. "No need to fret. They were named that because they were first found in underground catacombs. But any underground cave or space just below the surface will do. Too far down, though, and the walls are too hard for them to make their colonies."

"Huh, interesting." I stared down at my tea, unable to look at it the same again. It was still delicious though.

Alira plopped a big plate of food in front of me, snapping me back to reality. It was nothing fancy: bread, soup, and something that looked like jerky. I wasn't about to ask what it actually was, not after learning about how the tea was made.

"Thanks, Ali."

"No probs." She looked between us, frowning. "What happened while I was gone? What did you two talk about?" A laugh escaped me, confusing both Alira and Cordelia.

"Did you know this planet has beetles that make honey, Ali?"

She scrunched her nose. "Really? Gross."

Cordelia frowned. "What do you mean? Where does your honey come from?"

"Bees."

Cordelia's face remained blank.

"They're like beetles but they fly a lot more, pollinate flowers and such, and make their hives in trees."

"And a tree is?"

She had me there. How to explain a tree to someone who lived in a place that only had the occasional really small plant? Alira jumped in then.

"It's like a giant mushroom. Like a huge one. More than twice as tall as a person. But they're made of wood, like Cybele's desk."

"Fascinating. I'd always wondered where that material came from. It's rare enough out here that it's considered a luxury material, but we still find enough of it to make furniture."

We sat in relative silence as I started on breakfast, and Alira devoured another plate. When I was nearly done, Cybele emerged from her office holding Alira's bracelet, her expression and dark eyebags telling me she'd stayed up all night trying to finish it. I was planning on saying something about it, but I didn't have to. As soon as Cordelia saw her, she immediately started berating her for her recklessness, saying how she wouldn't be fit to travel like this, not if she risked passing out halfway in the middle of the desert. Cybele's only response was a sheepish grin.

"But I did it. Alira should be able to channel air magic now with this. Then I can have a nap while she whisks me away across the dunes."

Cordelia was still cross with her. "Only *if* it works, that is. And that's a terrible amount of pressure to put on her. You saw how difficult it was for Ender to get the hang of yesterday, and he's used to magic. Alira isn't."

Cybele shrugged, clearly having no energy to fight. "I'm sure Ender picked up enough to be a decent teacher."

And with that, she sat down, taking the remains of the cup of tea in front of Cordelia for herself. I looked to Alira, her gaze fixed on the bracelet Cybele was still clutching, seemingly having forgotten about it. I chuckled. Alira was no doubt going crazy with anticipation, wondering what using magic for the first time would be like.

8 – Alira

She actually did it! All I could think about the moment I saw Cybele with my upgraded bracelet was what it would be like to fly, just like that girl in the arena yesterday. But OMG, that was only the start. I could use all kinds of magic now—well, sort of. I couldn't wait to try out as many as possible. I was done with breakfast and ready to get going. Plus, I owed Dad an impromptu flight.

Dad saw me watching Cybele impatiently and started chuckling to himself. I wanted to ask Cybele for my bracelet back sooo bad, but I felt like it was rude to ask after she'd put so much work into it. She was clearly exhausted.

"Cybele," Dad started, "Ali and I have finished breakfast. Why don't we go and practise while you eat and get some rest?"

"Oh sure," Cybele said plainly, sitting idly in her chair. Dad stood awkwardly now, having expected Cybele to pass him the bracelet. Cordelia rolled her eyes and sighed. "She does this much too often. Here, take it, go practise. Come back when you think you can make it to Poenari."

Cordelia took the bracelet from Cybele's hand and handed it to Dad. It was so close now. I'd be flying through the air just minutes from now. Dad looked at me knowingly as he took the bracelet and turned toward the front door of the museum. I'm sure it was no secret how excited I was—it was no doubt written all over my face. I was almost skipping to the door as I followed Dad outside and into the square. The moment we stepped outside, I asked for the bracelet back.

"Ok, let's do this. Can I have my phone back now?"

Dad smiled, shaking his head lightly, having predicted that I would ask the moment we stepped outside.

"Sorry, Ali, but you'll have to wait until we get to the dunes first."

"But why? There's plenty of space in the square. And you were practising in a much smaller room underground. And we can fly to the dunes as soon as I get the hang of it."

"Well, for starters, we don't want to give away our position or wreck the museum. Practising here would draw too much attention, especially with the way air magic works." He stopped and thought for a moment. "But it is a long walk, and I know you can't wait that long."

I grinned. Dad slid back the top of the compartment in his sash, revealing his collection of gemstones. "We can, however, first practise connecting to gemstones."

Dad laughed as my face lit up. He handed me the bracelet and I immediately put it on, examining the beads to see if I could tell which one Cybele had made adjustments to, if any. Not finding anything, I brought up the home menu, the image projecting onto my forearm. The only new addition was an icon with no name—a red hexagonal crystal. I smiled and tapped the icon as soon as I recognised Cybele's gemstone.

Apparently, she had put in the effort to create a decent interface, with a catalogue of gemstones popping up once I clicked the icon. Most of them were empty presets, but she had loaded red beryl and indicolite already, their entries both showing the frequencies and harmonic series that would respond to those gems. I went to click on the indicolite, but Dad was watching and grabbed my wrist before I could.

"That'll cause a scene, and you might just blow us both up. I almost blew up your mother and me the first time I used magic. Which reminds me, choose the garnet preset instead and start tuning your frequency to slightly lower than whatever it says the red beryl base frequency is."

"You don't know?"

"I found all mine by listening. I could use my epicode to tell you exactly what frequency, sure, but then you wouldn't learn anything."

Typical Dad manoeuvre. I sighed but did as he suggested, taking note of the red beryl setting and using it as a starting point to look for the garnet. I was seconds away from throwing fireballs at anyone I wanted.

I heard the note ringing out through the connected earpiece hidden on the inside of my ear. I slowly tuned the frequency lower until suddenly another note was singing back. I turned my head a little bit to the left, and then to the right. Dad put his hand on his wrist, pulling his sleeve back to reveal the garnet set in a silver bracelet. "You've found it, I see."

"How did you know?"

"It's warm. And it gets hotter the more magic you use, so be careful, or you'll blow it up."

"Oh, ok." I stuck my hand out then, palm up, and tried to summon a fireball. Nothing happened.

Dad laughed. "You have to split the output frequency into harmonies, remember? You'll know it's working when new harmonies start singing without you having to create them manually."

I frowned, looking back at the projection on my forearm. Sure enough, Cybele had added a helpful little 'Save base frequency and add harmony' icon. I tapped it. Nothing sounded different, but when I started tuning again, I could hear both the original notes and the new one, all screeching against each other while I searched for the harmony.

A collection of sine waves popped up on my bracelet screen, the next two harmonies pinpointed along it, calculated using the preset information and the saved base frequency. No wonder Cybele was exhausted; she had thought of everything. I felt a little bit guilty then, thinking about Cybele staying up all night to make sure this app was perfect just for me. But soon enough, I had entered the next two harmonies and heard the next few spontaneously ring out and continue multiplying until they left the range of my hearing. Any guilt I felt vanished instantly—I was so ready to summon a ton of fireballs. I focused, holding out my palm, trying to conjure some flames. And... nothing happened.

I pouted. "Why can't I do it now?"

Dad laughed. "Because you're too happy?"

"What? That's a ridiculous answer."

"Fire magic uses anger. Just keep trying until you get frustrated. It should work then."

I huffed and tried again, my excitement turning to frustration after only two attempts. My palm lit up with fire, which immediately extinguished itself as I returned to being excited.

"I thought you said this one was easy. How'd you pick it up so fast?"

"Well, I was dying at the time. Panic sure helps expedite frustration."

"Great, so I'm too safe and happy to use magic?"

Dad laughed, but his expression quickly darkened. "For now, yes, but given our next destination, you won't always be. And besides, that's just fire magic. I think we should try topaz next; then you should have the strength to race me all the way to the dunes."

My jaw dropped. "But if we go back the way we came, it's over an hour's walk. I can't run that far."

"You can with strength magic."

I was conflicted. "Yeah, because I'm so thrilled that the first time I use magic is to make myself run really far. So much fun."

Dad rolled his eyes at my sarcasm. "Just think of it like this: the faster we get to the dunes, the quicker you can try air magic."

I grinned. "Now you're talking."

I followed the same steps for the topaz as I did for the garnet, eventually activating it and immediately feeling less tired, my feet not as sore as they were before from all the walking we did yesterday. I flexed my arms. They didn't look bigger, but I felt way stronger somehow. I looked down at my legs, jumping as high as I could to see if it made a difference, quickly finding that it did—and that I was unprepared to jump as high as I did, falling back to the ground and landing on my arse.

I groaned but got back up easily, my mind turning back to the image of the woman commanding a tornado at her own whim. "Ready, old man? You're so gonna lose in those ridiculous boots."

"Old man? You don't even know where you're going. How are you going to beat me?"

"I just will."

He rolled his eyes. "Ok then."

He started jogging to the far end of the square with me in tow, speeding up slowly as we got to the edge of the square. He looked back to make sure I was keeping up, able to adjust to the longer strides the strength magic allowed me to take. He grinned, seeing I was adapting quickly. It wasn't hard—it was just running. He shouted back at me, "The starting line is the row of buildings. We'll start sprinting as soon as we enter the streets."

I nodded as he looked back again, ready to beat his arse to the dunes. We were running slightly faster than I usually could once we reached the buildings, and the moment we did, Dad almost disappeared, speeding off into a maze I was much less familiar with than him. I sprinted to keep up, not realising that this was also a test of agility, trying to dodge buildings and make sharp turns as we sped through the streets. Dad's boots may not be made for running in, but they gave him way more grip than I had in my running shoes. Miraculously, I didn't hit any buildings despite involuntarily sliding through a few corners trying to keep up. The further we got from the museum, however, the buildings got smaller, and the streets opened up a little bit.

As I slid around the corner, nearly twisting my ankle but somehow staying on my feet, I ended up on a street that led straight into the sand. That's when I knew Dad was toast. I had fallen a bit behind, but not enough that I couldn't catch up on a straight bit of road. I booked it this last little stretch, only just now realising my breath was getting heavy. It amazed me how long it had taken to tire me. The look on Dad's face when I passed him right before the edge of the city was hilarious. But I also thought I caught a smirk twitch across his face right at the end. I would've been puzzled by this if the reason hadn't become immediately apparent.

The ground dropped away when I reached the edge of the city, my momentum keeping me going straight, eventually landing me in the middle of a river. I landed with a splash, rising quickly enough to see Dad leap over the river above me and land solidly on the other side.

"I win."

"I totally beat you. I just didn't see the river."

"That's what you get for being smug." He replied.

I pouted. I would have been mad if the adrenaline wasn't still pumping. I swam to the edge of the river and climbed up the dune on the other side to where Dad was. As I climbed, I saw him slide back the compartment of his chest and touch the topaz, jerking his finger back and shaking it in the air when he did. I reached him, finding him staring at his finger, his mouth a hard line.

"It seems that the topaz can't handle both of us being connected to it at the same time very well. It shouldn't be anywhere near this hot. We were cutting it pretty close there. For now, I think we should make the effort to avoid using the same gemstone simultaneously."

"What about the indicolite though? How are we both supposed to use air magic to get to Poenari?"

"I'm sure Cybele or Cordelia can find us another one. Or Brigitte even. We are saving her sister, after all."

I nodded, wondering what having magic like Brigitte would be like. Lightning magic. The most awesome magic I'd seen. And yet it was the only kind of magic that was too powerful for me to use, according to Dad.

"Ok then, ready for some air magic?"

I grinned. "Absolutely. What frequency should I start at?"

"It's not far below where you already are."

"Ok." I opened the Indicolite preset, finding it already full of harmonic sequences. "Oh yeah, I forgot Cybele already put it in." I tapped on the indicolite preset and I heard all the tones play, the harmonies growing exponentially higher until I could no longer hear them being added.

"Here goes." With the single thought of just, 'wind,' all the air around me started swirling, picking both me and Dad up off the ground and flinging us through the air.

I sat up, spitting sand out of my mouth. I looked over at Dad, who was holding his shoulder and rolling it around in the socket.

"At least the sand is softer than the training room walls," Dad said.

I chuckled. "You got off easy then."

He helped me up out of the sand, then suggested a better approach than just summoning the wind all at once. "What you want to do is start really constricted and tight, like tense up all your muscles and imagine a really small tornado swirling in front of you.

Then very slowly relax until the tornado forms in front of you. You have to stay tense once it's there though, if you keep relaxing it'll keep growing and get out of control."

"Ok, I can do that."

He nodded and took a few steps away from me, making sure to stand slightly behind me. I tensed up all the muscles I could and pictured the tiny tornado. When nothing happened, I started relaxing slowly. A gust of wind hit me in the face, and I tensed up again.

"Oh, you had it! You just have to focus on how tense your muscles are and not flinch when something changes."

I tried again, this time a little bit slower, anticipating the localized spiralling air in front of me. When the wind picked up, I froze but made sure not to tense up. The air stayed constant, not particularly strong or twisting, but it was more than a breeze.

I narrowed my image of the tornado in my mind, and I could feel the air shift, but the tornado still didn't form. I relaxed a little bit more, feeling the wind get incrementally stronger, until it was strong enough to start picking up sand from the ground, lifting it up and around itself, spiralling upwards in the same shape that I held in my mind. OMG, I was doing it! I just made a tornado! Now this was cool magic. I relaxed slightly more, widening the image of the tornado in my mind, playing with the tension and my image to see how they reacted to one another.

After ten minutes of doing this, my body was starting to shake. I was getting tired; I couldn't keep tensing like this. I relaxed all at once then, expecting the tornado to dissipate but instead, it expanded out, enveloping me and spitting me back out into the sand.

It dissipated then, after it had thrown me around. Dad stood over me, somehow unaffected by the sudden outburst.

"How are you still standing?"

"Magic. Now I know you were probably getting stiff standing there like that, but you can't relax like that unless you erase the image from your mind first. Otherwise, that happens."

"Gee, thanks for the heads up."

"Honestly, I thought it would take you a few more tries to get to that point, and I couldn't very well shout over the wind."

I sighed, smiling to myself. I had made a tornado. And a pretty solid one at that. My next one was going to be amazing.

We continued training, making sure to stretch after each conjuration, my subsequent tornados starting to move more fluidly—first moving around on the dunes, and then at different speeds, angles, and heights. At that point, Dad didn't have any more pointers, so he just sat on the sand and watched me play with the air. I couldn't tell if he was impressed or jealous. But the partial smirk told me he was at least proud of himself for his training. Not that he got any credit for my amazing tornadoes, but I was glad he threw himself around with air magic first so he could tell me how it worked. Otherwise, I might've blown myself back into the river a few more times before figuring it out. But now I could make a tornado and direct it any which way I wanted, changing its shape and everything about it while it moved. Now for the hard part, according to Dad anyway.

9 – Ender

Fire magic might not have been Alira's thing, but air magic certainly was. She had picked it up incredibly fast. Granted, she had the benefit of me explaining it to her, whereas I had to blow myself into a wall a couple of times before starting to understand. But regardless, she was already trying to fly. And I had no doubt she'd get it much faster than I did; my ability to fly was still questionable. I still hadn't tried it out in the open, and the air moved differently out here than it did in the training room. But I suppose that was to be expected. Maybe it was much easier out in the open.

The urge to test my own magic was rising, especially while I was watching Alira master it right in front of me. She was being careful now, as she tried to conjure strong enough winds around her feet to pick her up, and so far she hadn't tripped once, at least not spectacularly enough that she hadn't managed to catch herself right away. She was far better at this than I was. As much as I wanted to practice alongside her, I was worried after the topaz had gotten as hot as it did with us both connected, that we'd break the indicolite if we both practiced, especially with a magic this strong and unruly.

Once Alira got the hang of hovering, it didn't take long for her to apply all the tornado movements she had been working on before, moving herself up, down, and around on the dunes. She almost lost her balance a couple of times but quickly learned to catch herself with the air in her mind rather than her own muscles. She was clever.

I couldn't help myself then, watching Alira manage a tornado with a steep angle, sending her speeding off into the desert and back. Her face was beaming and flushed when she rushed back to me, the tornado slowly falling into the sand, dissipating as it laid her down softly, transitioning into a walk.

I raised my eyebrows. "Now you're just showing off."
She smiled in response, her hair windswept and tied in seemingly impossible knots. That was going to be a problem later.

"Looks like it's my turn then. You could probably give me some pointers with all the fancy moves you pulled out there."

Alira looked conflicted but resigned to her exhaustion, rubbing her sore muscles and stretching. "I guess so." She thought for a moment. "Well, I can't really give you any pointers if I don't know what you can do."

"Fair enough. How about you disconnect your bracelet, and I'll show you."

"Oh, right." Alira lifted her arm, tapping away on the projection on her skin. I felt the indicolite start cooling down seconds before Alira lowered her arms again. I opened the frequency augmenter on my epicode, activating the indicolite preset saved from yesterday. I started just like I had explained it to Alira, starting tense and slowly relaxing, remembering the feeling of the magic from yesterday, reacquainting myself with it.

After a few practice tornadoes, I summoned one around my feet, wobbly at first, but managing to get myself to hover. Alira looked unimpressed.

"This is what you spent hours working on yesterday?"

"Says the girl who can't summon a fireball," I retorted.

She rolled her eyes. "Anyway, it's no wonder you can't move about easily; you're focusing all the wind beneath you. You're essentially creating a tiny moving platform for yourself to stand on, which you fall off of as soon as you move it."

"Yes, and? How would you think about it?"

"I like to picture the tornadoes as a series of rings. One wrapped around my feet that stays in the centre of the tornado, and the other around my waist, supporting my hands. The trick is to get the image of the tornado's movement in your mind to sync up with the movement of your body."

"Oh, so kinda like Ironman then."

"Yeah, kinda."

That made more sense than what I was doing. Supporting my hands and feet equally, one stationary in the tornado, and the others free to help direct it, was much more stable than trying to ride it like a surfboard. Then again, I'm sure everyone had their own style. Alira seemed to be copying the woman from the arena to some extent. I tried a few times thinking about how Alira had described it and eventually managed to move around rapidly enough that I'd be able to get myself to Poenari well enough, although my reflexes weren't as fast as Alira's; her ability to reshape the wind so quickly still surprised me. I suppose that was the benefit of youth.

After a couple more practice rounds and the pair of us figuring out how to incorporate a second person into our personal tornadoes to transport Cybele and Cordelia, we returned to the Museum. It was four hours later, and both of us were hungry and sore from all the tense exercise. On the plus side, however, we didn't have to run back to the museum. Alira beat me this time fair and square, her ability to weave through the maze-like streets on her tornado greater than my own, slower movements. I took a gamble in an effort to keep up, flying over the rooftops for a short amount of time, but seeing the spires of the inner city and the cathedral beyond made me feel uneasy. I sank back to street level, albeit significantly closer to Alira's position.

We stopped in the square, Alira gliding down from her falling tornado into a graceful stroll, and myself closer to falling and landing in a run that my legs could barely keep up with. I didn't fall though, so that was good. When I stopped and caught my breath, I heard Alira laughing behind me.

"Definitely beat you that time. But it still doesn't make up for not telling me about the river."

I caught my breath a little longer, then responded, "Too bad you couldn't summon a fire to dry yourself off quickly."

She frowned and rolled her eyes, a little madder at me now.

"Yeah, just like that. Think about that feeling next time you try fire magic."

She rolled her eyes again but was smirking now. I quickly checked on the indicolite to make sure it wasn't too hot. It was scalding, but it had survived the trip. I knew it was risky pushing the gemstone like that, but I figured if we kept our tornados small and used them only for personal propulsion, it would be enough to make it back to the square.

I turned back to the museum, seeing a few people standing out the front around some sort of contraption that was set up. As we got closer, I recognised Cybele and Cordelia standing out front. Cybele waved as soon as she saw us, but Cordelia remained still, with her arms crossed.

"Hey Dad? I think I know what you mean about needing our own gems now. I couldn't feel it on our run, but when we were flying back, I could feel the magic get weaker when you were falling behind."

I thought about this, considering the ramifications more seriously now. I wanted Alira to learn magic partly so that she could protect herself better in this place, but without my gemstones to tap into, she couldn't use magic to protect herself anyway. I pushed back my sleeve and removed the garnet and silver bracelet.

"Here, take this. It was your mother's one anyway. You should have it."

She looked at it thoughtfully, holding her hand out. "But I can't even use it yet?"

"You will. Especially when you need it most. Fire magic is good for getting out of trouble."

She smiled. "And it was Mum's?"

"Yes. We had a matching set, but I stupidly traded mine away."

I sighed. What an idiot I was then. Alira smiled as I put it around her wrist. "Thanks." I smiled back, then continued towards the museum, Alira almost skipping, although how she had the energy after all that I had no idea. When we were close enough, Cybele called out to us, "You're both decent air sorcerers now, I presume?"

"Sure are!" Alira called back. "Now what's this big... thing?"

"It's how we're getting to Poenari, of course. You and Ender both go here and here, and Dels and I go here and here, as the passengers."

"It looks pretty heavy," I chimed in. The contraption looked a bit like a ballista, but made out of a collection of materials, including two stone chairs on the top and two woven hammocks below. The rest of the frame was covered in all sorts of stretched fabrics, presumably to act like little sails when the wind rushed up from underneath.

"It's a little heavy, but surely between the two of you we can pull it off."

"Maybe," Alira responded, "But I have a better idea."

"Oh?" was all Cybele said, watching Alira move towards the contraption and tear down the largest sail.

"If I can tear that off that easily, then my tornado would have shredded this thing."

Cybele raised her eyebrows. "I see."

Alira continued, folding the torn fabric into a triangle and holding it up behind her, so that the two points were in her hands and the fabric hung down her back, the third point of the triangle reaching down to the base of her spine. I could see what she was thinking now.

"Are you crazy? We can't fly all the way to Poenari with wingsuits—not carrying passengers at least."

"Sure we can. It's what the people in Telesto do, right? If the Indicolites have them, then they must be the way to go. Plus, once I've got my own gemstone, we won't have to worry about using too much magic simultaneously. It'll be great. And much stealthier, seeing as this *is* a covert mission."

She had us there. She was strong, and with her own stone, easily capable of flying herself and a passenger all the way there. Plus, this contraption wasn't exactly stealthy or speedy by the looks of things. I sighed.

"I agree, wingsuits will be much quicker, and Alira is capable enough that she won't drop anyone. I can't make any promises for myself though."

Cybele smirked, intrigued by the idea, but Cordelia's frown deepened, not liking where this was going. Cybele's head cocked slightly, like she was just remembering something. Then she looked down and shook her head slightly.

"Sorry about this morning, Alira. I was up all night working on your bracelet and when I came out this morning I was barely conscious. It didn't even occur to me that you might need your own stone. But at least it seems you guys managed to practice regardless?"

I responded, "Yes, but having two people connected strains the gems more than I would've expected. It's risky having two people connected to one stone, especially when only one can monitor it."

"I see. Well, luckily for you, I do have more. I will go get one and then we can be off."

Alira's stomach grumbled in protest. She smiled sheepishly.

"Or perhaps we'll leave after an early lunch instead?" Cybele offered. Both Alira and I were glad to hear that, and we proceeded to the museum to chow down on mystery jerky, tea, and bread.

10 – Alira

While Dad and I ate, Cybele sat with us, drawing the wingsuits based on what she could remember from the Indicolites from Telesto and my brief demonstration. The hard part was figuring out how the passenger was supposed to connect. Cybele asked me questions about how I planned to carry another person, trying to design something that would work with the way Dad and I had practiced but without the danger. They were tornadoes, after all. Cybele's designs were all rigid, mostly intended for the passenger to not have to do very much. But they were too heavy and kind of unfair.

"What about we both just wear the wingsuits and connect ourselves by rope? That's all we really need. It makes us smaller, we don't have to hide any equipment when we get there, and we can be really quick too."

Cybele seemed worried about the idea, repeatedly glancing at Cordelia, who seemed unfazed. Sensing Cybele's hesitation, Cordelia spoke up.

"Don't worry about me, Bele. I may be old, but I can handle a little bit of flying."

Cybele frowned. "You haven't flown a day in your life. How would you know?"

"We've all had to adapt. This is simply the latest adaptation."

This didn't seem to ease Cybele's concern, but I could see the hidden glint in her eye that said she was looking forward to it despite her worry.

"Alright then, four wingsuits coming right up." She disappeared into her workshop while the rest of us finished eating. A few minutes later she came back.

"Hey Dels, can I borrow you for a minute? These suits are all natural materials, so it would be way faster for you to stitch with your magic."

"Gladly," she replied.

But I was intrigued. I wanted to see more of my grandmother's magic, and I was done eating.

"Can I come too?"

"Of course."

Dad stood up then too. "Might as well."

And so we all went down through Cybele's office and into the workshop. Cybele had laid out four sets of leather garments, similar to what the guards at the entrance wore but without all the metal plating and additional armour components.

"I've drawn the stitch lines on each of the leathers and cut up the sails to fit. All you have to do, Dels, is stitch the two."

"I can see that, Cybele."

"Right, of course."

Cybele went quiet then, almost blushing as she stopped talking to let Cordelia work her magic.

They were weird... maybe they were—OMG, yes, they were dating. Definitely. I glanced at Dad and tugged on his sleeve. He leaned in close enough for me to whisper.

"I think Cybele's dating my grandmother."

He pulled back with a smile, saying nothing, but telling me everything. He already knew, and he didn't tell me!? I couldn't believe Dad figured it out before me, or maybe Cybele told him? They were strangely friendly for claiming they were trying to kill each other at one point. I stewed in these thoughts, daydreaming while Cordelia worked away, almost forgetting why I had come down here in the first place, until she was already on the last jacket. I snapped back to reality and moved in closer so that I could see what she was doing.

Cordelia was doing something similar to before on my hand, pinching the two fabrics. I watched as they weaved themselves together along the lines Cybele had drawn.

"Wow," I muttered. Cordelia heard it and smiled warmly. She finished, and before us were four wingsuit jackets. I was the first to try one on, quickly finding that it was much too large.

"Hey, um, I don't think this is going to stay on…"

But Cordelia was already on it, circling me and folding the fabric at the back of the jacket. She stitched along the folds with her magic until the suit fit nice and snug, although there were still folds of extra fabric hidden within it that weren't very comfortable.

"It's not perfect, but this is a time-sensitive mission. We can adjust them later, but for now, everyone put theirs on so I can make the final adjustments."

Everyone did as she said while I watched, thoroughly enjoying the small but enormously useful magic that Cordelia possessed. Eventually, we were all packed and ready to go, Dad and I with backpacks that had rations and some tools that we might need. I also had my indicolite that Cybele had given me, although I didn't have a convenient place for it just yet like Dad did. For now, I had it stitched into my wingsuit, courtesy of Cordelia, but in a way that made it easy enough to remove if necessary.

Now we were standing outside the museum, the four of us in hand-made wingsuits. Cybele and Dad were attached at the waist with rope, and I was attached to my grandmother. I grinned, so excited to show her what I could do. Dad saw my energy rising and gave me a non-verbal reminder to stay calm and in control of my muscles.

I took a few deep breaths, steadying myself. Cordelia looked ready too. I glanced back at Dad with an expression that said we were ready to go. I was to follow him and Cybele, as they had properly studied the way to get there. Dad was also worried I might get too eager and fly off faster than he could catch up, which was definitely a possibility.

Once Dad was hovering, I started slow, picturing the little tornadoes surrounding both myself and Cordelia. I had explained to her beforehand what to expect and how to stay inside the whirlwind. We lifted off, hovering for a few moments to let Cordelia get the hang of it. That was when Dad tilted their whirlwinds, and the air caught under their wings, the fabric arcing out like sails, and the two of them sped off over the dunes with surprising speed.

I hurried to catch up, but hastily remembered that I needed to stay as steady as I could for Cordelia's sake. I watched her as I started accelerating. She was wobbly at first, slightly more than Cybele was as I watched Dad drag her along for the ride. She found her balance and gave me a nod when she noticed me watching her. I grinned, taking it as permission to catch up to the others, and I did just that. Although at these speeds, I was quickly realising we should've worn goggles, especially with all the sand we were whipping up.

I squinted ahead, making our two tornadoes taller to get a little bit further away from the sand I was kicking up. This was a strange way to travel, that was for sure. I had never used a wingsuit before, and I didn't think I ever would. I had no reason to go jumping out of planes or off cliffs on Earth, but now here I was flying through the desert in a tornado of my own making.

I found that the rope connecting Cordelia to me was a little bit too short to travel as two standalone tornadoes like Dad and I had practised. Instead, we were close enough that the two air currents pulled on one another, trying to pull the other in. I pulled against this at first, but we ended up in a slow spiral dance with Cordelia's tornado, the two circling each other as we sped forward, so that each of us travelled in a corkscrew pattern. Honestly, the movement was making me a bit nauseous.

When I caught up to Dad, I purposely overtook them at top speed, grinning as I did so, not that anyone could see. I slowed down a bit once I did, letting Dad take the lead again. I could feel him rolling his eyes at me. They were circling each other now too, having also been too close because of the rope.

I was told Poenari wasn't too far away, the closest of the three new settlements, which made sense given that they seemed to want to take back the city. The other two groups, on the other hand, wandered off, leaving the city for good. I wondered how far the Indicolites went. If they had wingsuits and travelled like this, they could've gone much further than those who walked off into the desert. I wondered what their city looked like. I would love to visit it.

After twenty minutes of flying and speculation, Dad slowed down, and my focus returned to him as I matched his speed. I could see Poenari on the horizon now, sitting along a wide ridge—larger than the others that carved their way through the calico desert at odd angles. Dad flew closer to the ground, looking for somewhere to land so that we could sneak up on foot. He and Cybele landed on a light grey patch of sand; their landing was softer than I had imagined, mostly because the material wasn't stone or metal like I'd presumed.

I set Cordelia and me down much more gently, stumbling only slightly as I stepped out of the wind onto the ground. The sand sank a little as I did so before bouncing back, which surprised me. Dad laughed, "Not so graceful now, are you?"

I stared back and asked, "How was I supposed to know this was some kind of foam?"

"You think I'd go and land on crushed rocks—especially with my rough landings?" I sighed, recalling how I'd watched him land, knowing the surface wasn't as hard as it appeared.

"How'd you even know it was foam?"

He shrugged. "I've seen enough military-grade foam in my lifetime, as well as wandered these dunes enough to make an educated guess."

Cybele cut in then. "Come on you two, we don't know if the Painites saw us land or not. We have to stay quiet and out of sight for as long as possible."

Dad grinned. "Good thing you have two chameleons with you," he said before somehow turning a grey colour and completely blending in with the granulated foam we stood on.

I stared at him in shock, my expression creeping into an excited smile. "How'd you switch magic so fast?"

His colour returned. "I didn't. I simply turned my epicode off. We're Alexandrites, Alira. It's the kind of magic we inherently have."

I had forgotten I had natural magic, like the kind Mum had. I reached to feel for the gemstone around my neck. Mum didn't have all these fancy magics; she just had her own, and I had forgotten all about it. I wished I had met her. I looked over to Cordelia; her expression telling me she knew what I was thinking the moment I did so. For some reason, I was nervous now to use the magic I knew I was supposed to just have inherently—the magic my Mum had.

Cybele smiled. "I know it's a bit different, but I saw you do it as a baby, so I know you can do it."

I had forgotten I had done it before as a baby, and that Cybele had seen it. I wasn't sure how to feel about that. I looked to Dad.

"How do I use it?"

He smiled. "You simply wish to not be seen."

Like I hadn't wished that many times over in my life; why would it be different now? I sighed, finding it easy to wish to be invisible with three sets of eyes staring at me expectantly.

Cybele grinned. "And there it is, just like her mother, completely invisible except for those floating green eyes."

"Wait, you can still see my eyes? I thought I would look like Dad, like kinda camouflaged but still barely visible."

"No, Alira. Just like your mother, the rest of you is fully invisible, but your eyes give you away," Cybele replied.

Of course, the one thing that had been the reason I wanted to become invisible half the time were the only part of me that would never be. This magic was stupid. I immediately regretted that thought, feeling like I had offended a mother I never had. And that was the other reason I wanted to become invisible sometimes. I looked back to Dad, who blended back into the grey sand once more.

"Let's go. I'll use my epicode to scout out the perimeter and let everyone know if I see anything." Dad said as he walked off towards Poenari. He was difficult to see like this, and I kept losing him when I wasn't focusing, until I realised that I could just follow the footsteps he left behind in the sand.

Cybele was using her magic to make herself and Cordelia feel small. They didn't look any smaller, but more like they felt unimportant when I did look at them. It was good for anyone who might spot them from Poenari's ridge, but it was stirring up strange emotions—looking at my grandmother, whom I admired, and feeling like she was nothing. It was unsettling, so I focused on Dad's footsteps instead and set my sights on the city, although it was more of a small town. We were here to rescue a priestess. That was what I had to focus on.

11 – Ender

There it was. Poenari. The city of the painites, as well as where Akeldama took all of his prisoners and did who knows what else. He didn't seem like the kind of man to take many prisoners, just simply fashion his opponents into weapons for himself to cause more destruction. Perhaps I was being overzealous. Cybele had told me of the danger he posed and his threat towards the city, but I had personally only seen him fight those who fought him, people who put themselves into the arena, even if the kidnapping was uncalled for. That being said, he was dangerous, and this was his home. We were going to have to tread lightly.

As we reached the base of the final ridge that the settlement rested on, I used my epicode to scan the perimeter, using the optical zoom to see details of the outer border and its components in greater detail than the rest of the group could. Surprisingly, this place wasn't built at all like the fortress I thought it would be. I had expected some sort of heavily fortified medieval castle or something, but this place had no outer walls, no watchtowers, nothing.

Perhaps they simply expected to be left alone. Which was a fair assessment, as no one in their right mind would come here looking for a fight—not on purpose, knowing what Akeldama could do, and presumably many of the other painites. Perhaps they saw their abilities as the only defence they would need, fighting those who came to attack with their own magics and welcoming those who wished to join them. It was a risky move though, that was for sure.

But there had to be some sort of building that he was using to contain a diamond, and there was no wall to hide behind to look for it when we reached the top of the ridge. It was too open, too easy to see everything, including us. I pondered this as we climbed the last dune, Alira managing to keep up now that she had swapped out her runners for more sensible desert boots.

When we reached the top, I laid down in the sand, so that only my head would pop over the ridge when I scanned the settlement. I hoped the others would copy my example, seeing the shape my body made in the sand. Alira copied me, her eyes level with mine. I whispered to her, "If you see anyone look towards you, shut your eyes."

She nodded in response. The other two hung back, knowing they would be more obvious. I whispered down to them, "This place is too open. You two will be seen too easily. I will go alone and find the right building, and if it's close enough to the edge, I'll come back and we'll formulate a plan."

They both nodded, but Alira whispered back, "I'm coming with you."

"No, it's too dangerous."

"Not too dangerous for you."

"I know what I'm doing, and you're just a kid, a highly capable one, sure, but this is just too dangerous."

"I'm coming, and you can't stop me."

She was right, I couldn't stop her, but this was one hell of a time and place to decide to be rebellious. There were so many things that I would've preferred her to protest, but of course she chose to rebel against me trying to stop her from following me into the lair of a madman. I sighed.

"You're right, I can't. Just stay behind me and close your eyes the moment you think someone might see you."

I really hoped this would go smoothly, but knowing that Alira was following me now only made me more anxious to do this well and not be seen.

Here goes. I crept forward, rising to my feet but staying low. We crept to the front of the single-story house we had come up beside when we came over the ridge. The buildings here were similar to those in the city, but more spread out, allowing for wider buildings with fewer stories, the majority of the structures being only one or two stories tall. The main differences were the accents in the buildings, the stripes of red decorating them in various ways. As we moved along the outside walls of different structures, sneaking towards the centre, it became apparent that they didn't try very hard when it came to town planning, seemingly letting anyone build their house wherever they wanted, making it hard to navigate and potentially even harder to get back out the way we came.

As we passed buildings and people, most with deep red gemstones but some with other kinds, I started putting the pieces together. The red accents on the buildings were a type of code. Only the people with painite gemstones entered the buildings with stripes; those with different gems had regular sandstone houses.

My suspicions were further confirmed when I came across a building that had more stripes than usual, a deeper red with thicker lines running up and down the façade. We waited for a moment, and finally, we saw a man exit through the front door—a painite soldier, with armour not dissimilar to the red-scaled battle-dress that Jezebel used to wear, but sleeker and less showy. This guy was higher in the ranks of Akeldama's informal army, and thus had his rank painted on his house in the form of deep red stripes.

To find Akeldama, and wherever he was keeping Mellory, we just had to find the reddest building, or perhaps the darkest one. Soaked in the most blood was the style they were going for, I'd imagine. I didn't know if Alira had figured it out or not yet, but she was as clever as her mother, so it was likely, and she'd seen as much as I had. She tugged on my sleeve then, staring at me but doing nothing else. I frowned at her, then remembered that she couldn't see that. I felt her grab the rest of my arm, seeing by her eyes that she was shaking her head lightly. She straightened my arm, pointing it towards another part of the city.

I squinted to where she was pointing with my arm, chuckling as I realised she must have pointed to it first, forgetting that I couldn't see her. Sure enough, she had figured it out, as on a small hill at the other end of the little city was a single-story house. The outside of which was stained completely red, the roof so dark it was almost black, and not even a hint of the natural sandstone colour predominant in the rest of the city. That was the one. That was Akeldama's house.

I hesitated before starting to move in that direction. Were we really going to go right up to the house of the most dangerous man on the planet, and then go waltzing in there looking through all of his stuff? This seemed like a terrible idea, but at least we had found it.

As we got closer, I became increasingly concerned for Alira's safety, and my own, but that wasn't quite as important.

I whispered to her, "Ali, the house is close to the edge of the city. Why don't you sneak back around the edge and bring the others to this side of the city so we can make a plan for how to approach?"

"Ok," she responded, and then she was gone, her eyes turned away from me.

I continued past the last few buildings before the imposing red one, that was somehow more imposing than any of the others, despite its size. There was nothing left to do now but wait. Wait for the others, wait for Akeldama to show up, or wait for some sign of Mellory or where she was being kept. We didn't really know anything at all. I mean, why would Akeldama keep his victims in his own house? That seemed like a strange place to keep them, now that I thought about it. But what other leads did we have?

All I could do was hide and wait. I didn't have to wait long, however, as Akeldama exited the house soon thereafter, turning around to talk to someone inside that I couldn't see. I strained to listen, remembering then that my epicode microphone still worked this time around, allowing me to pick up on what they were saying from this distance. I focused my microphone on Akeldama until I could hear him clearly.

"—Just going down to the cellar for some more lightning, Ayuna. I've been going through it pretty quickly with all these experiments."

"Sure, just don't kill her before I get a turn."

"I won't, I promise."

Well, crap, that wasn't what I wanted to hear, and who was Ayuna? Akeldama turned back then and continued out of the house, moving towards the outskirts of the city. Whatever was going on, I at least knew he was about to lead me right to Mellory. I followed him silently, keeping my distance even though I was camouflaged.

Alira and the others would arrive close to the house soon, wondering where I'd gone, but I knew I couldn't lose Akeldama. I had to keep following him. This was the only lead we had on Mellory. As I followed him, I tried not to think of the kinds of experiments he was talking about to whoever Ayuna was, but my mind couldn't help but wander, conjuring images of him torturing people, seeing how much lightning they could take before they died, or combining it with air magic and conjuring up one hell of a storm. Who knew what this guy was capable of? It seemed like he could use magics almost simultaneously.

My focus returned as we left the edge of the city, the sands starting to vibrate again, and I wondered for a moment if he knew I was there, and was leading me out into the dunes to kill me quietly and leave my body there to dissolve. That didn't seem to be the case, however, as a small tower appeared into view—a solid sandstone tower built at the bottom of a large divot in the desert so that the top of the tower didn't rise higher than the edges of the basin, rendering it invisible from the city or across the horizon.

The tower had no red except for the door. It also appeared to be part of some sort of larger contraption, a metal foundation of sorts but with arms hidden just below the sand. They were exposed only when Akeldama took out a small vial filled with a red liquid, drank it, and then waved his hand in a motion that moved the sand away from the mechanism. A few more moments passed in which nothing seemed to happen, at least not from this distance, before he moved the sand back, and entered through the red door into the tower.

Once he entered, I slipped into the basin, leaving tracks down the side of the dune that Akeldama would see as soon as he left the tower. I would have to be in and out of there quickly, before he left again. When I got to the door, I stopped. If I opened this and he was standing on the other side, I would immediately be killed. I listened carefully, trying to figure out where he was in the tower. Nothing. I took a deep breath. There was no other way to do this. Perhaps if I had a sapphire on me, I would be able to figure out where he was, or maybe use the metal mechanism that the tower hid to my advantage, but unfortunately, I did not, and I had already left the footprints that would give me away, so there was no going back now to find one. I opened the door slowly and quietly, relieved to find no sign of Akeldama on the other side, but simultaneously concerned that I had lost him.

I entered quickly and shut the door behind me. The room was somewhat like what I was expecting, but less evil-looking. There was something that looked like a kitchenette, and a desk opposite, stacked with parchment and scribble that I didn't understand. A book of folklore stories sat on the corner of the desk. What drew my attention, however, was the large open trapdoor in the floor that I could hear the echoes of footsteps and the clinking of chains through. That was more like the creepy evil lair I was expecting.

I hesitantly approached the open door to 'the cellar' as Akeldama had called it. I slowly descended the stone steps, staying low to see as much of the room below as possible before I waltzed into what I assumed was a private prison. It pretty much was exactly that. The blood drained from my face at the sight of it, making me go almost paler than the people hanging from chains on the walls, drained of too much blood but somehow still alive. Clearly, many of Akeldama's experiments involved seeing how much blood he could drain from a person without killing them.

I felt nauseous, almost throwing up when I set my eyes on someone who had lost too much blood and hadn't made it, Akeldama having moved on to extracting their bone marrow. Oh, shit. I vomited onto the stone floor, my face lighting up the room as my paleness shone in the darkness, the chameleon magic disrupted.

Akeldama whipped his head towards me, stepping away from one of the bodies hanging on the wall. He looked shocked at first as I looked up at him, straightening up, gritting my teeth as I faced the consequences of my slip-up. His surprise quickly turned into a wicked grin. He stood there, flexing his fingers, my eyes drawn to his exposed arms, seeing that both of his forearms were entirely purple, unlike before. Now that I was closer, I realised that the discolouration was bruising. It seemed that blood magic wasn't kind to its users.

I faced Akeldama, taking in the scene, recognising the tattered clothes of the person he was standing in front of to be those of a diamond priestess. Mellory.

"How bold of you to come waltzing into your very own prison. You have guts, I'll give you that, but do you have magic worth keeping you alive?" He grinned, not giving me any time to respond, lunging towards me and ducking behind me. He grabbed my elbow for only a moment as he did so, but that brief contact was enough, leaving me feeling woozy as his hand left me. The room was still again, but I couldn't see him.

He reappeared right in front of me, my gaze fixing on him briefly before he blinked out of existence once more, and back.

"Ah, how interesting. I've heard of chameleon magic before, but I thought it was long dead. Unfortunately for you, I have no need of sneaking around in the shadows. Stealth is for the weak and the deceitful. Nice meeting you though."

He grinned before reaching his hand out to Mellory, her chest heaving as he extracted her magic, leaving behind little bruises where his fingertips had touched her. He swung that same hand around a moment later, pointing it at me as lightning shot out and hit me in the chest.

I landed hard on the stone floor, grateful that we were underground, knowing now how much that affected lightning magic. At least I had some experience in a fight like this. I activated my epicode, tuning to the obsidian around my neck, my fingernails flashing silver as I flexed my fingers. Akeldama took a step closer, throwing lightning with his other hand now.

I caught it, flexing all my muscles, redirecting the energy from one hand through my chest to the other, the lightning arcing out and hitting him in the thigh. He stumbled but didn't fall.

"Oh? Some knife magic I see. I wasn't expecting that. You're an interesting one indeed. Maybe I'll keep you around after all."

I wasn't planning on sticking around, and he had no intention of slowing down as he lunged towards one of the other bodies hanging on the wall, draining their blood with his fingertips, then throwing both lightning and fire at me simultaneously. All I could do was duck, having to flatten myself against the floor to avoid being hit by anything, the fire and lightning mixing and crashing into the wall behind me, evidently disrupting whatever mechanism was keeping this building from vibrating with the dunes, the room starting to shake a little bit.

Akeldama cursed, "Now look what you made me do." But he kept going, throwing both fire and lightning repeatedly, the vibrations getting worse as he damaged the walls. I had switched to strength magic, anticipating the collapse of the tower, Akeldama seemingly blinded by frustration at his inability to hit me. The next time he reached for Mellory, he took the last of her magic, her body going limp and lifeless, his attention switching to her instead.

"Well, shit. I promised my daughter I wouldn't kill her." He turned back to me. "Oh well, I'll find another," he said nonchalantly, wasting the last of Mellory's magic on a shot at me that I caught and sent back at him. He was expecting it this time, however, and managed to dodge, but the energy cracked the far wall, the last undamaged wall. The tower was now starting to sway, the vibrations of the desert quickening its demise, distracting Akeldama for long enough that I found the chance to duck back up the stairs and out of the tower altogether.

I sprinted out the red door and up the dunes walling in the hidden tower, the metal mechanism creaking underground as it failed to stop the desert from taking over the tower, crushing the room beneath it

The tower fell, but I didn't look back, didn't see its remains until I had reached the top of the ridge. I looked back to see the toppled tower, a man with almost completely purple arms and long black hair standing on top of the rubble, somehow maintaining a smirk as he watched me disappear over the edge of the basin, blending back into the sand and becoming invisible once more as I hurried back to where Alira, Cybele, and Cordelia hopefully still were.

I made my way hurriedly past the few buildings on the edge of the city, the red house once again in sight. I slowed down as I approached, my gut dropping as I took in the scene unfolding in front of the red house. There were three people: Cybele, Cordelia, and the girl holding a glowing red knife up to Cybele's throat. Cordelia struggled against the sand-coloured chains shackling her to the ground on her knees. This must have been Ayuna. I wasn't expecting her to look so young. She was almost Alira's age by the looks of it, but she looked very much like who I presume was her father, with her long dark hair and wicked grin.

Well, shit, this was bad. I didn't know how they were caught, but I couldn't see Alira anywhere. It was likely she hadn't made it back to them in time. If that was the case, she could still be out there looking for them. If that was true, then it was all up to me to save them. What the hell was I supposed to do here though?

I wracked my brain, trying to come up with a plan. The girl had me in checkmate. She hadn't seen me, so it was strange how focused she was on holding these two as strictly as she was. Maybe Alira was here somewhere after all. There was no way to know if she was doing like I said and keeping her eyes shut, but there was a chance. And that would mean all the girl's focus would be on her. It was slim and entirely circumstantial, but it was all I could come up with before Akeldama's inevitable return when I would definitely be outmatched. All I could do was hope that Alira was nearby, and ready.

12 – Alira

What just happened? Who was that, and how did she just appear like that? It all happened so fast. One moment I was leading Cybele and Cordelia around the edge of Poenari towards the red house, and the next they were gone from behind me. I had raced ahead to the house, unable to find them anywhere, only to come across the scene ahead of me—both Cybele and Cordelia somehow having been kidnapped right from behind me and were now held at knife point. And I couldn't do a thing about it, so I hid, hoping Dad would come back soon. But then again, maybe this girl, or Akeldama, had already gotten to him, and that's why he wasn't here.

I was starting to panic the longer I stared at the blade angled towards Cybele's throat, the blade getting sharper and assuming a red glow as the girl's other hand started bruising rapidly, Cybele's neck underneath it also bruising. I could just barely make out what she was saying from my hiding spot behind the edge of a nearby building.

"This is some interesting magic you've got here. I think we'll keep you for later."

This girl, she had to be related to Akeldama, right? I mean, the only explanation for her being able to use Cybele's magic was that she was a blood magic user too. Although, I suppose she was in Poenari, the home of blood magic users. Maybe all painites were this cruel.

I saw a familiar ripple off to my left, catching my gaze. Anyone else wouldn't have noticed, but I was almost used to the way Dad looked when he was near-invisible and moving over the sand dunes. He stopped, and I couldn't see him again, but I knew he was standing there, staring at the same scene that I had been unable to do anything about for the last few minutes. Even with both of us, there was nothing we could do. Even if we rushed her with our strongest magic, she would cut Cybele open, and she would die right in front of us. It wouldn't take much with a blade that sharp already hovering over her throat.

I stared at where I knew Dad was, still invisible, knowing that he would see my eyes, telling him I was there and ready to follow his lead. But I wasn't ready. I was terrified, and I just didn't want to watch Cordelia and Cybele struggle in the cruel grip of that witch. I sat there hiding, the tiny bit of relief I felt seeing that Dad had returned quickly dissolving as the scene remained the same, and Cordelia and Cybele had given up struggling against their restraints.

I shut my eyes, but opened them again, angry with myself for my cowardice, refusing to let myself hide from this, despite how much I wanted to. I had no plan here. All I could do was hope Dad could figure out something. He was the one used to fighting with magic after all, and I couldn't even manage to summon a fireball. But this girl was hurting my friend and my grandmother. If there was any time to be angry, it was now. If I tried summoning fire now,

I was sure I could do it. I'd have to if we were going to get out of this.

I made sure I was hidden in my spot, and that no one was around to see me reappear. But before I could activate the garnet around my wrist with my bracelet, a sudden rush of wind hit me in the face, coming from a tornado on the other side of the girl. My eyes locked on her. She was distracted, her head whipped around to look at the sudden tornado. Before I had a chance to act on this information, Dad appeared right next to her, lunging upwards and shoving his hand between the girl's knife and Cybele's throat. Her head whipped down to face him, but he had already wrapped his fingers around the blade of her knife, his fingernails silver. He ripped the knife away from her, stepping closer as he did so, putting his body between her and Cybele, his other arm coming up and swinging through, punching her right in the nose.

I winced. Even if this girl was evil, it felt weird to watch my Dad punch a girl in the nose. Even more uncomfortable considering that she looked to be about my age.

My pity was brief, however, as the girl jumped straight back up, grinning, seemingly unfazed by her obviously broken nose. The sand started to whip up around her then, and I could tell from Dad's expression that he wasn't prepared for whatever kind of magic she was using now.

Now it was my turn. I became visible once more, the girl too focused on Dad to see me. But Cordelia saw me, and the look of surprise and concern on her face was almost enough to stop me. Almost.

I activated the fire magic, knowing I wouldn't get another go at this, using the wild expression on Cordelia's face as she was shackled to the ground to fuel my anger. Not knowing entirely what would happen, I made sure that I balled all my anger up into my palm and threw it at the girl as hard as I could.

I surprised even myself as I noticed the flaming projectile only after I had thrown it, much bigger than I thought it would be. The basketball-sized ball of fury hit the girl, but not before she threw up a thin wall of sand to slow it down just enough that it didn't set her on fire. The thin sand walls started erecting in layers, stopping me from seeing where she was, the effects of my fireball unknown, until she burst through the layers of suspended sand riding a small tornado right towards me at a speed that didn't leave me any time to respond.

I raised my arms to block her, hoping to conjure some sort of flaming barrier, but there was nothing. My anger had turned to fear in the face of this girl with her bloody nose and sharp eyes staring me down as she got closer. She knocked me over the next instant, ramming into me and sending me flying, but grabbing my wrist and yanking me back down into the sand, winding me as I landed, and making me feel woozy.

I stared up at her, blinking into the sunlight, thinking that I was seeing things when she started flickering in and out of existence when I blinked. Oh no. I lifted my wrist weakly, the bruising from where she had grabbed it already visible. She had done to me what she had done to Cybele, and now she had my magic.

She looked down at me curiously, clicking her fingers and sparking a small fire that flickered on her fingertip. It only lasted a few seconds before it went out.

"Interesting. You seem to have the capacity for more than one magic. You can summon fire even though you naturally have chameleon magic. A long-lost kind of magic, I might add, and yet traces of fire still linger in your bloodstream." She smiled. "You should join us. I think you'd do well here, and we can teach you better ways of controlling more magic, better than however it is you're doing it now."

"Alira!" I whipped my head around to see Dad, staring back at me now that the sand this girl had whipped up as a smoke screen had settled. Cordelia was standing next to him, the shackles lying broken on the sand beside them. I could see him there, worrying, not sure whether to come and save me or not, sensing that his intervention might cause another knife-point hostage situation.

Dad's head whipped around then at the same time as the girl did, although the blood drained from Dad's face while the girl standing above me grinned. I followed their gaze, seeing a dark-haired man with completely bruised arms leaning against the wall of the red house. Akeldama.

Ok, it was time to go. While the girl was distracted, I shifted my wrist, tapping at Cybele's app projected on my arm, selecting the indicolite. I really needed a better way to switch; this way was too slow and too obvious, and it would never be as quick as an epicode. I mean, Dad just switched from chameleon magic to knife magic in one move, before this girl could even react. But now wasn't the time, and I was more than ready to get out of here.

The girl looked back down at me, sensing something was different, but wasn't quick enough to avoid the blast of wind that whipped up around me the moment I thought about it. I was too relaxed at first, but it did get rid of the girl. I narrowed the wind quickly and rode it, shooting myself across the distance between myself and the others. I angled my arms back and outwards, picking up speed now with the wingsuit working properly, ready to scoop up Cordelia as I flew by her. I could only hope they were ready by the time I reached them.

Dad was on it in no time, picking himself and Cybele up off the ground with his tornadoes. Cybele was a bit caught off guard, but she adjusted before they sped off into the desert. When I got to Cordelia, she jumped surprisingly high and found her balance in my tornado easily. Wow, I wasn't expecting that from her.

I followed Dad away from the city. I looked back, surprised that neither Akeldama nor the girl were following us, even though they could if they wanted to. I wonder why.

When we got back to the museum, questions were flying around, and Dad surprisingly had a lot of answers. He had followed Akeldama from the red house to where he was keeping Mellory.

"It was awful, the number of people he had chained to the walls down there and what he was doing to them." He shook his head sadly. "Mellory was alive when I got there, barely, but when Akeldama discovered me, he took the last of her power to fight me, and she died. So did anyone else down there who was still alive before the tower came crashing down."

Cybele looked lost in thought, mumbling to herself before she locked eyes with Dad and said, "Blood batteries. He was using them as blood batteries, his own personal collection of bodies pumping out various kinds of magic in the form of their blood."

I shivered. And to think that girl thought I would be a good fit for them.

"Akeldama mentioned the girl that caught you two as well; her name is Ayuna, his daughter."

His daughter!? I guess that explains why she looked so young. I wonder how old she was. Cybele chimed in again, thinking critically about the situation.

"If Akeldama's blood batteries are all gone, then he'll be looking for new ones, right? And it sounds like he's gotten used to lightning magic. It seems likely that he'll go for that first. But he also might have to rebuild his stores of blood with enough decent magic to take down another diamond, so he might be collecting other strong magics first…" Cybele trailed off when Cordelia rested her hand on her shoulder.

"Can we at least stop calling them blood batteries? They were people, after all, and one of them was a priestess."

Cordelia looked tired, and I realised then how tired I was too, the adrenaline finally wearing off. I started to yawn, but then a terrible thought hit me, bringing my adrenaline right back. I knew I wouldn't be able to get to sleep easily.

"Hey, uh, Dad? When Ayuna rushed at me and… borrowed my magic, she said my blood had traces of fire magic too, and wanted me to join them, to learn from them. I'm just now thinking that, well, if she and her father are trying to rebuild their magic collection, wouldn't it make sense to start with someone who could channel different kinds of magic without relying on blood, namely... us?"

The look on Dad's face when I said this did not help my anxiety. He turned to Cybele.

"Alira is right. They know what we can do now, and they let us go for a reason. I would guess they meant to let us go to lead them back here so they could capture us as well as anyone else they found. Hell, if they come at the wrong time they might even get Brigitte. I think we need to leave, to lead them away from here."

"But where would you go?" Cybele asked, but then seemed to answer her own question as her mind worked away at the problem, or a list of problems really that were rapidly increasing.

"Wait, Ender, do you still have your piece of the tail-key?"

"Yeah, right here, why?" Dad replied, pointing to the compartment in his strap.
"Well, I've been working on the problem of the diminishing magic for a few years now, and I've had some ideas, but without the tail-key or easy access to the world-ship, there's only so much that I can do. With your Parliamentarian access, and piece of the tail-key, I might be able to learn more, to find a way to boost the magic of this planet without luring pilots to their doom. If I could just find a way to selectively choose..."

Cordelia cut her off with a touch on the shoulder. "These ideas are highly speculative," she started, "But I believe Cybele—of all people—is capable of solving the problem. If we fix the diminishing magic, the Painites will lose their advantage, balance will be restored, and the people won't be so desperate that they follow Akeldama—the last hope they think they have for 'fixing' The City. Luckily, I know some people in Telesto. I'll accompany you two there, and we'll convince Teth, their leader, to give us her piece of the tail-key."

I looked back at Dad, who was deep in thought.

"Doesn't Akeldama have one of the pieces of the key, though? Won't that make fixing the tail-key a bit more of a challenge?" He said.

Cordelia sighed. "Hopefully, with enough of the key, Cybele can figure out how it works and bypass the system. But something tells me Akeldama isn't about to leave us alone anyway, so we might just run into the opportunity to take it."

"Hmm," Was all Dad said in response.

I found myself wondering what Telesto would be like—getting excited at the thought of visiting the city of air magic.
I even wondered if it was built in the sky. That would be awesome.

Dad was nodding now as he thought it over. "Telesto…Even if getting the tail-key piece from Teth is a long shot, it is the furthest city from here, right? If we do go there, it at least solves the immediate problem of Akeldama and Ayuna coming here and causing chaos. We could lure them there, far away, and to a city hopefully a little bit more prepared for a fight."

Cordelia nodded. "Telesto is full of adept warriors. I'm sure they could hold off the Painites for a time."

"And we could get real wingsuits and training too," I blurted out, picturing myself as the Indicolite warrior woman from the arena, wondering what secret air magic techniques I might learn from a woman like her. Everyone stared at me—Dad smiling, but Cybele frowning.

"What's wrong with my wingsuits?" Cybele asked.

"Oh, well, nothing. It's just that they're a bit, y'know, unconventional, to say the least, and ill-fitting. It would be nice to have a proper one that's my size and all, that's all."

Cybele sighed with a light smile. "They are a bit raggedy, aren't they?"

"So, Telesto. When do we leave?" I asked Dad excitedly, thinking more and more about fancy wingsuits and less about the psychopaths probably tracking us down as we spoke.

"Tomorrow. The three of us will go, and Cybele will stay here to protect the museum and work on the key problem," Cordelia cut in decisively.

Dad and Cybele nodded. Dad then turned to me. "Come on, Ali. We've got a long journey tomorrow by the sounds of it. Better get some rest."

13 – Ender

As much as I tried to hide it, seeing how well Alira was handling it all, I was terrified for her safety after the events in Poenari, especially because of her encounter with Ayuna. I had had a similar experience with Akeldama, fighting him with different magics, but his attitude was different—like my abilities were novel but nothing compared to his own. Ayuna, on the other hand, seemed to have taken an interest in Alira, or more specifically, the way her blood was able to contain different forms of magic simultaneously. It reminded me too much of the interest Cybele took in me when I first arrived, and while that turned out alright in the end, it was a rough ride involving multiple near-death experiences and a kidnapping.

I couldn't let the same happen to Alira. I was here to protect her, but Ayuna and Akeldama were much more powerful than Cybele, and they were hunting for power; an inherently more dangerous game than curiosity gone too far. At least in Telesto she could hone her air magic and other defensive magic. I really ought to give her an obsidian for protection. It wasn't hard to use, and it had saved me on countless occasions, including twice today already. Maybe I should've started Alira with knife magic instead. But then again, even though she struggled at first with fire magic, she made it work when she had to—and better than I ever did. That fireball was enormous. I'd have to make sure she was aware of the danger of using too much. I don't think she really understands the damage a garnet exploding on her wrist while she's holding fire can do. I shuddered just picturing it. Enough of that, we had to get to Telesto today.

Telesto was the furthest of the new cities from any of the others, purposely built to be harder to get to, making it easy only for those who could reach it with air magic. But even then, it would take a few hours and multiple stops for us to reach it, according to Cordelia. After breakfast, we packed the few things we would need for the journey on the backs of our wingsuits. It wasn't much, but I had the largest pack, considering I wouldn't need to carry Cybele anymore. After packing, we were on our way, following Cordelia's lead into the dunes in a completely different direction from Poenari.

The first stop we made was after about thirty minutes. When we landed, I checked my own indicolite as well as Alira's. They were concerningly warm, but I estimated we could go for about forty minutes before it became too risky.

Alira was happy to stick with flying in thirty-minute increments, saying so through panted breaths and a pink face. I smiled. She may have stronger magic, but she wasn't used to this kind of exercise. It was relatively easy at first, keeping your muscles flexed only as much as needed, but after a while, that level of muscle control became difficult. It was something I was used to from my military training, but I was honestly impressed that Alira hadn't faltered or slipped up yet. She was strong in more ways than one.

The gemstones cooled down quicker than Alira could catch her breath, and Cordelia was visibly worried about Alira's ability to do this roughly four more times.

"Perhaps I should go with Ender this time, to lessen the load for you, Alira?"

"No, no, that's okay. I'd actually have to tense my body more if I was by myself."

I nodded, and Cordelia resigned to being concerned in silence. We took off again, making a few more stops.

After about an hour and a half, we started making stops every fifteen minutes and included a few stretches in our breaks. Both of us were going stiff from the rigid poses we held in the air.

At last, we finally came upon Telesto—a big silver city at the edge of the world. From this distance, I couldn't make out many details, but it wasn't very city-shaped, comprised of more shiny, bulbous components than spires or boxy structures. The closer we got, the more I realised what Telesto was, why it looked so strange, and yet eerily familiar.

The city was entirely hidden inside one large structure, built within the carcass of an enormous starship. Its size wasn't immediately obvious, with only certain parts sticking up out of the ground—about a third of the ship, really. I could only know that much without seeing through the ground because the starship in question was the remains of the U.E.S. Cronus, the very ship I had been aboard when I first found my way to this planet, to this universe.

It was impossible that it was here now, buried under so much sand. The Cronus was still back home in our solar system, roughly near Neptune at the moment, I think, preparing for a trip over to Alpha Centauri. Or at least that's what I'd heard. Maybe their true destination was here all along. But that wouldn't explain how it was buried, or ruined in this state. No, something was definitely weird here, and I was going to find out exactly how this ship got here, and how the Indicolites found it. It wasn't exactly on the map.

As we got closer, Alira found a faded insignia on the outside of the ship and her head whipped around to face me, a shocked expression on her face, having come to the same conclusion as I had. We landed then, not sure how to approach the city inside a ruined starship.

When we landed, Cordelia immediately took the lead, trudging through the sand over to the giant hunk of steel separating us from the inside of the ship. We followed the outside of the ship for a few minutes before we came upon two guards, a particularly crumpled section of the ship's hull, and half of what used to be a turbine engine, used for landing the Cronus on planets with dense enough atmospheres.

The guards noticed us as soon as we noticed them, spinning around to face us as we approached from the side, whipping some sort of double-ended spear from their backs in the same fluid motion.

"Halt," the closest guard shouted, pointing his spear tip towards us.

Cordelia was unfazed as she continued forward, Alira and I stopping, the two of us as well as the guards raising our eyebrows at her.

"Tell Teth I've brought the one who killed Jezebel to her city. That should get her attention."

The guards eyed Alira and me suspiciously before the furthest guard from us lowered his spear and opened a panel on the outside of the ship, punching in something before speaking into the device. It seem they had figured out the intercom system at least. I wonder what other parts of the Cronus they had redesigned for their own purposes. The guard only holstered his spear-like weapon onto his back once a woman's voice responded through the intercom. The other guard did the same, and both of them moved to stand facing the remains of the turbine engine.

Wind whipped up all around us moments later before it focused into a whirlpool funnelling through the turbine blades, slowly starting to spin them, getting faster and faster until the more crumpled section of the ship that the guards seemed to be protecting started shifting, peeling back like a broken garage door—albeit an absolutely enormous one—revealing a large hollow chunk of the ship inside, full of life, including trees, people, and assorted other plant life. Clearly, this hole in the hull that was now a grand entrance was the entry point of a torpedo of some sort that had exploded just inside the hull of the ship, creating the enormous space that seemed to now serve as the city centre of Telesto.

Alira swivelled on the spot to face Cordelia, jaw hanging open. It seemed she wanted to say something but didn't. Eventually, she went with, "What!? Cordelia, I thought you said you didn't know what trees were!?"

Cordelia frowned at her, not sure what she meant. Alira's response was to stick out her arm, seemingly gesturing to the whole space. "Those are trees! And lots of different kinds too."

I could see something click in Alira's mind. She turned to me next. "Dad, did the Cronus have a garden?"

I took another look around at the plant life, seeing where she was going with this.

She was right, all the plant life here was easily recognisable, meaning they were from Earth. Or more specifically, from the gardens and plant research labs aboard Cronus. Although, it was a military vessel and so had nothing quite as grand as the trees and plants before us now. This ship had to have been here long before I was last aboard the Cronus, probably even before I was born given the size of some of these trees, but that was impossible.

"We actually had multiple, some for food, others for oxygen, and one or two for research purposes."

Alira's eyes lit up. "I've never been more excited for vegetables."

I laughed at this, and she smiled, still staring at the curated forest inside the ship's carcass.

Another set of guards found us then, offering, "This way to Teth please." But the way they held their spears indicated we didn't have a choice. Cordelia led the way, following the first guard while the second trailed us.

It was strange walking through a place like this; somewhere so familiar and yet so foreign, a place I could navigate in a heartbeat, but wouldn't know what I would find anywhere I went. Putting aside the impossible nature of where I was, I focused on the task ahead of us. Cordelia seemed to know what she was doing, but I got the feeling she was expecting me to play a certain part in this meeting. I wasn't entirely sure what, and acting wasn't my strong suit.

It was pretty clear when we reached Teth, as the main doors to what used to be the Bridge of the Cronus slid open, revealing a woman in the centre of the room with a dark blonde braid and a kind of armoured dress that looked like something halfway between what her guards wore and what Cordelia was wearing.

"Cordelia. What a… surprise to see you here. I assume not with good news, given who you claim to be here with." Teth eyed me suspiciously. I wasn't enjoying this reputation I seemed to have.

"Not particularly, no. Have you heard about Akeldama's recent appearance in the arena?"

Teth scoffed. "Of course I have. It's the only news of the city nowadays worth hearing about. Although I rather wish I hadn't heard about this last one. I assume you have more information regarding Akeldama and the priestess?"

Cordelia bowed her head. "The priestess was the sister of the High Priestess. She asked us to find her, and we did. Unfortunately, not before she had died and Akeldama and his daughter took an interest in Ender and my granddaughter here due to their… unique way with magic."

Teth's eyebrows raised slowly, a hard line spreading across her face, interrupted briefly by a fact she found interesting. "Akeldama has a daughter? Interesting. And she's much like him, it would seem."

Her frown returned. "And fearing they might come after your poorly defended museum, you've instead tried to lead them here to let my warriors die senselessly at the hands of them both."

"Only because you can fight, and we can't. I only came in the interest of saving the most innocent people from senselessly dying."

Alira stepped forward then, surprising both Cordelia and me. "And we can fight them too. I have air magic, but I only know what I taught myself. If you let me train with you, we won't have to hide from them."

Alira was standing strong, but I felt her voice crack slightly at the end, being brave despite her fear. I was proud of her then but terrified all the same, regretting my choice to drag my daughter into what was sure to become a civil war. Training with the Indicolites was the only way to make her strong enough to survive what was becoming of this place.

14 – Alira

Tomorrow I would become a magical warrior woman, soaring through the sky with her spear. The adrenaline of our arrival and meeting with Teth was finally wearing off as I lay down in the little bunk I would be staying in for however long we were here. It had been a long flight to get here, and my muscles were stiff. I wasn't sure how able for combat and flight training I would be tomorrow. But nevertheless, I was excited to get to use those cool spears, or yacharow as Teth had called them.

We walked past the training room, or really half a room as it was mostly open air, on the way to dinner and saw some of the warriors practising. Their yacharow flew through the air with fins jutting out from the centre, like a double-ended arrow with feathers in the middle rather than the end. I couldn't imagine being precise enough with my tornadoes to guide a flying spear so elegantly around the room like they were, but I couldn't wait to try.

When I made my way to the cafeteria the next morning, I was delighted to find that the Indicolites had figured out how to make actual fries. This place was awesome. My only complaint about this planet so far was the food, aside from the murderous psychopaths, and this place somehow had fried potatoes. I wasn't leaving this city, and I hadn't even gotten my wingsuit yet. Dad found me easily, knowing he was behind me after hearing him chuckle when he saw my plate stacked with fries and little else.

"Ali, I know it's been two whole days since you had any kind of fried food, but please eat something other than fries."

I rolled my eyes. "Fine, but I'm pretty sure I saw some peanut plants on the way in. You better teach them how to make peanut butter."

Dad frowned. "I don't know how to make peanut butter."

"Well, they figured out fries all on their own, so it can't be that hard."

Dad didn't seem convinced but replied, "I was planning on making a trip to see what they had anyway. I'll see what I can do."

I smiled at him. "Thankssss." I added a couple more things to my plate that weren't fries and sat back down to finish off breakfast. Then I was out the door and off to where Teth said I would be training before Dad was even half finished. My muscles ached from yesterday, but I was hoping the nutrients of fried potatoes would give me the boost I needed to not suck today.

I arrived at where I was supposed to be training, a little confused at first as I saw all the eight-year-olds running around tripping each other with gusts of wind.

I started to retreat back into the hallway, planning to check the next room down in case I had gotten it wrong. A voice rang out then from somewhere among the children, stopping me.

"You must be Alira."

I locked eyes with the man as he stood up from where he was kneeling to help one of the kids. He was really tall. And kinda hot. My face flushed a little bit.

"I… yes, that's me, Alira." Smooth, Alira, smooth.

The man started towards me. "My name is Evander. I hear you're a bit of a late bloomer. Well, don't worry, we'll have you flying around in no time."

I frowned, the man suddenly a little bit less hot. "I can already fly, thank you very much."

He smirked. "So can Billy." He retorted as he jabbed his thumb over his shoulder just as a little boy went flying through the air, his yelling echoing around the room.

Oh, I'll show this guy just how well I can fly. I went to launch myself into the air but stopped as the man spun around and shouted out over the sea of children.

"Alright everyone! It looks like everyone is here, so let's get started. I think we'll start with some pole rises, so if everyone could please spread out. Let's see who can get the highest today."

He turned back around to me, gesturing over to the corner where a space amongst the sea of eight-year-olds was forming.

"Let's see what you can do then."

I scoffed and strode over to the space, the kids all eyeing me with confused looks. I had no idea what a 'pole rise' was, but I grinned when I saw the kids start doing them. Evander was about to eat his words. Maybe then I'd get to go to a real air magic class. Pole rises were essentially cylindrical air currents that lifted you straight upwards off the ground, maintaining the shape of the column of air beneath you. Still grinning, I activated the indicolite via my bracelet, seeing Evander raise an eyebrow at me, curious. Ignoring him, I summoned the wind, swirling around me in tight circles about my waist.

Familiar with the feeling once more, I picked myself up and shot up towards the ceiling, almost falling out of the air when I realised I was going too fast and squeezed to slow down, cutting off the tornado altogether. I caught myself quickly, rising more slowly this time back up to the ceiling, smirking as I reached it.

Deciding to show off a little bit, my tornado twisted me upside-down and pinned me against the ceiling so that it appeared like I was standing on it. The intense air rushing at me to keep me there was hard to maintain and was starting to hurt, but it was worth it to see the look on Evander's face. The competition among the kids died out when they saw me too, all collectively giving up and floating back down to the ground.

The embarrassment hit once I was the only one still in the air, and I quickly flipped myself back around and came down, my face flushed from both embarrassment and being upside-down.

"It seems I misjudged you, Miss Alira. Clearly Teth has sent you to the wrong class," Evander said with an impressed smirk.

He turned back to the kids then. "Keep practising while I escort Alira here to somewhere more fitting for her level."

I followed Evander out into the hall and we began towards another part of the ship, him asking me questions to gauge my true level.

"So, Alira. It seems you're stronger than Teth led me to believe. What did you tell her about your skill?"

I thought for a moment. "Well, my grandmother said I had a unique way with magic, and then I said I only knew what I had taught myself. Other than that, not a whole lot."

"You really taught yourself to do that back there?"

"I mean, my dad helped me figure out the basics first, but then I was the one who figured out how to fly with a passenger and how to get us all the way here from the city. The others were against wingsuits at first, but it worked out pretty well, I think."

Evander had a look of bewilderment on his face. "You flew here all the way from the city with a wingsuit and carrying a passenger?"

"I… Yes?"

Evander grinned. "Oh, Freya is going to love you. You know, we don't even teach passenger flight. It's deemed too much effort for how often it's used, which, given that this is Telesto, is almost never."

"Who is Freya?"

"She's the Captain of the Telesto Guard, but she also teaches the new recruits and decides who makes it into the guard and who doesn't. I believe she's teaching an advanced wingsuit aerobatics class right now, which is perfect."

"Wait, you want me to join *that* class? But all I can do is get from point A to B, not exactly what I'd call advanced aerobatics."

Evander smiled. "I know you said you have a unique way with magic, and that it's pretty new for you. Tell me, how long have you been practising with air magic?"

"Well, about three days."

He stopped and stared at me. "Three days!?" He shook his head and continued on. "Three days, and you've already taught yourself how to fly across the desert in a wingsuit with a passenger."

He looked me up and down then, and I got suddenly self-conscious, seeing a man as beautiful as him look at me like that.

"You may be a bit younger than Freya's mob, but you'll be flying circles around them in no time. They're a bit full of themselves, so they need someone like you to put them in their place."

"When you say a bit older, what exactly do you mean?"

"They're about sixteen to eighteen. Eighteen is typically when you would graduate and become a member of the guard."

"But I'm only fifteen!?"

Evander smiled. "Then you'll damage their egos all the more easily."

I blushed then, his confidence in me totally misplaced but endearing. I was nervous as I saw where we were heading—almost to the outside of the ship near what used to be the main engine thrusters. Evander held up the back side of his hand where a nicely cut clear indicolite crystal was embedded in the leather cuff wrapping his wrist and sticking out over the back of his hand to a point. He saw me frown as the door clicked after scanning his gemstone and opening.

"We all have one gemstone in Telesto encoded with all of our details. It lets us go wherever we have access. You'll get one if you stick around long enough. You might even get special access if you get into the guard."

I wasn't sure how to respond to that. We didn't exactly have many future plans right now. Our only plan was for me and Dad to get stronger so we could protect ourselves from Akeldama and Ayuna. And that was exactly what I was going to do.

We stepped outside into the awfully bright sunlight, the rippling watercolour sky above us shockingly pretty as always.

"Come on, it's this way," Evander said, making me realise that I'd stopped to stare at the alien sky. "Right, yes."

The first thing I heard as we approached Freya's training ground was a woman shouting. As we got closer, I realised that the woman was shouting at all the teenagers flying through the sky exceptionally fast and hard to keep track of. Freya didn't stop yelling at them long after we had stopped in front of her. I followed Evander's example, patiently waiting for her attention. When we finally got it, she was straight to the point.

"Yes, Evander, can I help you?"

"It seems Teth has misjudged Alira here and placed her with me. After seeing what she's capable of, I believe she belongs with you."

"Is that so?" She turned to me then, eyeing me up and down. I tried to exude confidence, but I was getting a lot of attention today and I wasn't a fan of it all that much.

"Well then, girl, prove to me you belong here."

I froze, glancing at Evander, who only gestured to the open sky before us, the people flying around just before having come down one by one, now all watching Freya and me. Embarrassed as I was, it was easy to launch into the sky to show what I could do, given that the sky was much further away from all the eyeballs staring at me on the ground.

I stepped away from Evander and Freya, exploding into the sky a little more aggressively than I had planned to, my unease spurring me up and away. Once there, however, I locked in, not wearing a wingsuit, but still able to throw myself around through the sky, bending air currents around and around, trying to remember the hardest stuff that I had practised days earlier. I lost my balance a couple of times, getting close enough to the ground more than once to see the scrutinising gaze of Freya. It was much harder to balance without the wingsuit to align my body properly with the air. Not seeing much change in Freya's stony expression, I decided to try one last thing. A properly practised move that was more than carving random shapes into the sky. I just had to hope that Evander would understand what I was doing.

I conjured a second tornado, only realising as I was already diving to scoop Evander up that this could end catastrophically with both of us not having wingsuits or being tied to each other. But it was too late for that now. Evander's eyes widened, but he adopted a strong stance facing away from me, ready to be at the whim of my magic. I scooped him up, trying to adjust for his movement but then stopped, realising that he was much more practised than Cordelia and could adjust himself much more easily, letting me concentrate on keeping myself upright and our tornadoes close but not crashing into one another.

I brought us back down in front of Freya, Evander opting for a swift exit, thumping down in the sand, the motion surprising me and causing me to waver enough that I tripped forward on my own landing, falling forward onto my hands, panting, hesitating to look up into Freya's stony face, fearing the worst. When I had stopped panting so hard, I stood up, raising my chin and trying to look confident, whatever judgement I faced. Freya's stony gaze remained, but I thought I saw her eyebrow slightly raised.

"How long have you been practising that last move, girl?"

"Since two days ago, ma'am," I responded, not sure how to address the captain of the Telesto Guard. Her other eyebrow definitely moved then, raising slightly to meet the other one, confirming my suspicions that she had, in fact, raised her eyebrow before. She turned to Evander then.

"Thank you, Evander, I'll take it from here."

Evander bowed slightly with a grin, returning to his class after shooting me a look.

"Alira, was it? I look forward to seeing how you do in a wingsuit."

Freya immediately turned to the group standing, whispering, on the other side of the training grounds.

"Emma!" she shouted over at the group, "Please take Alira here to get a wingsuit and return as quickly as possible."

Finally, now my real training would begin.

15 – Ender

I could tell that Alira was excited for training today, but learning that Telesto had fries had made her like this place even more. I had started wondering what would happen if Alira decided she liked this place too much to leave, but decided that training wouldn't be so exciting once she had learned as much as she could. The food might be harder to drag her away from though.

With Alira now at training, after eating a plate of mostly fries as quickly as possible, and Cordelia catching up with Teth, discussing the current political climate or something like that, I was left to finish breakfast by myself and plan for the day. I had focused so much on making sure Alira could protect herself that I hadn't planned a whole lot for myself while I was here. Teth had told me where I could go to practise air magic and gave me some names of people who might want to train me, but because I was older there weren't any classes I could join. All the older people who had suddenly gained air magic had done so fifteen years ago, after all. Nowadays, everyone was trained as a kid, and Alira still fit into the training schedule. But I wasn't as fast to pick up air magic as Alira, nor did I need to since I already had other types of magic at my disposal. Other than going to have my indicolite properly cut and encoded with biometrics so I could access the city more easily, and visiting the kitchens, I didn't have much else planned for the day. Encoding my Indicolite gemstone didn't take very long, but I quickly found that it was slightly awkward to hold my chest up to the scanner every time I wanted to go somewhere outside of the main public facilities.

After that, I made my way to the kitchens easily enough, knowing exactly where they were on the original Cronus and finding them in the same place here, although stocked mostly with ingredients I didn't recognise. After asking around, I discovered that the head chefs didn't do as much experimentation as I had thought and instead used the knowledge that one particular botanist had gathered to inform the way they used the various foreign plants that grew on the Cronus. Curious, I sought out this botanist, unsurprised when I found her in the remains of the largest garden on Cronus, which was now much bigger given the caved-in walls and extra time the plants had had to grow, wherever that impossible time had come from.

I must have caught her eye, gawking at the huge garden in foreign clothes, as she came over and introduced herself, her appearance leaving no doubt that she was exactly who I was looking for.

"Hiya. You must be new to Telesto. There aren't more exotic plants anywhere else on this dried-up planet. It truly is a miracle how they've flourished."

The botanist joined me in my wide-eyed assessment of the garden. "It's really something. I never thought I'd see anything like this here. This garden was so much smaller last time I saw it."

She frowned then, not sure what I meant, but questioned, "Not your first time to Telesto then?"

"Well, yes and no."

She raised her eyebrows in response but said nothing.

"I came here looking for you after hearing from the kitchens that you know the most about the plants here. I'd like to share what I know about some of the more edible plants I know of."

"Oh? A fellow botanist are you? With knowledge of the plants that only seem to exist here in Telesto where you claim to have been before but maybe not?"

I chuckled. Clearly, I wasn't great at the whole 'air of mystery' thing. I seemed to just be confusing. But then again, the origins of this place confused me too.

"I'm not a botanist, no, but I am from the planet where these plants originated. I've been to this garden before because I used to live here, back when this city was still a spaceship."

Her frown remained, still sceptical. "Given our archaeological records of this place, that would make you much, much older than you look."

"Admittedly, I am confused on that point too."

This seemed to appease her scepticism a little bit, making her more keen to hear what I knew about her plants.

"So, what is it you think you can tell me about these plants that I haven't already discovered in my decade or so of studying them?"

"My knowledge is mostly of a culinary nature, but for starters, there are some plants in the lobby with seeds that taste great mashed up and spread on toast."

16 – Alira

Uuurrnghhh. Everything hurt. My arms were stiff from hours of being stuck out from my side supporting wingsuit flaps, and my whole body hurt almost as much from all the constant clenching, unclenching, and then crashing into various things, including but not limited to: the ground, other students, and then the ground as I fell out of the sky from crashing into other students. I had never been this bruised in my entire life. My excitement for getting to try out a yacharow was rapidly dwindling, afraid of what I would do to myself with something so sharp if I was going to be this beat up after flying around in just a wingsuit.

Flying with Freya's recruits was much harder than with Dad, or even carrying Cordelia. Flying through the open sky was easy enough with some practice, but as soon as a bunch of other students start whipping by you, the air currents go haywire and the constant readjusting and predicting is exhausting. And I was totally exhausted.

I hadn't seen Dad all day, and I almost didn't see him as I blearily wandered over to a table in the dining hall, which just happened to be the one he was sitting at, along with some other woman who looked like she had dirt in her hair and… everywhere else.

Dad was grinning, and when I didn't have the energy to ask why, or the concentration left to see what was on the two plates in front of him, he chuckled,

"I see they've been working you hard."

"I am deceased," I mumbled as I sat down, wincing as I eased into the bruises on my butt.

"Well, maybe some of this will revive you," Dad said as he pushed one of the plates towards me, now realising what was on it. My eyes shot up at him, and back down to the plate of peanut butter toast with a drizzle of honey on top. Finally, something to be excited about that wasn't about to beat me up.

I bit into the toast ravenously. It had a bit of a strange flavour, but that made sense given that it was this planet's first attempt at peanut butter. But then again, the flavour could have been the honey. It was made by beetles, after all. Nevertheless, I devoured the toast, finding the energy now to ask Dad about the dirt-covered woman sitting next to him.

"So, Dad. Who's this?"

"Oh, this is Chantrelle. She's the botanist who figured out that potatoes would taste great cooked in a big pot of oil."

"OMG, you are a HERO. You single-handedly saved this place from being just as culinarily destitute as the rest of this planet seems to be."

Chantrelle seemed to be momentarily offended by this introduction but seemed to understand it after my immediate reaction was to praise her as the genius who invented fries.

"And thanks for the peanut butter. I can't imagine Dad could've figured it out by himself."

Dad responded with a sarcastic frown, unable to hold it after I grinned back at him. It was then that a fourth person appeared at our table, sitting down gracefully and looking much less covered in dirt and grime than the rest of us.

"Cordelia! I was wondering where you had been all day." I exclaimed as my grandmother sat down with us, wearing much fancier clothes than the rest of us, and in the Telesto colours of teal, blue, white, and brown.

"Hello, Alira. I've been discussing the political situation with Teth. There has been a lot to discuss, especially since the last person she sent to the city to gather information was that poor woman who fell to Akeldama in the arena." She sighed a long sigh before continuing. "Nevertheless, I have yet to explain the…"

Cordelia's gaze found Dad's botanist friend then, hesitant to reveal certain facts in her presence.

Dad noticed immediately and turned to Chantrelle, "Cordelia, this is Chantrelle. She's a local botanist responsible for the various foods here made from Earth plants."

"Like peanut butter! Cordelia, you have to try some, it's an Earth delicacy." I blurted out, quickly realising that I had none to offer her as I stared at my polished-off plate. I glanced to Dad, who chuckled, pushing the second plate towards Cordelia across the table. She seemed to not know what to think of the offer, treating it with suspicion. She hesitantly took a bite of the toast, her eyebrows raising as she took a second bite.

"Dad spent all day with Chantrelle making it after I told him I had seen peanuts in the lobby."

"Your father certainly is full of surprises. All right then."

Cordelia, having accepted the peanut butter toast as a bribe to win her trust, continued with her summary of her discussions with Teth and the current plan.

As for the matter of the tail-key and why we need it, I have yet to explain this to Teth, but I think she would be willing to part with her piece if the conditions are right. She's a shrewd negotiator and whatever she chooses to ask for in return would not be anything small. That being said, I sense that there is some sort of technical issue happening relating to the ship Telesto is built within, and I am hoping Ender will have enough knowledge of this ship to be able to trade for the piece. I am, of course, hesitant to suggest such a deal, not knowing much more about the problem or the extent of Ender's knowledge."

Cordelia finished then, expecting Dad to respond, to try and fill in his half of the puzzle, but it was Chantrelle who drew everyone's attention. Her eyes were suddenly scanning the room, her head tilted down, like she was worried she was being watched all of a sudden. Noticing the attention she was ironically drawing, she spoke up softly, "I might know something about the problem, actually, but we can't speak here. Teth is very careful to make Telesto look strong, and I'm afraid after recent events, she would be even more desperate to keep any weaknesses under wraps."

Dad and Cordelia both looked at Chantrelle stunned, but I instead smiled smugly. Of course this lady knew what was going on. She was the genius that re-invented peanut butter *and* fries and who knows what else. If she could discover the secrets of potatoes, of course she could figure out the secrets of Telesto.

Chantrelle stood up then and turned to leave the cafeteria. We all followed, unsure where we were being led. Cordelia looked concerned, like she was wondering if this was a trap, but the ease with which Dad followed Chantrelle was enough for me to dispel any doubt. Somewhat unsurprisingly, we ended up in a large biodome of sorts. At least that's what it looked like it used to be before the walls were torn apart and the plants grew beyond the bounds of the space.

I tried to restrain my wide-eyed looks as the rest of the group marched on between the various trees and plants, most of which were unexpectedly ripe with fruit. We took a detour off the central path, shuffling down a narrow gap between two rows of overgrown garden beds. At the other end was a heavily shaded pocket of space, the large tree close by casting the majority of the shade, and raining down some kind of nut all over the space. There were a few pillows on the floor of the secret garden, Chantrelle going and sitting down cross-legged on one of them before explaining anything.

"I wasn't sure at first what had kept this little pocket from being overgrown, but it turned out to be a broken battery that had leaked over the floor, the liquid slowly evaporating over time and preventing anything from growing into this space without poisoning itself. Don't worry, the battery has long been empty, but the plants have already grown beyond here, leaving this little pocket behind."

Chantrelle leaned forward then, sweeping the nuts and leaves aside from a panel on the floor before popping it open to reveal a collection of pipes and wires beneath the floor. On the back of the panel was a kind of tablet, wired into the floor, clearly having been done without proper permission. Cordelia looked conflicted, like she knew this was probably exactly what we were looking for, but that if Teth found out how we'd found out, we would never get the piece. We would most likely get kicked out, along with Chantrelle, given what I knew of Teth.

Chantrelle continued as she navigated the tablet, "I was having trouble matching up the health of the plants and their growth with the numbers the system was giving me about the various biosphere systems. Y'know, like water and filtration and such. Anyway, as I do my best thinking here, I patched in a tablet so I could work on the problem, and discovered the raw system data, which was much different than what the official diagnostics were saying. That's when I realised the diagnostics were being faked, making the city look like it was in better health than it really was."

Cordelia was still on edge, her worry starting to show more, whispering sharply, "This is all very interesting, but what exactly is the problem here?"

Chantrelle sighed, "Essentially, the population of Telesto has exceeded the maximum energy output of the original ship systems, and without the resources of the ships from the sky, they can't create more energy or build more generators."

Cordelia paused, thinking about the problem, relaxing a little more now that she knew exactly what the stakes were.

Dad frowned, thinking too, "Are there no sapphires here? Could they not increase the power output that way? Maybe by rerouting energy from other systems?"

"That's exactly what they have been doing, which is why my garden is starting to suffer. Eventually they won't be able to take anymore and there will be brownouts. When that happens, everyone will know that Telesto is weak."

"I see," Dad replied.

Cordelia then looked back up and directly at Ender. "Well, it's definitely a problem, if solved, worthy of Teth's piece of the key. In order to move forward, though, it sounds like we need to get Ender to the generators to see if he can do something about it. If not, it's not worth us exposing ourselves to Teth that we discovered this knowledge."

Chantrelle nodded, and they both looked at Dad expectantly, a weird look on his face.

"Uh, you guys know I'm not an engineer or anything, right? I just lived here for a little bit, is all. I can't promise I'll even know what I'm looking at. I've only been to the engine room once, and that was before the Cronus got an antimatter drive."

Cordelia sighed. "Even so, I'm hoping your familiarity with Earth technology, as well as your ability to use sapphire magic, will be enough to find a solution."

"It's worth a shot. Where to then?"

Cordelia blinked absently back at him until Dad scrunched his face in embarrassment.

"Oh, right. Follow me, I guess."

Chantrelle stuck with us as we made our way through the wonky steel corridors towards the energy generators near the very back of the ship, buried far underground. She clearly wasn't afraid of the danger. Dad didn't seem to be either, but knowing Cordelia was the most aware of the full situation, and seeing her following firmly but hesitantly behind, was a worrying sight.

The sun was starting to set when we entered the part of the ship with no windows. Or at least none that weren't buried. Chantrelle got us past a couple of doors that the rest of us guests didn't have access to, but the door into maintenance was locked for her too, meaning we couldn't progress further as easily.

"We won't be able to get much further without setting off alarms. The encoded indicolites make it hard to hack into anything."

We all stood awkwardly in the dimly lit room in front of the door like we were waiting for it to magically open. I knew everyone was trying to think of a plan, but still. It was a weird moment. Dad randomly raised his wrist up, his sleeve falling back to reveal his parliamentarian tattoo. Two loosely braided cords were printed on his wrist. One a deep purple, and the other navy. The tattoo was supposedly able to teleport him to parliament aboard the ship at the centre of the planet. I had my doubts though, given what I knew about gravity, and the state of disrepair this much smaller ship was in, let alone one old enough to grow a whole planet around it.

Chantrelle stared at it, intrigued. When she realised what it was, she snatched his wrist out of the air and drew it closer to her face, startling Dad as she did so.

"Whoa. You're a parliamentarian? That's what this is, right? It's been so long."

"Yes, I am. Not that I agree with the rest of them on much, if anything. I've only been there once. Well, twice technically, but the second time I was breaking in."

"Now that's some crazy shit right there. I don't know much about parliamentarians, but I do know that their security is waaaay better than Telesto's. I assume that means these tattoos are much more complex than our encoded indicolites. Especially since they have to communicate with teleporters. I'm no expert myself, but I know a guy that's good with these kinds of things, and he absolutely loves a puzzle. I should be able to download its encryption and send it to him. Best of all is that he won't know what it is he's deciphering, and he won't really care as long as it's a good challenge. It will take a couple of days, though."

Dad and Cordelia were nodding, both of them surprised at Chantrelle once again.

"That sounds good. Alira will be able to get in some more training. I assume a couple of days won't make your situation more difficult, Cordelia?" Dad asked.

Cordelia thought, a hard line on her face. "It won't make things more difficult, no. However, it does change the timeline a little bit. I had planned to discuss our situation at length with Teth tomorrow, but I won't be doing that anymore. She knows I want to talk about something, however, so I will have to come up with something for now. But never mind that, that's my problem. You worry about the tattoo. Now let's get out of here."

"There is one more thing you should know too. Because Telesto's security system is identification-based, you'll still have to assign a person to the tattoo. That being said, it's likely that they give the same tattoo to every parliamentarian, meaning that we'll be adding all of them to the system, and not just Ender. I could be wrong, though."

Cordelia's brow furrowed further. She was starting to look exhausted. I know I was.

"Until we know more, it's pointless to discuss. Everyone go get some sleep; we've all got long and increasingly complicated days tomorrow. Ender, if you wouldn't mind leading us back?"

"Of course, this way."

17 – Ender

It had been nine days since we discovered the energy problem in Telesto and made plans to get inside and figure out what was happening and whether or not I could help fix it. It had taken this long for Chantrelle's hacker friend to crack the encryption on my tattoo. Apparently, he could've done it much faster, but Chantrelle presented it to him pretty casually so as to not raise suspicions, and so he had only worked on it after his shifts, working away at it like a puzzle. Chantrelle had said the only thing he asked about it was whether she had any more that difficult.

Alira had spent her time training. Apparently, the class she was in was pretty intense as she hadn't got a day off since we'd been here, and it sounded like she wasn't going to get any anytime soon. Cordelia had ended up feigning sickness in her attempts to slow down discussions with Teth, which was okay to begin with, but after nearly a week, she couldn't fake it any longer. Fortunately, by then, Telesto had gotten used to our presence, and no-one eyed us as outsiders anymore.

Alira, particularly after the first few days, seemed to start enjoying herself, even if she did practically pass out the moment she had any free time. It was strange seeing her in uniform and working so hard while I sat around and waited. I tried to help Chantrelle as much as I could, but outside of describing Earth foods, I wasn't much help. She was in charge of maintaining the gardens after all, and I wasn't much help there outside of manual labour. I found myself for the majority of my days having not very much to do.

Left to my own devices, I tended to spend my time exploring Telesto, wondering what I would find at the end of each steel corridor where I knew something different used to be.

It wasn't until today when I reached the remains of the hangar that I actually started to get any answers as to how Telesto was possible, and what had happened to the U.E.S Cronus. I entered the hangar, somewhat surprised to find that it was significantly smaller than I remembered as most of the walls had crumpled in the landing. I suppose not all the spaces could decay into larger ones like the garden and main halls seemed to have done. I could see when I entered it why not much had been done with the place. The crumbled walls made almost everything in the room exposed, sharp and dangerous, which was particularly problematic in the floor. I had to be careful where I stepped, not sure how far I would fall if the floor gave out. As I wandered around the space, slipping between fallen beams and shuffling around exploded fighters, one ship in particular caught my attention. The small ship was pressed against an exposed wall where the edge of the desert vibrated enough to slowly chew through the exterior wall of the Cronus and subsequently the smaller ships within. While the wall and the front half of the ship had been eaten by the desert, the cockpit and the semi-preserved body within remained.

At first, I was amazed that a corpse had managed to stay so intact after so long, before slowly realising that half of the point of the cockpit was protecting life from dead, empty space.

What was more astonishing was the moment I realised that I recognised the corpse. It was none other than Colonel Amir Summanus. As I stared at the corpse, my astonishment slowly turned to curiosity as I noticed details about him that were unfamiliar. Unfortunately, it was hard to tell how old he was when he died or even if he was, in fact, Colonel Summanus. Strangely, he seemed to have two full-sleeve tattoos when he died. Not that I could make out any of the art on his skin with it as decayed as it was. But the Summanus I knew didn't have any tattoos. The only way to confirm what had happened, and that this was at least a version of Summanus, was to open the cockpit. I took a deep breath of the corpse-free air and braced myself as I reached for the quick-release handle.

The moment I turned it, the cockpit window grunted forcefully in steely protest, the window jolting to the side and shattering under the stress, the glass raining down all over the corpse as well as the jagged floor of the hangar. I guess the cockpit was under a lot of stress, and the release was too sudden for it to take any more of the pressure. I used my sleeve to brush away the tiny shards of glass from the edge of the cockpit so that I could reach inside. It was then that I realised my face felt a bit hot and itchy. Looking down at myself, I saw that I too was also covered in a fine silicate dust and realised what must have happened. I reached up to my face, my hand coming away covered in tiny pinpricks of blood. Good, nothing serious, just a whole lot of tiny cuts that made it look a bit like I was bleeding out of my pores.

Not having a handkerchief on me, and wanting to get away from the condensed smell of old corpse as fast as possible, I turned my attention back to Summanus and reached into the cockpit, holding my breath. I reached first around his neck for his dog tags, having to fish them out of his chest after his ribs crumbled to dust the moment I touched them. I was going to need to seriously sanitise my hand, and probably everything, after this. Pulling out his dog tags, I read them, finding nothing unusual and confirming that this was, in fact, Colonel Amir Summanus. The only other item I found on him that could identify him was a badge, recognising him as being in command of the ship, although it looked different somehow, like it was different to the design I remembered. It wasn't until I spotted the dark brown bag by his feet that I knew that this was a very different man than the one I knew. I pulled out the bag and hopped away from the ship to look inside it, taking deep, relatively corpse-free breaths once I was away from the body. The bag held a few of his personal items—things that he clearly didn't want to leave behind as he attempted to escape whatever it was that had caused the ship to crash, realising too late that fighting against this planet's ability to crash ships onto itself was futile.

There wasn't much here that told me anything, but there were a couple of photos. One of them showed Colonel Summanus as I had known him, with his dark hair and tan skin, although he still had his sleeve tattoos, so that was throwing me off. The other photo, however, must have been more recent, showing an older Summanus with grey hair, still relatively dark, but his face showed his age, his wrinkled smile unusual on a man of his build. Although some of those muscles had shrunken since the last photo was taken. This man was definitely much older when he died than the one I knew, and also an entirely different man. It was starting to seem possible that the world ship not only stole ships from other universes for their anti-matter power sources but also stole them out of time.

Just then the lights flickered, and the constant background electrical hum of Telesto faltered, pitching lower, and sputtering for a few moments before rising again and blending back into the background. The lights flicked back to life seconds later. This was a bad sign. This was exactly what Teth was trying to avoid, knowing that brownouts would make it suddenly clear to the world that Telesto wasn't as strong as it appeared. Whatever I was going to do to try and fix it, I was going to have to try now, before the next one confirmed undoubtedly that there was a big problem.

I rushed out of the hangar as fast as I could, almost tripping on the jagged floor. I picked up speed when I reached the hallway, heading for our secret garden, knowing that at the very least Chantrelle would be there and would hopefully have finished doing whatever it was she was doing to get my tattoo to open the door into maintenance.

I slowed back down to a brisk walk once there were too many people about, hoping not to draw attention, but everyone was pretty on edge anyway, whispering about what had just happened. As I crossed the lobby and turned down another corridor towards the biosphere garden, I thought I saw a smirk on the face of a man across the room. But I was too focused to wonder about it. Besides, I had probably imagined it anyway.

I found Chantrelle in the secret garden just as I predicted. She was laser-focused on the tablet, but as soon as I sat down, she spoke,

"Give me your arm."

Her stern tone, strange coming from her, caused me to stick out my arm in front of her instinctively.

"Other arm, dummy. I need your tattoo. Now that we've had a brownout, we need to get into maintenance now. There's no time for a stealth plan. We need to get you down there as soon as possible."

"I know, but what about Teth?"

"If she finds out, she'll probably thank us for fixing her city. Unless we don't. But then she can't accuse us of spying, given that the whole city probably knows something is up now."

"True. I still don't know what to do if we happen to run into her though."

"Well, hopefully Cordelia had the same idea as you and she'll be here soon. She can do the talking if we run into Teth."

I nodded, watching Chantrelle work away, stuck between worrying about the myriad consequences of everything that may or may not be about to happen and wondering how the tech worked that Chantrelle seemed to be using to add my parliamentary tattoo to the door system with full access. The device was a big tube I had stuck my wrist into with a laser show going off inside.

Just as Chantrelle finished and I removed my arm, Cordelia entered the garden, opening her mouth to speak, but being cut off by Chantrelle as she led the way back out into the main garden, "Perfect, you're here. Let's go, time's a wastin'."

Stunned by her sudden take-charge attitude, Cordelia followed as Chantrelle retraced the path I had led us down to the engines before. Once we were out of the garden, Cordelia had mentally caught up and spoke, "I assume you two already have some sort of plan and that Ender's tattoo is ready to go?"

"Yep. Ender's tattoo should work to open the doors, and our plan so far is pretty much to get him to the generators and get you to deal with Teth if we do cross paths with her."

"That's the whole plan?"

"We were a little short on time and have no idea what we'll really find down there."

"Hmm, right."

Cordelia spent the rest of the journey in contemplation, trying to figure out what might happen and how to still get what we came for: Teth's piece of the tail-key. I, myself, having had not much to do all week other than make plans for what I would do when I finally got myself to the generators, had exhausted all the possibilities I could come up with and found my mind instead worrying about Alira. We had pretty much left her behind. It was probably for the best. Besides, she was most likely training outside when the brownout happened, meaning she might not have even noticed it. Not like that Freya woman would let her run off if she did know about it. Freya was strict, but a good teacher. Alira was learning a lot. She was even decent with a yacharow now, those crazy air staff things. She had tried to teach me once, but I couldn't keep it from spinning out and crashing whenever I did manage to keep it in the air, and the amount of concentration and finesse it required just to accomplish that heated up my indicolite pretty quickly, so I couldn't maintain it for long.

Alira said she had almost burned her Indicolite out in training a few times, but that once Freya understood this limitation, she focused her training into shorter, more explosive manoeuvres, rather than endurance training. Alira would be fine. Plus, it took us nearly a whole day to get to Telesto. Any news of the brownout would take at least that long to get out, and the same again for any curious painites to show up.

We finally approached the door that had prevented us from progressing towards the engine last time. Chantrelle stepped back, and I found both sets of eyes staring at me expectantly. A bit nervously, I stepped forward and held my wrist up to the scanner, hoping Chantrelle had worked enough of her magic. She had, and the door slid open with ease. I grinned, hearing the collective sigh escape from the other two. I led the way into maintenance, treading softly on the steel to avoid alerting anyone to our presence, even if we were in a hurry and somewhat abandoning stealth. The others followed suit, and we continued down into the ship towards the engines at a brisk tip-toe. Surprisingly, I found that the further we went down into the ship, the more intact it was until I almost knew exactly where I was going despite the ominous glow coming from the generator room that was new. I opened the door and crouched to sneak through, the other two doing the same. We were in the generator room now, right at the very back, or now the very bottom, I suppose, of the ship. We were crouched up against a wall at the top of a set of steel stairs leading down to the main floor where the four large, now glowing, generators were positioned, and a small crowd of people stood around wearing teal lab coats. I instantly recognised the voice echoing through the chamber above the others.

"We have to sort this out now! Is there no way to add another generator? We've been at this for years, and you're telling me we still can't figure out how these things work? Even after we adapted them for a completely different fuel source?"

Teth sounded a bit panicked.

"No, Ma'am. Creating a fuel source that would suit the machine is entirely different from building an entirely new generator. It might be possible, but we would also have to entirely disassemble one of the existing generators, causing the city to completely shut down."

"Yes, thank you. I'm fully aware that the city is on the brink of shutdown."

Teth was pinching her nose now and scrunching her face. She was stressed. I started to rise, feeling like now might be a good time to step in and help, but a hand grabbed my sleeve and yanked me back down. It was Cordelia.

"Ender, what are you doing!? You can't just walk down there. Did you even use sapphire magic to figure out the generators first?"

"Oh, right. I'll need to connect to yours if you don't mind. I don't have any blue sapphires on me."

"That's alright. You just need to learn enough for us to present Teth with a plan to fix her problem. If we go down there without one, we'll be locked up for sure."

"Ok, on it," I replied, feeling silly that I had forgotten I didn't actually know how the generators worked yet. As soon as I activated the yellow sapphire and changed the harmonies so that I could channel blue sapphire magic, I understood the generators on a certain level. Trying to understand the complexity of them gave me a headache, but I could sense how they worked well enough to remember the kinds of generators they used to be and why Teth's scientists' alternate fuel source was nowhere near as potent as the intended fuel. It was an honest mistake, and a relatively easy fix. At least I thought so while I had the mind of a sapphire.

I grinned and stood up confidently then, saying over my shoulder, "This might be easier than I thought," before striding over and down the stairs before the other two could respond. My sudden confidence, however, seemed to give them enough hope to follow, although clearly nervous that our charade was finally coming to an end.

"Teth! Sorry for the intrusion, but after discovering the energy problem with Telesto and seeing these generators and understanding why, I thought it imperative that I help as soon as possible."

Teth stared wide-eyed at me, shocked, her eyes soon flicking to the two behind me, resting on Cordelia the longest, before her brow furrowed and flicked back to me.

"This is highly illegal and a problematic way to get my attention. But as you seem to have discovered, the situation is dire, and if you really do understand the problem and can help, then I would be willing to overlook your transgressions in return."

"We would've broached the topic more conventionally given more time, but Telesto has already reached its limit, so here we are."

"Mmm. And how exactly do you plan on fixing it?"

"Actually, it's a rather simple fix."

I gestured to the generators. "These generators were originally designed as fusion reactors, capable of powering the entire U.E.S Cronus three times over. In your attempts to utilise them, you've turned them instead into fission reactors, which generate significantly less energy."

"Daniel, did that make any sense to you?" Teth asked the engineer in the teal lab coat she had been talking to before.

"Well, somewhat yes. We did adapt the machines in order to use the fuel sources we thought were viable. It's entirely likely that a different fuel source would generate more energy. We just haven't been able to find anything more efficient that works with our current machines."

I responded then before Teth could. "It's true that fission is somewhat easier to achieve, and once you'd converted the generators for fission fuel, it wouldn't have made sense to use hydrogen-based fuel over whatever it is you have been using."

Teth continued frowning. "And how is it that you know so much about these machines, and what exactly is the U.E.S Cronus you mentioned?"

"Right. This is hard to explain, but Telesto is built inside a ship that I used to live on, back when it was floating through space in my solar system. At least a version of this ship. This one appears to be from another part of the multiverse or something."

"I see. So that's why you're so familiar with how these generators originally ran."

Teth stopped and thought for a moment. "Very well. How do we switch to fusion energy then?"

"I, well…" Shit, I might have the understanding to figure out their generators, but I wasn't truly an engineer or a physicist. I could only do so much. All I could really do was the same thing I had done with Chantrelle: explain how the food tasted and what it was made of, and hope that she could figure out how to make it. I turned my attention to Daniel.

"Daniel, was it? Do you understand what I mean when I said you need hydrogen fuel to turn these into fusion reactors?"

"I… Theoretically, I understand that rather than splitting heavy particles to make energy, you could also combine smaller particles, but we've never done it, and I wouldn't know if the energy would be any more or less."

"Well, trust me on this when I say it works. It produces much more energy, and these machines were originally designed to do exactly that. All you have to do is revert one of them and make a suitable hydrogen fuel cell. I don't know exactly how to do that, but the design of the machine should tell you roughly what the fuel cell should look like."

"Right. I'll get right on it." Daniel turned to Teth then with a pained look on his face. "I think we might be able to pull this off if what this guy says is true. However, it still means that we have to pull one of the generators offline for a few hours at least, and I'm sure you know the effects that will have on Telesto."

"Yes. Quite acutely. But it's our only option. So do it, and get it done as soon as pos—"

The ship grumbled suddenly, a low haunting set of creaks echoing through the chamber.

"What the hell was that?" Teth yelled in the direction of a man in front of a tablet similar to Chantrelle's.

"Ma'am, the turbine that operates the front gates of Telesto has just exploded."

"It what!? How is that possible?"

"Ma'am, the security system has also detected the presence of painite gemstones in that same part of the city," the same man added.

Teth's face went white. Daniel and the rest of the engineers had stopped when the explosion rattled the ship, but now they were rushing around as fast as ever, knowing that they had to do their job quicker than they had thought. I looked back at Cordelia and Chantrelle, Cordelia's expression mimicking Teth's. She whispered quietly to me, "They're here. Akeldama and Ayuna are here. And Alira is still outside."

18 – Alira

I was outside when I heard the explosion. Before I could even guess what was going on, Freya had launched herself into the air for a bird's-eye view of Telesto. She swooped back down a moment later, only to shout at us to follow before she sped off over Telesto towards where Dad, Cordelia, and I had first entered the city. When Freya took her yacharow from off her back, was when I started to be concerned about what we were heading into, and whether Dad had been hurt by whatever it was that exploded. The fear only hit me fully, not when we saw the group of rebels dressed in red below us, or when Freya dove straight down towards them, but when we were close enough that I could see the grin on the girl's face below, staring up straight at me. Ayuna.

The fear hit me all at once, but I was already in a dive with my yacharow poised to strike, and my newly acquired muscle memory was keeping me in place. Speeding towards the ground with the devil upon it, I let my mind focus solely on the battle formations Freya had taught us. In an instant, yacharow were flying everywhere. Both towards the Painite rebels and back at us, the painites using our magic against us, snatching our own weapons out of the sky. I hadn't even had time to direct my own weapon before

I was forcibly broken from our formation. I was panicking. I couldn't see what was happening. I'd somehow ended up spinning out of control, like my own tornado had swallowed me, the traitor.

The world stopped spinning only as I hit the sand, my vision blurry, but slowly focusing on the figure in front of me. Unsurprisingly, it was Ayuna, hovering in the air with two thin and wild tornadoes writhing beneath her palms keeping her afloat. My eyes widened seeing the flames within the wind. She was using two magics simultaneously, both wind and fire, and for no real reason other than to look more intimidating. Although, she was succeeding.

"We meet again, chameleon-girl. And it looks like you've gotten a few upgrades. How cute."
Ayuna set herself down slowly, starting to approach where I was sprawled out in the sand. My vision clear now, I looked around, pushing myself away from Ayuna as I did so, but only discovering that we had flown quite far from the front gates. Too far for anyone to easily spot me and come to help. Wait, what was I saying? Seeing the bodies and yacharow fly through the air in the distance reminded me that I was a soldier. I had been trained by the best of the best in Telesto. This girl was no match for me anymore, even if she did have flaming tornadoes.

I jumped to my feet and focused on my yacharow. I hadn't seen it, but I had had an indicolite embedded in it so that I could tell what direction it was just by moving my wrist around. I was still figuring out how to gauge how far away it was based on the intensity of its responding harmonies, but I didn't have to be too precise right now. I moved my wrist subtly in a circle, feeling the vibrational waves, using a tornado from as far away as I could to whip up anything that might be resting on the sand as it barrelled towards us.

Ayuna didn't flinch as the whirlwind of sand stopped suddenly right beside her, the motion spraying her lightly with sand, revealing the yacharow poised to strike, hovering right by her head. I grinned. I had the advantage now. Ayuna turned her head to admire the point of the yacharow, my confidence fading as she treated it like a toy, flicking the point before turning back to me.

"Impressive. But wouldn't it be sooo much cooler with a little bit of fire? I mean, where's the fun if the wind itself can't even do any damage, and you have to rely on a stick to do it for you."

She shook her head condescendingly, but it was enough to make the point of my yacharow dip for a moment, causing her to smile before I tightened up my form once more.

"It's not too late to join us, y'know. You'd even get to train directly under myself, and you'd have all the magic this world has to offer."

I was starting to get sick of her 'join the dark side' speech. Gritting my teeth and sick of Ayuna's nonsense, I pushed my spear forward, right at Ayuna's neck, almost gagging as I saw the image of her being ripped in two by my hand flash through my mind. I was almost relieved when I realised that she had dodged my attack and the yacharow had lodged itself into the sand between us. Ayuna laughed.

"You really thought something so obvious would work? It's pitiful, really. But regardless, you did just try to kill me, so when the day comes when all that's left is our magic, you'll beg to join me then, and I'll kill you anyway."

"Oh yeah? And how are you supposed to accomplish that? You'd have to get through all of parliament to even try."

"Parliament, you say…"

Oh shit. She didn't know about the world-ship. She probably just meant when they took over the city and, well, that would require fighting off all of parliament, right? I can salvage this.

"Yeah, parliament. In case you'd forgotten, they protect the city as much as the diamonds do. So you'd have to get rid of parliament *and* the diamonds for any chance of being the strongest left."

"True… but your body language tells me there's something else, isn't there? Besides, after everything, no-one has any faith in parliament anymore."

My breathing was a bit shaky now, thinking that I might've just doomed the world. Or would they have figured it out soon enough anyway?

Ayuna kept going when I stayed silent, "How interesting. I'm sure my father will have no trouble discovering whatever secret is hiding within parliament, seeing as you clearly have no intention of saying any more. Regardless, as a thanks, I'll leave you with your life and this little present."

Ayuna flicked a tiny red crystal towards me with a smirk. It landed on the sand at my feet.

"I hope you have fun with that." She said, her smirk widening as flames twisted out from her palms, picking up speed until they blasted her into the air and towards the front entrance to Telesto.

I went to jump into the sky after her, but instead my knees buckled, falling into the sand, my eyes fixed on the smooth crimson gemstone, its dark hue the colour of blood. What had I done? The painites didn't even know anything about the world ship or its ability to control the magic. If they found out and figured out how to work it, it could spell disaster for this planet and ships all throughout the multiverse. This was bad. And it was all my fault.

Dark spots appeared on the sand by the painite crystal, and I realised I was crying. No. I couldn't just let this happen. I could still reach Ayuna before she got to her father. I could take her down. Then they would never know.

I cried harder, the mental image of my yacharow splitting Ayuna in half flashing through my mind again. I knew that this was war. But could I really kill someone? Even a bitch like her? She had let me live, after all. She could've killed me so easily. I thought about Dad then and where he was. That was enough. My fear turned to anger, and I found myself fixated on the crystal. This was war. I had to take her out before she doomed this world, or worse, got to Dad. But to do that, I would have to be stronger. I was too weak. But maybe I didn't have to be.

I grabbed the crystal along with a fistful of sand and shot into the sky. I made a new preset for the crystal as I flew, but left it untitled. Not thinking, I switched to it, immediately falling out of the sky. I panicked, but I knew I didn't have time to switch back to indicolite. So I found the harmonies and, on a whim, focused on my own blood as a power source, hoping to use the air magic inside it like the painites did.

Moments before I hit the ground, the air came back, almost like nothing had happened. The only thing that felt different was that my indicolite wasn't warm, and neither was the painite. Gradually, as I flew, I started to feel like I was getting hotter. Realising what I had done, I tensed suddenly, not wanting to explode, and fell out of the sky again, this time much closer to the sand, and hit the ground, sliding relatively painlessly. I was an expert at it after falling so much in practice, after all. Blood magic was dangerous, especially for me. It wasn't the crystals that heated up, but my own blood. If I pushed too far, I'd explode myself rather than just a rock. I was starting to regret my choice, raising my arm back up to switch back to indicolite, but I stopped, my eyes fixed on the corpses of my classmates in front of me. They had died in the skirmish at the entrance.

No. I had to do this. The painites had killed my friends, and they deserved to die for it.

I tensed just enough to hover, intending to fly into Telesto, metaphorical guns blazing, but I was too angry, for so many reasons. I tried to stay calm, but it was too much. It was making my blood warm and my skin catch on fire. Wait. I stared at my arm, the flames dying out as I focused on it. I grinned. This was it. This bitch had it coming now.

Looking at my fallen friends as I approached the entrance to Telesto, now a big hole rather than the big door it was before, I was feeling the anger again. I hopped into a tornado, letting it wrap itself around me as I sped up towards the entrance, my arms flickering more and more with flames, setting the tornado around me on fire, engulfing me in flames. Now we'd really see how much damage I could do with wind.

19 – Ender

If we were on Earth, it would take weeks, if not months, to take apart a fission reactor and rebuild it into a fusion one, even if most of the machine was fairly similar. Luckily, here we had the benefit of sapphire magic.

All was quiet after the initial explosion, the intruders too far away for us to hear anything, but we knew where they were, and it was only a matter of time before they came down to this end of the ship looking for us. Since I was one of the few sapphires in the room, or able to use their abilities anyway, I was helping to dismantle and rebuild one of the generators.

Fortunately, because this used to be a fusion reactor, I could sense what it used to be, and knew which parts to remove, and what the new parts needed to look like. Not enough to recreate them, but when the group of scientists returned with a trolley load of old parts, I knew what went where.

Eventually, the painites turned their attention to the back of the ship, the number of casualties unknown. Teth was on edge the entire time.

We had finished taking the fission reactor apart and had started rebuilding it when the painites were close enough for us to hear the bombs they were setting off to force open the locked doors between us and them. We were already working lightning fast, impossibly so by Earth standards, but at this rate, we might not be done in time. Furthermore, the team who went to try and produce a suitable hydrogen fuel cell were nowhere to be seen.

A second explosion went off. I could picture the doors as the painites broke through them, the man with the tablet confirming their location after each one. After an unusually quiet period of time, I started feeling more nervous. It was likely they had run out of bombs, which gave us a little more time, but at least before we knew exactly what they were doing.
Now we didn't know their plan at all.

After a few moments of painful silence, the entire room trying to hear where the painites were, the man with the tablet gave us an update. They were apparently now trying to melt their way through the doors. The sensors burned out pretty quickly, leaving us in the dark once more, but given the rate at which the steel was melting, I'd wager they were simultaneously using fire and strength magic— one to burn a hole in the door and the other to widen that hole to human-size as fast as possible.

It would still be much slower than bombs, but there were only a couple of doors left until they reached us. As the time we had grew shorter, I found myself wondering how a room of scientists planned to defend itself, and why we were trying so hard to fix the generator before they got here. It was clearly too late to pretend Telesto wasn't weak. Shouldn't we be more focused on defending ourselves than on putting this thing back together?

"Teth? Given that the Painites are only a few doors away, shouldn't we be more focused on defending ourselves? I can't see what good fixing the generator will do before they get here."

Teth grinned. "Fixing the generator is our best defense. You see, if the fusion reactor does what you say and produces more energy than before, then we will be able to bring back online defensive systems that have been dormant for years, to conserve power. One system in particular which has been programmed to alert and detain any traces of painite."

Teth's grin faded. "It hasn't really been tested though. There was only a short period of time where the threat of the painites and Telesto having enough power overlapped."

"So you're saying if we can get the generator up and running in time, the ship will be able to fight for us?"

"Precisely, especially underground here where more of this ship is intact. Our defenses in the more open areas are quite spotty, so we will still have to drive them out from there."

"I see."

"The sensor in the second last door has burnt out, ma'am," the tablet guy said suddenly. Shit, better keep working. I turned my focus back to the generator, putting in the last few fusion reactor parts with the help of the engineers and scientists. Now, where did the fuel-cell group go?

"The last door, ma'am…" The tablet guy trailed off as he became fixated on the glowing orange spot in the middle of the same door that Chantrelle, Cordelia, and I had entered through. The spot grew rapidly until a flaming fist punched through it. I could see a man on the other side now, his fingers gripping the edge of the hole to widen it as fast as his heat and enhanced strength would allow him. A familiar voice soon rang out, laughing.

"There you all are. I was starting to wonder if Telesto's leadership was so cowardly as to abandon their people to slaughter."

When the hole had been stretched to wider than a face, Akeldama stooped, the glowing ring outlining his grin. Seeing into the room properly now, he locked eyes with me.

"Oh, and I see you've adopted a stranger. I did some research on you since we last met." He was speaking directly to me now. "It seems you're the one I should thank for my daughter and her immense power. You see, we painites were powerless before you, a forgotten gemstone living in poverty. Then one day you survived crashing onto this planet and taught a genocidal priestess how to eradicate magics. Eventually, she did just that, and right when my daughter Ayuna was born nonetheless. Thus the painites were blessed with blood magic, and a power vacuum was created. It was like a divine sign that she and I were supposed to take our place as the next rulers of the city. But as it turns out, it was all thanks to you. So thank you, Ender, for granting me purpose and power."

The hole was almost wide enough for him to step through now.

"I will apologise in advance, though, for killing you. I know Ayuna was especially interested in your unique way with magic, but she found a suitable playmate outside, so it shouldn't matter if one of you dies."

With that, he stepped through the hole, and the group around him followed with haste until seven of them, including Akeldama, were standing on the platform above us, looking down on the room. Wait, did he just say Ayuna was fighting Alira? I was more afraid then of

Alira getting hurt than of the seven painites in front of us. I felt powerless. All I could do was hope that Alira had learnt enough air magic to escape her. But that said, Ayuna had been raised as a weapon to help Akeldama take over the city. I had faith in Alira, but that didn't stop me from being terrified for her.

Movement at the edge of the room drew everyone's attention. The group stopped immediately, the front runner holding a thin translucent case in front of him with two hands. In the centre of the case was something that looked like a small glass ball, or maybe a large marble, with numerous bubbles inside. That's right, the reactor. The hydrogen fuel cell had arrived. All we had to do now was get the fuel cell loaded and the reactor powering the city's defense systems, all before the painites could cross the room and kill us all. Sounded easy enough.

As Akeldama started to make a move, crouching in preparation to jump straight off the balcony, I switched to Indicolite as quickly as I could, making sure to focus as much as possible on retaining what I needed to know about the reactor to load the fuel cell properly. I yelled out as Akeldama leapt over the railing.

"Daniel, throw it here now!"

Daniel's head swivelled, ripping his terrified eyes away from the vampire in mid-air, to stare at me, but shaking himself out of it quickly enough to throw the case across the room before Akeldama had hit the floor. Akeldama watched the case as he landed, curious, but clearly too smug to think any last-ditch attempt of ours would save us. I caught the case, hesitating to do anything with it, not wanting to take my eyes off Akeldama as the rest of the painites joined him on the floor.

As Teth stepped up to face him, I found myself surprised, but after she threw him across the room with a tornado and fighting erupted between her guards and the rest of the painites, I knew she could hold him for long enough.

I got to work, wishing momentarily that I had kept the sapphire active. I thought Daniel's throw might be frantic and need to be caught with the help of some air magic, but it was a surprisingly perfect throw, and I hadn't needed it at all. There was no time to switch though, and I remembered enough to load the cell. Luckily, these reactors had been designed for easy fuel-cell replacement, in case they became depleted during battle. The fuel cell might be different, but Daniel was smart enough to create a new one with hydrogen fuel and fit it into the original fission fuel-cell case. That made my job way easier. All I had to do now was slide the new one in, lock it, and shout,

"Tablet guy! Start it up!"

He was sitting on the floor staring at the violence of yacharow and fireballs whizzing around the room, but the moment he heard me, he was head down in his tablet as usual. The generator flickered to life behind me soon after, the giant magnet inside it starting to spin faster and faster, making me feel a bit woozy standing this close to it. I took a step away from the generator, expecting Akeldama and the painites to turn their attention to it as it started up, but a firestorm blew through the hole in the wall seconds later, drawing their attention instead, and stopping me in my tracks.

Ayuna. It had to be. I couldn't see her face behind the flaming tornado she was engulfed in, but her silhouette and dramatic entrance told me it had to be her. And if she was here, then Alira was… Where was Alira?

I tried to focus, standing my ground against her, sweat starting to drip into my eyes from the heat of the fires and the generator starting to get hot, the atoms exploding inside and bringing Telesto slowly back to life. I stood my ground, facing Ayuna, assuming she would come for me and the generator first, but she instead started flying around the room in an apparent rage, which was good because the heat was too much now, and I was too close to the generator, passing out as I tried to take another step away from it.

20 – Alira

I was sitting in the infirmary with Dad unconscious in the bed. The nurse said he'd be fine and that it was just a bit of heatstroke. Cordelia had confirmed what the nurse said, using her magic to examine Dad's injuries. I was more concerned about hers, though, as the fight between Telesto and the Painites in the engine room had left her with a myriad of new cuts and bruises. Although she stitched herself back together afterwards, the fresh set of scars and the state of her usually formal attire were concerning, especially with her knives now exposed.

Even knowing Dad would be fine, I was still worried. Namely, my entrance to the engine room, wielding both air and fire magic, which was only possible for the Painites. I had no doubt I was in big trouble once he woke up. I was disappointed I never found Ayuna, but kind of relieved at the same time. I thought for sure she would have run straight to Akeldama, but she wasn't there when I arrived. I didn't have time after the battle either when the Painites fled once the ship's defence systems were finally activated. It was the only reason many of us survived. The battle in the engine room was a losing one, the Painites easily blindsiding us the moment they switched to a new kind of magic. My entrance seemed to be the only thing that caught them off guard, but it was hard to maintain that advantage once they were wary of me. At first, they seemed to think I was Ayuna, but once I started knocking them down, they realised I wasn't on their side, and I found myself running away faster than I had stormed in.

Fortunately, Dad's plan worked soon after, and suddenly the ship was going crazy. I remember the smirk on Teth's face when the alarm went off. She was on the ground, Akeldama looming over her, grinning wickedly as he does, but their expressions flipped once the alarm sounded, the walls humming with new energy. It was then that I started feeling feverish, like my blood had gotten too hot, like I had used too much magic, and this was the price. I turned off my connection straight away, dropping from my flaming fury to my knees at Dad's side, seeing that he had passed out. I quickly realised why as I felt the heat from the generator, my fire tolerance gone with my magic. I had disconnected from the tiny painite stone just in time, feeling the nausea fade just in time to avoid vomiting. The rest of the painites, however, weren't so lucky, and that's when I realised what Teth was so smug about. Whatever it was that Dad and Teth had been working to fix when the painites showed up, had finally started up, and it seemed to specifically target painites, making them too sick to fight. Really, it was just super high-tech pest control, but it was effective, leaving soldiers throwing up all over the place.

Akeldama had raised his wrist to his mouth, but I never saw him vomit. He led the retreat quickly after that, saying unusually little given his typical talkative villain act. I suspect it was purely so that he didn't throw up his guts. It seemed like a total victory as they ran away, afraid of their own stomachs, but the thought of Ayuna and my slip-up left me feeling less optimistic, knowing that I'd given something away that could potentially give them control of the whole planet. Not to mention I had used blood magic to try and stop Ayuna and rectify my mistake, only to fail and expose myself in the process.

Dad groaned, his eyes blinking slowly as he started to sit up. I squeezed his hand, waiting apprehensively for him to be okay, and to berate me. Dad scrunched his whole face as he sat up, wincing. He took his hand back from me to rub the back of his head, wincing again when he did so. Looks like he whacked his head on the floor when he passed out.

"Dad."

He turned to me, his eyes taking a moment to adjust before he smiled. "Hi Ali."

Then all at once, he seemed to remember everything that happened, turning unexpectedly swiftly to Cordelia.

"What happened? Are they gone? Is everyone okay?"

Cordelia smiled weakly in response. "Most of us survived, yes. And the ship's defence systems worked once they started up, driving them away instantly."

"How so? Are they dead?"

"No. I'm not sure exactly how it works, but the painites were suddenly too sick to fight. They all ran away whilst vomiting everywhere. It was quite disturbing."

Dad thought for a moment before chuckling to himself. "I think I know what they've done. They must have fused the sterilisation system with the gemstone recognition in the security doors.

Essentially, they reclassified painite gemstones as bacteria, and the ship did the rest to try and sterilise them. Brilliant."

I watched Dad, waiting for him to remember what I did. He looked back to me. "And Alira, I am so relieved that you're okay. I worried that Ayuna got to you, and when she showed up in her flaming tornado in the engine room, I feared that meant you weren't able to stop her. But I see now that you're okay. I'm so glad. I don't know what I would've done without you."

Cordelia cut in then, "Now, now, that's enough, Ender. She's okay."

Dad smiled at me, then cocked his head slightly, making me realise that the look on my face must not have been what he was expecting. I bit my tongue, stopping myself from probing into exactly what he saw. He thought I was Ayuna, and that was my get-out-of-jail-free card. That didn't solve my other big mistake, though.

"Hey Dad, So... You see... I did fight with Ayuna, kind of. I couldn't beat her, but she didn't seem to want to kill me. But I... Well, I kind of accidentally let slip that Parliament had something that they needed to conquer the world."

As soon as I said it, I panicked and tried to make it sound like less of a big deal.

"I didn't really say it like that, though, obviously. All I said was that she'd have to fight all of parliament if she wanted to control the city, which, y'know, makes sense, right? But she figured me out somehow and thinks that there was something else. She doesn't know what, but if she figured out that much then I doubt it will take her long to interfere with parliament once she tells Akeldama."

Dad opened and closed his mouth repeatedly before laying back in his hospital bed and closing his eyes, taking a deep breath like he'd just had another blow to the head. Which he kind of had. Whoops. I was sitting quietly, waiting, when Dad sat back up, gathering his thoughts.

"Right. Well, obviously we need to tell Cybele all of this, and find out from her the current state of parliament. I could go myself, but that might stir up unwanted trouble. We'll have to move quickly before the painites can make a move. I think it'll be more efficient if we meet Cybele in the tiger's eye city. We'll still need to get their piece of the tail-key, right? Obviously, we'll have to convince Teth to give up her piece of the tail-key before we leave, which shouldn't be too hard given how we just saved her city both from painites and total power failure. Alira, go pack up your things. And bring the yacharow; I'm sure it'll come in handy once you've mastered it. Cordelia and I will go see Teth."

As Dad swung his legs out of the bed to stand up, Chantrelle walked in, and everyone froze for a moment, realising we'd all forgotten about her. Dad was the first to relax.

"Hi Chantrelle, I'm glad you're okay."

Chantrelle rolled her eyes. "I'm fine. You're the one in the hospital bed. I can't believe you were smart enough to solve the energy problem but stupid enough to pass out from standing too close to it. Honestly."

She said this like she was berating a child, but her glassy eyes betrayed her true feelings.

Dad smiled in response. "Yeah. But it worked out in the end." A shadow crossed his face. "With a few complications."

Chantrelle frowned, cocking her head slightly. Dad sighed.

"It's a long story, but we have to leave Telesto right away. Cordelia and I will go and discuss Teth's piece of the tail-key with her while Alira gets ready. It might be beneficial if you came too. Your perspective as a resident who can vouch for us might help."

Chantrelle smiled, glancing at me instead. "I think you've done enough for Telesto that Teth will give you whatever you ask of her. As for me, if you're leaving so soon, I think I'd rather chat with Alira about some recipes I've been thinking up if that's okay?"

"Of course. We'll see you two soon then," Dad finished, getting out of the bed and continuing to the door, rubbing the back of his head with his palm. Chantrelle and I were alone in the room now. I was intrigued to hear what recipes she was thinking up. If they were anything as perfect as fries or peanut butter, they were sure to be winners.

"Alira, I know it was you in the engine room and not Ayuna."

"Oh," I replied softly, realising there were no new recipes. She stretched out her hand to the door. "Shall we go somewhere more private? You do have to pack after all."

"Right," I responded absently, worrying what it was exactly she wanted to say about my appearance in the engine room. She knew I didn't want to tell Dad, and that he didn't realise. Otherwise, she would've said something. I pondered this on the silent walk back to my room, leading Chantrelle through steel corridors that she knew better than I did.

Chantrelle shut the door behind us as we slid into my room. I immediately started packing but stopped the moment she spoke.

"So, you can use blood magic too, huh?"

"Yeah."

"I guess I knew you could, given how you and your dad's magic works, but I didn't think you would."

"Me neither, I just…"

Chantrelle didn't respond, forcing me to finish my sentence. I sighed before doing so.

"Please don't tell Dad. I know I shouldn't have, but I felt powerless otherwise, and I thought Ayuna was coming for you guys."

I looked her in the eye properly now, remembering how helpless I felt as I faced Ayuna.

"She was too powerful. She laughed when I launched my yacharow at her. I just wanted to get on her level, to be able to do more. And it was the only way."

"Turning to power like that is never the only way. You've only just started learning. In time you'll be a better fighter, more powerful. You can't rush it with dangerous magic."

"I know. You're right. Dad does fine with his system, I just…"

"I know. And you learn quickly, you'll be wielding the elements in no time; I'm sure of it."

I smiled weakly back at her. "I hope so. I'm going to need to after what I've done."

She frowned at that, so I elaborated, remembering her missing the conversation in the hospital.

"I may have accidentally given Ayuna a piece of the puzzle. If they figure it out and beat us to the puzzle pieces, the whole planet might be screwed."

"Right, I see. Something to do with the tail-key pieces?"

I nodded.

"In any case, given how Ender explained his magic to me, I take it you have a painite gemstone somehow? If I were you, I would get rid of it as soon as possible. Good luck."

Chantrelle left with a worried smile, leaving me alone in the silence of my empty room. She was right, I had to get rid of it. But what if I needed it? I thought about this the whole time I was packing, weighing the risks. There wasn't much to pack, just some clothes really. I was already wearing my wingsuit. It was much more elegant than the ones Cybele had whipped up, and much easier to walk around in, making it better suited for soldiers' everyday wear. Most of my belongings were part of this suit now, or easily attached to it. I didn't know how far the tiger's eye city was from here, but the flight would be much easier than the way here. This wingsuit was way better, and I had a longer rope for towing people along now.

I grabbed the last of my things, shoving them into a small bag and tying it to my back. I caught a glimpse of myself in the mirror as I went to leave the room. It wasn't much of a mirror, more like thoroughly polished steel, but I looked cool nonetheless. I looked like a warrior in the Telesto wingsuit uniform, a yacharow positioned along my spine. It was then that I finally decided to keep the small painite stone. I didn't plan to use it, but it served as a reminder of what I needed to be. What I would become. With that, I smiled at the strong figure in the mirror and strode out the door, the small red crystal buried in the cuff of my uniform.

When I arrived at the room where we had first met Teth, I walked in on the end of the conversation between Dad, Cordelia, and Teth.

"…Very well. I understand the situation and can't dispute the value of your actions in solving Telesto's energy crisis. I will give you my piece of the High Priestess staff, and wish you well in restoring the magic of this world. If your efforts here are any indication, I believe you'll succeed."

Teth stood up, my own stride slowing down as I entered to not interrupt.

"I had my piece of the staff turned into a yacharow. It seemed fitting given that it was once a part of the staff of a diamond. If you don't mind, I'll give you the whole thing. I've been meaning to get myself an upgrade anyway. This one is over a decade out of date now."

As Teth said this, she was holding out her hand, waiting. Before she finished speaking, a guard had brought her a beautiful yacharow, made with two-tone wood and thinner spear tips, much sharper looking than what I was used to seeing. Teth locked eyes with me then, noticing my arrival.

"Oh, you're here. Perfect timing."

She held out the yacharow in my direction. "A gift for you, for helping to defend our city. I'm sure you know the significance of this particular weapon?"

I stared at the beautifully crafted alien spear. Teth chuckled, making me remember myself.

"Yes, of course. The tail key." I said as I gestured to the section of the pole that had been replaced with a strange, crystallised sort of material.

"Yes. I trust that you'll take good care of this. It might take some extra practice as well. I had this made before we fully refined the design of the yacharow, and so the thinner spear tips tend to stick into the sand and get stuck. That being said, that should be no problem for you given what I have heard from Freya."

She smiled as she handed me the weapon. Staring at it, I felt the strange urge to curtsey out of respect. The reactions of the room made me blush and realise that curtseying wasn't a thing here. The only differing reaction was Dad's, who chuckled quietly. He was so going to tease me for this later.

"Thank you. I'll take good care of it."

"If you ever find yourself back in Telesto, you're welcome to a place in the city guard. Freya would have no objections."

"Seriously? That would be awesome." I had no idea what the world would be like that far into the future. We were trying to fix it, after all. But it was cool to think I had a place in this world waiting for me.

I joined Dad and Cordelia, holding the fancy yacharow, eyeing it thoroughly. The crystallised tail section was a bit rough, and it wasn't all that pleasant to hold. We'd probably want to cover it anyway so that people didn't get the wrong idea. I wasn't really listening to the rest of the conversation between Dad and Teth, but soon enough we were being escorted to the big hole in the wall where there used to be a big turbine-powered door. There were extra guards at the entrance now. No surprise there. I was surprised, however, to find a few of Freya's students guarding the entrance. They immediately noticed my yacharow when they spotted me, and I ended up having to explain why I had the fanciest weapon ever made in Telesto, which was supposed to indicate the current ruler. I didn't tell them the truth, of course, except the part where it was given to Dad in gratitude for saving the city. I tried to give Dad as much credit as possible to avoid it being too awkward.

Nevertheless, Dad and Cordelia gathered their things while I explained this and said some goodbyes. Chantrelle showed up to see us off, giving me a knowing look as the three of us left Telesto through the big hole.

"Right then," Dad started, "I'll see you two in a day or so. Remember, we will meet outside the house of the guy that runs the tiger's eye city. What was his name again?"

"Navoi," Cordelia answered.

"Right. Navoi."

"Wait, wait, what? Aren't you coming with us?" I demanded of Dad, stunned that it seemed they'd suddenly made plans for us to split up without even telling me.

Dad looked at me surprised at first, but his expression quickly became more apologetic. "Oh, sorry Ali. Cordelia and I ironed out some details while on the way to meet Teth. We have to split up so that we can get to the tiger's eye city as quickly as possible. You two will fly there from here while Cybele and I will fly from the city."

"That doesn't make any sense. How are you supposed to get to Cybele then?"

Dad held up his parliamentarian tattoo. "I can teleport directly to Parliament. Then I'll hopefully be able to teleport from there straight into the museum. But if not, I can just blip up to the city and make my way from there."

"Oh. I guess that makes sense."

I thought about it for a moment, absorbing the fact that I was going to an entirely new city on an alien world with a woman I'd just met a couple of weeks ago. Even if she was my grandmother. I was also trying to figure out a different way. A better way, that meant I could stay with Dad, but he was right. This was the only way that made sense. He was the only one who could teleport, and Cordelia couldn't fly herself.

I sighed, multiple emotions welling up as I accepted defeat in an argument that never actually began, and chose to bury my face in Dad's shirt, simultaneously hiding my tears from him as well as giving him a good-bye hug. It was only a day. But I already knew everything would feel different without Dad there experiencing it all alongside me.

I pulled back, wiping my face quickly with my sleeve, feeling the painite hidden there momentarily, and feeling slightly ashamed. But if he was leaving, I needed as much protection as I could get. Dad smiled, bringing his fingers up to his tattooed wrist.

"I'll see you soon, Ali."

He circled his wrist with his middle finger before dragging it down his palm. Dad disappeared from right in front of me the moment the tips of his middle fingers touched, the air where he used to be shifting uncomfortably. There really was teleportation here. What a crazy planet.

21 – Ender

It was chilling being back in the halls of Parliament. I couldn't imagine the drama that had unfolded here after Cybele and I sabotaged the tail-key and the city started falling into disrepair. If any one of them saw me here, they would immediately try to kill me. That I was pretty confident about. Luckily, the teleporting tattoo had dropped me right where I had been the last time I was in Parliament, which happened to be outside of the very teleporter that had taken me to Cybele's museum basement. I opened the map on the teleporter screen, looking both ways down the corridor for anyone passing by. It was strangely silent here. Maybe there were generally fewer people here when they weren't expecting newcomers. It was also possible that something similar had happened to them that had happened to the rest of the city. I didn't need to think about that now though.

I zoomed in on the museum on the map, mimicking what I had seen Cybele do before. That was about as far as I got though. I was recalling something from fifteen years ago, but I remembered enough to realise whatever kind of scan Cybele did to make her teleporter pop up was not something I was going to be able to replicate. In lieu of going straight to the museum, I went instead to the same exit I had used the first time I left Parliament. Hopefully, this Telesto outfit wouldn't stand out too much in the middle of the city. I hesitated before I tapped the button and stepped in, remembering the extra guards standing between the inner city and the limbs. I should make myself invisible before I teleport, just in case.

I climbed into the teleporter, my presence only seen as ripples as I moved, my natural alexandrite magic in effect.

The streets above were almost exactly as I had remembered them, albeit now empty. It felt strange being in a place so metropolitan as this and there being no people. It wasn't totally unfamiliar, however, somewhat reminding me of the last time the global economy crashed on Earth. There were signs of people, movement from windows higher up in buildings, but the shops and stalls at street level were all closed, having no new merchandise to sell. I made my way through the empty city, occasionally finding people on the street huddled in alleyways and curled up in pockets of space littered around the city. They didn't notice me as I passed, but I noticed them. Some of them could have been lower gems that had snuck in here. It was entirely possible. But the majority of them still displayed their gem types, sparkling jewels stitched onto tattered clothing. I suppose not all of upper gem society was wealthy. I imagined anyone who owned one of the various deserted shops I wandered by was likely to have gone broke. I can't imagine where they would have gone. Given what I knew of the downfall of the city, their only options likely would have been living on the street, seeking refuge in the museum, or fighting in the arena. There didn't seem to be much else going on around here.

I could see the entrance to the limbs now, the row of guards blocking the path as stoic as before. They were all facing the other way, clearly focusing on people trying to sneak in rather than out. Although why they bothered was beyond me, there wasn't any more happening on one side of the wall than on the other. I slowed down as I approached the wall, not particularly worried about being seen. The safest option seemed to be slipping through the gap on the side of the row of soldiers and following the wall along for the distance of one building before slipping through the space between them, soon emerging onto the road out of their sight. When I knew I was in the clear, I became fully visible once more, setting my epicode to harmonise with my topaz, allowing me to run to the museum at top speed without tiring.

I arrived not long after, relieved at the sight of the golden chryacal statues guarding the entrance, remembering how Cybele could bring them to life with such realism. Even if they weren't as real-looking as they might've been before the magic weakened, they were still plenty scary as a hunk of golden claws bounding towards you.

The guards at the entrance didn't seem to know what to think of me as I approached, but eventually, as I got closer, one of them seemed to recognise me and went to push open the door, the other guard frowning at him warily.

"I'm a friend of Cybele's, there's no need to worry. Do either of you know where she is?"

The one who seemed to recognise me responded, "Yes, she's in her lab I think. Do you know the way?"

"I do, thanks."

He nodded, and I slipped through the door. The museum inside looked about as unchanged as the outside. I guess the painites hadn't found the museum after all. I made my way to Cybele's office and through the bookshelf, down into the basement. I found Cybele hunched over a screen connected to a large device that I couldn't even begin to describe. I suppose it might've looked a little bit like the original Apollo lunar lander, but smaller, about five feet tall. Cybele hadn't noticed me enter the room.

"What's this you've cooked up?"

Cybele jumped, swivelling around, relaxing as she saw me, but momentarily tensing up again, sensing something must have been wrong for me to be here alone.

"Why are you here? Where's Del?"

"She's with Alira, on the way to the Tiger's eye city."

"Muruntau."

"Is that what it's called?"

"Yes."

"Huh. What's this thing you're working on?"

Cybele's eyes lit up as I asked that question, seemingly forgetting about the million questions she should have for me.

"It's a telescope of sorts, like one that can see the stars up close. The main difference is that this one is tuned specifically to look for sources of anti-matter."

"I see, kind of like what the world ship does."

"Yes, although I haven't quite been able to make the jump to searching the multiverse, but I am getting there. I'm currently writing the program that tracks found anti-matter sources, so that we can build a map of sorts."

"Wow, that's amazing. How does one detect anti-matter anyway?"

"Oh, it's quite fascinating. Given the composition and trajectory of a combination of positrons, gamma radiation, and the cosmic rays that encompass them, you can find the origin of the energy source producing these particular rays, and it's usually antimatter. Although I haven't quite tuned it very finely yet, so I've only detected about two larger sources in this universe, and I can't tell yet what the sources actually are. They could be ships, but at least one of them looks large enough to be some sort of celestial body."

"In other words, it's a good start."

"Yes. I've been working on it non-stop since you left." The concern returned to Cybele's face. "Wait, so why have you sent the other two to Muruntau? Did you get the piece of the tail-key from Telesto?"

"We did. Alira has it for now. I'll explain everything on the way, but we should get going if we are going to meet them there on time. Alira will fly much quicker than me too, so we'll already be there after them even though we have shorter to go."

Cybele's expression started shifting, becoming more and more entranced in her own ideas. Knowing her, that kind of expression was worrying.

"Well... they'll be safe in Muruntau. I have another idea first. It'll be quick, I promise."

I already didn't like where this was going. Cybele was smart, but her curiosity could all too easily get away from her, as I knew all too well. I watched her sceptically before responding.

"What is it?"

190

She jovially started explaining, seeming to take my obviously apprehensive question to mean total agreement.

"Well, I managed to sneak onto the world-ship once before, back when magic was stronger and the Cathedral was in total disarray. That's when I snuck aboard to see if I could find anything out about the magic. I didn't really find anything useful in that regard, but I did see the same antimatter acquisition log—the final entry being a manual entry programmed by yours truly. I couldn't do much without the key, and it was honestly a miracle that Parliament seemed to have started up the console without it. Even so, without the key not much could be done other than poring over logs and ship systems. Anyway, I noted down the full coordinates and all the information the ship would tell me about its universe-jumping capabilities, and I eventually used that information to connect to the radio. A radio is hardly enough to solve the magic problem, but I did see a map of the entire ship while I was there. I didn't think much of it then—other than being impressed by its sheer size. But after thinking about it for many years, I've decided that the only way to truly fix the magic is to find a way to replicate how it locates antimatter. And the only way to do that is to go back to the ship— specifically to the engine room. I think I can get more information if we go directly to the engine."

I paused for a moment, absorbing everything Cybele had just said, my mind trying to catch up with her rapid rambling.

"I see. I guess we have to go then. If you think you really can fix the magic this way, then we have to try. Especially if it will help us turn the tide against Akeldama. But we have to be quick. I wouldn't want Alira to think something bad had happened to us."

"We'll be in and out in no time with your teleporter tattoo."

"And how exactly do you plan on making that work? I'm pretty sure it only transports myself."

"Well, in my research trying to connect my teleporter to the world-ship, albeit unsuccessfully, I found a little bit about how the system sees the tattoos, and it gave me an idea that I think should work. I need you to connect to my magic though."

"You want me to connect to your red beryl?"

"Yep."

I looked at her sceptically but did as she said. Being connected to her magic was confusing at first, my perception of the world around me starting to warp softly, but I found that focusing on how it should be helped return everything to normal.

"Are you ready?"

"What, now? How is this supposed to work?"

"Just get ready to go."

I lifted my fingers to my wrist, watching Cybele and waiting. Seeing that I was ready, she stepped forward towards me and wrapped her arms around me tightly, startling me.

"What… is this?"

She sighed, still hugging me. "The ship uses resonant frequencies to find and teleport people to it, meaning that if we are close enough together and vibrating at the same frequency, it'll see us as one entity and take both of us."

"Oh… I see. Why didn't you just say that?"

"Can you just take us already?"

I blushed, knowing Cybele couldn't see it but still getting embarrassed from standing here like this so awkwardly. Even if we were friends now, this was still new and very strange, especially for us.

"Um, right, okay."

I lifted my fingers back to my wrist and traced the gesture, both of us finding ourselves standing aboard the ship moments later. Rather than teleporting to where I last was, however, I found myself in the remains of the High Priestess chambers, a wave of emotions washing over me as I remembered everything that had happened here. Cybele released me the moment we spawned in the room, taking steps towards where her genocide machine used to be, before stopping and turning back, wondering why I wasn't following. She realised moments later as she saw me staring into the room, tears starting to escape from the corners of my eyes.

"Oh, right. I had forgotten. I… I'll give you a minute."
Cybele walked off, bowing her head, continuing the way she was going. I hadn't expected to feel so strongly just seeing this room again. But then again, my eyes were failing to tear themselves away from the spot on the floor where Nadira had died, and Alira was born. Two insane events happening at one time. The worst loss I had ever felt. And the greatest blessing.

I fell to my knees. Thinking of it that way, of course I would break down seeing this room again. The image of Alira's big purple eyes the first time I saw them popped into my head, and it gave me the strength to stand. That's why I was here. I was here to fix this planet so that Alira wouldn't be in danger, and we had to do this as quickly as possible so that I could get right back to protecting her.

I stood, looking instead to the far wall where Cybele was waiting, wiping away my tears so that I could see her. We didn't have time to stand around crying. We had things to do. I started walking towards Cybele, having to steady my breathing as I went. By the time I reached her, I had managed to distract myself enough with planning our way down to the engine, though the image of Nadira's soft smile as her body broke down pulled at the edge of my mind.

"Ready?"

"Ready. Which way?"

"Well… I'm not entirely sure. I know which direction the engine is from here, based on that map I saw. But I have no idea how to get there. We'll just have to improvise in that general direction."

This did not sound like the quick and easy mission she had promised. I sighed, thinking hard.

"Oh, the teleporters. They have a map on them, and I think the old guy who showed me around this place said that they were originally for getting around the ship because it was so big."

"Perfect, we should be able to teleport straight there then. In that case, follow me."

I nodded, and we left the old high priestess quarters and all the memories in it behind in search of the engine of the world ship.

22 – Alira

Now this was flying. I had gotten so much faster and sharper thanks to all of Freya's training. Cordelia looked like she was struggling at first, so I had made sure to speed up gradually. She had scoffed at the idea of wearing goggles when I presented them to her before we took off, but when we made our first stop, she was quick to note how glad she was that I made her put them on. Hearing Cordelia tell me how surprised she was at my speed had only made me want to race Dad across the desert even more. Although it wouldn't be much of a race because he would've been too far behind to see after a minute or less.

Between Cordelia's polite request and the thought of what we would even do in Muruntau if we got there too far ahead of them, I slowed down considerably for the rest of the journey. We flew across the calico landscape leisurely, but still fast enough for Cordelia to want to leave her goggles on, despite how unflattering she thought they were. I thought they were more unflattering when she took them off, a big red squiggle pressed into her face. Although I figured I must've had one too.

Now we were almost there, according to Cordelia. I had no idea where we were going. I just flew as straight as I could in whatever direction she told me to when we took a break.

After almost two hours, I noticed something up ahead that could only have been Muruntau. As we flew over the calico desert, I admired its patchy terrain and the myriad of strange angles of the desert as it vibrated below, but amid the chaotic landscape, one vast patch of greyish-beige—nearly a perfect circle—stood out as an unmistakable anomaly. I'd seen all the other cities so far, and none resembled this; it had to be Muruntau. We had finally arrived.

I set us down well before the city, where I thought we were far enough away that it was unlikely anyone in Muruntau had spotted us in the sky already.

"Well, it looks like we're here. What's the plan for when we get there? Are we sneaking in or just walking up to the gates like in Telesto or…?"

Cordelia didn't respond right away, her head down and her hands on her knees, panting hard. Oh, right. I was quite fit now from all the training with Freya, but Cordelia wasn't exactly used to this kind of exercise. I didn't know how old she was either, but it was old enough to be a grandmother to a teenager, and getting in shape at that age couldn't have been easy.

After a few minutes, she had caught her breath, taking another moment to compose herself.

"Right, I suppose we have to come up with an approach now don't we. I have a bit of a headache after that, not to mention a myriad of other aches." I gave her a moment, finding myself wondering how Muruntau would receive visitors looking the way we did; sweaty, in Telesto uniform, and clearly carrying a weapon that we had no right to have. At least, that's probably what they would see at first glance. This might be harder than we first thought. Cordelia seemed to have reached the same conclusion.

"I don't think we will be able to approach the front gates directly. Not looking like this."

She looked down at herself with disgust, clearly hating being covered in so much sweat and sand.

"And definitely not with that new weapon of yours. People will think we stole it if we don't explain the situation to Navoi first."

She sighed with a tired smile. "I don't have any sway here like I do in Telesto. We'll immediately be treated like outsiders and have no right to talk to Navoi in person. Our only chance is to get inside and wait until the others arrive. I'm sure your father's infamous reputation will be enough to get an audience, even if not under ideal circumstances."

"So what do we do before then? We can't wait out here."

"No, we can't." Cordelia looked me over for a moment, thinking. "Darling, would you mind using your chameleon magic for a moment?"

"Um, sure."

Not entirely sure what she was thinking, I did as she asked. Her eyes continued to look me over but seemed to focus beyond me for a moment, before settling on mine again. A small, sad smile crossed Cordelia's face before she turned her head away. It wasn't hard to guess why—Dad often told me how much my eyes looked like my mother's.

Cordelia spoke before looking back at me, managing to stay as composed as ever, though it took more effort than usual.

"I thought as much. You should be able to sneak into the city with no problem, yacharow and all. All you have to do is close your eyes while you walk past the guards. I, on the other hand, will have to enter the hard way and hope they pity an old woman wandering in from the wasteland."

I went to object, but Cordelia's expression was resolute, and I couldn't think of a better plan. This way, we'd draw less suspicion and wouldn't have to leave the yacharow behind or risk fighting our way in. It wasn't a perfect plan—a lone woman emerging from the desert was still suspicious—but it was less risky than entering together. If she was escorted by a Telesto guard carrying Teth's yacharow, we'd have no chance.

I sighed. "You're right. That's probably the best way for now. Once I get in, I'll stay as close as I can in case you need help."

She nodded. "Very well. Shall we go then?"

I nodded slowly, thinking about how easily this could go wrong. I really hoped it would go smoothly; otherwise, we'd be in quite a pickle. Soon after, we took to the sky briefly before touching back down behind the last sand dune before the main gate. From there, Cordelia would have to walk to make it look like she had arrived on foot by herself. I walked nearby but kept my distance, ensuring that any guards watching Cordelia wouldn't notice the flashes of green as I approached. This way, all eyes would be on Cordelia while I slipped through the main gate from the side.

As I approached the entrance, I noticed the confused expressions on the guards' faces. They were all fixated on the lone woman approaching the gates, seemingly having crossed the calico desert on foot and alone. The closer I got, the more intrigued I became with the soldiers themselves, observing their uniforms and weapons. Their uniforms were fairly plain—certainly not as stylish or unique as the Telesto wingsuit—but their staffs caught my attention. Each staff bore a unique design, with bands of colour arranged in a distinct combination, making every pole individual to its owner. It was hard to decipher much about them, but I noticed a trend—the older warriors' staffs had more intricate patterns, with numerous bands of varying thicknesses, while the younger ones carried staffs with more uniform and consistent designs. One detail that stood out, however, was the black band at the top of most of the guards' poles. As dark as coal, it seemed to be standard for all but the youngest among them.

While I was busy analysing the guards, one of them glanced my way. My heart skipped a beat as I ducked my head, shielding my eyes instinctively. Adrenaline surged through me, but when no one shouted or called out, I realised I might have gone unnoticed. I let out a long breath as my adrenaline calmed back down, and decided it was best to stick to the plan and keep my head down from now on.

I glanced forward once more, carefully aligning my body with a clear path through the archway. I aimed for the blank wall of a nearby building, figuring I'd know I was safely inside once I touched it. With a deep breath, I quickly checked on Cordelia's progress before making a beeline for the wall.

Eyes closed, I strained my ears, listening intently for any sound that might warn me of danger—whether it was the shuffle of a guard's footsteps or an alarmed shout. But it only took a few seconds for my pounding heart and shaky breaths to drown out everything else. I quickened my pace, careful not to break into a full run, my fingertips stretched out in front of me. I could only hope they met with the cool bricks instead of the armour of a startled guard.

Moments later, my fingers jammed against the rough stone. I recognised the brick and let out a deep sigh—too carelessly. Realising my mistake, I pressed myself against the wall, scanning the entrance for any sign that someone had noticed.

Nothing. All eyes remained fixed on Cordelia, who was now just steps away from the archway.

One of the two guards standing outside the wall stepped forward to greet her. There were six guards in total: two outside the archway, two inside, and two stationed atop the wall. If they shouted, no doubt more guards along the wall's perimeter would come running.

"Welcome to Muruntau. What is your reason for travel?" The guard's tone was stern and suspicious, though he seemed to be following a rehearsed script.

"My family was killed recently in a raid on Telesto by the painites. I came here seeking refuge."

Cordelia's reply was calm, and it was clear she had thought this through.

"Telesto was raided as well?"

The guard sounded genuinely surprised. Wait—Telesto *too*? How could the painites have reached Muruntau so quickly?

"Yes, sir."

The man scoffed, muttering under his breath, "Those bastards." Then, raising his voice, he continued, "Would you recount the events of the attack for us, including how you managed to make it here all by yourself?" His suspicion returned, evident in his tone.

"Of course. But it is a painful story, and I'd rather only tell it once. Perhaps I should recount it to Navoi directly."

"Navoi!?" The guard's reaction was sharp and offended—clearly, that wasn't the right thing to say. He followed with a menacing laugh, and my hope that this encounter might go smoothly began to crumble.

"You can tell *The Commander* your story, sure, but only after a lengthy stay in the dungeon. Any true refugee would be glad of free food and shelter, even at the… costs they might come with."

The way he said 'costs' sent a chill up my spine. I didn't like this brute—not his tone, not his words, and certainly not his attitude. There was no way I was going to let them throw my grandmother into prison simply for seeking refuge. What kind of twisted policy was that?

Anger burned in my chest, and I was ready to spring into action. Cordelia, on the other hand, looked conflicted but maintained her usual composure. Somehow, she always managed to keep her cool, no matter the situation. The guard took a step closer to her, then grabbed her arm.

I moved forward instinctively, creeping closer while trying to think rationally. Yet, as composed as I tried to remain, the look of fear on Cordelia's face shattered any calm I had left. His grip was firm and deliberate, and there was no mistaking his intent—to drag her away, kicking and screaming if necessary.

I wasn't going to let that happen.

I pounced, switching to my air magic as I lunged. For a brief moment, I was irritated by the extra effort it took to channel it through a bracelet rather than an epicode… or even blood magic. Still, I was fully visible for only a few seconds—just long enough for all the guards to turn their heads and see me launch forward. Swirling gusts of wind propelled me, separating the brute from my grandmother as my fist connected with his nose.

I'd assumed that the combined force of my punch and the wind would send him flying, but he was sturdier than I anticipated. Though I managed to break his nose, he didn't budge. Spinning away somewhat awkwardly, caught off guard by his resilience, I planted myself between him and Cordelia. Blood was streaming from his nose now as he stared at me, bewildered. So much for sneaking in without a fight.

The rest of the guards wasted no time, raising their staffs and pointing them in my direction. The man with the broken nose glared at me, anger burning in his expression, but only for a fleeting moment. His eyes darted upward, glancing over my head, and his expression shifted dramatically—a strange grin of surprise spreading across his face, almost as if he had just seen an unexpected ally.

"Who would've thought. We've found the thief. Mind telling us how you acquired that fancy yacharow on your back…" His expression darkened. "…and where you've hidden The Commander's stratum staff?"

Although it sounded like a question, he didn't give me the chance to respond before lunging at me. Great—not only do they think I stole Teth's yacharow, but now they think I've taken something called a stratum staff. That must be what they call those banded poles they're carrying around. And if Navoi's staff was missing, it meant we were already too late.

The man threw a forceful punch, but his lack of speed made it easy to dodge—at least, until a banded staff erupted from the ground straight into his waiting hand. With a sharp twist, he swung it back, and the pole's length made it impossible to avoid completely. The end struck my ribs with the force of a block of iron, sending pain ricocheting through me. I stumbled forward, twisting as quickly as I could. Falling was something I'd become skilled at by now, but that didn't make it any less terrifying. And I had every reason to be afraid. This was the city of sand magic, after all, and I was lying right in the middle of it.

Right, time to move. I summoned a tornado as he raised his staff to strike again. The swirling air didn't slow him down at all. He slammed the grey end of his staff down with alarming precision, narrowly missing my head and embedding it deep into the sand.

Luckily, I had only intended to kick up sand to escape. The man swivelled towards Cordelia as he realised he'd missed. Then, with a sharp motion of his pole, the ground between us began to shift, like it was opening up to swallow us. But it was already too late for that—Cordelia and I were hovering above the sand in my tornadoes. Without a second thought, we zoomed off into the city, just above the rooftops. Not exactly a great start to what was supposed to be a diplomatic mission, but hopefully we could turn it around. Then again, if Navoi's piece of the tail-key had already been stolen, maybe we wouldn't need to bargain for it after all.

A sudden explosion rang out behind us, right around where the gate was. I glanced down at Cordelia, bewildered by the sound. Her shocked expression told me explosives mustn't be too common in this world. Moments later, something struck my foot, causing me to flip and lose control. I spun wildly before crashing into the street, landing directly on my broken ribs. A scream tore from my throat, but Cordelia was on me in an instant, hurriedly clamping her hand over my mouth.

Her actions startled me, but her vigilance was even more striking. Her face was smeared with blood from the fall, yet her expression didn't waver—utterly focused, she seemed determined to push past the pain, as if she didn't even notice the injury.

I shut up as best I could, blinking away tears as I tried to focus on her face. She helped me up, and we limped into an alley, my eyes catching sight of a silver cylinder lying in the street where I'd fallen. One end was smeared with fresh blood—it was the iron tip of the guard's pole. But how had it ended up here? Was that what caused the explosion?

My head was swimming. Just hobbling on a shattered foot and with broken ribs was a challenge in itself, but trying to stay quiet as we ducked through streets and alleys, as inconspicuously as possible, took every ounce of strength I had left. Finally, Cordelia let me stop to rest. Without a word, she turned and unzipped my jacket. The initial pained confusion I felt gave way to teary relief as I remembered the kind of magic she possessed.

There I was, lying in an alley, hiding from guards with my uniform undone and half my bare chest exposed to the open sky. Meanwhile, my new grandmother calmly used her magic to stitch my bones back together while I slowly bled out from my foot. A soft chuckle escaped me—one I immediately regretted as it turned into a garbled cough. This wasn't at all what I thought being fifteen would be like.

We stayed huddled in that alley for hours.

With the adrenaline rush gone and most of the pain dulled after Cordelia stitched me up, I was still far from recovered. The wounds were fresh, and the bruises told a whole other story. I was more than content to stay still for as long as I could get.

"Alira, are you awake?" Cordelia whispered, her eyes fixed on the section of street visible from our hiding spot.

"Yes."

"I've been thinking about what our next move should be," she began. "It's been a few hours, so Cybele and Ender should already be here. I haven't heard any commotion, so it's likely they made it in far smoother than we did. They'll be waiting for us, so we need to make our way to Navoi—or The Commander, as that brutish man insisted on calling him."

"Right, but how? Do we even know where it is? And you still can't go invisible."

"True," she admitted, "But I don't stand out as much as you do with those eyes and that yacharow. All I need is a cloak or something, and I'll blend in well enough."

"So you need a cloak?"

Cordelia hesitated, her voice carrying a reluctant edge. "I really hate to suggest this, but it seems we don't have much choice. I've heard what sounds like a market about three streets over. If you could turn invisible and… well, *borrow* me a cloak, I'd be able to move around much more easily."

She was clearly uncomfortable with the idea of stealing, but she was right—we didn't have much of a choice.

"I get it. I'll go find you a cloak."

I began sitting up slowly, testing out Cordelia's handiwork. My side was sore, but it was no longer broken. I smiled, confident in her work, but stumbled as I tried to stand. A sharp pain shot up my foot. Resting against the wall of the alley, I looked down at my healed foot. Nothing seemed wrong with it. Cordelia winced when she saw me stumble.

"Are you alright? I'm sorry I couldn't do better. Stitching bones and tendons together is tricky enough, but nerves are even harder."

I flexed my foot tentatively. It shook a little as I moved it, but otherwise seemed functional.

"It should heal in time. It's not damaged anymore, per se, but it's in a kind of shock. My magic isn't quite as effective at healing as pearl water was."

"I see," I replied, not really knowing much about either kind of magic. Testing it again, I shifted more weight onto my foot.

"I can manage this. Walking to the market and back should be easy enough."

I spoke through gritted teeth, ignoring my foot's protests despite the fact there wasn't much left for it to complain about.

"Good luck."

With that, I left the alley, leaving Cordelia behind. The thought of her being found while I was gone gnawed at me. I was going to have to move quickly.

I kept my head down as I hobbled along the street, the pain in my foot gradually fading into a strange tingling sensation. By the time I reached what I assumed was the market, I was almost walking normally again, though the tingle remained persistent.

Navigating through the market, I took care to avert my gaze whenever people glanced my way and sidestepped if anyone drew too close. The market appeared to sit on the edge of some sort of cliff, which didn't make much sense given that this was supposed to be the edge of the desert. Intrigued, I weaved my way through the crowd and the rows of stalls until I reached the very last row, beyond which there was nothing but sky.

In the distance, I could see more of the city and the sandy landscape stretching beyond it. Whatever lay between here and there, however, remained a mystery. Shuffling forward cautiously, I tried to peer beyond the edge of the stalls. Though I couldn't get too close, I was near enough to glimpse what lay beyond the horizon on the other side of the chasm. It was like another tier of the city— and below that, another, and then another—like the whole of Muruntau was an upside-down tier cake pressed into the desert.

Eventually, I found a gap between the stalls and slipped into it, peering further down into the city. All I could see were smaller and smaller layers. Squinting closer, I realised the only two differences between the tiers were their sizes and, of course, their overall fanciness. I grinned. That's how we were going to find Navoi. He'd probably be in the largest house on the smallest tier—maybe even at the very centre of the city, right at the bottom.

That said, I couldn't just fly down there. It was going to be a long walk. I groaned, shuffling back out from between the stalls and onto the street. That's when I spotted a clothing merchant and remembered why I was here. Standing by the stall, I squinted at the ground to stay invisible, watching the merchant out of the corner of my eye. Eventually, he turned his head away, and I seized the moment to snag what looked like a cloak from the table. I held it close to my chest before turning and hurrying back towards Cordelia.

I relaxed a little after rounding the corner, relieved not to hear any commotion behind me. Nearing the alley, I held up the cloak in front of me, inspecting it to ensure it was suitable. I glanced at the passersby, checking that it wouldn't stand out too much. It was perfect. It was a simple, loose cloak, held together by three toggle buttons at the front. I peered closer at them—they were stripy brown stones, carved into long, smooth shapes. I wasn't entirely sure what kind of stone they were, but this was the tiger's eye city after all, so that seemed like a safe bet.

After ducking back into the alley and reappearing, I held the cloak up for Cordelia to inspect. She was understandably on edge and jumped slightly when I appeared, before chuckling to herself.

"Your mother used to scare me like that all the time as a little girl—disappearing and reappearing out of nowhere. It's terrifying as a mother. Anyway, how did you go?"

"It looks pretty similar to what others are wearing, although these buttons are kind of unique, I think."

Cordelia squinted at the buttons. "Ah, yes. Those are tiger's eye. How fortuitous. Perhaps you can use one for sand magic. I don't know what your father has taught you so far, but I have a feeling sand magic will come in particularly useful here."

Heck yes. I wanted sand magic. I'd only seen it do simple things so far—like what Ayuna and that guard had done—but if that explosion that hit me was sand magic based, then this kind of magic clearly had some secrets worth discovering. Definitely worth a shot.

Cordelia noticed me fiddling with my bracelet and quickly placed a hand over it to stop me. I looked up at her, confused.

"Be very careful," she warned. "This is far from the ideal place to test new magic—especially given our position. You do remember how you got started with the indicolite, right?"

"Of course I do. I'll be careful, I promise. But just in case, you might want to put on your cloak and step back—just in case we need to make a run for it."

Cordelia nodded, though a pained expression crossed her face.

"I've done enough running for today. I wouldn't mind a nice stroll instead. It would be even nicer if it happened to be in the direction of Cybele."

"Oh, about that. I might know where we can find Navoi."

"That's a relief. I assume that means you can lead the way?"

"Probably, but I should really test this magic here first while we're still hidden and on the edge of the city. I think Navoi lives right in the heart of it."

"I see."

Cordelia took a few cautious steps back, throwing the cloak around her shoulders and buttoning it up—minus the third button, which she ripped off and tossed to me. By the time I caught the gemstone, she had already re-stitched the fabric to look as though it had never had a third button at all.

I turned the gemstone over in my palm, feeling the tiny painite stone still tucked in my sleeve. I really needed something to store these in—carrying loose stones like this was becoming a hassle. Pulling up a new preset on my bracelet, I hesitated. I had no idea where to even start looking for the resonant frequency of tiger's eye.

Now that I thought about it, it was a complete fluke that I'd found the Painite frequency so quickly. I must've just happened to start near the right tone. Focusing on the stone again, I began with the indicolite frequency, tuning it slightly higher—only to feel a sudden flush of warmth spreading through my skin. Realising what that meant, I reversed course, searching below the indicolite frequency instead.

Cordelia frowned slightly, probably wondering why I looked so flushed all of a sudden. The tiger's eye frequency wasn't far below. Surprisingly close, actually. It was curious how near these three stones seemed to be in their harmonics. Then again, maybe it was just because I didn't have enough gems to map all the frequencies in between.

Nevertheless, the button in my hand began to get warm, humming harmonically as it resonated. I completed the sequence, the harmonies ringing in my ears as I felt the vibrations of the desert more vividly than before—the motion of the sands outside the city and the eerie stillness of the grains within its borders. I couldn't help but chuckle.

"I can feel the vibrations of the desert outside the city."

"Really? The range for sand magic is more impressive than I thought."

I nodded, still grinning, and turned my attention to the grains of sand scattered in front of me. The grains had been compacted to form a dense ground, yet I could still sense the individual particles. I imagined floating a handful of it into the air, but the small patch of ground in front of me barely twitched. Nothing else moved.

I sighed. "Well, at least it's not explosive, but figuring this out from scratch might take a while."

"Even so, it's better to at least understand how it works before we start heading deeper into the city."

I sighed again. "You're right."

Sitting there, frowning at the dirt, I started to think about what to try next. I began experimenting with different ways of visualising shapes—starting with how I pictured tornadoes when using indicolite, and tweaking my thoughts from there. I was really hoping this wasn't emotional magic like fire magic. That would make things a lot harder. It clearly wasn't passive magic like alexandrite or topaz either.

I sighed frustratedly, feeling defeated. But at the exact moment I exhaled, I felt the sand shift—like a single pulse echoed through the ground in front of me. I sighed again, this time with more intent, and felt the sand move again, shifting in time with my breath.

Intrigued, I began focusing on my breathing, feeling the rhythmic pulse of the sand aligning with it. As I concentrated, I started to understand what was happening. It wasn't a heartbeat, but rather the sand expanding and compressing in time with my breathing. The act of sighing had simply made it feel more sudden.

Now all I had to figure out was how this revelation could actually help me. I cycled through my visualisation methods again, this time incorporating breathing techniques to bring the sand to life. I managed to shift it here and there in front of me—just enough to break up the dense ground, discolouring it from the surrounding dirt. Nothing more significant happened until I tried picturing a spherical stone hovering in front of me, projecting the image onto the ground where I wanted it to form.

The sand wouldn't budge—at least, not until I sighed sharply as I gave up. The result was unexpected: ripples spread outward, like those on a pond, except they moved in reverse. Intrigued, I tried again, this time exhaling more forcefully. The ripples returned, flowing to the centre until they formed a sphere. Its density increased the more air I pushed out of my lungs.

Out of breath, I inhaled deeply, only to watch as the sphere exploded outward, scattering in all directions. If I wanted to keep my creations, I'd have to figure out how to disconnect the magic before inhaling. I repeated the process a few more times, gradually managing to maintain my shapes even after breathing back in. It was tricky—disconnecting my breathing from the sand magic for just one breath before reconnecting—but I was getting the hang of it.

It took a while to match the frequency again, but I was sure I'd get faster with practice. For now, my experimentation had taught me enough to know how to practise without causing anything to explode—and it had even given me an idea for a disguise.
I stood up, grinning from ear to ear as Cordelia chuckled.

"Watching you work away at that was quite fascinating. You're quite remarkable, you know."

I blushed. "If you say so."

Refocusing on my idea, I took a deep, slow breath, pulling a cloud of sand up from the ground around me. I choked almost immediately, realising too late that I couldn't actually breathe sand, no matter how the magic felt. My coughing sent the cloud scattering violently, tiny rocks spraying outwards everywhere as the grains clumped together mid-air. I glanced at Cordelia, embarrassed, but her expression was unreadable. She didn't say anything, which somehow made it worse.

Alright, attempt number two. This time, I remembered not to try breathing sand. Carefully, I drew up another cloud, keeping it well away from my face. It only really needed to reach my neck, anyway. Slowly, I began breathing out, drawing the cloud towards me and condensing it over my body. I made an extra effort to focus on separating my breathing from the sand as I inhaled again.

Looking down at my clothes, I couldn't help but grin. My Telesto wingsuit uniform was now a single colour—the pale yellow of the surrounding sand.

I could blend into the crowds and surroundings now, without the risk of bumping into people or being unable to use other magic while invisible.

"Oh, I see—a disguise." Cordelia let out a brief laugh. "The first thing you do with your new magic is recreate chameleon magic. I suppose even if you can use other magics, you're still an alexandrite at heart."

She gave me a smile, and I immediately knew she was thinking about Mum. I wished I had known her.

"Regardless, we still need to do something about those wings and that yacharow."

"Well, I was hoping you could help remove the wings for me, but as for the yacharow..." Feeling the sand through my breath again, I took a deep breath, softening a patch of ground in the alley. Holding my breath, I slid the yacharow slowly into the softened sand until it had completely disappeared. As I exhaled, the sand fell back in on itself, swallowing the yacharow.

"Now I just have to remember where I left it."

Cordelia nodded and stepped forward to examine my wings. She quickly got to work, unstitching the fabric stretched between my limbs until she had three folded triangles of material. Then, with a few moments of weaving with her magic, she handed me a tiny pouch on a string, crafted entirely from part of my wings.

"You're going to need something to carry that tige's eye in. You can't very well carry it around like that," she said.

I looked down at the stripy button clutched in my hand and smiled. She'd just solved more than one problem for me. Slipping the button into the pouch, I looped the string around my neck. Next, I added the leftover fabric to the yacharow hiding spot beneath the sand. As Cordelia turned to face the street, I seized the opportunity to slip the tiny painite gemstone from my sleeve and pop it in the pouch alongside the button.

With our disguises complete and my newly acquired magic, I took the lead, venturing into the heart of Muruntau.

23 – Ender

Most of the floors on the world-ship were eerily similar, which, I suppose, was to be expected on such a massive vessel. The few floors near the engine were a little different, though—likely adapted to accommodate the engine systems in and around them. According to the teleporter map, the place Cybele estimated we needed to reach was heavily damaged, or so we assumed.

Cybele had examined the map to assess the extent of the intact teleporter network, finding—unsurprisingly—that the teleporters closest to the ship's exterior were inactive. The pattern suggested that the ship had been compressed by gravity, forcing it into a more spherical shape. Unfortunately for us, that meant the corridors were far from neat or intact as we ventured out towards the engine.

The teleporter for the engine room itself was offline, so we'd had to walk from the nearest active one, memorising the route before we set off. Seeing the map again had also reminded me of something I'd been meaning to ask Cybele, so I brought it up as we continued our journey towards the engine.

"Hey, Cybele. How much do you know about the multiverse? Like, do you know if there are differences between universes?"

"Of course there are differences. Otherwise, it wouldn't be a multiverse."

"Right, of course. But like…" How was I supposed to phrase this? I wasn't even sure what I was trying to ask. I sighed, resigning myself to just telling Cybele the story.

"So, in Telesto, I went exploring and found someone I knew. They were a corpse at that point, obviously, but when I saw that they'd died on the Cronus—and that they were much older than the version of him I knew—it got me wondering. Did that mean the world-ship was snatching ships out of time as well as from across the multiverse? And that made me worry—does that mean my Cronus is doomed to crash on this planet one day? Or, y'know, a planet like this one in another multiverse, if it exists?"

Cybele whipped around to face me, staring. "Wait, wait, wait. You're telling me Telesto was built inside the same ship you came from? That military Earth ship?"

"Oh, yeah. I forgot I hadn't told you about that."

"That's so interesting. And that ship has been there for decades—longer than Telesto has existed, that's for sure. Who knew that when you first came here, there might already have been another version of you buried in the sand on this planet—assuming that version of you stayed on the ship that long. But hey, that guy you knew did, so it's possible."

"Right. That's not weird to think about at all. So, do you think the world-ship was taking ships out of time as well?"

"Oh no, definitely not. Time doesn't work that way. It's more like the universe that ship came from was further along the timeline than yours. Actually, based on what I've been able to deduce about your history and ours, I'd wager that this universe is slightly ahead of yours on the timeline too. That means there's probably an Earth just like yours in this universe, doing its thing—albeit a few decades or more ahead. Hey, who knows? Maybe the ship at Telesto wasn't even from another universe but from this one."

"That's also weird to think about. I'm not sure I can wrap my head around all that, but I'll try."

Cybele smiled cheerfully and turned back, continuing towards the engine room in a noticeably lighter mood. The same history and scientific discovery that was stimulating her mind was giving me a bit of a headache.

Finally, we arrived at what we assumed was the engine room. Cybele led the way, ducking under steel beams and navigating through crushed debris of all kinds. I wasn't entirely convinced we'd made it until I followed Cybele through a sharp, triangular opening into a room that was unexpectedly bright and far more intact than the rest of the ship. The wall panels were pristine white, and the room was bathed in light, which was unusual for this part of the ship, or really any part of the ship we'd seen so far. Something about this place felt almost sterile.

"Huh, interesting," Cybele said as she stared at the room's centrepiece, pacing around it and analysing every detail.

"What do you think it is? Is this what we were looking for?"

"Not quite," she replied, "But it might actually be even better. Given the size of the ship and what I've seen of its technology so far, I'm hoping this room is a kind of... black box, I think you'd call it."

My eyes widened. A black box? If that's what this was, could it mean we'd finally be able to uncover more about the beings who built this ship? My mind raced with possibilities, and I could tell Cybele's did too, as I watched her continue to analyse the large device in the centre of the room. It wasn't hard to see why she thought this might be even better than what we'd originally been searching for. Black boxes were supposed to be recorders—storage devices that documented events aboard a ship, especially those that had crashed or suffered catastrophic damage. And information from a heavily damaged ship was exactly what we were after.

"Alright then. Where do we start?"

"Mmmm. I'm not sure yet. This one's a bit clunkier than the main console upstairs, and it doesn't seem to have an obvious display. Oh, wait—this might be something."

Cybele stepped towards the device, which stood almost taller than she was, covered in all sorts of patterns and what could have been the alien equivalent of USB ports. She started fiddling with something on the outside of the device. Curious, I peered around to see what she was doing and realised she was pressing segments of the pattern I hadn't noticed were physical buttons.

When Cybele finished, the new pattern almost resembled a chequered keyboard. Then, the buttons popped up again, and the top slab of the device shifted slightly, releasing a low hiss. Slowly, the entire top section floated upwards until it refixed itself on the ceiling. Between the two slabs, a holographic display flickered to life, projecting a 3D image of the entire ship—or at least, what it used to look like.

It was a truly impressive ship back in its day. I couldn't help but imagine how incredible it must have been to see it then. Cybele, meanwhile, was beaming as she navigated the console, pressing the same patterns she'd used earlier, which now appeared to act as some sort of keyboard.

A moment later, the holographic ship disappeared, replaced by what looked like engine schematics. There was far too much information for me to process, but the drawings of the thruster were unmistakable—that's the only reason I knew what I was looking at.

Cybele continued navigating through more schematics for various systems, though they were all far too complex and much harder to recognise than the thrusters. Eventually, she stopped on one that also looked incomprehensible to me, but by the expression on her face, it must have been exactly what she was looking for.

"Is that it? Is that the schematic for whatever device this ship uses to search for anti-matter throughout the universe?" I asked.

"Well, it takes more than one device for that," she said, "But yes, all of them are here. This contains all the information I need to build my own multiversal anti-matter telescope, as well as how to program the ship to only target the sources I identify. I'd already nearly sorted out the mapping system, but it looks like I should be able to reprogram the ship's system to redirect its energy acquisition to only come from designated sources."

She paused, a wry smile forming. "Well, I say 'easily,' but it's actually ridiculously complicated. It's somewhat simple in theory, but factoring in the reduced scale of my telescope compared to the one on this ship, as well as the two entirely different coding languages they operate on—not to mention the fact that I'm just barely fluent enough in this ship's coding language to navigate menus at this point and—"

"Whoa, okay. I get it. But we don't have time for all that right now. Did you have a plan to get the information you need so we can get out of here? Ali and Cordelia are definitely waiting for us by now."

"Well, not exactly. I wasn't familiar enough with the storage ports here to design a device I could just plug in. I wasn't expecting to find this much information. I thought I'd be able to memorise what we found, but this is far more than I can remember."

Cybele paused, thinking for a moment as I groaned.

"It's okay though," she continued. "Like I said, I already have most of the telescope built. There were only a few key things I needed to figure out, and they're all right here. As long as I remember the parts I couldn't solve myself, I should be fine. And it wouldn't hurt to learn a bit more of the ship's coding language while we're here."

I sighed again. "And how long do you think it'll take to go through all of this and learn what you need?"

"It is quite a lot, isn't it? Maybe… a couple of hours?"

"Hours!? You do realise that Alira and Cordelia are waiting for us, by themselves, in a foreign city, right? They're probably already wondering where we are."

"Exactly. And by now, they'll have realised we're running late and found somewhere safe to camp out. It'd be a waste to hurry back to meet them now with nothing to show for it.

"Let's at least show up late having solved the mystery of how to ethically draw antimatter from the multiverse to power the planet—

and subsequently its magic. Is that not worth being a few hours late?"

I grumbled in agreement. It was hard to argue when she put it like that. But I was still worried about Alira. We were relying somewhat on my infamous reputation to secure an audience with Navoi. Without that, Alira and Cordelia would probably seem quite suspicious in Muruntau, especially carrying around Teth's yacharow.

I knew Alira could slip in easily enough with her chameleon magic, but Cordelia would've been a problem in that regard, and there was no way Alira would've left her behind. I could only hope they'd managed to make it in and had found somewhere safe to camp out for a little while.

24 – Alira

Making our way down to the second ring of the city proved to be more difficult than I expected. Once we eventually found the stairs carved into the side of the stone, it wasn't too difficult to figure out where the next set might be when we searched for the way down to the third ring. Unfortunately, the stairs weren't all in one spot, nor were they particularly wide. It was almost like they didn't want people to travel between layers. At least not often.

I felt exposed as we descended the narrow stairs from one layer to the next, as though my disguise had temporarily vanished. But once we reached the next level, we blended back into the crowds again. Muruntau was definitely more crowded than either The City or Telesto. It was hard to figure out why, though—considering how much I'd enjoyed my time in Telesto and how little I'd enjoyed my time here so far. That being said, it was a much shorter walk from The City to Muruntau than it was to Telesto. I couldn't imagine making that journey without air magic.

It wasn't until we reached the third layer that I noticed people moving in and out of dark entrances carved into the stone walls of the tiered city.

I was tempted to follow some people into one of the openings to see what they were, but it felt too risky. After the fourth layer down, I began noticing proper doors, some even with family names carved above them, indicating that most of these must have been homes. No wonder I hadn't seen many houses around Muruntau—the people were living in the walls.

Except for those on the lower layers. Their large houses were unmistakable, clearly visible as we moved closer to the centre of the pit. The sixth layer of Muruntau was as far as we made it. The seventh layer was guarded, and the stairs there were much nicer and wider than those we had used before. I supposed the smaller the layers became, the greater the need for movement between them was.

Still, there was no getting past those guards, at least not without causing another scene—and it was starting to get dark. Dad and Cybele would've realised by now that we couldn't make it past the guards, so they were probably somewhere around here. I turned to tell Cordelia, but she seemed to have come to the same conclusion already.

"Alira, it's likely your dad and Bele would've waited on this level for us once they realised we couldn't get through," she said. "We should go look for them. This level is relatively small. If we stick to the edge, we could probably walk it in a few hours, although it'll be quite dark by then. Hopefully, we run into them before that."

I nodded, understanding what she was saying without her having to spell it out. If we didn't find them soon, we'd be stuck on this level, out on the street for the night. They had to be here somewhere.

We turned left at the stairs and began making our way along the sixth level, both of us scanning the crowd for any sign of Dad or Cybele. As the sun began to set, its light crept higher up the tiers of Muruntau, gradually leaving us behind in the shadows. Gradually, strings of electric lights I hadn't noticed before flickered to life. Rows of multi-coloured bulbs, like stained glass, lined the streets, and light spilled out from some of the more open establishments hidden within the rock walls.

One of the first places I noticed that was clearly not a house was definitely a bar, complete with wild-west sound effects. I shuddered. I was not ready to spend the night sleeping on a street like this—not that I'd be able to sleep, even if I tried. I hoped we'd find them soon.

We kept walking along the increasingly darkening street, the air turning colder now that the sunlight had vanished. I scanned the crowd as best I could in the mix of shadows and the multi-coloured glow bathing the streets.

At first, I thought nothing of the figure passing close by us on the street, but their pitch-black cloak caught my attention. They seemed a bit suspicious, and I was admittedly a bit intrigued, but I forgot about them as they came closer, returning to scanning the crowds for Dad. Then, the figure subtly changed trajectory and brushed against my hand as they pushed by me, like a pickpocket.

Instinctively, I whipped around, trying to grab their hand, wondering if they'd stolen something—though I didn't even have pockets in these clothes. I missed, but the figure turned around anyway, a bewildered expression on his face as he stared at me from beneath his cloak. His dark-brown eyes flicked over me quickly, as though searching for something, but it felt uncomfortably like I was being undressed.

Before I could say a word, he pulled his hood up and vanished before my eyes, his cloak blending even more perfectly into the darkness than before. Confused, I glanced down at my hand where he'd touched me—and fear jolted through me. A large bruise was already spreading across the back of my hand.

He was a painite. A painite was here in Muruntau. And he knew I was here.

Even if he didn't know exactly who I was, he must've felt the magic in my blood, just like Ayuna had—the multiple kinds of magic waiting to be activated. I knew he'd felt it. The way he vanished was too quick—it had to have been chameleon magic.

Nothing else could have made him disappear that quickly. Failing to spot him in the darkness, I felt Cordelia place her hand on my arm. Reluctantly, I gave up searching the street and turned back to her, noting the deep frown on her face.

"What was that? A pickpocket?"

"No, not quite."

I held up my hand, showing her the bruise that had already formed. I didn't need to say any more—the fear spreading across Cordelia's face told me she understood.

"Well, it is rather dark now. Perhaps we should find somewhere to stay the night."

An idea struck, still thinking about the boy, distracted from whatever Cordelia was saying.

"Wait. Do you think that boy was the real thief? The one who stole Navoi's stratum staff?"

"You're right—it's possible. But why would he still be wandering around the city?"

"I imagine it's because it would be really hard to escape a city like this without being noticed. Although, now that he's stolen a bit of my magic, he might make a run for it."

Cordelia sighed. "Regardless, we should find somewhere to hide."

She took the lead, guiding us through the colourfully lit streets. The crowds were slowly thinning out, but the voices and sounds coming from within the rock walls only seemed to grow louder.

This level of Muruntau must have been some sort of nightlife hub—perhaps a red-light district of sorts. I followed Cordelia, scanning the area but seeing nowhere suitable to curl up for the night. We hadn't brought any money with us for a place to stay.

When I noticed Cordelia slowing down, her legs beginning to tremble, I took her hand, and we found a spot to sit between two small buildings. Whatever these places were, they looked like they were only open during the day, so I figured we could manage a few hours of sleep here. It was hard to tell, though—this planet's days were longer than Earth's, but its nights were much shorter. That hadn't mattered much in Telesto, but here I could see how it might be a problem, especially if we were stuck outside.

As we settled into the narrow space between the buildings, I thought I saw a shadow move out of the corner of my eye. I searched the street, only to convince myself I'd imagined it. The streets were so lively here that all the shadows seemed to shift and flicker.

Then I flinched again, feeling a prickle of unease, as though someone was watching me. Turning, I glanced down the quieter street on the other side of the shops we were nestled between.

It was the painite thief. I shuffled back instinctively, clutching at Cordelia's arm, which made her notice the boy for the first time.

I felt a wave of helplessness wash over me. But then I remembered—I was a warrior of Telesto, armed with all kinds of magic. The helplessness morphed into a surge of resolve, anger igniting within me. I jumped to my feet, tapping into the garnet in my mum's silver bracelet around my wrist. Summoning fire, I raised a flaming fist to the boy's face.

He stepped back immediately, hands raised in surrender. He looked genuinely frightened, which confused me even more. Why would he approach us if he was so afraid?

I let the tension in my body ease slightly, realising that if he was going to attack, he probably would have done so already—or at the very least, he'd wait until after he said whatever it was he was so eager to tell us.

"What do you want?" I snapped, the flames on my fist dimming slightly. The boy exhaled in visible relief.

"My name is Maximon," he said calmly, though his fear hadn't entirely subsided. "And as I'm sure you know, I'm a painite—as I believe you are as well."

I hesitated, taken aback. But I quickly responded, eager to make it absolutely clear that I was not a painite. I was not like him.

"You're wrong. I'm not a painite, but I understand why you think I am. Now, why are you going around stealing magic?"

A small pang of guilt flickered across his face, making him look genuinely remorseful.

"I am sorry about that. I was only looking for healing magic for my mother. There were thieves at the city entrance earlier today, and the guards went wild searching for them, attacking anyone who looked remotely like them. Apparently, they thought my mother was one of them and broke her leg."

His words made my chest tighten.

He continued, "Even if you aren't a painite, I know you have multiple magics in your bloodstream somehow. I won't ask how—despite how intriguing that chameleon magic might be—but if you have any kind of healing magic at all, then I politely request your assistance."

He seemed sincere, and I couldn't help feeling a twinge of guilt. The guards had probably mistaken his mother for Cordelia. Even if he was a painite, it was clear he wasn't aligned with Akeldama. Still, it was a lot to process, and I wasn't sure what to say anymore. Cordelia, however, responded before I could.

"We can help," she said firmly, "But only on the condition that you provide somewhere for us to stay the night. We haven't yet acquired any local currency."

The boy's face lit up with a hopeful smile, and I couldn't help but wonder how old he was.

I couldn't see his hair beneath the hood of his cloak, but he had the wispy beginnings of a dark beard, so he couldn't be much older than me.

"Now that I can do. In fact, if you're staying with us for the night, you might find the time to tell me about your magic—and your names even?"

I peered at him suspiciously over my still flaming hand. Why was he so persistent about my magic?

"I'm Cordelia, and this is Alira. Now, would you kindly lead the way," Cordelia said.

I spun my head towards her, feeling momentarily betrayed but more curious than anything else. Why was she suddenly trusting this stranger? That wasn't like her at all.

He smiled again, clearly trying to soften me up.

"Of course. It's not far from here."

With that, he stepped onto the quieter street, his cloak blending into the dim light and making him hard to follow, even with my flaming hand outstretched. I extinguished it when we turned a corner through the buildings onto the brighter streets along the wall leading back up to the fifth layer of Muruntau.

He led us to what looked like a hole in the wall, its entrance covered by a relatively simple door compared to some of the elaborate ones I'd seen around the city. Inside, the walls were lit, though only dimly.

Maximon led us through a large hallway, wider than I had expected, before it branched off into slopes that reminded me of how I imagined an ant nest might look underground. From there, he guided us down a smaller, windier corridor until we reached a small, rounded pocket with three doors set in the walls. Two of the doors had family names carved above them. Maximon, however, took us to the unmarked entrance. Clearly, he didn't want to advertise his family name. It only made him seem more suspicious—what was he hiding?

He smiled warmly as he held the door open, and I followed Cordelia hesitantly inside. Behind the door was a hallway, the same sandstone material as the rest of the walls, both inside and out. At the far end, we found the equivalent of a lounge room. Sand furniture, draped with various rugs and blankets, softened the harshness of the unwelcoming stone.

Lying on the couch was a woman I assumed to be Maximon's mother. Her breathing was shallow, and a red blanket was tied around her thigh. Her shin was unmistakably broken, the fractured bone fragments aggravating the skin and causing severe bruising that spread wildly across her leg. Cordelia winced and immediately knelt down beside Maximon's mother, who cried out in pain as Cordelia gently touched the break. Closing her eyes, Cordelia breathed deeply, focusing.

I glanced at Maximon, noticing the frown on his face as he looked at me, seemingly surprised it was Cordelia helping and not me.

He leaned closer and whispered, "Is she like you?"

I whispered back, "No."

"What kind of magic does she have?"

"Just watch and stop asking so many questions," I snapped quietly. He went silent after that, watching Cordelia intently as the leg straightened under her touch. When she finished, Cordelia rested her hands in her lap and exhaled.

"There's not much I can do about the bruising, but it should heal faster than usual now that I've stitched the bones back together."

Maximon's mother stared at her, finally coming to her senses and realising there were strangers in the room.

"Stitched…" I heard Maximon mumble, before he turned to me again. I braced myself for another barrage of questions.

"She's a yellow sapphire," he said, more to himself than to me. It wasn't exactly a question, but the subtle hint of surprise on my face seemed to satisfy him.

"How curious," he murmured, loud enough for only me to hear.

"A painite and a yellow sapphire wandering around Muruntau."

I elbowed him lightly in the ribs.

"I'm not a painite. And you're one to talk—you're the one stalking people with the whole cloak-and-dagger act."

He sighed, rubbing his ribs. "Well, painites aren't exactly welcome here."

"So why are you here then? Shouldn't you go live in Poenari like the rest of you?"

Maximon unexpectedly grinned, and for a moment, it frightened me—until it became clear he was just being smug.

"Now who's asking too many questions?"

I rolled my eyes at him, realising it was probably better for both of us not to know too much about each other. Still, if we were going to stay here for the night, it would've been nice to know we weren't living with war criminals or something.

Maximon's mother finally broke the silence, her voice wary yet kind.

"Maximon. Who is this you've brought into our house?"

She smiled at Cordelia with an expression of gratitude that didn't quite match her tone.

"Mother, this is Cordelia and Alira. They're healers."

"I'd gathered that much, given that my leg is magically straight again," she replied with a polite smile.

"What I'm more interested in is where they came from—and whether or not we owe them money."

Maximon chuckled. "No, Mother, don't worry. They're new to the city and just want a place to stay for the night in return. I thought a nice floor for a healed leg was a good trade."

"Maximon, don't be ridiculous. Even if that is the case, these two get the beds tonight. It'll be us sleeping out here."

Maximon grumbled but didn't argue. "Right, right, of course. Alira, I'll show you to my room if you'd like."

He almost managed to finish that sentence without smirking. I hesitated, unsure if I wanted to follow a teenage painite boy into his bedroom. Sensing my reluctance, he smirked again.

"Unless you'd rather sleep out here on the floor?"

I sighed and followed him, acutely aware of the warm garnet hanging from my wrist and the infinite thickness of the walls around us. My mind wandered—how long would it take to find our bodies if we were buried under all this sand?

Maximon's room was slightly smaller than the lounge room, but otherwise not much different, except for the pile of excess blankets covering what looked like the sandstone equivalent of a box spring. "Is there a reason all your furniture is just rocks covered in blankets?" I asked.

"Oh, you couldn't tell? We're poor," he replied sarcastically, his tone oddly cheerful. I frowned, unimpressed by his strange humour. He rolled his eyes before elaborating.

"Well, sandstone is free when you've got sand magic. But, as you can imagine, it's not particularly comfortable."

"But you're a painite. Surely there's a million things you could do to make money."

He scoffed. "Yeah, because being a painite means I've got unlimited magic," he said mockingly.

I was growing more curious now—finally, I was getting close to real answers about painite magic that weren't just propaganda spouted by Ayuna.

"So, what is painite magic like then?" I asked.

He looked me up and down, as if trying to figure out my angle. After a moment, having seemingly come to a conclusion, he replied, "I'll tell you if you really want to know. But first, tell me what you are."

I hesitated, weighing my options. Then I decided I had the upper hand in this little game, and it was worth playing.

"I'm an Alexandrite. My turn."

As I expected, he looked puzzled, clearly unfamiliar with my gemstone.

"What is painite magic like for you?" I repeated.

He grinned, shaking his head slightly, perhaps realising this would be a somewhat one-sided conversation.

"It's like a forced dependence on other people. When you have those you can share with, you have everything. But when you have no one, you have nothing."

It was a vague answer, but it hinted at exactly what I wanted to know. He knew how to play this game, and I realised he was matching me move for move.

"My turn," he said. "What kind of magic do alexandrites have, and why have I never heard of them?"

"You only get one question. But we have chameleon magic—the kind you used to slip away from us earlier. And you've never heard of alexandrites because there are only two of us at the moment."

"I see. How curious." He paused briefly before attempting another question. "How is it that I felt other—"

"Nope, my turn." I cut him off. "If you claim that having no one feels like having nothing, then why do you live here and not in Poenari, where you could be with everyone?"

A pained expression crossed his face. "Pass."

I scoffed, surprised. "What? You can't pass."

"I just did."

"But don't you want to know how I use multiple magics?"

"Oh, so you can? I wasn't just imagining that, then."

"You know I can. I literally used fire magic."

"True. But hearing you say yourself that you can use even more than just those two is… intriguing."

I blushed. He had won this round, though he didn't need to look so smug about it.

He grinned as my face flushed—part embarrassment, part anger. I grinned back, deciding to change tactics. With the garnet still warm on my wrist, I lit up my forearms with soft flames, startling Maximon just enough to see his confidence falter.

"I could always just burn your room down until you told me everything," I said, half-teasing.

His eyes betrayed a flicker of fear as he tried to determine if I was serious, and I suddenly remembered that we were strangers.

He'd picked me up off the street not long ago. Guilt washed over me, and I snuffed out the flames.

"Sorry, I got carried away," I mumbled.

He let out a light chuckle after sighing.

"I'm jealous of you," he admitted unexpectedly. "I've tried to hold onto magic long enough to bring it home—to practice with, or to make something useful to sell. But every time I try, it fades before I get the chance to do anything with it. I've worked especially hard with fire magic, having these grand delusions of being a glass sculptor. But by the time I get home, it's no longer strong enough to melt the sand—and then it's gone altogether."

There were no games now. He was speaking honestly, his usual smirk replaced by something raw and vulnerable. He still hadn't answered why he chose to live here in solitude instead of in Poenari, but I was no longer afraid of what that could mean. Two painites living away from their kind sounded suspicious and had scared me before. But after getting to know Max a little better, maybe it wasn't such a bad thing. Maybe they were so strongly opposed to what Akeldama was doing that they refused to live in his city. But then again, why would he be so quiet about it if that were the case?

"I… I have conditions to my magic too," I admitted.

"There's a cool-down period of sorts, but it's otherwise pretty constant."

"Can you do this with any kind of magic?" he asked.

"No. I need a physical gemstone to connect. Oh, and no lightning magic either. But I can't remember the reason—I haven't actually ever tried."

"Oh? How do you know then?"

"My dad is like me. He tried once and couldn't do it."

"Is he the other alexandrite? You said before there were only two?"

"Yes."

"Why aren't you with him?"

He had me there. Dad should have been here. But he wasn't. And now we were sleeping in a hole in the ground.

Max noticed the hesitation in my response and the way my thoughts turned inward. My worry bubbled to the surface. Why was Dad late? Was he here somewhere, and we just couldn't find him?

How were we supposed to find him now? Maximon's presence suddenly felt awkward, and I realised, as a tear slid down my cheek, that it was my fault. I was crying in a stranger's bedroom, and the more tears fell, the faster new ones began to well up.

I slid to the floor, sand falling down my shoulders. I couldn't tell if I was sanding down the wall behind me or if the sand I'd stuck to my clothes to hide the Telesto colours was wearing off. I'd forgotten I was still wearing my Telesto uniform. That was going to be a separate problem soon. Besides, I couldn't very well sleep in it.

Maximon frowned at me, and I frowned back, confused about what he was looking at. Then I realised I'd stopped crying, distracted by thoughts about my clothes. We'd find Dad first thing tomorrow. We had to. There was no point worrying about it now.

"Are you… okay now?" Maximon asked hesitantly.

I scoffed, rolling my eyes as I wiped the last tear away with my sleeve. How smooth this guy was.

"Yes, I'm okay. Just worried about Dad."

I couldn't stand the look of concern in his eyes, so I looked away, fiddling with the floor. I rolled some loose grains of sand between my fingers. The sand here had a reddish tinge, and I tried to guess why that might be, but I wasn't a geologist. To me, it was just reddish sand.

Maximon, noticing I was in no rush to stand up, decided to sit on the floor with me. The garnet was still warm against my wrist, and as I absentmindedly fiddled with the sand, an idea sparked in my mind.

I looked up into Maximon's eyes, hesitant to trust him, but all I saw was concern, mixed with a hint of curiosity. I sighed. If anyone could understand, it would be this boy. He knew the limitations and struggles of painite magic—how it sometimes made the world hate him. He was still a stranger, but he'd been kind, and so I decided I could trust him with this.

Lifting my arm, I activated the screen projected from my bracelet, the interface flickering to life against my skin. Maximon stared, his expression shifting into one of undisguised fascination. Ignoring him, I focused on the bracelet, the garnet's warmth fading and feeling weird, almost cold, after being warm for so long.

Moments later, warmth spread through my entire body, my blood seeming to sizzle with latent fire. It wasn't from overuse, but rather an awareness of the fire magic still coursing within me—its energy lingering after being active most recently. I frowned, unsure where to start. Maximon, however, gave up waiting.

"Okay, what are you doing? You've been strangely quiet for too long. And what did you just do to your arm?"

I looked up at him, and a slow smile crept across my face. I realised how much he would both love and hate this—if I managed to figure it out. But combining magics was tricky. The last time I managed it was only because I had followed my Telesto guard training, fuelled by a little—or rather, quite a lot—of anger.

Sand magic, on the other hand, was entirely new to me. Its reliance on steady breath control was typically a calming technique, designed to pacify anger rather than harness it. Two magics that didn't seem particularly compatible. But then again, I had a painite right here who might know a few tricks.

I finally addressed Maximon.

"How do you use two magics simultaneously when they don't fundamentally go well together?"

His eyebrows shot up dramatically. "Well… you mean like fire and water?"

"Sure, that works."

He narrowed his eyes at me thoughtfully before continuing, "I guess you just have to kind of draw from them simultaneously."

I frowned, unsatisfied with his answer.

"Well, obviously. But how do I do that when I'm 'drawing' from two places that contradict one another?"

A slow smile spread across Maximon's face.

"That's the best part about our kind of magic," Maximon said. "There are no contradictions. There's always room for more; you just have to figure out how to make the pieces fit within yourself."

"Okay, that sounded a little too much like something some kind of monk might say—or one of those pseudo-spiritual yoga instructors."

"I don't know what either of those things are," he admitted. "But you're right. It's something my dad used to say when he was teaching me. In other words, there are no opposites in magic. Like fire magic, which is based in anger—there's no such thing as sadness magic. But even if there was, could you honestly say you've never felt both angry and sad at the same time?"

"I see your point now. I guess I'll just have to give it a try."

"Try what exactly?"

I smirked. "You'll just have to wait and see."

The smirk faded as I turned my attention to the flat patch of ground in front of me. I inhaled slowly, watching the tightly packed sand begin to loosen. Grains floated upward, forming a small dust cloud. Now for the hard part.

I exhaled, slowly but forcefully, pushing harder than necessary to condense the sand again. I focused on the imaginary pressure, allowing the frustration to simmer and directing that anger toward the rock beginning to form before me. I refused to let the building heat dissipate, channelling it instead into the rippling surface of the emerging ball.

The sand condensed. The rock I created twinkled faintly, its surface rippling in a way no ordinary stone ever could. The twinkling faded as my excitement surged, frustrating me, which in turn re-ignited the fire once more, but not before I ran out of breath. I inhaled carefully, steadying myself as I had practised, ensuring my breath only influenced the warm, rippling ball of magic when I intended it to.

One more push.

I exhaled slowly, painfully, forcing myself to focus on the opaque glass ball in front of me. I channelled as much heat as I could muster, letting my frustration fuel the flames, crushing the air from my lungs with deliberate force. As the heat built within me, I refused to let the growing energy dissipate.

Finally, I cut the connection. Gasping for air, I fell back, my chest heaving. Relief mingled with pride as the edges of my vision started clearing. The ball hadn't exploded when I drew in a quick, desperate breath.

I pushed myself upright, my gaze landing on Maximon's gobsmacked expression. His astonishment almost felt more rewarding than the result itself.

I picked up the glass ball, holding it to the light to examine it properly. It was smooth, transparent with metallic streaks, and still warm to the touch.

"You don't even know how many times I've tried to do exactly that," Maximon said, his voice tinged with awe.

"There's never enough heat."

"Maybe you aren't getting angry enough?" I suggested with a grin.

His face darkened slightly. "Trust me. I have plenty to be angry about. It's the magic that gets too weak in my bloodstream."

"Oh. Well, I don't know how to help you there."

I yawned, a wave of exhaustion washing over me. That last effort had drained everything I had left.

"Feel free to keep that," I said, gesturing to the glass ball,

"in exchange for your bed. But I need to sleep before I pass out on the floor. I've had a hell of a day."

"I can imagine. You look like you've broken a rib, even."

I stared at him, surprised, suspicion creeping into my voice. "How did you know that?"

He shrugged. "I didn't. But while you were doing that intense breathing thing, I noticed you wince a bit when you inhaled. Plus, you tended to lean a little, probably to avoid the pain on the broken side. I imagine your friend stitched you up pretty well, though."

I knew I'd chosen to let my guard down a bit with him, but seeing just how perceptive he was made me second-guess that decision. What else had he figured out about me? I tried to push the thought away—it was only making my headache worse.

Standing up, I looked blearily around the room before flopping onto the bed. My headache spiked as I landed, having forgotten that despite the inviting pile of blankets, there was nothing but a slab of stone underneath. I heard Maximon wince.

"I guess I'll leave you to it. Don't knock yourself out, though."

"Goodnight, Maximon," I mumbled through a pile of blankets.

"Call me Max."

"Okay, Max," I murmured once more before drifting into a dreamless sleep, too tired to worry about tomorrow—or how we were ever going to find Dad and Cybele again.

25 – Ender

"Okay… I think I'm good," Cybele said slowly, after spending hours staring at the dozens of diagrams and notes she claimed she had to memorise.

I was sitting on the floor, half-asleep and slumped against the wall of the white room. Rubbing my eyes, I realised I had drifted off.

"How long has it been?" I asked, blinking groggily, feeling like I might've slept more than just a little.

"About seven hours," she replied. "We probably could've left two hours ago, but you were asleep. It was dark outside, so I figured I'd wait until morning and keep learning more of the ship's code."

I groaned, feeling like I'd been taken advantage of. Her logic wasn't wrong—leaving while it was dark wasn't exactly ideal. Still, sleeping in a steel box had clearly soured my mood. I rubbed my eyes again.

"How do you even know it's still dark? We're at the centre of the planet. And this planet doesn't even have clocks, which I've always found ridiculous."

"We don't need them," Cybele said, shrugging. "The days are so consistent, everyone just kind of knows what time it is. Or at least where the sun is in the sky. Only the machines use actual time. Plus, the city has at least one clock."

Cybele pouted as she said this, her energy far too high after staying up all night.

"Yes, yes, I know—you built that fancy clock into the façade of the museum that you make a show of using sometimes. Not that anyone but you knows how to read it."

"I'll teach you. Maybe then you'll stop complaining about time," she teased.

I rolled my eyes and pushed myself to my feet, my back protesting with a dull ache. I wasn't young enough to sleep on the floor anymore. Cybele winced in sympathy, clearly noticing my discomfort. I tried to massage my back, working my hand down my side in an attempt to loosen my stiff muscles.

"You wouldn't happen to have some sort of magical remedy for sore muscles, would you, Cybele?" I asked hopefully.

"Why are you asking me? You're the one with all the different types of magic. Use some of that."

I paused, considering her suggestion. Maybe she was right. Although, the only one that came to mind was fire magic which could at least warm my muscles enough to stretch them out. But I doubted it would be sufficient. Not with a trip to Muruntau ahead of me. I wouldn't last twenty minutes like this.

Sighing, I tried to activate the garnet's harmonic sequence through my epicode. Nothing happened. Oh, right—I'd given my garnet to Alira. Well, I was out of ideas.

"I've got nothing. And until I get some strength back in my muscles, I don't think I'll make it to Muruntau without cramping and falling out of the sky."

Cybele chuckled. "Fine, you win. I've got a yellow sapphire on me. If you connect to that, you should be able to give yourself the most rejuvenating internal massage of your life."

I gave her a suspicious look, wondering why she was so reluctant to share this earlier. Then it clicked. Her face flushed slightly as I smiled with realisation.

"Ah, so that's how you and Cordelia stay so agile and fit despite your age. I suppose there's no limit to which muscles you can massage either." I added with a wry smile.

Cybele looked away, clearly embarrassed. "Just fix yourself already so we can go."

Still smiling, I glanced at the epicode display and activated the yellow sapphire, hidden somewhere on Cybele. Yellow sapphire magic felt similar to blue sapphire magic. But instead of the hidden components of machines tugging at my attention, it was myself— and Cybele too.

I focused inward, becoming acutely aware of my blood flowing, the sensation almost making me nauseous. Instinctively, I dissipated the discomfort with magic, letting the warmth spread through me. Relief and focus returned. I took a deep breath, wondering how it would feel, and noticed it briefly drew my attention away from my circulatory system. Experimenting, I chose a muscle to focus on. I picked one that was a bit sore but non-essential for flying, just in case I made things worse.

Cybele was right, it felt just like an internal massage. I could sense every muscle fibre and how they sat in relation to other muscles, bones, and even capillaries. It was bizarre. But I could also feel the knots and knew exactly where to direct my energy to relax them.

Because I was doing it to myself, all I needed was focus. Once I figured that out, I laid down flat on the floor, making sure none of my muscles were engaged at all. Sprawled out, I worked systematically, moving from muscle to muscle, priming myself for the day ahead while the sun slowly rose far above us on the surface.

"All right. I'm good to go," I said, jumping up and swinging my shoulders around. "Wow. I think I'm going to start doing this every morning. I feel great."

Cybele smiled sheepishly.

"I'm glad, because you're going to have to carry me to Muruntau. I'm sure I'll fall asleep the moment I stop walking."

The sun had risen, and we were almost at Muruntau. As Cybele had warned, she'd practically passed out from exhaustion after we stopped on the edge of the city to prepare for take-off. She was now asleep on my back as we flew across the calico desert.

I'd thought it would be harder to fly this way, but it turned out to be less effort than I expected. With the wind doing most of the heavy lifting, it was probably even a bit easier. Still, I spent the journey torn between figuring out what I was going to say when I got there and worrying whether I was even going in the right direction.

After almost exactly as long as Cybele had said it would take at my typical flight speed, I saw it. Muruntau was nothing like the other cities I'd been to. From here, it looked more like a vast hole in the ground, carved neatly out of the desert.

As I drew closer, details started to take shape. Soldiers were stationed along the walls that marked the city's border, and bustling market streets hugged the edges of the pit. The city teemed with life, even at this early hour.

I decided on a bold entrance. Either Navoi was already waiting for me—likely informed by Alira and Cordelia—or, if not, I had news about Telesto that he would undoubtedly want to hear.

Either way, boldly flying down and announcing myself seemed like the quickest way to meet with Navoi and find Alira. The guards looked on edge as I descended toward the main entrance—a grand archway breaking up the monotony of the singular, circular defensive wall that surrounded the city.

Cybele hopped off my back as we landed, having woken up when I first spotted the city in the distance. As expected, the soldiers wore unique garments, but their staffs caught my attention the most. They were long, banded poles featuring a collection of colours from the calico desert sands. However, the chunks of black material that seemed to be commonly affixed to the ends of their staffs were a rare sight out in the desert.

"What's your business here?" one of the guards shouted when I was close enough for them to address me. Clearly, they weren't all that friendly. I could only hope this wasn't a bad omen for Alira and Cordelia.

"My name is Ender Herman, and this is Cybele," I called back. "We've come on behalf of Teth of Telesto. I bring news of the painites and their recent attack on Telesto, along with reason to believe they'll target this city next."

"We know," the guard replied, cutting me off. "You're a bit late there. We found and pursued the thieves yesterday morning, but they escaped into the city. They also claimed to have been fleeing a painite attack on Telesto."

He eyed me suspiciously, clearly undecided in whether to trust me or not.

"Who were the thieves you mentioned? What did they steal?"

"If you truly are here on behalf of the leader of Telesto, then I'm sure you can guess—it's the same thing that was stolen from her."

Well, that confirmed it. They were talking about the tail-key. Navoi's piece had already been taken by the painites. Even worse, it seemed they had seen Alira with Teth's yacharow and assumed she was the thief. I dreaded to think what that could mean for her and Cordelia, but at least it seemed they'd managed to escape. Unfortunately, that would probably make them much harder to find now. And who knew the state they were in.

For the time being, I needed as much information from this guard as I could get. Even if it meant entertaining the ridiculous notion that my daughter was some kind of master thief— responsible for not one, but two symbolic weapons of power. I could only assume Navoi's fragment of the tail-key had been crafted into a weapon like Teth's, perhaps one of the staffs the guards were carrying.

"Ah, I see I am too late with my information, then," I said. "Once Teth's yacharow was stolen, we feared they would come here next in search of the High Priestess's staff piece in your possession. In any case, I would greatly appreciate a guide through your city to speak with Navoi about this matter. I believe Telesto and Muruntau would benefit immensely from forming a proper alliance—especially if this painite problem continues to escalate."
The guard nodded slowly, clearly processing everything I had said, though he seemed a little dissatisfied. I ran over my words in my head, worrying I had said something wrong.

Nothing stood out as problematic, but then again, it had been many years since I was trained in diplomacy by HITNE. Even then, I'd been only a recruit and hadn't taken those classes as seriously as the combat-focused ones.

"Very well," the guard said at last. "But please refer to him as *The Commander* in the future. Follow Gordo—he'll take you to meet with The Commander when he finds time."

He nodded again, gesturing toward a large man standing just inside the gate.

"Thank you very much. I appreciate it—and I do hope you find those thieves soon," I added.

The guard smiled for the first time, a subtle but reassuring sign that he no longer viewed me as a threat.

"Don't worry, we'll catch them soon enough. They have nowhere to run."

I very much did not hope they found the thieves—well, not the ones *they* thought were the thieves. Whoever had actually managed to steal Navoi's piece of the Tail-key was probably stealthy enough to have left the city already. As for finding Alira and Cordelia, I had no idea how we were going to manage that now. They certainly wouldn't be hanging around outside Navoi's house or whatever government building he might be stationed in. Not now that they were wanted criminals. Just great.

Cybele followed me in silence as I approached the man called Gordo. My initial shock at seeing him was hard to hide. He had the same greyish skin that Araysh used to have, along with the same bald head. I couldn't tell if he shared Araysh's scale-like lumps, given how much of him was concealed by armour, but it seemed likely they were from the same planet.

How many different species in the universe could have invented anti-matter-based space travel, after all? It couldn't be too many, or this planet would look a lot less human than it did.

The large grey man turned and began moving further into the city. Watching him was almost surreal. He moved like a boulder— just a massive slab of rock pushing its way through the narrow streets, reminiscent of a scene from *Indiana Jones*. It didn't help that Gordo's grey skin made him look even more boulder-like.

We followed him through the bustling crowds, enjoying plenty of space to stroll in his wake. This place was far livelier than any of the other cities I'd seen so far. I couldn't help but wonder what this place had that Telesto and The City were missing.

As we moved deeper, I had a sense we were approaching the edge of the city. From the sky, Muruntau had looked like a vast pit, and so far we'd only travelled inwards on level ground. The sky loomed behind the last row of market stalls, confirming my suspicions. We turned, following the curve of the pit's edge, though I still couldn't see down into the city below.

It wasn't until Gordo led us to the stairs that I began to grasp the true complexity of Muruntau. We were descending from the uppermost ring of the city to the next. As the view opened up, the hierarchy of Muruntau became starkly apparent. The lower levels housed the wealthy, while the surface—where we had started—was home to the poor. That much was obvious, even from the vantage point of the second layer.

It wasn't until we descended even further that I noticed something else. Subtle doorways and hidden entrances dotted the walls of the city itself, hinting at an even larger network of structures and homes buried deep within. These hidden spaces were likely central to Muruntau's culture, an unseen heart of the city

This place seemed to lay everything bare, yet kept so many secrets. What an interesting place. I could only hope it had kept the secret of Alira and Cordelia safe through the night—that they hadn't descended to depths beyond my reach. This felt like the kind of city where things were either easily found or hidden so deeply they might never resurface. I could only hope Alira had managed to tread the fine line between those extremes—staying out of sight from those they needed to hide from, but not so well-hidden that I'd never find them.

The further I descended into the city on my way to meet Navoi, the more I worried they might already be lost to its depths forever.

26 – Alira

Maximon's mother, Perdita, was kind enough to provide us with breakfast before we resumed wandering the streets of Muruntau. It was nothing special—just the typical meat, bread, and tea that seemed standard fare here. How I already missed Telesto and its burgeoning culinary scene.

Breakfast was quiet. It was clear that Perdita and Cordelia hadn't said much to each other beyond pleasantries and expressions of gratitude. Not like the conversation Maximon and I had shared— which lingered at the edge of my mind. I was uneasy when I thought about what he might do with the things I'd told him. It wasn't as though he could do much with the information, but somehow it still left me feeling exposed.

After the awkward breakfast, Max led us outside, as instructed by his mother. We left the underground apartment and began winding our way back to the singular door that opened onto the layered pit that was Muruntau. As we approached the exit, Max looked as though he wanted to say something, but held back.

He was looking at me, though his eyes kept flicking toward Cordelia, who seemed oblivious to the situation. She was scanning the streets, already searching for the others. Turning away from

Max—who, it was obvious, wasn't going to say whatever was on his mind in front of Cordelia—I waved goodbye and mimicked her actions, hoping to spot Dad in the crowd by chance.

When I glanced back at the door moments later to see if Max was still there, he was gone. I guessed that was that. There was no time to dwell on it—we had more important things to do. The fate of the planet was at stake, and we were still completely lost.

Cordelia started moving into the city.

"If I remember correctly, the stairs down to the next level are back this way. We should probably hide out as close as we can until Cybele and Ender show up."

I nodded in agreement when she glanced back at me, then followed as she led the way through the streets. She moved as though she remembered exactly where to go, despite how different everything looked in the daylight.

It didn't take long to get my bearings once we reached the edge of level six. Looking down onto the gated seventh level, I could orient myself properly. All we needed to do now was follow the edge until we found the stairs again.

I spotted the guards first, stationed by the stairs leading to the next level. Peering over the edge, I tried to get a better view down the staircase. I wasn't sure what I'd been expecting—but it all looked the same as it had yesterday.

As we got closer, a tall man moving in the general direction of the stairs caught my eye. He was tall. Really tall. I first noticed him when his grey head appeared, floating above the rooftops of the small buildings between us and him.

The street Cordelia and I were walking along followed the curve of the level, hugging the edge. By the time the tall grey man reached the end of the street, where the curve straightened slightly, I could see just how massive he really was. With his grey skin, bald head, and earthy armour, he resembled a boulder—an imposing, solid rock of a man.

The boulder stopped briefly in front of the guards stationed at the stairs. After a moment, they nodded and let him pass, allowing him to descend to the seventh level.

He wasn't alone. A few smaller figures followed him, though from this distance, they were much harder to make out. I squinted, focusing on their shapes until it hit me—I knew them.

I ran. Sprinting as fast as I could, I didn't care about the strangers staring at me. I had to reach them. I had to get to them before they descended further—before they disappeared beyond my reach. Dad and Cybele passed the guards, starting to descend the stairs. I yelled out, trying desperately to get their attention.

"Dad, wait!" But he didn't hear me—I wasn't close enough yet.

I kept running, finally reaching the stairs, only to nearly collide with the stratum staff of a guard as he thrust it out to block my path.

"Dad, stop! Ender!" I shouted again. But he was gone. He wasn't on the stairs anymore. Even the tall grey man had vanished. Where had they gone?

"You can't enter without…" one of the guards began, trailing off. His free hand shot out suddenly, and the sand at his feet began to swirl. A column of twisting sand rose up, spinning into a thick roll of parchment that emerged from the centre. The sand fell away as he caught the parchment, which unfurled in his hand. My stomach sank when I recognised the crude drawing staring back at me. It was me.

The guard turned his head sharply back to me, snarling.

"You're the thief," he growled through gritted teeth. Without hesitation, he dropped the parchment and gripped his staff with both hands, shoving me to the ground as he did so. I stared up at him in shock, cursing myself as I remembered just how precarious my situation was. His staff came crashing down on me. I spun to the side at the last moment, narrowly dodging the blow as the silver-tipped end struck the compacted ground with a sharp *clink*. Glancing past the guard to where Cordelia stood, still uninvolved, I found my next move easy to decide. With no need to worry about her, I willed myself to disappear and turned to run, hearing the guard shout, "What the!?" behind me as I sped away.

I smirked, thinking I had escaped, and turned to see what I'd left behind as I began to slow down. The guard locked eyes with me, and I instantly knew I had made a huge mistake.

"There!" he yelled. I spun around to run again, but the sand shifted like lightning across the ground, as though the earth had cracked apart without the surface breaking. By the time I tore my gaze from the first guard, my eyes fell on another—this one standing directly in front of me. Before I could react, he grabbed me as I ran into him.

I realised then that I'd forgotten about the second guard stationed by the stairs. Somehow, he had appeared in front of me in the blink of an eye.

I instinctively reached for my arm to switch magics, but the guard wrenched it down and twisted it behind my back, forcing me to stay still. I couldn't move except to step in the direction he pushed me.

I was stuck. Without access to an epicode, I couldn't activate any other magic. I was trapped with only my alexandrite magic—and in this situation, it was utterly useless.

Out of desperation, I disappeared again, hoping the guard would be shocked enough to loosen his grip. But it didn't faze him. If anything, I thought I saw him smirk, as though he knew I had run out of tricks.

"Well, well, well," the guard by the stairs sneered. "Lucky us. We've caught the thief." He laughed, thoroughly pleased with himself.

"You might have managed to flee the guards at the city border and sneak into The Commander's quarters with that fancy disappearing magic, but you were no match for us."

This guy was absolutely full of himself.

"The Commander is going to love this. And then you can tell him yourself where you've stashed his staff."

A wave of fear swept over me. I really couldn't escape now. But then, maybe this wasn't so bad after all. If he was taking me to Navoi, perhaps—with Dad and Cybele there—we'd finally be able to set things straight. Or, just as easily, he might assume they were my accomplices, and we'd all get executed, leaving Cordelia wondering what had happened to us. The thought made my stomach churn.

I gulped, staring blankly into space as the silent guard began dragging me down the stairs. Halfway down, I caught Cordelia's eye. She had crept closer, standing right at the edge. Her posture made it clear she wanted to yell out, but she seemed to know that would be a terrible idea. That was what had gotten me into this mess in the first place.

I mustered a weak smile to console Cordelia, however briefly, before her brow furrowed, and her gaze stopped following me, lingering instead at the base of the stairs.

I frowned, but then the crowds roared to life. Whipping my head around to see the sudden commotion on the seventh level, I was met instead with a sharp tug from the guard. I winced, worrying about how much hair I'd just lost in the process. The pain, at least, gave me an excuse to cry. Helpless and all alone, the tears spilled out as I was dragged through alien streets.

Even if I did see Dad at the other end of this ordeal, I didn't want him to see me like this. I'd tried so hard to be a warrior, a soldier—just like him. And here I was, being dragged along as if I were nothing. It was infuriating. My face flushed, and for a fleeting moment, my skin prickled with heat.

My eyes widened. The sensation was fleeting but unmistakable. It had felt, for the briefest moment, like fire magic. But not just any fire magic—the kind that lingered in my blood.

Confused, I let my thoughts swirl as the guard dragged me further, now descending to the eighth level. Maybe Max had been right—that magic lingered but faded in one's bloodstream over time. In my case, that probably meant the last time I was connected to the garnet. Or... would it be the painite?

Argh, how did this all work? It was so complicated.

It was so much easier when all I had to do was select a magic to use, and then use it. But then again, if it were that simple, I wouldn't have felt that fleeting flash of fire just now. The painite might not be active, but its harmonies tapped directly into my bloodstream—not the stone itself.

I tried to feel it again, to summon the sensation, but it wasn't the same as when the garnet was active. I couldn't force it to make fire for me; anger wasn't enough. My blood had to literally boil.

We descended to the ninth level as I concentrated harder, trying to summon the fire somehow—to harmonise myself with my own blood without relying on my phone or any external device. It was in my blood, after all. It was there—I just had to rip it out somehow.

Approaching the final set of stairs, leading down to what appeared to be the very centre of Muruntau, I braced for the pain and attempted to break away from the guard's grip. My arm barely budged, the twisting motion sending sharp jolts of pain shooting up my arm and frustration surging to the surface.

I strained, muscles tensing as I tried to pull my arms forward. His grip tightened. My heart began pounding, the rhythm loud and persistent. It helped me visualise the blood pumping through my body, every beat sharp and clear.

With one final push, I screamed, the sound resonating in my skull—a strange sense of déjà vu accompanying the burst of flames that engulfed my body. My own scream echoed in my head at a familiar frequency, lingering long after the sound itself faded.

The guard released me at last, stepping back while squeezing his hands tightly, his palms an ugly, blistered red and the fabric beneath his armour charred. I grinned as I pulled my arms forward, rubbing my sore wrists. Time to go.

Turning to flee, I decided sneaking around level ten would be more productive than returning to Cordelia. I broke into a sprint, only to collide head-first with a solid grey slab before I even took two steps. My vision instantly blurred. I think I hit the floor, but it was hard to tell until I found myself sprawled out across smooth cobblestone, staring up at the bald, grey head of an exceptionally large man.

My vision dipped again, returning blurry and distorted. This time, I was looking down at the heels of someone very tall. Waves of pain from my new migraine overtook me. By the time I realised I was being carried over someone's shoulder, the throbbing pain in my head dragged me back into unconsciousness.

Another glimpse of lucidity came, though fleeting. The heels had stopped moving, and I could faintly discern the pattern on the tiled floor—a muddled mix of reds and browns. My head spun too much to see anything clearly.

Suddenly, air rushed around my body as the scenery changed, the tiles and heels vanishing from view. My eyes struggled to focus, but a new figure emerged—a man lunging at me. No, kneeling in front of me.

I looked into his eyes, and a wave of calmness washed over me. Their familiarity brought a sense of safety I hadn't felt in days. It was enough to let my defences drop, surrendering to the concussion-induced haze and slipping into a deep, unconscious nap.

27 – Ender

The deeper Gordo the boulder led us into Muruntau, the more lavish everything became. The seventh level was the first to be officially segregated from the rest of the city, dividing the inner city from the outer rings—much like The City did. Honestly, it really needed a proper name now that there was more than one settlement on this planet. Maybe I'd mention it to Brigitte the next time I saw her.

In any case, Muruntau's segregation operated in a similar way. However, to combat the exposure of the lower levels to the prying eyes of those above, it appeared the city had implemented bubbles. They were a lot like the one at the arena in The City; the moment we stepped inside, the noise and activity within the bubble sprang to life. Descending from level six to seven had been just like that— the seventh level appearing lifeless from one end of the stairs but bustling with energy at the other. And it wasn't the only one.

Levels seven and eight seemed to share the same bubble, creating a space that resembled what I'd imagine high society might look like in a place like this.

Levels nine and ten each had their own bubbles, but they were far less leisurely or residential. Instead, they appeared to house more significant structures. It was hard to discern the purpose of level nine from just a brief wander through, especially when many of the buildings rose all the way up to the eighth level. In some areas, these rooftops even served as extensions of level eight. The maze of tall, blocky buildings definitely gave off a distinctly industrial vibe.

This made the transition to level ten all the more jarring. The final level was some sort of diplomatic zone, with a clear hierarchy reflected in the uniquely designed and meticulously maintained buildings. It was evident that someone had put a great deal of thought into this space.

What surprised me most, however, was the abundance of plants. There were only a few varieties, but they were thriving and well-maintained. They felt out of place here at the bottom of a sandstone pit, but they brought a special quality to the space.

I wasn't sure what to expect from Navoi, but if he had masterminded a space like this, it spoke volumes about his character and vision. Of course, I supposed that was precisely the impression he was trying to create with such a meticulously crafted landscape. Despite the many potential problems with this meeting, I was genuinely curious to meet this Navoi.

Gordo continued leading the way, winding through simple gardens and small buildings that looked like they might serve as guest cabins.

At last, we reached the steps of the grandest building in the entire city. It wasn't the largest by any stretch, but it was undeniably the most intricately detailed and thoughtfully designed. Subtle hints of gold and copper were embedded in unexpected places, catching the light in a way that commanded attention. The building was unusually open, lacking a front door and featuring an abundance of windows—large, deliberate holes in the walls, often framed with mosaic patterns. It had the aura of a large, modern beach house, spliced with some kind of ancient Spanish design, and nestled in an oasis, though I couldn't recall seeing anything quite like it on Earth.

We followed Gordo up a few steps onto a long porch. The exterior walls were made of a white, plaster-like material, punctured by the mosaic-lined windows evenly spaced along the façade. Gordo exchanged words with the two guards stationed on either side of the entrance.

Interestingly, the absence of doors didn't grant much insight into what was going on inside. From where we stood, I could see a tiled lobby, lavishly decorated, and a small courtyard featuring a singular tree. Beyond that, any additional rooms remained purposely hidden around corners. There wasn't a door in sight.

Gordo stepped aside, motioning with his long, grey arm for us to follow another guard inside. I glanced at Cybele, who shrugged sheepishly in response. She still looked half-asleep, which wasn't surprising given she'd only had about an hour of rest. It also explained her unusually quietude.

Cybele trailed behind me as we entered, her steps sluggish. I couldn't help but take in the surroundings, my curiosity piqued with every detail. The more we moved through the space, the more I noticed. The guard led us through a boxy corridor to the left, revealing a set of red-brick stairs. The corridor itself was entirely red-brick, from the floor to the ceiling. It lacked the grandeur of the lavishly decorated lobby, where gold sparkled in the grout between the tiles, but it had its own novel charm.

The stairs opened into a lavish corner room. Two of its walls were lined with empty windows, offering stunning views of the gardens, the cabins, and, farther in the distance, the concentric bands of the city rising toward the surface.

When the guard instructed us to wait there until Navoi was ready, I was more than happy to oblige. Wandering over to the nearest window, I gazed out at the view, marvelling at the tiered cityscape.

"I don't think I've ever seen a view like this. Maybe the one from the Cathedral footbridge, but…" I trailed off, turning back to Cybele as I spoke, only to find her curled up on a kind of Grecian-style couch that blended into the pale green and silver wallpaper behind it. Cybele was already asleep.

I was starting to get the feeling that either Navoi or someone in his circle had very eccentric tastes. Sitting down on a smaller couch by the window, I gazed out at the long grasses and sturdy shrubs that flourished here. They had to have been imported from Telesto—I couldn't think of anywhere else they might have come from. After all, we were at the bottom of a man-made pit; these plants couldn't possibly have grown here naturally.

As I stared out, my lack of sleep began catching up to me. Daydreams started to blur my focus, but I knew I couldn't allow myself to sleep—not here, not now. This was an important moment, and somehow, I'd ended up taking the lead. I wasn't exactly the best person for this job, and pulling it off without someone like Cordelia around—and with Cybele fast asleep—felt far from ideal. Adding to the problems was the fact that my daughter was a wanted criminal.

Lost in thought, I found myself staring at a patch of watercolour sky, its hues oddly mimicking the silver and pale green tones of the room. It was only when someone cleared their throat that I realised I hadn't heard them enter.

"Excuse me, Sir, Miss," the man said politely. "The Commander has been notified of your presence and will meet with you shortly. Please follow me."

I rose from the couch to follow him but hesitated, turning instead toward Cybele. She was still fast asleep.

"Cybele," I said plainly as I approached her. "Cybele," I repeated, more loudly this time, directly into her ear. She jolted awake, scanning the room instinctively before her now wide-open eyes locked with mine. She stared for a few seconds, as though trying to process the situation, before the rest of her finally woke up. Rubbing her eyes, she grumbled, "That time already, is it?"

Still rubbing her eyes, Cybele suddenly jumped up off the couch with unexpected energy.

"Alrighty then, let's get to it."

Somehow, she was full of life once more. I had to assume her body had grown accustomed to functioning on so little sleep. She took the lead, following the man out of the room and leaving me trailing behind, momentarily stunned by her transformation. Shaking my head, I forced myself to refocus on the all-important meeting with Navoi.

Following Cybele and the man, we ventured into another red-brick corridor. This one was longer than necessary, with far too many twists and turns. Unlike before, we remained on the second floor. The next room we entered was noticeably darker than the others. Small, square windows were wedged high in the corners, almost pressed up against the ceiling, allowing only a little light to spill in. The majority of the light in the room came from firelight. Two long, narrow trenches ran along either side of the rectangular space, filled with smooth stones from which flames flickered and danced, casting an uneven, shifting glow across the walls. Even without anything else, this dramatic lighting made the room feel intimidating—but it was far from the centrepiece.

Sunlight streamed through the tiny back windows, positioned in the corners, illuminating the gold and copper that featured heavily in the garb of the lone figure standing in the centre of the room. He was the only one not pressed against the walls, and the only one barefoot—a detail I found oddly disconcerting. Even more unnerving, however, was the fact that his feet were not human.

My gaze travelled upwards, taking in the thick, earthy fabrics adorned with gold and copper scales, as well as what appeared to be textured embroidery crafted from gold thread. All of this was draped over the shoulders of a man—or creature—whose slitted golden eyes gleamed in the firelight as they bore into us. A shiver ran down my spine.

There was no question about it—this was a commander. Just his presence made it abundantly clear that Akeldama would stand no chance against Muruntau. Yet somehow, Akeldama had managed to steal this man's most prized possession: his staff.

"Greetings, friends. I understand that you have important news to share. If not, you wouldn't have made it this far," Navoi said, his tone carrying a slightly menacing undertone. It seemed he didn't know much about what we had to say—only that it was important enough for his guards to grant us passage. This might be more of a challenge than I'd anticipated. I couldn't shake the feeling that one wrong move would result in swift and deadly repercussions.

My eyes lingered a little too long on the colourful slices of sand radiating out from Navoi's feet.

"Ah, curious about my throne, are you?" he asked, his slitted golden eyes narrowing slightly. "I suppose I should mention that if I don't like what you have to say, then, well..."

He exhaled sharply through his thin, reptilian nostrils. At the same time, his foot shifted ever so slightly, and the silver sand beneath it erupted. It shot out in the shape of a pike, aimed directly between my eyes, before dissolving back into grains that coated Cybele and me in a fine silver dust. The radial pattern of the sand on the floor was disrupted, but the warning was crystal clear—this entire room was his weapon. If we slipped up, we wouldn't stand a chance.

Navoi's grin at my terrified expression was short-lived, quickly replaced by impatience. His facial expressions were peculiarly human, as was his overall form, though marked by reptilian traits like the tail extending from him. It hung low, barely grazing the ground, and was mostly concealed beneath thick white fabric adorned with copper stripes cascading from his belt.

"Speak!"

Navoi's voice echoed sharply through the stone chamber, reverberating off the walls with a force that made me gulp.

"My apologies, Commander. I was ill-prepared for your formidable strength," I said, bowing slightly in an awkward attempt at deference. "As you may already be aware, the painites, led by

Akeldama, recently launched an attack on Telesto, resulting in significant casualties. I have travelled here on behalf of Teth to warn you of a possible attack from the painites, though I fear I may already be too late to prevent it. Additionally, I have come to explore the possibility of establishing diplomatic relations, with the hope of forming a unified front against Poenari."

Navoi's lips curled into a grin. "So, we're going to war then—finally."

For a moment, his expression turned wistful, as though he had been anticipating this moment for some time. But just as quickly, his demeanour shifted. His eyes narrowed, and he fixed me with a piercing, suspicious stare.

"Although," he began, "Teth doesn't strike me as the type to be the first to declare war. She built her city far out in the desert, where hardly anyone can reach her. How do I know this is truly her will? For all I know, you could be a spy."

"You're right. We are not explicitly subordinates of Teth. Instead, we have allied ourselves with Telesto in order to fight off the painites. Teth would not want to leave her city to launch a direct attack on Poenari—I believe you're correct about that. However, after their assault on Telesto, she has every reason to want them gone, as I'm sure you do too."

I had the feeling Teth wasn't going to appreciate hearing that she had essentially declared war on Poenari. But for men like Navoi, it was necessary. It wasn't that she didn't want to fight—there was no denying her resolve. But there was also a reason she had built her city so far out of reach, and it certainly wasn't to dabble in war or politics. Both of which, unfortunately, we were dragging her into.

"If what you say is true," Navoi said, his voice sharp and probing, "Then who exactly are you? I have not yet heard your name."

"My name is Ender Herman, and this is Cybele," I replied steadily. "You might know me as the man who killed Jezebel and stopped the instant genocides fifteen years ago. Cybele here is from The City and is a personal friend of the current High Priestess, Brigitte Tahtinen."

Navoi's brow ridges shot up, the only visible sign of his surprise. He remained silent for a moment, deep in thought. Then, a faint, calculating smile crept onto his face.

"How interesting," he said at last. "You must be quite powerful then, to have been the one to truly kill the mad priestess. Although I suppose Teth wouldn't ally herself with anyone less. She's quite selective when it comes to allies. I could never sway her. And yet, somehow, you have."

His suspicion was evident as his piercing gaze remained fixed on me.

"And how, then, do I know you are who you say you are? You don't seem particularly powerful to me."

"In truth, it's my allies who make me strong. However..."

I paused, lifting my wrist to reveal the parliamentarian tattoo etched into my skin.

"I assume you understand how difficult these are to acquire."

Navoi's golden, slitted eyes flicked to my wrist.

"Yes, quite," he replied, his voice carrying a begrudging note of acknowledgment. "Although why you bothered with that useless group, I'll never understand. Still though..." His words lingered as his suspicious demeanour softened slightly. He finally seemed to be coming around.

For a moment, silence filled the chamber, broken only by the sound of heavy footsteps growing louder. All eyes turned toward the entrance—the same one Cybele and I had walked through moments earlier.

A massive figure emerged, hunching to make it through the narrow red-brick passageway. The giant boulder of a man straightened up once inside, a girl slung over his shoulder like she weighed nothing. Without ceremony, he shouldered her off, flinging her forward until she crumpled onto the stone floor, clearly unconscious. At first, I didn't recognise her. Her clothes were caked in a thick crust of sand, obscuring her identity. But as soon as I saw her face, I knew immediately—it was Alira.

Without hesitation, I ran to her, sliding onto my knees to scoop her up from the rough tiles.

"Alira!" I yelled, my voice thick with surprise and concern. Her eyes fluttered open, her pupils unusually large as they struggled to focus on mine. The faintest smile crossed her face, and with an almost inaudible whisper, she said, "Dad…" before collapsing completely, slipping into unconsciousness. Panic surged through me as I jerked my head up toward Gordo.

"What did you do to her?" I snarled, cradling Alira protectively in my arms. Gordo, unfazed by my outburst, ignored me and turned instead to Navoi, speaking in his usual stoic manner.

"We've caught the thief, Commander."

Oh. Right. Shit. This looked really bad.

I turned slowly toward Navoi, still clutching Alira tightly and refusing to let go. To my surprise, he remained calmer than I had expected, though it was clear he was struggling to maintain his composure. Through gritted teeth, he finally spoke, his words sharp and cutting.

"Explain yourself."

"Your men have it wrong, Commander. This is no thief. She's my daughter. She was supposed to meet me here, but it seems she's had a rough time reuniting with me."

Navoi's golden eyes narrowed. "Then how do you explain the Yacharow she was seen with?"

"As I mentioned earlier, Teth owed us for helping defend her city. We requested her Yacharow in return, as we believe it could be a vital piece of the puzzle in defeating Akeldama. He has no doubt discovered enough of our plan to come after your staff. In all honesty, we came here intending to negotiate to borrow it."

Navoi bared his teeth, his posture rigid and unmoving. His suspicion had not wavered.

"You've seen our army, our city. Why do we need you? Akeldama didn't have the courage to attack us the way he attacked Telesto because he knew he'd lose. We should just take him on ourselves!" he spat, his voice echoing with defiance. The guards stationed around the edges of the room shifted subtly. I couldn't tell whether it was out of fear or preparation for a fight, but the tension was evident.

"Perhaps I should kill you now and be rid of all this diplomatic nonsense. We don't need you or Telesto," Navoi growled, his voice thick with menace.

"You're wrong," I said firmly.

"Excuse me?"

His tail began to rise, his hands flexing in agitation. The light filtering through the tiny windows glinted off his scales, revealing its dark brown tone and his pale palms. Beneath his clothing, the brown scales transitioned into a slightly darker shade, the darker scales covering most of his body. He was angry—dangerously so. But I had no choice. He needed to understand.

"If you kill me," I began, steadying my voice, "You will never know why we and Akeldama are both after the remaining pieces of the High Priestess's staff. Furthermore, Alira doesn't have Teth's Yacharow on her, meaning she's hidden it somewhere you'll never find. Knowing this, don't you think Teth might come looking for it? Especially if she finds out that the allies she's so grateful for have been brutally murdered over what's clearly a misunderstanding."

He stood frozen, his golden, slitted eyes boring into me for what felt like an eternity. His gaze was sharp, unrelenting, and it made the silence suffocating. Still, I refused to back down, staring right back at him with a mask of determination carved into my face. I couldn't falter now, not even as the sight of his flexed claws and glimmering reptilian eyes sent my stomach flipping in protest.

It was his move.

It was hard not to feel weak kneeling on the floor beneath Navoi, cradling my unconscious daughter. His posture eased slightly, his hands relaxing, but his piercing eyes remained cold and unyielding.

"Before this thief was thrown in, you had me close to convinced of your legitimacy. That being said, I can't ignore this turn of events. It would also seem that you withheld key information until it was vital to your survival."

His smirk was sharp, but his nose twitched with distaste. You certainly are a worthy opponent, if nothing else. If you agree to be imprisoned until we can verify your story, then I'll let you leave alive. I'll make sure to provide a healer for—"

"Actually," Cybele interjected, her voice awkward but firm. Navoi's golden eyes snapped to her, glaring suspiciously—this was the first time he had even acknowledged her presence. For a moment, she faltered under the weight of his intimidating stare, but she recovered quickly and continued.

"We have a healer in our party," Cybele explained, "She was accompanying the girl, but it seems they've gotten separated."

"I see. I did think it suspicious that one would send their daughter, as young as yours appears, to a place like Muruntau alone." Navoi remarked, his tone edged with scepticism.

"Now that I think about it, an older woman was reported to have been with her at the border. I will send someone to retrieve her from where the girl was picked up. Although, whether or not she chooses to reveal herself is another matter."

His gaze shifted from me to Gordo then, dismissing Cybele as soon as she finished speaking. He had looked at her only briefly, engaging with me directly instead. I felt a pang of guilt for Cybele— it was clear Navoi only respected power, and Cybele had offered him no reason to view her as such. His respect was hard-earned, and she hadn't yet given him cause to extend it.

Cybele, however, didn't seem bothered. As Navoi spoke of Cordelia, she released a quiet sigh of relief—one I hadn't realised she was holding, reassured that Cordelia was most likely unharmed.

With a wave of his hand, Navoi dismissed Gordo, who left the room without a word. Moments later, we were silently escorted away, into another red-brick corridor on the opposite side of the chamber. This passage was steep, lined with stairs that wound further and further down until we finally reached our prison, presumably buried deep underground.

We were left alone there, an unconscious Alira cradled in my arms. My thoughts churned as I gazed down at her face. I couldn't imagine what she had endured—fighting for her life in an alien city, against Navoi's soldiers. Alira was a skilled fighter now, and yet they had managed to catch her and beat her badly. It was then that I noticed the hole in her shoe. I saw the coin-sized scar on her foot when I peered closer, a shiver running down my spine, painfully aware of how little I knew about her experience in Muruntau. All I could do as I waited for Alira to wake up, was worry and send my infinite gratitude out to Cordelia for being with Alira through whatever they had been through. Clearly it was her who had stitched up her foot and who knows what else. I could only imagine the worst as I sat there in Navoi's prison cell, waiting, Cybele already asleep in the corner.

28 – Alira

I woke, my vision completely obscured by a collection of lines on a wrinkly palm. I blinked a few times, the wrinkly palms moving away, having felt my eyelashes brush them, to reveal three familiar faces staring down at me. Cordelia let out a sigh of relief.

"Thank goodness. I was starting to worry my magic might not be enough. You seem to have gotten into quite the fight after being dragged off."

"So, what happened to you two anyway? Looks like we missed a party," Cybele said, her comment earning a soft elbow to the ribs from Cordelia. The movement drew my attention to their laced hands.

I tried to sit up, Dad immediately leaning forward to help me. He hadn't taken his eyes off me since I'd woken up.

"It's okay, I'm fine," I reassured him.

He scoffed. "Thanks to Cordelia. You were in pretty bad shape otherwise. And that's not even taking into account the hole in your foot."

I chuckled, glad to see he wasn't so worried that he'd lost his sarcasm.

"It wasn't a hole, just a dent."

"A dent?" Dad repeated, his tone sceptical.

"Yeah, just a dent."

"And what exactly caused this dent? I understand you had to flee from some guards, but I thought you'd easily outmanoeuvre them in the sky."

"Well… I'm not entirely sure how it happened, but it was basically like a bullet. From those stratum staffs, I think."

"You got shot with a bullet!?"

"It wasn't a bullet! It just made a dent remember, not a hole."

Dad shook his head, smirking—but then he froze, his expression shifting as he pieced something together.

"The staffs… Was there some kind of explosion when you got hit?"

"Yep."

"I see. The black section of the staff many of the guards carry must be gunpowder. That's why they keep it at the very tip—to stop it from blowing off their hands or destroying the staff entirely."

"But how did they use it to shoot the other end of the staff at me? Wouldn't they need fire or some way to aim?" I asked, still puzzled.

"True," Dad replied. "I can't say I know for sure, but based on what I've seen, it'd be fairly easy for them to modify their staffs to fire projectiles."

"Correct!" Cybele chimed in. "Sand magic allows the free manipulation of sediment—within certain limits—into practically any shape the user desires, provided they have the skill. Something as basic as a tube to fire a cylinder wouldn't be too complicated for most guards."

"So, this planet has finally invented guns," Dad muttered. "That's mildly concerning."

"They seem like one-shot weapons, though," I pointed out. "The guard who hit me fired the entire silver end of his staff. I saw it lying on the ground afterward."

"Maybe," Dad agreed. "But I doubt Muruntau's most skilled fighters are stationed at the border."

A moment of silence followed, giving me time to glance around and take stock of where we were.

"Um, why are we all in prison? I get why I might be, but how did the rest of you end up here?"

"Well, funny story," Dad began with an awkward smile. "I was in the middle of explaining things to Navoi, trying to earn his trust, when you were thrown in front of us. That kind of... complicated things. Everything should work out, though. We just have to wait for Navoi to confirm our story."

"Oh."

Guilt washed over me as I realised my recklessness hadn't just gotten me captured—it had derailed our only other chance of making a good impression on Navoi.

"It'll be alright, Ali. It's not your fault," Dad said gently. "Although, where exactly did you leave Teth's Yacharow? I hope you remember, because it's become an important bargaining chip."

I frowned. "I know where it is, but it's hard to explain. Also, when did you get good at bargaining? It sounds like you've been running the show with Navoi. I thought for sure you'd make Cybele explain everything."

"Well, Cybele wasn't at Telesto, for one. Besides, I picked up a few diplomacy skills at HITNE—I just don't use them much. Plus, Cybele was practically asleep during that entire conversation."

"I was not!" Cybele snapped.

"No? Just directly before and after, then?"

"Maybe," she grumbled. Then, with sudden enthusiasm, she exclaimed, "Oh, that reminds me! Ender and I went to the world-ship and—" Cordelia's sharp glare cut her off.

"That's why you were late? You went to that bloody ship?" I don't think I'd ever heard Cordelia as genuinely mad as she was right now.

"I… Yes? It was important, okay? You know how what's down there could help my research," Cybele said, trying to defend herself.

"Yes. Your research," Cordelia shot back, her tone icy.

"No, but it's for everyone! We can save the planet with what we found!"

"That's what you always say," Cordelia replied. Dad, of course, felt the need to butt in.

"Cordelia, I actually believe what we found could help save the planet. The timing might've been poor—especially with everything you both were going through—but we might finally be able to revitalise the magic without randomly pulling ships out of space."

Cordelia fell silent, clearly considering his words. After a long sigh, she finally said, "Yes. Extremely poor timing. Ender, next time, don't let her convince you. It can always wait."

"You're right," Dad admitted. "It could've."

"Very well. Explain how it was all worth it then, Bele."

Cybele perked up again, relieved to have dodged the full force of Cordelia's wrath—for now.

"Well, you know the multiversal anti-matter telescope I've been working on?"

"You mean the one that's just a regular telescope?" Cordelia asked, unimpressed. Cybele went red.

"Well… yes. But not for much longer! We found schematics on the world-ship for multiversal astronomy tech. Once I apply those to my telescope, we'll be looking across the multiverse for a new anti-matter power source in no time!"

"But even if you can build it, there's no way to implement it without the tail-key," Dad said, his tone heavy. "So, as long as Akeldama has a piece—or now two—he has the upper hand. Even if he doesn't realise it."

Cybele visibly deflated. "I know."

Dad jumped in again, his voice more urgent.

"Speaking of, does anyone have ideas for our new predicament? How are we going to get those pieces back from Akeldama?"

No one said a word at first, the silence stretching awkwardly. Finally, I spoke up, trying to offer something helpful.

"Do you think Akeldama turned his piece of the staff into a weapon, like the others did?"

Dad shook his head slightly, considering.

"Well, he's not exactly like the others, and I haven't seen him carrying anything like that around, but it's possible. Although his piece would've been the section between the handle and the blade tip, which would make it the most awkward to turn into a weapon."

"Oh. Oh yeah, isn't the tail-key meant to look like the tails of the chryacals on Cybele's museum?"

"Yep, pretty much exactly like that."

"I see what you mean about having the awkward bit then. But what about the other one? How do you think the real thief stole it from Navoi?"

"I have no idea," Dad admitted. "And I doubt Navoi does either, which is why our chameleon magic makes us highly suspicious. Cordelia, Cybele—any ideas?"

"Hmm," Cybele began thoughtfully. "I'd say shadow magic is the next most likely. But, since it was eradicated fifteen years ago, the thief would either have to be a child or the painites have replenished their blood-batteries—including an onyx child."

Everyone winced at some part of Cybele's explanation.

"I told you to stop calling them blood-batteries. They're people," Cordelia said sharply, scrunching her nose in discomfort.
"Wait, so does that mean the onyx in the arena was younger than me?" I asked, wide-eyed, even though I really didn't want an answer.

"Unfortunately, yes. That kid looked about fourteen. Tall though," Cybele replied, far too unsympathetically. She seemed to realise the weight of her words later, spacing out as the silence continued. So Akeldama wasn't just a killer—he was a child killer. How someone could have children and then go on to murder someone even younger and more innocent than his own daughter was beyond me. Akeldama was a psychopath. We had to stop him before he pieced it all together.

First things first, though—we needed to get out of this cell. I opened my mouth to say something to Dad but froze as a woman appeared from a brick passageway. I watched as she marched towards us, stopping with precise, military-like movements before addressing us.

"The Commander has revised your story and wishes to speak with you all," she announced crisply.

Holding her hand out towards the lock, I noticed how simple the lock actually was. We could have easily busted out. Of course, Dad had probably thought the same but decided breaking out wouldn't do much to get us on Navoi's good side.

A thin column of sand rose from the floor, delivering a key into the woman's hand. I watched the trick, intrigued—this was the second time I'd seen it. It made me wonder… Could I do something like that? Could I summon Teth's staff through the ground? Not only would it be super helpful, but it'd also impress the hell out of Dad. I tried to hide my grin as we stood and followed the woman out of the cell into the brick passageway. I hadn't seen much of this building yet, but it was already clear how ridiculous it was— especially after encountering the skinny staircase made entirely of bricks that wound from the prison to Navoi's dark and broody throne room.

Although, 'throne room' didn't feel quite right, given there was no throne. Still, seeing Navoi's bare feet planted amidst the myriad of coloured sands, I didn't doubt for a second that he could kill me in an instant. And that was before I met his slitted golden eyes. Just one look was enough to send a shiver through me. This man—this creature—was terrifying. The fact that Dad had somehow managed to keep civil negotiations going with him was honestly astounding. Suddenly, my grand idea of summoning Teth's staff didn't feel so impressive.

"Ah! Ender Herman, the diamond killer, has returned," Navoi exclaimed, his voice echoing through the room with unsettling enthusiasm.

"We've confirmed your story and uncovered a few other things about you. The indicolites at Telesto seemed... surprised by our visit, which was curious. But a woman named Chantrelle spoke very highly of you. Said you could use different types of magic but weren't a painite. Care to explain that one to me? Your friend tried, but her explanation was awfully scientific for magic."

Dad nodded slightly and replied calmly,

"I'm afraid Chantrelle's explanation was likely quite accurate. But to put it simply: my planet doesn't have magic. So, when I arrived here, my body wasn't attuned to any single type, allowing me to practise with several magics."

"How interesting. And you can just do whatever magic you like then?"

"Well, no. But the explanation for that part is probably what Chantrelle tried explaining."

"Yes I see. As interesting at that all is, Telesto seemed to have no knowledge of the theft of my staff, but they did say you were smart enough to solve their problem, so why don't you solve mine. Who do you think the thief was if not your daughter?"

"I have no idea. But we do suspect them of using shadow magic to do so."

"Shadow magic, you say. That would make sense," Navoi said thoughtfully. "The only problem with that theory is that my staff was in this very room when it was stolen. The amount of shadow magic required to enter this room illuminated by these flames would exceed what even the most adept of the older onyxes could muster. As for the onyx children running around today—they'd have no chance."

Cybele made a sound that drew both Dad's and my attention.

"Oh! I have an idea. It's pretty unlikely, but it does tick all the boxes so far."

"Out with it, then," Navoi snapped impatiently.

"Right," Cybele began. "There aren't many things that could boost shadow magic enough to allow someone to stay entirely engulfed in shadow while entering a room like this. But the most likely explanation is that there were two thieves—an onyx and a red beryl."

"A red beryl, you say. What an unexpected answer," Navoi said, pausing to think. "We are dealing with painites, after all. Could it be that the thief was one person, using both onyx and red beryl magics simultaneously?"

He shifted his focus to Dad as he posed the question.

Cybele, seemingly oblivious—or just not caring—jumped in before Dad could respond.

"No, it's not possible. Painite magic is evenly distributed, meaning someone using both magics would still only be half as strong as two people working together. Plus, the natural harmony created by a single person with both magics doesn't create the energy feedback loop that forms when red beryl energy is funnelled through another magic."

Navoi's irritation with Cybele was clear, but he turned to her with his next question regardless.

"And what makes you so certain? How can you claim to know so much about feedback loops and red beryls?"

"Because I am one," Cybele said simply. Her tone was defiant, but guilt flickered across her face as she added, "And because I once used my power to enhance a diamond." Her gaze faltered, breaking the brief stare she had held with Navoi.

"The very same one that Ender killed. While they were fighting."

Navoi's laugh echoed through the chamber.

"You were helping the diamond that Ender killed?"

"Yes," Cybele whispered, her voice barely audible.

"Now that's an unexpected twist," Navoi mused, a curious gleam in his golden eyes.

"What an interesting lot you are. And tell me, Ender Herman—how have you come to trust someone like her?"

"In truth, I'm not entirely sure myself," Dad admitted. "But she did save my life—and my daughter's—when she defied Jezebel. And, in the end, she was the one who got us home."

"I see," Navoi said, his tone contemplative. "So how can you be certain she won't turn on you like she did Jezebel?"

"Well… it might sound simple," Dad replied, a faint smile playing on his lips. "But Cybele's obsessed with inventing and tinkering, and what could be a grander project than restoring the magic of this planet? Besides, I believe Cordelia keeps her in line pretty well these days.”

Cybele blushed at that but didn’t argue. Cybele and Cordelia were so cute together. Navoi laughed again, his deep voice reverberating through the room.

“How peculiar. Regardless, I too am invested in the restoration of the magic in this world,” Navoi said thoughtfully.

“This city is becoming overcrowded, and expansion grows harder as the magic slowly dwindles. We’re nearing the point where the entire city might collapse from the abundance of unauthorised tunnels popping up. People seem to think they can simply dig themselves a hole to live in, but the ground can only sustain so many before the whole thing comes crashing down.”

He leaned in, his golden eyes piercing as he continued.

“Tell me, Ender Herman. How do you plan to save this world—and my city?”

Finally, it felt like we were getting somewhere. I glanced up at Dad, eager to hear how he’d answer. I already knew the gist of his plan, but the way he’d been framing everything for Navoi was unexpectedly effective—almost heroic. I’d never known him to be such a good talker, and it was kind of impressive to watch.

“The first step, of course,” Dad began confidently, “is to acquire both your staff and Akeldama’s piece of the tail-key. Then—”

“Wait. Tail-key?” Navoi interrupted, his brow ridge lifting slightly.

“Ah, right. Excuse me,” Dad said, his tone polite yet steady.

“The reason we’re after the staff of the High Priestess is because it’s actually a key—a tool that grants access to the World-ship at the planet's core. That ship is what controls the flow of magic on this planet."

"I see, so you need all the pieces of the key to turn the magic back on?"

"It's only part of the process, but yes," Dad replied evenly.

"I have a myriad of questions about this world-ship, but please, continue," Navoi said, gesturing for Dad to go on.

"Thank you. Once we've acquired all the pieces of the key, we'll travel to the world-ship and connect it to a special telescope Cybele is working on. This telescope will allow us to siphon anti-matter from the universe, effectively producing more magic. Of course, we'll need to do all of this before Akeldama gets there."

Navoi considered this, his expression unreadable.

"I can't say I fully understand this plan, but you seem sincere. I do have one vital question, though. If Akeldama is also attempting to access this world-ship, and thus the magic, wouldn't his success lead to the same outcome? That is, restoring the magic to its original state and allowing me to expand my city once more?"

"Unfortunately, I don't think so," Dad said firmly. "Akeldama's goals are very different from ours. Access to the World-ship offers much more than just control over the flow of magic. The knowledge down there… if Akeldama got his hands on it, he could take over this entire planet—or even rampage across the multiverse. He doesn't know much yet, but if he finds his way down there, I believe his ambition would grow far beyond conquering The City and the diamonds. Not to mention he'd be able to hoard the magic for himself, making his army unstoppable."

Navoi's expression darkened slightly as he listened.

"I see. But your plan is instead to return the magic to normal—for everyone?"

"Yes," Dad replied steadily. "Which would, in turn, strip the painites of some of their power, since their ability to combine magics wouldn't be as impossible to fight against as it seems now."

"This plan of yours seems awfully generous. How do I know you don't intend to build an empire of your own?"

"I suppose that's a hard guarantee to make," Dad admitted with a slight shrug. "But guilt is a powerful motivator. I am, after all, partly responsible for both the birth of the painites and the dwindling magic in the first place."

Navoi laughed, the sound echoing through the room.

"It seems there's much more to the story of the mad priestess Jezebel's death than the world knows. I'd like to hear the full tale someday. For now, however, I will allow you to retrieve my staff—under strict conditions, of course."

"Yes, I understand," Dad said.

"Firstly, before you leave my city, you will give me Teth's staff to hold onto until you return with mine to trade," Navoi began, his tone firm. "Secondly, this telescope will be built here in Muruntau under my supervision. I want to keep a close eye on the project to ensure it is completed and functions as you claim. In return, I will offer my protection and resources."

Cybele's eyes lit up, brimming with enthusiasm as she glanced at Dad, clearly hoping he'd agree just as excitedly. Dad didn't turn to her but smiled faintly, catching her expression from the corner of his eye.

"A fine proposal," Dad replied. "I only have one small amendment I'd like to add."

As he spoke, he reached for the compartment on his chest and slid it open.

"Teth's Yacharow is currently my daughter's weapon of choice, and we don't have the luxury of travelling back to Telesto for a replacement. So Instead, I offer my own piece of the tail-key."

He held up a thin, fossilised blade, its design intricate and ancient—the very tip of what must have once been the tail of a chryacal. Navoi's gaze sharpened as he examined it, suspicion flickering across his face.

"A bold proposal," Navoi remarked, his tone cool. "That artifact you're holding isn't one of the pieces of the staff distributed by the Fovan Church. And yet, it appears to be the exact shape of a chryacal's tail tip—a piece thought to have been lost or kept hidden by the church. Tell me, Ender Herman, how exactly did you come into possession of such a prize?"

"It is like you said. There is much more to High Priestess Jezebel's death than the world knows," Dad admitted.

Navoi let out one of his echoing, bone-chilling laughs.

"Of course! You slew the mad priestess. Naturally, you took a prize with you. It seems you have proof of your accomplishments after all. Very well, I accept your offer. You are free to go. Cybele, please see Bueller on your way out. He will show you where you'll construct the telescope. And the rest of you—be sure to get my staff back, and kill the bastards who stole it."

"Yes, sir," Dad replied with an odd smile, adding a sharp salute. Diplomatic Dad had been fascinating to watch, but this soldier Dad? He was a little unnerving.

We left the room through the maze-like brick hallways that made no sense, passing through random rooms that made even less sense—like one that was obnoxiously posh, decorated in green and silver of all colours. Bleh.

When we finally stepped outside, I glanced up at Dad's face again, trying to understand the strange expression he'd made when essentially promising to kill for Navoi. It didn't sit well with me, and I couldn't shake the unease it left behind.

"Dad, did you mean it when you said you would kill whoever stole from Navoi?" I asked hesitantly.

He smiled weakly. "Not if I can help it. Sorry to freak you out, Ali. I was probably just a bit caught up in the promise of freedom and finally earning Navoi's trust and aid. I've already had a hand in the eradication of the Onyxes. I don't need to kill another—even if they're one of the thieves. They're probably just a child."

He looked genuinely concerned, and that helped me relax a bit. This was the Dad I knew—not some soldier spouting promises of bloodshed.

At the entrance to the building, a man stood waiting for us. It was yet another archway with no doors—like the windows, which also lacked any actual glass. The whole building felt strangely open for something meant to be Navoi's fortress.

Cybele practically bounded toward the man, her excitement obvious, and Cordelia followed close behind. She noticed my frown as she drifted closer.

"Alira, Ender," she began, her voice calm. "I think it's best if I stay with Cybele this time. You don't seem to need my help with diplomacy here, and I won't be able to contribute much to another raid on Poenari, if that's what you're planning."

"I understand," Dad said, throwing a glance at Cybele and trying to suppress a smirk. "Though I think we'll head back to the museum first. I could've sworn I heard Cybele mention in her endless chatter that Akeldama is supposed to fight in the arena in a day or two. My guess? He'll use Navoi's staff to show off, trying to prove he's stronger and gain more supporters. Don't worry—I don't plan to fight him. But knowing exactly where he is and that he has at least one piece of the tail-key gives us the upper hand."

Cordelia nodded, her expression calm. "I have no doubt you and Alira will come up with a plan to reacquire both pieces. Good luck."

"You too."

"Bye, Grandma!" I chimed in with a grin, delighted when her cheeks turned pink. "Don't have too much fun alone with Bele," I added, pushing her blush even deeper.

Dad looked down at me, both shocked and amused. "Alira!" he said, exasperated but laughing all the same.

"Cordelia, ever composed, exhaled slowly through her nose and nodded once more before turning to follow Cybele and Bueller. Together, they headed toward where the telescope was to be built.

Dad shook his head at me, a mix of disbelief and amusement in his expression.

"I can't believe you."

I just smiled innocently, resting my chin on my hands.

Dad chuckled. "Right, let's get going then."

29 – Ender

Alira flew circles around me on our way back to the museum. As we ascended to the surface level of Muruntau, she filled me in on a few things, diverting through the crowded streets on the first level to retrieve the yacharow. Apparently, she'd had time to teach herself sand magic and had used it both to bury the yacharow and to cake herself in sand, hiding the Telesto colours she wore. I'd been wondering how and why she was crusted in sand.

Once we passed through the outer wall of the city, she released the sand from her body, revealing her Telesto wingsuit again—although it seemed she'd detached the actual wings when she buried the yacharow. I made a mental note to ask her to teach me sand magic when we next had time. It was hard to say when that would be, though, with Akeldama's fight in the arena looming and the uncertainty of how much time we had to plan our next move.

We arrived back in The City a little slower than we would've if we'd had wingsuits. I had changed into more appropriate attire, and Alira had evidently detached her wings beforehand. We flew up to the outskirts of The City, dipping lower to weave through the buildings as we headed back to the museum. Nothing had changed—it was just as quiet as it had been for probably a decade.

We landed at the base of the stairs leading up to the museum, the guards looking visibly relieved at our arrival. I chuckled to myself, realising how much we'd dealt with hostile guards recently. This was a refreshing change of pace.

As we stepped inside, the museum felt oddly quiet without Cybele's presence. Or maybe there were just fewer people here now? I pressed further into the building with Alira trailing behind, not entirely sure where to start. I reasoned that if Cybele knew about Akeldama's appearance in the arena, she would've written it down somewhere in her workshop. With that as my only lead, I headed for Cybele's office and made my way past the bookshelf into the basement.

Alira, as usual, was a little too impatient to wait.

"Sooo, what now? It didn't seem like you had much of a plan before we came here. Plus, it kind of feels weird being here without the others."

"Well, we have to find out exactly when Akeldama is supposed to be in the arena first. We can't really make any plans until we know that much. So, help me look, would you? Surely Cybele has a calendar or something around here. Not that this planet has seasons or months or anything, to my knowledge. It's always kind of just the same."

"Well, I like it. It's warm, and I don't have to worry about it raining," Alira replied.

"I suppose that's true. Although, you haven't had to sleep outside in the cold before. It's not quite as warm in the dunes at night."

Alira fell a little quiet then. I wasn't sure why at first, but I ventured a guess that she was probably thinking about Nadira.

She'd asked me plenty of times to recount how we met, and I always obliged. I mean, meeting the love of your life as you lay dying in the desert is wild. But that's how life is I suppose. Well, mine anyway.

I turned my attention back to the basement room, which was furnished with a large wooden table and the cabinets Cybele had pulled an indicolite from when we first arrived. Alira floated around the edges of the room, slowly examining everything. I mirrored her movements, circling the room from the opposite direction.

There was no sign of a calendar or anything useful. The room was far too tidy to be where Cybele would do her work or jot down notes. My curiosity was piqued, however, when I reached the large wooden cabinet that seemed to be brimming with trinkets and gemstones. I tried to recall which drawer Cybele had pulled the indicolite from but evidently got it wrong, as the one I opened was filled with an assortment of cloudy green gemstones. Probably some kind of jade. I wondered briefly if jade held any magic connected with it. The temptation to connect to it and find out pulled at me, but I dismissed the thought, knowing it could be counterproductive—or even destructive—if paired with the wrong type of magic.

I slid open the next drawer and found a single, familiar blue crystal inside. It looked like Alira and I had nearly depleted Cybele's indicolite supply. Thankfully, she seemed to have a habit of hoarding anything she came across.

Alira caught up to me as I opened another drawer at random. It was empty. I tried another, and this time I found a handful of stripy brown stones. Alira leaned over to peer inside, her face lighting up with recognition. Her reaction sparked something in my mind—I should know this one too. I didn't have to think hard, having just been in Muruntau where so much of the population wore this exact stone. It had to be tiger's eye. That would explain why Alira recognised it so quickly.

"Ali, I didn't ask earlier, but how exactly did you happen to get a tiger's eye to use for your sand magic?" I asked, raising an eyebrow.

She avoided my gaze, her hands fidgeting as she replied hesitantly, "Well… we didn't have any money, and we were kind of fugitives, and I needed to hide the yacharow, and…"

"Yes, I know all that. You stole it, didn't you?" I asked, raising an eyebrow.

"Technically," Alira admitted, "But I didn't steal it for me! I could disguise myself, but Cordelia couldn't, so I stole a cloak for her. The tiger's eye just happened to be what the buttons were made of."

"I see. It's hard to argue with that, but still—stealing is bad."

"Yeah, I know that."

She rolled her eyes, shrugging off any lingering guilt as she wandered off to another room.

Once she left, I took one of the tiger's eye stones from the drawer, resolving to tell Cybele I'd taken it later. I returned to the corridor in the basement and picked another room to explore. It took some time, but eventually, Alira and I both converged on the final room likely to contain what we were searching for.

We stood in the doorway, staring blankly at the chaos before us. It was Cybele's actual workshop, cluttered with ship parts, piles of unidentifiable junk, and who knows what else. Neither of us had any idea where to start.

"Well, at least we know it's definitely in here. This is what I imagine it looks like inside Cybele's head," Alira said, her tone playful as she stepped cautiously into the room, her gaze flitting over the various heaps.

"Although," she added with a sigh, "Akeldama will have come and gone by the time we find anything useful in this mess."

I wandered into the room, just as unsure of where to begin as Alira had been. The space looked different from the last time I'd seen it, but when I reached what I thought was the centre, my eyes landed on a black rectangular box sitting on a bench. A brass key rested on top of it, shining under the glare of a nearby lamp. The workshop itself might have changed, but the box was exactly the same.

A chill ran down my spine as a suppressed memory surfaced, sharper now—the moment Cybele had tried, with unsettling sincerity, to slice my skull open. I was forever grateful to Ava and Nadira for their timely rescue. And strangely, I was thankful Ava had decided not to kill Cybele. It left me feeling a little conflicted, but I couldn't ignore my curiosity as it pulled me towards the box.

I picked up the brass key gingerly, turning it over in my hands before unlocking the box. As I lifted the hatch and peered inside, I wasn't sure what to expect. One thing was certain—I hadn't expected to find a piece of paper with my name scrawled on it. Bewildered, I picked up the note, staring at my name written neatly on the outside.

I hesitated before unfolding it, still processing the surprise. Alira, who had noticed my discovery by this point, wandered over quietly, her curiosity clearly piqued.

"What is it?"

"I'm not sure yet."

I unfolded the note, finding a short scribble that read: *I knew I'd forget about this, so I left it where you might find it.*

I chuckled to myself. How very Cybele. Setting the note aside, I reached into the box to see what she'd left for me—however long ago. I pulled out a pair of fingerless leather gauntlets, looking them over. I found a row of five circles running along the back part of the forearm, and embedded within were what appeared to be small metal discs.

Curious, I popped open one of the circles, revealing a tiny pocket beneath it. At the bottom of the pocket sat a flat metallic disc with a slight dent in its surface. The disc was intricate, appearing to house multiple hidden components, like it were some sort of device.

I couldn't quite make sense of it, but that didn't stop me from sliding the gauntlets on. They fit surprisingly well. The leather-like material was flexible despite the hidden technology, and a strange weave layered over the top added to their unique feel. I flexed my fingers experimentally. They were comfortable, moulding to my movements with ease.

The gauntlets only covered part of my forearm and wrist, ending at the base of my thumb. They looped around it neatly, leaving my fingers and most of my palm exposed. I slid on the other gauntlet, starting to piece together why Cybele made these. Sliding back the compartment on my chest, I revealed the collection of gemstones hidden inside. I removed the topaz and carefully placed it into one of the circular pockets on my wrist, fitting it snugly into the divot in the metal disc before covering it with the circular patch.

Curious to see if anything had changed, I went to connect to the topaz. As I opened the frequency augmenter on my epicode, a faint, random frequency buzzing in the background caught my attention. Switching into scanning mode, I honed in on the signal, quickly realising it was coming directly from my wrist. I couldn't help but smile.

Decrypting the signal took a few minutes—a perfect opportunity to explain to Alira what was happening and what I suspected the gauntlets were capable of. I was partially right.

Once I'd finished decrypting the signal, I found I could connect to the gauntlets and access the specific data they were collecting. The interface was rough, but I could tell the gloves were analysing the composition of the gemstone, its temperature, and even its strength—allowing them to determine the breaking point of the stone. The gauntlets were now feeding me data, telling me that they contained one topaz, which was incrementally increasing in heat—perfectly corresponding with the flexing of my muscles. Cybele had designed a way for me to track my gemstones and monitor their integrity before they shattered. This was a lifesaver.
Even more convenient was the fact that my epicode allowed me to prioritise this stream of data, placing it unobtrusively in the corner of my vision where I could monitor it constantly.

Whenever I activated a gemstone, its energy levels would appear, allowing me to track how close I was to pushing it past its limit. This was perfect; I no longer had to hold back out of caution, worrying I might accidentally break a stone.

As I flexed absently, watching the little bar rise and fall in sync with my movements, I noticed Alira frowning at me. Her curious gaze was locked on the gauntlets. It made me wonder if Cybele had added a similar feature to Alira's bracelet phone, but trying to figure out how that would work made me reconsider its feasibility.

"Looks like I don't need this compartment anymore," I said, removing the sash from my chest. I folded it neatly and tucked it into the box after removing the remaining gemstones and fitting them into the gauntlets. I knew I'd thank Cybele when I saw her next, but I wanted to acknowledge it now as well.

I glanced around the bench, searching for a pen or something to leave her a note. As I rummaged, I lifted a random set of sketches for some device or another but didn't find a pen anywhere. What I did find, however, was a large grid hidden beneath the papers, with key events scrawled across several boxes. This was it—the calendar.

I pushed the sketches aside, pulling out the calendar and laying it flat on the bench. Alira popped back up beside me, holding out a pencil.

"Oh hey, you found it," she said, surprised.

I took the pencil and quickly wrote a thank-you on the back of Cybele's note before placing it back into the box and locking it with the brass key. My attention snapped back to the calendar, though I couldn't help glancing down at my new gear.

"Dad, the calendar," Alira said, unimpressed.

"Right, yes, I know," I replied, pretending I hadn't been admiring my new toys. Honestly, why wasn't I allowed to be excited about something for once? She had been just as thrilled when she got her Telesto wingsuit and yacharow.

I turned back to the calendar, only to be greeted by disappointment. There were no numbers, no dates, and no names for months or days—just a simple grid.

"There! That's the last one," Alira exclaimed, jabbing her finger at some scribbles that read 'Akeldama Arena' and, beneath it in the same box, 'Ender Arrival.'

"So that was the day we arrived, which was…" Alira began, trailing off as she started calculating how long we had been here and where that would place us on the grid.

"Wow, we've only been here for, like, two weeks. It feels like way longer," Alira said. "Anyway, that puts us right… here!" She exclaimed, jabbing her finger at another scribble on the calendar. The box she pointed at was empty, but two boxes to the right, the words 'Akeldama Arena' were written again. So, two days from now, he'd be back. That's how long we had to prepare.

No specific time was noted, of course, but I vividly recalled Cybele's face lit by the red gemstone as sunlight streamed through the museum's front façade. I could only assume whatever time that had been would align with Akeldama's appearance in two days. It was all we had to go on. Neither Alira nor I had the absurd body clocks the locals here seemed to possess.

"Alright," I said, determination building, "We've got two days to figure out how we're gonna do this."

A spark of hope fluttered through me. This time, we were on the offensive. So far, we'd only been on the defensive. Even during the Poenari raid to find Mellory—Brigitte's sister—we weren't truly prepared for a fight and wound up retreating as fast as we could. But now? Now we were ready. We were going straight to Akeldama, taking back Navoi's staff—and, if possible, his piece of the tail-key too.

We had time to plan this time. Even though there were only two of us, we had enough magic between us to pull off just about anything. That being said, entering the arena as contestants was definitely off the table. There was no way we could win that way. Not only had Akeldama bested us multiple times before, but he'd have fresh magic coursing through him—collected from fallen challengers. He'd be at the peak of his ability. We needed to catch him off-guard, ideally stealing back the staff and tail-key without him even noticing. Though even with two alexandrites, that seemed unlikely. He knew what we could do and would undoubtedly be on guard for us. Still, it was a good start.

"I think our best course of action is to scope out the arena first," I said. "It'll be easier to plan if we know the layout—and roughly where Akeldama might be before and after the match."

"Okay, but I can't promise I'll be able to do much else today," Alira replied. "That sounds like a whole adventure, and I've already had about three of those today. Not to mention the hole in my foot."

I raised my eyebrows at her, half in concern and half teasing. She quickly realised her mistake.

"Dent! I meant dent—not a hole," she corrected hurriedly.

I chuckled. "Best case scenario, it'll be more of an invisible sightseeing tour than an adventure. I don't think it'll be particularly eventful, but I know you've been through a lot today. If you're too tired, you could stay here while I go."

She nodded, and with that settled, we turned and left the workshop. I had planned to head straight to the arena, making sure I wouldn't get stuck out there in the dark. But Alira's stomach grumbled on our way out of the basement, prompting a quick detour to scrounge up some rations. It had been a while since I'd had the chance to sit down and enjoy a meal with my daughter, so we took the time to do just that.

Alira sighed but didn't complain as I passed her some jerky and bread.

"Missing Telesto, are you?" I asked.

"Why are they the only ones with good food?" she groaned.

"Well, I'm sure you've noticed there's not a whole lot of plants or animals around here. After learning about the mushroom beetle tea, I'm a bit afraid to ask where this jerky comes from," I replied.

Alira shuddered. "Stop. I don't want to think about what beetles making honey even looks like," she said through a mouthful of bread.

I finished my rations fairly quickly and stood, telling Alira I'd be back as soon as I could and that I'd try to draw a map we could use to make a plan. From there, I left the museum, stepping into the maze-like streets of The City once again. Disguised as nothing more than a ripple of the light, I made my way toward the arena.

30 – Alira

Dad had been gone for hours by the time he finally returned. I'd spent the time chatting with some of the people hanging around the museum. At first, it was casual small talk, but then I met a boy playing a board game he called Proelium. He eagerly explained the game to me, walking me through a round of my own. After that, I was hooked. We played a few more rounds, and with each one, I got better—advancing further and learning plenty about The City as we played. The boy explained the different symbols as they appeared, tying them to various aspects of The City's history and culture.

Dad re-entered the museum just as my piece was eaten by a chryacal. A weird chill ran down my spine as the memory surfaced—the moment Dad had nearly died in a similar fashion, battling a chryacal on a real-life Proelium board just to get into parliament.

I got up and hurried over to him, eager to find out what he had discovered.

"Dad! What did you find? Anything useful?"

"I mean, I've got a pretty solid map of the arena now, including where I think Akeldama and his crew might stay—or at least stash their stuff when they arrive. But it's just a guess. I took a nice long walk and started working on a plan, though, and I think I've made a good start," Dad explained.

I grinned. "Tell me everything."

"Actually," he replied, "I was hoping to get some info from you first. My plan is going to need that little trick you pulled with the yacharow. Do you think you can teach me some sand magic?"

"Absolutely. It's super easy once you know how it works," I said casually. It wasn't. It was harder than both air and fire magic. But hey, making magic look easy was kind of my thing. Well, except maybe with fire magic—still, I figured it out eventually.

"Perfect. It's getting dark now, so why don't you get some rest? I'll draw up a map tonight, and in the morning, you can teach me some sand magic, and I'll explain my idea," he suggested.

"Okay," I said, already starting to wonder what I'd be able to with a little bit of space to really test what I could do with sand magic. My thoughts wandered to the glass ball I'd made with Max, wondering if he was staring at it right now, thinking about me. But, of course, Dad was here now, and he couldn't know I even had a painite gemstone on me—let alone that I'd actually practiced with it multiple times. I wandered over to Cybele's office, spotting the thin mattress I'd slept on before, shoved up against the wall with a few others. I yanked it out, wondering if I'd be able to get any sleep with so much swirling around in my head. After all, so much had happened today. We had an entire plan forming for taking on Akeldama and Ayuna, and tomorrow I'd finally get to properly practise sand magic.

Despite my worrying, the moment I lay down on the thin mattress, it felt like utter bliss compared to the night before. To my surprise, I drifted into a deep sleep with no trouble at all.

Or so I thought.

It was strange. I knew I was still asleep, and I could tell I was dreaming—but even for a lucid dream, this one felt unusually vivid. I blinked, confused, as I realised I was standing in our backyard on Earth. The grass, the fence—it was all slightly fuzzy, like a picture taken with a smudged lens. For whatever reason Dad was also here, standing in the middle of the backyard, clear as day, wearing his Telesto gear.

I barely remembered what his new gauntlets looked like in real life, but here, I could see them in an uncanny amount of detail—far sharper than the backyard itself.

"Hey, Ali," Dad said, his tone apologetic. "Sorry to scare you like this, but while I was drawing the map, I remembered I had an amethyst and figured I could just show you what the arena layout looks like."

"Oh. I wasn't scared. But this is pretty weird. So, amethyst is some kind of dream magic, is it? What else can it do?" I asked.

"Well, so far I've only used it for things like this, but it can also put people to sleep," Dad replied.

"That sounds like it would've been pretty useful up until now. Why haven't you tried it?"

"Honestly, I keep forgetting I even have a stone like this. I guess I'm so used to using fire and knife magic to fight that I fall back on those whenever something happens."

"Maybe you should let me take it then. I'll knock some painites out easy" I said with a grin.

Dad made a face. "Maybe. Anyway, I conjured this dream so I could show you the arena layout—so you wouldn't have to just rely on the map."

As he spoke, the silhouette of the arena appeared in the background, looming like a shadow in Dad's subconscious mind.

"Alright, show me then."

I woke up groggy, my mind slowly piecing together the awfully long dream I'd had. The fragments came together bit by bit until I remembered mostly everything Dad had shown me—especially the part where he'd promised to lend me the amethyst so I could try out dream magic for myself.

Bouncing up from the mattress, I wandered over to check on Dad, only to find him still asleep. Instead, I wandered past him to grab some breakfast, including tea that was perfectly normal tea as far as I was concerned. I sat down to eat, letting my mind wander as I daydreamed about all sorts of random things.

It wasn't long before I heard Dad groan, in that typical old-man way, as he hauled himself up off his mattress on the floor.

"Good morning!" I piped up, not quite finishing my mouthful of bread.

"Good morning, Ali," he replied, rubbing his eyes. "I see you're in a good mood. Do you remember everything from the dream last night?"

"Yup, I think so."

"Good. Some people have a hard time recalling dreams, even when they're magic-induced."

"Not me," I said, trying to sound nonchalant. "I'm basically a pro at magic stuff by this point."

Dad rolled his eyes. "Just because you have a knack for air magic doesn't make you a 'pro at magic stuff,'" he said, finishing with a mocking tone, motioning air quotes.

I opened my mouth to refute him but caught myself. Proving myself would only mean spilling my secret about using blood magic—so instead, I just pouted.

Once Dad had sorted his breakfast, he gave me a brief rundown of the plan. Then, we headed outside and made our way across the city, toward the edge of the desert where we'd first practised air magic.

"Sooo, you want to use sand magic to bury modified resonance scanners around the arena, so you'll know when Akeldama arrives and roughly where he is?" I asked after we finished our race to the city limits. Naturally, I won, seeing as it was an air race.

"Pretty much, yep," Dad replied.

"But how will you know what the scanners are reading? Won't it be hard to connect your epicode to all of them? And even if you manage it, won't the crowds mess with the signals?"

"Not necessarily," he replied. "I don't want to modify the scanners too much. We don't really have the time—even if I borrow a sapphire, assuming Cybele has one somewhere. The scanners will only work within a really short radius, like a single hallway, so the crowds shouldn't be an issue. As long as we stay at ground level, beneath the crowds, and not too far from any of the scanners, I should be able to read all the signals clearly."

"Okay, sure. Then what again?"

Dad rolled his eyes. "Well, there are a few different options after that, depending on who we detect first and where. It'll be impossible to tell one painite from another using this method, but I doubt they'll be too spread out. The giveaway I'm hoping for will be the presence of the onyx and red beryl thieves. Although even that is still just a guess. Regardless, based on the situation, we either—"

I cut him off. "Yeah, I kind of remember, generally speaking. But you went through so many scenarios it's impossible to keep track of them all. I think I'll just wait until it happens, and then you can tell me the plan. It's probably a better use of my time getting better at sand magic than trying to remember a million scenarios that won't even happen."

Dad frowned, sighing as he finally gave in. "I suppose you're right about that. I suppose for this mission, I'll be the brains, and you'll be the brawn."

"Hey! Don't call me the brawn!" I protested.

He grinned. "I thought you liked having stronger magic than me?"

"Well, yeah, but… I have brains too. I just don't waste them on pointless possibilities."

"I know. I'm just teasing," he said with a chuckle.

"Well, tease this," I said smugly, summoning the wind without tensing a single muscle, effectively sending Dad and a wave of sand flying in all directions.

He caught himself mid-air, floating back down gracefully on his own personal tornado.

"You should focus that energy on learning instead. Now, teach me how sand magic works."

I obliged, switching over to sand magic. I noticed Dad switch too, but caught him sneaking a glance at his shiny new gloves.

"Are you done?" I asked, raising an eyebrow at him.

"For now," he replied with a grin.

I rolled my eyes and dove into a quick intro to sand magic. Dad nodded along as I spoke, looking almost too studious.

"It sounds a bit like water magic but with a twist," he said once I'd finished. "Might be a bit tricky. Especially considering I was never particularly good with water magic."

I demonstrated for him next, knowing I couldn't show and talk at the same time since it required precise lung control.

First, I condensed a small pile of sand into a rock, then shattered it into pieces, exaggerating my breathing to make it easier to see. After that, I recreated my camouflage trick—kicking up a cloud of sand before sticking it to my clothes. Unfortunately, we were standing on a patch of orange sand, which made me stand out way more than blend in.

Dad frowned thoughtfully, then started trying it himself. With everything I knew already laid out for him, I turned back to practising too. The orange sand had sparked an wanted to try out.

I stood over the division between two distinct patches of the desert—one bright orange, the other a dark brown that was unusually gritty. I inhaled slowly, separating the sand in my mind as I tried to draw two distinct streams from the ground. I felt the sand stir, but they didn't rise. Recalling the visual aspects of sand magic, I kept my eyes fixed on the hard line between the two-tone desert before me. I inhaled once more, picturing the streams rising right where I wanted them. The sand obliged—one orange tendril and one dark brown, each drawing themselves up from the dunes. I experimented further, compressing and re-compressing the different colours until I achieved my goal.

Now I held a small cylinder—one end orange and the other brown—and it didn't snap in the middle like my previous iterations. This one was strong. The two materials had bonded flawlessly, leaving no weak points. This was how they made stratum staffs, and now, I could make my own. It wasn't like I needed one—I had Teth's yacharow after all—but it was a useful skill nonetheless. Especially if it helped me figure out how to manipulate other sand magic users' staffs. Or even Navoi's stratum staff. I might even be able to dissolve it right out of Akeldama's possession, pulling the piece of the tail-key within it straight through the ground to where we were. Although I hadn't moved anything underground yet, only buried it, so I figured I should probably practise that next.

Dad came over to me while I was practising, moving my tiny two-tone staff around underground.

"Ali, what are you doing? It looks like you're just meditating."

I opened my eyes slowly, trying to maintain the tiny staff moving in increasingly large circles beneath the surface of the dunes. It stopped moving the moment I decided to reply,

"I'm moving things underground. It's actually much easier than trying to get the sand to rise into the air."

"Oh really, are you?" Dad said, raising an eyebrow. It was pretty clear he wanted proof. I stared at the spot on the sand where I was pretty sure the tiny staff was currently at, then exhaled swiftly through my nose, launching the little cylinder out of the sand and into the sky in my general direction.

Dad and I both watched it as it reached its peak and began to fall back towards us. He briefly glanced down at the sand, which shifted subtly under his gaze, before refocusing on the cylinder. A large orange bowl rose from the sand, adjusting its position constantly based on where Dad thought the little staff would land. He caught it in the bowl, about two meters to my left. Looks like my aim was pretty good too—although I probably would've missed if I had tried to aim at a person. How that guard managed to hit me in the foot while I was speeding away was still astounding to me.

"Oh, I see. And you've tried making yourself a little staff too— not that you need one. Although I might like one. I don't have much in terms of weapons, but I'm pretty good with a staff," Dad said.

"Yes, Dad, I know. You made me train with you back at home using big sticks. Although I can see why now, given the types of weapons I've seen here," I replied.

He nodded, leaning forward to hold the little staff out to me, but froze and pulled it back before I could grab it. Instead, he threw it as hard as he could into the desert.

"Hey! What was that for?" I shouted at him.

"Quick, feel the vibrations of the desert before it lands. It'll be much harder to find once it's sitting still," he said.
I let out an annoyed groan, accompanied by an eyeroll, but did as he said, not having time to complain before it landed.

Everything was quiet for a couple of seconds. Then, suddenly, ripples in the constant background vibrations of the desert made their way outward from a single point. With enough effort, I found I could pinpoint it. I felt the little staff through my connection to the sand—in a way I imagined was like echo-location—and pulled it through the sand toward me, popping it out of the ground right in front of me and up into my hand. I couldn't help but grin, aiming it at Dad, who I couldn't decide whether he looked more proud or defeated.

"Now that ability might just come in extremely handy, especially in a place like the arena."

"I'll get back to practising it then," I said as I threw the little staff back into the desert without bothering to look where.

We continued like that for a little while before Dad decided to head back to the museum to work on modifying enough resonance scanners for tomorrow's plan. By that point, he'd put together his own full-sized staff, crafted from three different kinds of sand. He'd tried transporting it underground but found it too awkward to manoeuvre properly, although he did manage to sink it far enough to hide it from sight.

He let me try next, and I managed to move it around beneath the surface, but I couldn't launch it like the tiny one—it would only resurface and fall flat on the ground. Still, it was more than Dad could manage, so that was good enough for me.

He left me there to practise for a few more hours, and I found myself trying out everything I could think of, including moving off the ridge we were practising on to the part of the desert that vibrated fully. The experience was a little different, but not enough that it was worth standing around there with my vision slowly going blurry.

When I had exhausted all my ideas and was absolutely sure that Dad wouldn't show up, I finally caved and switched to blood magic, curious about what I could do if I combined it with fire or air magic. I quickly realised that blending wind and sand magic was extremely difficult and not worth the extra effort, given that the best I could manage was whipping up a dust-storm. While that might come in handy, throwing fire into the mix with sand magic was waaaay cooler.

I could create more than just glass as I heated sand while drawing it from the earth, shaping it into bizarre, fluid sculptures. Some patches of the desert revealed metallic properties, melting into steely, twisted forms when I set the metallic grains ablaze. Of course, the desert wasn't entirely made up of silicate and metal—something I was reminded of when I set a patch of some ugly yellow material on fire.

Holding it as it twisted into an obscure form, it immediately exploded in my face like a bright blue firework and reeked of burnt garbage.

After that, I made sure to start small when testing my combination magic on new materials. Shortly after nearly blowing myself up, I'd seemingly exhausted all the combinations of gemstones I had on me—which only made me want to borrow Dad's amethyst even more. I had no idea how dream magic would combine with anything—it seemed so separate and intangible. As I pondered the possibilities, I found myself fiddling with my mother's necklace, the one with the alexandrite gemstone. I began wondering if I could combine my natural magic with any of the others, but I wasn't sure where to start. Wishing to be invisible was pretty self-contained and, at best, would just let me perform other magics while invisible.

Wanting to at least give it a shot, I took out my little staff and tried to tap into both my own magic and sand magic. Then, I simply wished for the staff to be invisible instead. At first, I also turned invisible along with the staff, which wasn't new. But eventually, I figured out how to make myself visible and render only the little staff invisible. Proud of myself, I brought the staff back into full colour, its stark juxtaposition of colour even more pronounced as it suddenly popped back into existence.

Seeing this gave me another idea—it was curiously called chameleon magic, not invisible magic. Chameleons weren't specifically known for being invisible but for changing the colour of their skin. With this in mind, I repeated my experiment, trying to turn the little staff into ridiculous colours like red and blue. Nothing happened. Convinced that I could do it, I began walking back to the museum, now mindful of how low the sun was getting, while staring at the little staff and willing it to change colours. It wasn't until I focused on just one colour that I started seeing some progress.

My little staff went completely orange. I felt along the join, confirming it was still made of two distinct materials. I tried switching the entire staff to brown, but for some reason, it failed. Frustrated but curious, I returned it to normal and then successfully turned the staff brown. Still confused, I randomly picked another colour to try, but this didn't work either.

It wasn't until the staff turned the exact same shade as the patch of deep-purple sand I walked over that I realised the flaw in my thinking. I had forgotten once again that it was chameleon magic— not colour magic.

By the time I reached the museum, I had managed to change the staff multiple times, both into a single colour and into two different colours. I discovered I could only change the colours of objects to other colours within my sight, which made sense as that's exactly what chameleons do, I was just too stupid to stop and think about it for a second. I hadn't yet figured out how this would be more useful than simply turning myself or objects invisible, but something about it felt promising—like it would become invaluable soon enough.

31 – Ender

Today was the day. The resonance scanners had all been modified, thanks to a sapphire I'd borrowed from Cybele's cabinet, and their locations all mapped out. Alira had come back later than I'd expected yesterday but still had plenty of energy—she must have gotten carried away practising. If she'd come up with many more sand magic tricks beyond what she already seemed to have mastered when I left then this mission might actually go nice and smoothly

All that was left for today was to quickly bury all the scanners underground at the arena, and then wait for Akeldama to show up before making our move. Naturally, I'd devised a number of potential courses of action, but like Alira had said, we wouldn't truly know what we were up against until the moment came. Any good plan always needed room for improvisation.

"You ready, Ali?"

"Yup," Alira said, pulling on her boots and hopping to her feet.

I led the way out of the museum and toward the arena, becoming invisible almost immediately—just in case. Alira seemed to follow me easily enough, despite us both being invisible. It was early when we arrived at the arena, so there were no crowds yet—just a handful of people beneath the grandstands, scurrying about. Some of them looked like competitors, while others appeared to be running the place.

The first scanner I sunk beneath the sand was directly below the doorway we'd entered through. It disappeared into the ground seamlessly. The next few placements were slightly trickier; I had to wait for people to pass or move away before becoming visible and switching to sand magic to sink the scanners. We made our way through the labyrinth beneath the arena until there was only one scanner left to place.

We had tried earlier but skipped it, as this spot seemed to be where the most activity was. Now, we stood silently at the edge of the training ground, watching competitors spar as we waited for an opportunity to sneak in and bury the scanner. The sparring matches seemed endless, and since all the competitors knew who they'd be facing, I doubted there'd be any gaps in activity until he arrived.

It wasn't until the end of about the third sparring match that it occurred to me this was as good a spot as any to sit and wait for any sign of painites on our scanner system. I found myself enjoying these friendly fights—they were much more entertaining than the death matches.

I sat down, trying to signal to Alira that this was where I was settling in, without showing or telling her outright. I could only see her eyes, but after a moment, they sunk to my level—probably accompanied by a frown. I activated the last scanner, the one I hadn't been able to hide, and checked the training arena for any signs of painite gemstones. Finding none, I used my epicode to tap into the new detection system hidden throughout the arena's underbelly. Still nothing. I couldn't decide whether to feel relieved or uneasy.

Alira and I continued watching the sparring matches, occasionally checking the scanners. I didn't need to, having set up an alert for any detected painites, but it didn't hurt to double-check. After a while, I glanced at the scanner and noticed something unusual. I couldn't remember if the presences I was seeing had been there before.

Two faint but confirmed signatures appeared at the edge of the training ground, much like where we were sitting, but somewhere on the opposite side.

I looked up but couldn't see any sign of them. Curious, I got up and stalked along the edge of the mini arena, trying to peer into the shaded area on the other side where the supposed people were. There was nothing but shadow. Hold on a second. I weighed the risks and decided to whisper the situation to Alira.

"Alira, there's someone over there hiding in the shadows. I'm moving closer. Be on your guard." I whispered. I saw her eyes bob, indicating a nod, and turned my attention back to the shadows. I stalked along the shaded edge of the sparring arena, keeping an eye on the spot where the two presences were and double-checking the scanner constantly.

The signal was still unusually faint as I approached. By now, I should have been able to identify their gemstones, but for some reason, they still weren't registering properly. I crept closer, moving slower now, knowing that if there were people where there was supposed to be, they would definitely be able to spot Alira's eyes— and the slower I moved, the less distortion I would appear as.

Finally, the scanner beeped, indicating the gemstones hiding somewhere ahead. Shit. It was exactly what I had feared. Akeldama did have a pair of spies—a combination of onyx and red beryl—and they were right in front of us, concealed in the shadows. That explained why they were so hard to detect on the scanner; the red beryl was likely minimizing their presence while amplifying the onyx's shadow magic, rendering them invisible even though I knew exactly where they were.

We had the upper hand here. We knew about them, but they didn't know about us. Now I just needed to figure what to do about it. I'd made rough plans for similar situations, but this was different. There were no signs of any painites yet, and as far as I could tell, they didn't have Navoi's staff.

I had no idea why these two were here, what they were doing, or why they weren't with the painites. Could we have been completely wrong about them? Or were they some sort of bait, set specifically for us? I couldn't tell if Akeldama would plan something like that. He was smart, and he probably suspected we might show up at the arena looking for him today. But the chances of us finding these two were incredibly slim on their own. Either this wasn't a trap, or Akeldama was extremely clever. Either way, we couldn't ignore them.

The painite alert went off suddenly, making me flinch. Only I could hear it as it echoed softly through my epicode. Quickly, I brought up the map, scanning for the exact location of the alert. It was exactly where I'd expected. It had to be Akeldama. The only question was, why was he alone?

My focus shifted back to the problem ahead. The onyx and red beryl signals were moving—slowly but surely—away from us. Likely heading to meet Akeldama. If that was the case, it was entirely possible they did have Navoi's staff, keeping it hidden until Akeldama wanted to unveil it in the arena, proving his dominance to the world. I went to switch to knife magic but remembered what Alira had said the other day, and instead connected to the amethyst, only to find it was already warm.

Two bodies suddenly appeared in front of me mid-fall, as if they were dropping straight out of the shadow of a column supporting the place. They quickly disappeared again, and I saw Alira's bright green eyes flick up to me from where the invisible bodies were.

"What did you do!" I demanded in a sharp whisper.

"I took action. You were taking too long, and they were leaving, so I put them to sleep," she replied impatiently.

I rubbed my head. She was right, I was overthinking. But we didn't have time to argue. Akeldama had arrived, just in time for his fight. I doubted he would do much else but head straight to the main stage.

"I don't know how you just made them both invisible like that, but as long as you've knocked them out for a good while, Akeldama is here, and we have to go," I said.

She nodded, and the amethyst cooled down again.

"I've buried them, so they shouldn't be in anyone's way. Let's go."

"You can't bury people—they'll die!" I hissed, trying to keep my voice low.

"Chill, their heads aren't buried—they'll be fine," Alira shot back. I grumbled, but it was the best we could do for now.

"Fine, let's go."

I hurried off as quickly and quietly as I could toward Akeldama. I didn't see the staff during the brief moment the spies had been visible, which meant Akeldama likely had it on him already. We had to get to him before he entered the arena floor. We wouldn't be able to reach him easily once he was inside, and afterwards he'd have all the magic of his enemies flowing through him—so that option was off the table too.

The halls were far too crowded now, but we ran when we could until it became more inconvenient to dodge people than to simply blend in and push past. So, that's what we did.

We turned the final corner only to find the hall completely packed. The end of this hall opened out onto a wide, somewhat ceremonial passageway that directly connected the outer city straight to the arena floor. And, of course, this was where Akeldama had entered, making his way slowly but directly to the exact spot we didn't want him to be.

I checked the scanner while we pushed through the crowd, but the moment I saw Akeldama walk past the end of the hall was also the moment the crowd became too dense to move through. Everyone was inexplicably scrambling for a closer look at the world's most infamous murderer.

As Akeldama passed, I knew we'd lost this race. But there was always a backup plan. I'd assumed it was unlikely we'd reach Akeldama if he entered somewhere unexpected—but the real issue turned out to be that we weren't where I'd expected us to be. And Akeldama was.

Plan B was less decisive, but it would give us more information before making our next move. Plus, we now had hostages who might provide exactly what we needed to know. I turned to the now-visible Alira.

"Back to the hostages," I said with a curt nod.

She nodded back and led the way. We stayed visible, knowing that there were suspiciously no other painites around and that we already knew where the key pieces were. Still, I couldn't help but feel concerned that I didn't know where Ayuna was. Akeldama was rarely without her—aside from the last arena match—which I hoped was a good sign somehow.

We arrived back at the training ground, now deserted with the main event underway.

"Wake them up but keep them buried," I instructed Alira.

She obliged, revealing their heads poking out just above the sand at the base of the wall, where no one would trip over them. Moments later, the heads spluttered to life, coughing up sand in the process. Cybele had told us the onyx would likely be younger than Alira, but it was still a shock to see the head of a thirteen-year-old boy staring angrily up at us. Next to him was an even younger girl, maybe ten years old, staring at the ground as though ashamed.

"You'll pay for this!" the boy spat.

"Where is the staff you stole?" I demanded calmly. The boy's angry expression flickered with brief surprise before settling back into pure hatred. He grinned maliciously as he answered.

"He's got it now. He's killing all the weaklings with it as we speak."

Just as I suspected. "And where is Ayuna?" I pressed.

The boy scoffed. "I don't know what you mean," he said, more calmly this time, with a look of triumph spreading across his face.

We didn't have time for this. Begrudgingly, I activated my tiger's eye. My stomach churned with guilt as I began sinking the boy lower into the sand. A look of shock and fear flashed across his face before the girl beside him yelled out, and I stopped.

"No! Don't hurt him!" she cried. Her hair still hung over most of her face, but now she was looking up at us, pleading. The boy's expression hardened again into determined defiance. Hoping the girl would give in, I directed my question at them once more, this time slightly more aggressively.

"Where is Ayuna?"

"A mission!" the girl suddenly shouted.

"Where to?" I demanded.

"We don't know," she said quickly. "It's a secret mission. All he said was that she'd be gone for a few days."

The boy turned to glare at her, his face contorted in betrayal, and the girl hung her head in shame again. I lifted the boy slightly back through the sand, enough to restore him to his earlier position. If for no other reason, I hoped it would ease the girl for her cooperation.

There weren't many things I could think of that Ayuna would be sent off to do alone. But one particular possibility came to mind— something that would take a couple of days. In any case, it was clear these kids weren't privy to Akeldama's grand plans.

"If Ayuna is on a secret mission somewhere, then what's your mission here exactly?" I asked.

The boy responded eagerly this time, his angry expression melting into smug satisfaction.

"Oh, just scoping out the competition, making sure Akeldama can mop the floor with all these idiots. We were supposed to warn him if there was anyone who looked really strong or if there were any diamonds ready to challenge him, but there weren't. So his fight is probably already over. All these losers practising here before are dead now," he said with a grin, seemingly oblivious to how bad of a spy he was by admitting things like that. I couldn't blame him, though. He was young and had absolute faith in Akeldama. The girl, on the other hand, was harder to read. She seemed less confident and more cautious, her gaze often lowered.

In any case, Akeldama was proving to be more careful and calculating than he appeared. Ensuring he could win fights before stepping into the arena was a move that spoke to his strategic mindset. I could only imagine how infuriated he must have been after his failed attempt at Telesto. Still, even with what we knew now, something felt off. It was too quiet. There should have been other painites here—anyone but just these two. Why was it only them?

"Where are all the other painites? It can't just be you two and Akeldama?" I pressed.

The boy smirked briefly, then tried to mask it.

"I don't know. I'm just doing my job," he said, his tone turning coy.

Frustrated, I started to sink him into the sand again, catching the girl's attention.

"Wait! They are here, they're just…" she started, only to be cut off by the boy.

"NO! You can't!" he screeched at her, making her drop her head instantly.

I sank the boy further, stopping when the sand covered his mouth. He glared at me with a fury I couldn't quite understand. He could still breathe through his nose, but now he couldn't yell at the girl again. Ignoring him, I knelt in front of her, lifting her slightly out of the sand.

"Where are the painites?" I asked her, keeping my voice as gentle as I could manage.

The girl glanced nervously at the onyx boy, her eyes glistening with tears.

"You promise you won't hurt him if I tell you?" she whispered shakily.

"I promise I won't hurt either of you," I assured her.

She hesitated, conflicted, but finally gave in, her shaking more evident now. She spoke slowly,

"They're outside the arena in the city. I don't know why. I think they're waiting for something. Now please let him go!" the girl pleaded.

So they were here, but why were they… Oh no. I felt stupid for not realising it sooner. Akeldama had always planned to take over the city. Even with the introduction of the world-ship and the tail-key, they had only added another layer to his conquest.

Now that he'd attacked both Telesto and Muruntau in attempts to seize their tail-key weapons, his next move would be attacking the city. He probably believed Brigitte had a fourth piece of the High-Priestess staff. I mean, why wouldn't she? He'd seen all the pieces now and had likely realised the tip was missing. But Brigitte didn't have it—I did.

Akeldama had his entire army on standby, ready to strike the cathedral. It was insane how quickly everything was happening, but Akeldama was clever, and we were playing catch-up trying to figure it all out. He'd likely planned it this way from the beginning. And if Ayuna was on a journey spanning multiple days, it could only mean one thing: she was travelling north towards the desert entrance to the parliamentary trials. She was getting into position, preparing to meet Akeldama when he arrived with his complete tail-key staff.

I glanced at Alira, who was staring at me intensely, likely trying to piece together everything running through my head.

"Put them back to sleep. We need to stop Akeldama now, before he signals the attack," I said.

She acted with lightning speed, not letting her bracelet navigation slow her down like it had before. Then we ran, this time heading up into the stands where we'd have a better view—and could fly upwards to intercept him if the need arose. If we reached him before he signalled the others, it would be two against one.

As we ran, I shouted over my shoulder to Alira, uncertain how much she had pieced together herself—though knowing her, she had probably figured it all out before I did.

"Ali, Akeldama is going to attack the cathedral. If he succeeds, he'll gain access to unlimited lightning magic, as well as the backdoor to the world-ship. I don't even know if he realises there is a backdoor, which is why he's sent Ayuna to challenge parliament the old-fashioned way. She might already be down there, waiting. We have to stop him before he signals the attack."

"Right!" She yelled back raring to go as she ran behind me. We finally burst out into the crowds, seeing the carnage of the arena in full view. I had never seen so much blood before. It was like Akeldama had been painting the arena floor using his opponents' bodies as paint brushes. And yet the crowd cheered on as he crushed the neck of an obsidian, blood spraying out and adding to his canvas, but even more so when he flipped the dead man upside down with one hand, both of their bodies flashing silver as he swung the corpse at another challenger, slicing him in half with the corpse's steely shins. I saw Alira gag.

We couldn't just rush down there. It was like he was in a flow state, killing left and right, not even using Navoi's staff which stood there near him poking up out of the arena floor. Maybe if I grabbed it, he'd second guess his invasion plan.

Probably not, but we still needed that key, and it was right there where I could sneak down and get it.

"Alira, stay here. I'm going to grab the staff."

"Wait what!? Dad, You can't do that! You saw what he just did to those two guys?"

"I know, but I have to try. He won't even see me, don't worry."

And with that I went invisible, not giving Alira time to argue further. I hopped down onto the arena floor, stumbling a little bit from the height, suddenly remembering all the traps hidden beneath the floor. I let out a steadying breath. All I had to do was follow the bodies and blood patterns, and I'd only step on deactivated tiles.

I carefully but swiftly made my way toward the staff, slowing down whenever Akeldama faced in my direction to avoid the rippling light betraying my presence. The closer I got, the clearer his expressions became—the glee shining in his eyes was almost more sickening than the bodies flying around him.

I was mere metres from the staff now. I reached out my arm, taking the final steps.

"I was wondering if I was going to see you here, Ender," Akeldama said suddenly, spinning through the air. His foot connected with someone's face so hard that if their neck hadn't snapped instantly, it certainly would've when the body spun half a turn, and smashed their face into the arena floor.

Terror gripped me, but I lunged for the staff anyway, confident he couldn't see me. I was wrong. Red ice burst from the fresh corpse, shooting out from where its head had been moments ago. The sharp icicle skewered my hand just before I could grab the staff.

Shit. He could see me.

I spun around, switching to knife magic as I gritted my teeth and pulled my hand off the icicle with a muffled yell. Facing Akeldama head-on, I saw him land gracefully on the arena floor, radiating a confidence that sent a shiver down my spine.

"Fortunately, I've found a way around your little invisibility trick. Unfortunately, for you at least, you can't stop me this late in the game," Akeldama said.

Another icicle shot through me, straight into my gut, and I keeled over. The knife magic had stopped the blow from penetrating my skin, but it didn't mean my organs weren't bleeding internally. I coughed up blood, struggling to push myself onto my elbow—standing was completely out of the question.

Akeldama stared down at me with a wicked grin, the sand and wind at his feet both picking up wildly.

"Now watch me take everything I want, Ender. This city and everything beyond will soon be mine."

Akeldama calmly took the staff, and pure chaos erupted from the ground. The force launched him into the sky, where he could deliver one of his grand speeches. Without lightning magic, he used wind and sand magic to float a chunk of earth as a platform in the sky, a wild tornado spinning furiously beneath it to keep it airborne.

He paced around the platform like it was solid ground, his mouth starting to take on a faint red glow as he projected his voice across the entire stadium. He shoved Navoi's staff into the air.

"Today I am the ruler of this city. Today I will bring back the prosperity we once enjoyed—but not just for upper gems. For everyone."

The crowd roared.

"Muruntau couldn't hold us back, and neither could Telesto. It's time for the diamonds to fall, and for the ships that once rained from the heavens to once again fertilise this wasteland. Our new city will be like nothing you've ever seen!"

I could tell he'd written this speech before his failure in Telesto. I coughed up more blood.

He snapped Navoi's staff, the pieces shifting between solid and grains as they rearranged themselves. They formed into a contraption whose purpose I could already guess, noticing the distinctly familiar black cylinder nestled behind a silver one that sat at the tip, pointing skyward.

Akeldama swung part of the staff outwards, preparing to strike the match. The contraption gave off a faint red glow before he struck, making the resulting explosion louder and flashier than it would have otherwise been.

I couldn't help but think of the red beryl girl who was supposed to be Akeldama's spy. Even his own disciples weren't exempt from becoming his blood batteries. We had to save both her and the boy from Akeldama if we could.

I wretched, choking on my own blood. But first, I'd have to save myself. I switched to the sapphire I had borrowed from Cybele, trying to focus the harmonies toward yellow-sapphire magic. But I hadn't made that specific connection yet, and the tones were making my head feel fuzzier. I fell onto my back, trying to focus, but feeling an impending sense of dread.

As I lay dying, I locked eyes with Akeldama when he peered down from his platform, savouring my pain. Suddenly, the platform fell out of the sky, cut off, and Akeldama took his wild tornado with him as he sped out of the arena toward the cathedral.

It was over. I would die here. And it wouldn't be long before Akeldama finished off the diamonds and stormed Muruntau, slaughtering everyone until Navoi surrendered the piece we had loaned him. After that, I doubted Alira would be able to keep Teth's yacharow from him forever.

I tried to focus on the harmonies again, but it was no use—it only made everything worse. I thought I was finally losing it when I saw Alira pop up in front of me, crying. But after focusing a little harder, I realised she must have come down from the stands. I mean, why wouldn't she?

She started looking me over, trying to figure out where I was hurt. I tried to tell her, but I was winded, only managing to cough up more blood when I tried to speak. She must have found something, though, because I saw her smile. The next moment, she was checking me more gently with her eyes closed and I started feeling something like a warm massage start flowing over my organs. I felt queasy at first, but I took deeper and deeper breaths as Alira figured out how to stitch me back up from the inside. I found the energy to look down and find one of the circles on my gauntlets popped open, revealing the sapphire. I smiled. Alira was doing what I had tried to do, finding the warm stone to figure out what I was trying to do, and doing it herself.

"You're amazing" I managed to squeeze out, but that only made her lose her composure and the tears fell harder, leaning into me as I gave her a painful hug. She had at least mended my broken ribs, so it wasn't too bad, despite my organs still being pretty beat up.

"I don't care where we go but we have to leave. He's too strong," She said tearfully, trying to act tough as she wiped away tears. With some effort, and Alira's help, I stood.

"Back to the museum then. We can't fight in this state. But we have to bring the others too."

"What others?"

"The children."

"Oh, right. But… no I think I can do it, but only if you can fly yourself home?"

I smiled, trying to make my hobble look more like a proper walk as we left the arena floor.

"I'll be fine. Just please get the kids."

She nodded, not wanting to leave, but doing as I asked eventually, once I could use the wall to help me through the arena's underbelly. I took over trying to heal myself too, trying to do a similar thing to what Cybele had shown me with the morning massage. Although, this wasn't quite the same.

I was ready enough, by the time I hobbled out of the arena, to fly the short distance to the museum. Although, when I arrived, it felt like my landing had undone everything I worked on, my ribs breaking all over again. Luckily, impossibly, the real healer came running over to me as I once again lay on my back, dying.

Cordelia looked down at me, shocked, but didn't hesitate to stoop down and fix Alira and I's shoddy healing work. I chuckled, which seemed to concern Cordelia, and Cybele as well who also seemed to be here. I couldn't imagine why they were here, but I was infinitely grateful that they were.

32 – Alira

I can't believe he would just jump down there and try to grab the staff. It was an insane thing to do, and now he was hobbling around pretending like he wasn't dying. I hadn't used Cordelia's magic before, but I could figure out how to fix bones well enough. The organs, however, felt confusing. There was no way I put them back together right. I couldn't even guess how long he would last, but hopefully he could fix himself a bit better than I could now that he was conscious. I seriously doubted his ability to make it back to the museum though.

I eventually decided to deliver the spy childern and come back to find Dad. I found, however, that I didn't need to, as I found him outside the museum sprawled out on the ground. As I flew down with the two limp bodies of our prisoners orbiting me in little tornadoes, I felt the urge to switch to painite magic so that I could re-bury our prisoners with sand magic while I landed simultaneously. I didn't, having locked eyes with Cybele, who, with Cordelia, was standing over Dad's body.

I was immensely relieved. I wondered briefly why they were here but didn't dwell on it as I landed and ran the rest of the way to Dad.

"He'll be okay. Although I take it you attempted to heal him first, did you?" Cordelia asked.

"I did. I know I messed it up, but it was all I could do," I replied.

"I know. I'm surprised you managed what you did. He would've died earlier if you hadn't tried, but he wouldn't have lasted long like that either."

I knelt beside Dad, holding his hand. After a moment, I glanced up at Cybele, following her gaze to the unconscious spies lying on the ground where I had landed. A chuckle escaped me—an inappropriate reaction, considering the situation—but I couldn't help imagining what Cybele must have been thinking. Me, showing up with unconscious children in tow.

"We found the spies. That's them—the onyx and red beryl. I know we expected the onyx to be young, but the girl is even younger."

Cybele stared at them, her expression unreadable—a rarity for her, as she usually voiced her thoughts without hesitation. Slowly, she approached them. I stood and followed, casting one last hopeful glance over Dad, knowing he was in Cordelia's capable hands. Cybele knelt in front of the red beryl girl, her touch surprisingly gentle as she brushed a strand of hair away from the child's face. Her gaze shifted to the boy, and a pang of guilt flashed across her face. In that moment, I began to understand what she was feeling.

"Did you learn anything useful from them?" Cybele asked without looking away.

"Nothing that isn't obvious now that the painites are full-on sieging the cathedral. Although we did discover that Ayuna is heading to parliament—if she's not already there waiting."

I had briefly forgotten this last point, but now it was slowly making its way to the front of my mind, making me uneasy.

"I see. Then, one way or another, the painites will find their way onto the world ship. Even if they fail with their siege, I have no doubt someone like Ayuna will get through parliament's trials. I'm more worried about what she'll do once inside. It's too late to stop her now, though, if she's already there."

"Well, we don't know for sure how far she's gotten."

"Even so, finding the entrance to parliament is a closely guarded secret in itself. Sending someone after her would be fruitless. Everyone should focus on protecting the cathedral."

For some reason, I felt somewhat responsible for Ayuna's actions, as though I was supposed to be keeping her in cheque— much like how Dad seemed to feel about Akeldama. Plus, Cybele was right, it was a challenge just to find parliament. But I'd heard enough stories from Dad to know how to find it, and with my air magic, I had no doubt I could get there in record time. I looked to Dad again, his breathing looking more even now, and his face no longer held a pained expression. I reminded myself that he would be okay in Cordelia's hands, before turning back to Cybele with a determined look on my face.

"I'll stop her. I'm the only one that can. I have to try."

"Alira..." Cybele started, but stopped, examining my face. Eventually, she sighed.

"I know I can't stop you. And that if anyone has a chance of stopping her it's you, but still. What would your father say? It's too dangerous."

"He doesn't have a say right now. I'm the only one who can, and so I will. I'm going. I'll see you all when I get back," I explained stubbornly. My face remained fixed as I turned around and took a few steps, ready to take off. I stopped for a moment, reassessing what I was about to do. If I was going to fight Ayuna, I would need as much of an advantage as I could get. I briskly walked back over to Dad.

Cordelia had her eyes closed, moving her fingers slowly over Dad's chest. I opened up some of the spots on his gauntlets, deciding to take only the amethyst, knowing how it worked already. I considered the sapphire as well, but figured it would be pointless if we were fighting out in the desert. Besides, sapphire magic was complicated, and Dad might need it for whatever he planned to do about Akeldama when he woke up.

Confident in my choice, I took off. Cybele's worried look lingered in my mind, but she hadn't argued since I told her I'd already made up my mind. I knew she'd understand. The way she looked at the onyx boy said it all—like it was her fault he ended up like that. Which, honestly, made sense, given her role in the annihilation of the onyxes.

I'd fought Ayuna more than anyone, so I already knew what I'd be up against if I had to face her at parliament. Hopefully, though, I'd catch her before she got inside. It didn't seem like I'd even be able to follow her in anyway. All I could do now was fly north as fast as possible and hope for the best.

Flying this fast without my wingsuit was harder than I'd expected, but at least I still had goggles. Once I'd stabilised my speed, I switched to painite magic. I dropped a few metres at first before catching myself again—I was getting better at that.

From there, I let desperation fuel my fire magic, desperation turning to exhilaration as the air behind me burst into flames. I shot forward like I was riding some kind of flaming vortex. It had actually worked. The fire acted as a thruster, speeding me up way more than I'd expected. No wonder this was Ayuna's go-to magic combo.

For a moment, I wondered why Dad thought it'd take Ayuna days to get here. Flying like this, she could've easily made the journey in no time at all. But Ayuna was from this planet, after all, and there were plenty of traditions and rules—especially when it came to Parliament. Akeldama was an anarchist, but he was still careful, and he must've figured sending Ayuna to Parliament the traditional way was less risky than sending her in the way I was heading there now. I could only thank him for his superstitions. Otherwise, this chase might have been even more of a lost cause.

Instead, I was now grinning, seeing on the dunes ahead of me four distinct shapes: one large triangle, two rectangles, and a tiny little line standing between them. As I got closer, I registered the little line as Ayuna, standing between a tent and two teleporters, staring back at me with a smug grin like she was expecting me.

I gritted my teeth. She might pretend to have been expecting me, but it was more likely she'd spotted my flames shooting through the sky and guessed it was me—underestimating me enough to not care that I had come to mess her up. She was about to be so wrong.

I only noticed, when I tried to slow down to land, just how much my anger was fuelling me, propelling me forward—now towards the ground faster than I'd have preferred. Rather than frantically flail about trying not to crash, I went with it instead, glad I did when I found myself moments later crashing with some force into the sand, staring into the surprised eyes of Ayuna. I met her gaze defiantly, catching the glint of the glass crater in my peripheral vision—the one I'd created in the sand and now stood in the centre of. I tried not to grin too much, but let's be honest: that was a badass entrance.

"Look who decided to show up. And just in time too. Well, unless you were trying to save that guy. You were too late for that," she said, jabbing a thumb towards the tent.

I ignored her, forcing myself to stay focused.

"You're not getting through Parliament. I won't let you."

"Oh yeah? And how are you going to do that?" she shot back with a smirk.

I hesitated for too long, fumbling for a comeback that wouldn't sound completely awkward. Ayuna laughed.

"That's what I thought. You'd have more luck saving the dead guy over there than stopping me," she taunted, jabbing her thumb at the tent again.

Instinctively, I glanced in the tent's direction, only realising too late what she was trying to do. The moment I looked away, she launched herself toward one of the teleporters, propelled by sand magic. Thankfully, I was already in flight mode and reacted instantly. I shot after her with full force, managing to grab her ankle just before it could pass through the teleporter along with the rest of her. I shot through the teleporter, my magic instantly thrown out of whack and cutting off. My explosive momentum carried me forward—dragging Ayuna along by the ankle—and practically throwing her over my head as I landed on the hard rock awaiting me on the other side.

Snapping my head up to search for Ayuna, I stared into the apparent darkness. I whipped up my hand, summoning fire. The flame burst to life larger than I expected, nearly setting my eyebrows on fire. The magic down here seemed stronger than on the surface. That made sense if it was somehow being generated by the big ship that was supposed to be around here somehwhere. I wondered if this was more like how strong magic had been when Dad came here for the first time.

My gaze settled on the rocky ground and the absence of much else that my flames could illuminate. The supposed cavern was too large to see into, with only dark rock in front of me—and the girl sitting a few steps ahead, rubbing her ankle. It was bruised.

I quickly glanced at my hand—the one that had held Ayuna's ankle—and found my fingers purple.

"You bitch!" Ayuna called out, "You really had to throw me like that *and* steal my magic right before whatever this big parliamentary trial is. I'm going to kill you before I leave here," she snapped, standing and dusting herself off.

Remembering why I was there, I took a step towards her, my flames flaring larger momentarily. I stopped before I got much further, however, as the enormous hangar doors started opening and pouring light into the cave—it was hard to look away. I had seen some big ships and some impressive hangars, but this was on a whole other level. Although, I guess it made sense if this ship was so big it had somehow turned into a planet.

Ayuna glanced back at me, and my flames flared again as I took another step towards her. She ran. My flames flared once more, but this time, I threw them after her instead, not needing the light with the hangar opening like it was. I missed, not that I expected to hit her, and I chased after her, trying to catch up before she reached the ship.

I hadn't closed the gap at all, so I started hurling fireballs, hoping to slow her down—or ideally vaporise her. A few slowed her, but my final shot actually hit her, sending her sprawling into the hangar.

I tried to stop before stepping into the hangar myself but was running too aggressively. I ended up planting a single foot onto the sandstone tiles covering the hangar floor. Ayuna landed on her back the same moment my foot hit the tile, sending ripples of ink spreading across the sandstone grid from both of our locations.

The ink slowly filled the board with a collection of simple designs—some pictures, some numbers, and some words. For the most part, it was an indecipherable mess and looked nothing like the patterns on Proelium boards I had seen before. But this was still unmistakably a Proelium board.

A sandy chryacal rose up from the squares in front of both Ayuna and me, somehow taking on a fleshier appearance after forming. I had never seen two-player Proelium before, and Dad had seemed to imply that it was impossible. Clearly, that was not the case.

I scanned the board, wondering how it would be possible to play with two people. My eyes settled on what I assumed was supposed to be the door on the far side of the board. Its warped appearance made me second-guess the legitimacy of this game—the door looked like some sort of glitch out of a video game. It was clearly still a door, but there was a second one superimposed over the top of it, cutting through it at an awkward angle and obscuring some of the symbols that were supposed to tell you the endgame items you needed.

The symbols that weren't cut through weren't much better either. Their sizes and shapes were too varied for a proper game of Proelium, turning what should have been a clear set of goals into an abstract, impressionist mess that made no sense.

Ayuna was staring at the door too. She turned to me angrily as she noticed its condition.

"Look what you've done! How am I supposed to finish this with you breaking the game? Proelium isn't supposed to be two-player. Oh, wait. Brilliant idea. If I kill you, your door will disappear, and the board will go back to normal. I'll just have to take you down first."

She took a step towards me, glancing at the chryacal near her, and made a last-minute pivot to the next tile on her right. The chryacal immediately pounced, landing on the square beside her— the one she had been about to step on. Damn. That was almost an easy win.

The board suddenly started shifting, though not before my own chryacal leapt over me, moving to the same square relative to me that Ayuna's chryacal was to her. That fact didn't matter much once the board shifted. Ayuna hadn't bothered to decipher the image on the tile before stepping on it, too focused on trying to kill me instead.

It was hard to describe how the board shifted. Tiles floated up at strange angles, their surfaces taking on mirror-like qualities until I was surrounded, stuck in what felt like a hall of mirrors. At least, that's what I imagined the original design was supposed to be. This version, however, was severely warped—somehow making my reflections appear as though I was Ayuna, and Ayuna was me, like a ghost in the machine.

Directly above me, I could see Ayuna looking down at me, but my own reflection only appeared in the corners of various mirrors, small and distant. I couldn't wrap my head around the physics of it, but given the door's glitchy appearance, I guessed I should start getting used to whatever nonsense this game was going to throw at me.

I looked at my feet, finding the tiles surrounding me at least seemed to make some sense. I wondered then if Ayuna would take another step and mess everything up again. Whatever tile I chose— if I wanted to be in control—I'd have to make my move before she did. None of the options were particularly obvious.

The symbols were super weird for a Proelium game. Not that I'd expected them to be normal, given how this was playing out, but still. One of the tiles near me looked like a baby surrounded by a vaguely human-shaped cloud of mist. What kind of obstacle that could be describing, I had no idea. Another symbol resembled a campfire. I rationalised that if I switched to fire magic, I'd probably be impervious to whatever the board threw at me from that one, and it might catch Ayuna off guard.

I stepped onto the tile decisively, but as my leg crossed over the line between my tile and the campfire tile, it vanished—like I was stepping through an impossibly thin teleporter.

When my foot landed, it wasn't on the campfire tile at all. I guessed what had happened when I heard Ayuna yell out, "No, not that one!"

I whipped my head to the ceiling, noticing the tiles around Ayuna looked completely different. One had a random leg sticking out from nowhere onto a tile beside her.

I understood then why our reflections made us look like we were the other, and what a grave mistake I had made by choosing the tile I did.

My vision went black instantly, and I heard the distinct sound of chryacal claws on sandstone—one set landing milliseconds after the other. My vision then seemed to glitch, everything distorting and breaking along strange lines before settling and looking relatively normal. However, after that I could no longer see colour, and had no depth perception, as one eye was still completely dark.

I looked up, seeing Ayuna glancing around frantically, her inability to focus her eyes on me giving away that her vision hadn't glitched like mine—she still had fully blacked-out vision. I could also see the chryacal right beside her.

Given the weird mirror-teleporty thing, I guessed that if it launched itself at Ayuna, it would maul me instead. Not that it mattered when the other chryacal mirrored its movements and was also right beside me on my side of the board.

"Ayuna," I called out, "My eye glitched. I can still see a little bit. If we work together, we might be able to make a smart move for once."

I hated the taste that sentence left in my mouth, but instinctively, I wanted to work together, knowing it was the only way we would both get out of this—even if she was the last person I'd ever want to cooperate with.

"Seriously!? You blind me and then suggest that we work together? Are you insane?" she snapped.

"I know. I hate it too. But I can see the tiles around both of us, and I can only step on the ones near you. If the best option is close to me, you'll have to take the step."

Ayuna stayed silent for a few moments before responding begrudgingly, her voice quiet and grumbling.

"Well, if you insist. Before you rudely interrupted, I was going to choose the one that looks like a stratum staff but with a block on the end of it."

I squinted at the ceiling, not seeing anything that matched her description, until I realised she was talking about the tile the chryacal was standing on. Also, it was clearly a sledgehammer.

"That's a sledgehammer—and it's also got a chryacal standing on it."

"Whatever that is. It's still a weapon, right?"

"Kind of. But it doesn't matter now. We need to choose another one."

Ayuna scoffed, "Well, don't expect me to be much help. You blinded me, remember."

I didn't bother replying. Instead, I sighed and turned my attention to the tiles around me. Looks like my options were: the baby, a dice, two overlapping octagons, the number five-hundred and thirty-seven, a gemstone-studded gauntlet that looked like it was about to click, the campfire, the blank square that must have been where I started, and the tile the chryacal was standing on. Most of these didn't make much sense to me, but the one that was obviously a pop culture reference pulled straight out of my head was definitely a no.

The rest were harder to determine. I wasn't even sure if this planet had dice, and I wondered how many of these symbols were meant just for me, and which ones were Ayuna's.

"Hey, does the number five-hundred and thirty-seven mean anything to you?"

"Nope."

Okay, so not that one. As curious as I was about the baby, I felt like the dice was the best option, even though I had no real reason to back that up.

"Okay, I think I'm going to go with the dice, but you'll need to step on it."

Ayuna sighed and shrugged dramatically.

"Sure, whatever that is. Which way is it?"

"Diagonally to your left. Or my left? It should work if you step diagonally left is what I mean."

Ayuna scoffed, "How trustworthy you sound right now."

She paused for a moment before taking the step.

"And this isn't going to put me right where the chryacal is, is it? Trying to kill me before I get the chance to kill you?"

"If I did that, we would both get mauled," I replied.

She smirked in response.

"I'm glad you're stupid." She said before confidently stepping where I had told her too. I felt stupid once I realised what she meant. Even if the chryacals moved simultaneously, only one of us moved at a time, meaning that only one of us would get mauled. I couldn't decide if Ayuna thinking I was stupid was a good or bad thing. Maybe it meant she would underestimate me when it counted, or maybe it would make getting through this a whole lot harder.

I lost track of those thoughts as a giant dice appeared, rolling onto the board but visible only in a million angles through the reflections—without actually being anywhere. It landed on a two.

Immediately, both chryacals moved. Then they moved again, but one glitched mid-jump and disappeared from the immediate vicinity, replacing the dice in the million reflections. I guessed the mirror movements were officially broken—or at least one of them was. We were still stuck in this warped hall of mirrors.

"What happened?" Ayuna asked quickly, looking like she was trying to listen for whatever had changed.

"The chryacal both moved twice, that's all," I replied.

"Well, not great, but we're still alive, I guess."

After the chryacal moved, the campfire square was free of danger—it had been one of the squares the chryacal could have landed on before.

"I have another option that might bring our sight back. Although, it might be a bit of a stretch to think so."

"What is it?"

"It's a campfire."

"Ah, perfect. I love fire. This should be good. Where am I going now?"

Not exactly what I wanted to hear, but she did say I had drained her magic when I grabbed her, so maybe she wasn't as fireproof as she thought. In any case, it was a win-win for me.

"If you turn forty-five degrees to your right, it's the tile directly on your right," I told her while looking up at the ceiling, my fire magic already prepared for whatever was about to happen.

Ayuna stepped on the tile, her leg disappearing as it crossed the threshold between tiles, reappearing beside me and stepping onto the campfire tile. My vision went white instantly.

After a few seconds, my eyes readjusted, and I could see the room through a flickering orange haze, Ayuna's laughter pouring from the background.

"A perfect choice," she said enthusiastically. "You fixed my vision and set yourself on fire."

She laughed some more. "How perfect."

I stared up at her, feeling stupid but also glad I had activated the fire magic. Now we could both see, and I was entirely unaffected despite spontaneously combusting. The only problem now seemed to be that the heat had melted the mirrors—or whatever reflective charms were creating this mess—making everything far too warped to decipher anymore.

Ayuna realised this too after she finished laughing.

"I don't suppose you can see through all this crap, can you?" she asked with a frustrated sigh.

"Nope."

"Ah well, I suppose it doesn't matter then."

I saw Ayuna move.

"Wait, what? Stop!" I yelled, but it was too late. Ayuna had randomly chosen a tile, and even as she stepped and her leg disappeared, I saw it reappear somewhere in the tangle of mirrors, an indeterminable distance away.

The board shifted, and both chryacal leapt, but where they landed was impossible to know until the board had stopped moving. I had to close my eyes as it shifted—the melted mirrors and teleporting veils were doing my head in as they moved through one another.

When I opened them again, the board was slowly clicking back into place. The original sandstone grid was now visible once more, the symbols all recognisable but unfamiliar. Ayuna, however, was still on the ceiling with half of the board.

I glanced under her to the tile she had chosen. It was a fairly straightforward silhouette depicting two square planes.

Ayuna's gamble had somehow paid off, and now the board was relatively normal, with both chryacal in sight. Luckily, they were both pretty far away from us. Not that I cared if Ayuna got mauled—in fact, I'd appreciate it if she did. She was scanning the tiles around her.

"Before you go blindly risking our lives again, maybe we should be more careful with our choices and work together to not die."

She scoffed again, "Work with you? No thanks. Besides, my choices have worked out pretty good so far."

She chose another tile then, stepping onto one with a small grid covered in squiggles and lines. As mad as I wanted to be, I didn't have time to berate Ayuna as the board started shifting. I peered closer, trying to figure out what was happening as sand rose from the entire board, finishing its strange transformation. The squiggles were actually snakes, and the straighter lines, ladders.

I couldn't decide if I was relieved or not, but then the tile glitched, merging with the one beside it and becoming one long rectangle. That particular tile showed the image of a spider.

I didn't have time to guess what that meant for the board, as sand whipped out from all the tiles, forming grey strings that stitched the ceiling and floor together. Spiders almost as big as the chryacal began appearing on the webbed ladders, connecting my side of the board with Ayuna's. We were now essentially both stuck inside a gravitationally challenged but well-structured spider nest. Just great.

I sighed, "You idiot. I could've told you what both of those symbols were," I shouted at the ceiling, watching Ayuna eye one of the spiders with caution. Although, watching Ayuna see a spider for the first time was admittedly entertaining.

"You know what these things are!?"

"Obviously. They're from my world. Which I could've told you before you chose to step on it."

"I didn't step on that one!" she retorted, glancing back at the spider. "Your world is creepy."

I grinned. It was more fun not telling Ayuna that spiders were supposed to be much smaller. But it was also really hard pretending to not be absolutely terrified right now.

"I'm moving next. You're too rash for Proelium. You're gonna get us both killed."

Ayuna rolled her eyes and crossed her arms. "We're fine. Stop complaining."

Trying to ignore her, I looked down at my own tile options, not seeing anything particularly exciting or new, given that Ayuna had taken the last two moves.

Finally having some time to think, I remembered the door. Glancing at it, I found it was still very broken, but I was closer now and could see the symbols more clearly. Although, some of them looked like they had changed. It wouldn't surprise me, given how broken this game already was, but that was going to make this impossible without ensuring Ayuna died first. It seemed, though, no matter what choice I made, I endangered myself as well—or even more so. As long as I figured out how to stop doing that, I might not have to fight Ayuna directly, but I'd still need to overcome an obstacle that she couldn't.

The real game, then, was finding and choosing the right obstacle—one that would take her out but that I could pass. I had no clues. The symbols on the door(s) didn't help either. In fact, they were even vaguer than usual. One of them looked like a handshake. What the fuck was that supposed to mean?

Having no idea what to choose given my limited options, I feigned confidence and stepped forward onto the number five-hundred and thirty-seven. The sand started forming our new obstacle in the centre of the board, filing into the shape of a man that I realised looked suspiciously like Akeldama.

Before I could fully process it, one of the spiders—which seemed to get their own turns—crawled along a webbed ladder straight through the figure. The spider's movement caused an immediate glitch, fusing together the spider and Akeldama into one being. It flipped upside down, then back, and repeated this over and over again, seemingly unable to choose which version of gravity to follow.

In the end, it chose both—eight spidery legs protruding from the half-man to touch tiles both on the floor and ceiling. There were definitely man parts and spider parts in there, but they were so jumbled now that I couldn't tell which way the creature thought 'up' was. It was like a mirror image of itself.

One of the chryacal moved into a webbed thread, which snapped as it got stuck, flinging it from Ayuna's side of the board to mine. I guess this webbed mess had 'snakes' after all.

"Ohhhh," Ayuna exclaimed, "Five-hundred and thirty-seven. That is a familiar number actually. It's how many days in a row Dad made me fight him until I landed a blow."

"That would have been nice to know before I chose it," I muttered frustratedly. I'd been trying to find obstacles that only I could overcome, but I'd just done the exact opposite—or at least, that was before the spider got in the way. What a nightmare this was.

"Okay, my turn," Ayuna said, her hand catching fire without warning. She then proceeded to torch the entire board with a sinister look in her eye, like she was enjoying burning everything down. A little too much.

For someone who claimed I'd drained her magic, she sure seemed to have plenty left. That was more fire magic than I'd ever conjured at once. But then again, I wasn't the arsonist Ayuna was.

When the flames were extinguished, the webs were gone, but the spiders and spider-creature remained, along with the chryacal. The heat had evidently affected their softer parts—their scales intact, but parts of their faces charred. They both looked blind now. One had solid white eyes, while the other had no eyes at all, the goo that used to be its eyes now dripping from the empty sockets, exposing some of the bones that made up its head, along with chunks of skin that hadn't withstood the heat.

I gagged. Why were sand-creatures this realistic? I gagged again. I couldn't imagine what would've happened to the chryacal if it had been on Ayuna's board, even closer to her. I was just glad that one was nearer to her than it was to me.

All the creatures moved next. I watched as remnants of the chryacal's skin and dripping eye goo flung out of its face when it leapt to its next square.

Ayuna screamed, and I tore my gaze away from the zombified cat to see one of the spiders launch itself directly at her face. She held up a flaming forearm to block it, but its hard, black exoskeleton was surprisingly fire-resistant.

"This thing has fangs!?" she yelled, throwing it off. But the spider was already on her square, and it launched itself at her again. I saw her take a sharp breath, staring at the spider as it leapt toward her. This time, nothing stopped it. Pure terror shot across Ayuna's face as the spider sank its fangs into her outstretched hand. She screamed and threw the spider again, this time more directly at the ground, bashing it repeatedly as it refused to let go of her hand. With her free hand, she pulled out a knife and started stabbing straight through its abdomen.

The creature finally let go, but it couldn't leave Ayuna's square and had no choice but to submit to her enraged stabbing—even after it was already dead.

When she was done, Ayuna knelt, breathing hard and covered in all sorts of spider guts. She held up her wounded hand to me, surprisingly calm.

"Do these things have venom?"

"Usually," I responded casually, though I knew my expression betrayed my astonishment.

Without a second thought, Ayuna set herself on fire again. The guts on her sizzled and charred, while the venom—and probably a good amount of her own blood—poured and bubbled from the holes in her hand where the fangs had pierced it. The wound stitched itself back together once it was done oozing, and Ayuna let the flames fade.

I had to admit, she had incredible control over her magic. She'd just burnt away all the spider bits without harming her clothes, all while stitching her hand back together and cauterising the wound. Probably not the most effective way of doing things, but it was incredibly quick and did the job better than I could've imagined myself doing.

"Ok fine," she grunted. "You win. We'll work together, but only to avoid crap like that happening again. We've already summoned enough abominations messing around—we don't need any more."

I smiled smugly. Looks like we might finally get somewhere with this game. Although, finally playing seriously when the board was already full of spiders, a spidery abomination, and two levels of zombie-chryacal was far from a great start.

33 – Ender

I woke up staring at the ceiling of the museum lobby. I sat up frantically, remembering everything that was going on when I apparently fell asleep. It didn't feel like I had been out that long, but my injuries were all healed—Cordelia was good at what she did.

Now the question was why they were here in the first place. Had they known that Akeldama was about to attack the cathedral?

I noticed Cybele across the room and stood up suddenly, calling out to her, "Cybele!"

She looked over, quickly excusing herself from whoever she was talking to, and hustled over to me.

"Ender, you're awake."

"Yes, now what happened? Why are you here?" I asked bluntly.

"Well, initially we came back to collect my telescope and all my research to take back to the laboratory in Muruntau, but when we got here, we saw the explosions from the arena, and soon after, lightning was striking around the cathedral like crazy."

"Right. Makes sense. How long was I out? Have Alira and the children arrived?"

A strange expression crossed Cybele's face.

"You've only been out an hour, and yes, Alira arrived with the children. They're downstairs in the basement."

I got the feeling Cybele wasn't telling me something. "What's wrong? Are they hurt or something?"

"What? No, nothing like that. The children are fine."

The way she emphasised that sentence made me worried. Why had she singled out the children?

"And Alira?" I questioned, my concern growing.

Cybele sighed, giving in, "She thought she could get to Ayuna before she reached parliament. So she chased after her."

"She what!? Why did you let her do that? Ayuna will kill her!"

"I couldn't stop her. She was determined to go. And the chances of Ayuna not already being in parliament seemed low anyway, and Alira isn't stupid enough to enter parliament blindly."

"Did you even try to stop her?" I asked furiously.

Her wince told me everything before she even spoke.

"Not really. I knew you'd object, but I wasn't going to fight her on it—not when she was the only chance we had at stopping Ayuna at the time, even if it was only a slim chance."

I was still mad, but she was at least somewhat right. If Alira was determined to go, it would've been pointless to try and stop her. She was probably the only one fast enough to catch up in time, and if she wasn't, she'd just have to come back. The chances of her even fighting Ayuna were pretty low, and Alira would likely have the advantage if Ayuna was in the same exhausted condition I was in when I arrived at parliament. Not that that had stopped me from beating the trials and taking down a parliamentarian.

I sighed, deciding to focus on the current battle and leave Alira to deal with Ayuna. She was capable a young woman after all. I hated the thought, but if it came down to it, Alira could beat Ayuna in the end. She had to.

I shook my head. "Fine. What about the children? Are they still asleep?"

"Yes. It seems whoever put them to sleep knocked them out pretty good."

I smiled just a little, the subtle reminder of Alira's ability to pick up magic so quickly reassuring.

"It was Alira, with dream magic."

Cybele smiled. "Always full of surprises, that one."

I chuckled. She was right about that.

"Okay then, we'll leave them for now. If the Diamonds are still fighting off Akeldama, we have to go and help."

"I agree. I would've gone myself, but I thought it would be more prudent to wait for you to wake up so we could join the fray together. If we ambush them from behind while they're fighting the Diamonds, we might be able to turn the tide."

I nodded. "As good a plan as any, I suppose. Let's go then."

Cybele nodded and led the way out of the museum. She glowed red the moment she stepped outside, taking me aback momentarily—especially after almost dying at the hands of Akeldama while he was using the same kind of magic.

The golden chryacal statue leapt off the column of the museum's façade, turning to face us, its golden sheen shining through its attempt to take on more natural colours.

"I figured this would come in handy," Cybele said plainly.

Composing myself after the initial surprise, I had to agree with her, "Definitely. Although, it's probably too heavy to lift it there with us on a tornado. Too heavy for me, at least."

"What about sand magic? You could use that, and we could ride it like a wave."

I eyed her curiously. "Interesting. I assume you're suggesting that because you've seen it done before?"

"More or less. Sand magic users that aren't strong enough to travel underground tend to travel by riding a wave of sand," she explained.

"I see. It's work a shot then," I replied, shifting my focus to the vibrations of the sand as I started to sync my breathing with them. My lungs still felt a bit raw, but I pushed through, knowing I needed full control to handle something this powerful. The strength of the tiger's eye in my gauntlet conveniently appeared in the corner of my vision, letting me push its limit more easily as I summoned a massive wave of sand to propel us toward the cathedral.

The plaza in front of the museum broke apart. The ground was too hard and compact, unlike the shifting sands beneath the plaza. We were standing on the edge of one of the larger chunks and had to re-adjust toward the centre as I balanced the chunk of stone and set it in motion. I concentrated, propelling us toward the city's outskirts, knowing I wouldn't be able to cut through all the dense structures at its centre.

It was difficult enough crushing the smaller buildings and houses being destroyed under us now, though I reassured myself that they were all empty—the city's outskirts were the first to leave for the newer cities.

When we reached the edge, our speed increased considerably as the ground moved more smoothly under us. The change was as stark as driving over rocky terrain to brand-new asphalt. Surfing the dunes this way, we circled the city until we reached the northern side.

The thunder came immediately after the lightning now, almost simultaneous as we closed in on the cathedral. Luckily, everyone seemed too distracted to notice us approaching. Diamonds hurled thunderbolts at painites, while the painites spewed rainbows in their defence, throwing every bit of magic they had at their disposal.

For a moment, I wondered how we were supposed to locate Akeldama amidst all this chaos, but a single flash of red lightning instantly revealed his position. I knew in that moment exactly what he was doing—it was almost identical to something I had done before, and in his presence no less.

The red lightning flashed again, and this time I saw the motions clearly: the lightning struck Akeldama's fingertips, zipping around his arms in rapid loops before shooting out from the tips of his other hand. A beryl-enhanced red bolt struck down a stunned diamond, sending them plummeting from the sky above the cathedral into the blood-streaked dunes below.

It was then I noticed the bodies scattered across sand. The dunes painted red in violent brushstrokes—a grim echo of the arena only moments ago.

I stared at the battlefield in the sky as we closed in, trying to make sense of the tactics at play. Were the painites simply trying to eliminate the diamonds first? And what, exactly, were the diamonds doing? They weren't using the cathedral as a defensive stronghold or anything. Instead, they had flown up above the cathedral to meet each other in a chaotic brawl. No ground was being lost or gained—only the growing pile of bodies indicated how the battle was progressing.

Another diamond fell.

It was only after this that the tide began turning in favour of the painites. The fallen diamonds provided the painites with enough blood to power their wicked magic, enabling them to combine lightning magic with other magics. This devastating combination rendered the diamonds' magic all but inert.

Akeldama had now switched to firing off his own red lightning, soaking up the blood of the diamond he felled before her body even hit the ground. I knew we couldn't stand idly by anymore. Lightning-powered painites seemed unstoppable, but if we did nothing, Akeldama would rule this world, and more lives would be lost.

I pushed our platform higher, starting the ascent from the dunes to the heights of the cathedral. Our best bet was to eliminate Akeldama as quickly as possible with a surprise attack. I could only hope that springing Cybele's metal chryacal on him would be enough. His lightning magic might even energise the beast, with the additional red-beryl magic improving its realism.

It was wishful thinking, but it was the best plan we had.

As we ascended, I caught a glint of something in the window of the covered walkway connecting the main cathedral to the tower that housed the priestesses' rooms. I zoomed in with my epicode, noticing the intentional back-and-forth movement signalling me. It was Brigitte. She hadn't joined the fray and had spotted us approaching, now waving to me. I knew whatever Brigitte had to say was likely super important, but I couldn't waste this chance to surprise Akeldama. Fortunately, my plan didn't particularly require my intervention.

"Cybele!" I yelled over the thunder and wind roaring around us.

"I'm going inside the cathedral to meet Brigitte. You attack Akeldama with your chryacal, but don't stick around if a surprise attack doesn't work."

Cybele nodded with determined focus, and I nodded back in acknowledgment. I made sure to first concentrate on the acceleration of the platform and calculated its trajectory for when I cut off the sand magic. Once we reached a height and velocity sufficient to take Cybele up into the fight, I disengaged the magic and jumped off the platform, activating my chameleon magic so no one would notice me slipping into the cathedral.

I was falling.

There wasn't much time before I hit the ground, but luckily, I'd practised enough with air magic and wingsuits that I wasn't afraid of dying from this height—even though I wasn't wearing a wingsuit or using air magic now. I was just falling.

I angled my body as best I could toward where I'd seen Brigitte, aiming for the windows of the bridge. They were relatively small targets, and I could only hope I wouldn't hit Brigitte. But there was no time to adjust my trajectory—I would only just make it as it was.

My adrenaline spiked as the building rushed toward me, fully aware I was about to attempt smashing through a window with my body. Failure would mean instant death and splattering against the stone below.

At the last moment, I switched to air magic, activating it just a split second after crashing through the glass with my forearms. The magic softened my fall without preventing the window from shattering as I needed it to. I still had only a few metres to slow down, so the landing was rough. I slammed against the windows on the opposite side of the walkway.

I was alive. In one piece.

And, miraculously, I hadn't broken the opposite windows. Groaning, I peeled myself off the wall, noticing the cracks I'd left behind as I stretched out the pain radiating through my limbs. Nailed it.

Brigitte stared at me wide-eyed, her voice tentative but concerned.

"Are you… okay?"

"Yup," I replied, though my tone was strained enough to betray the truth.

"I… okay, well," Brigitte stammered, shaking off her initial shock before refocusing on the reason she'd signalled me.

"I need your help to destroy the east wing. I can't allow Akeldama access to the centre of the world."

I nodded, already understanding what she meant: the world-ship.

"Do you have explosives or something we can use?" I asked.

Her brow furrowed in confusion. "Explosives?"

Right—who needed explosives in a world full of magic? "Never mind," I said quickly. "How were you planning to destroy the teleporter?"

"I have obtained an unusual substance that seems to cause a great deal of destruction when hit with lightning. I've seen much less of the stuff create craters far larger than the circumference of this tower," she explained, her voice calm yet laced with a subtle intensity. Her description sounded familiar too.

"Does this substance happen to be a slightly yellowish powder?" I asked, narrowing my eyes. Brigitte looked back at me in surprise.

"I didn't realise you were familiar with such curiosities."

So that was a yes. She had explosives—or more specifically, TNT.

"Right, okay," I began, speaking more quickly now as the plan began forming in my mind. "This should be easy then. All we have to do is pack the powder into the corners of the room so that the pressure pushes directly on the walls. It might be quicker to collapse the inside of the tower where the teleporter is rather than going in and out of all the rooms trying to topple the whole thing."

Brigitte blinked at me absently. That was when I realised I'd been speaking out loud. My rambling probably wasn't very helpful to someone who had never used explosives before either.

"I'll place the powder. All you have to do is be ready to light it up with your lightning from outside. I'll give the signal," I said firmly.

She nodded, then pulled out an overly embroidered bag from somewhere within her billowy white folds. Handing it to me, she said, "May Varanasi watch over you," before floating down the hall towards the main cathedral.

Right, time to get to work.

I headed down the hall towards the east wing of the cathedral, where the priestesses lived. This wing also housed the teleporter to the chambers of the High Priestess aboard the world-ship. Once I destroyed it, the only way to reach the chambers would be to pass the parliamentary trials—or to have already completed them and bear a tattoo.

My thoughts drifted to Alira, wondering if all this effort would be in vain if Ayuna managed to obtain a parliamentarian tattoo herself. But we could only do so much, and I had to focus on my job right now. Hopefully, Alira had gotten to her in time.

What was I saying? Ayuna might kill her.

I shook my head, trying to refocus and not fall down the rabbit hole of worry. I was anxious, but I couldn't change anything from here—not now. All I could do was my job, which at the moment was blowing up a teleporter and, inevitably, a good chunk of the cathedral given how much TNT Brigitte had handed over.

I entered the tower proper, walking through its curved halls, past the rooms where the priestesses once lived. All were empty now. Finally, I came across the all-too-familiar door to the room at the centre of the tower that housed the teleporter. To everyone else— including the other priestesses—this was just an ordinary room. I found it unlocked this time around.

A wave of old dread washed over me as I spotted the teleporter, its heavily distorted image showing the rooms it connected to. Tearing my eyes away from it, I pulled out the bag and opened it, visually confirming its contents.

It was pure trinitrotoluene—TNT.

I was suddenly very glad I hadn't crashed into that patch of sand in the dunes earlier. That would've ended me instantly.

I stuck my hand into the bag and began compressing the granulated explosive, knowing its capabilities from my time at

HITNE. I never thought I'd be blowing up a building—let alone a church—by hand with nothing but raw TNT. Life was wild.

I knelt down and pushed the putty into the join where the wall met the floor, continuing around the entire circular room until I'd run out of TNT. Now all Brigitte had to do was unleash her fury on the building once I was clear.

Assuming it didn't get hit by stray lightning from the battle above. Each wave of thunder made me acutely aware of just how easily I could die simply from standing too close to this room. Time to go.

I walked out of the room, casting a final glance at the teleporter before sprinting down the remaining halls. I felt slightly less anxious about my proximity to so much explosive and the abundance of stray detonators lighting up the sky as I got further away from the loaded room.

Lightning struck the bridge then, making me trip as my legs spasmed from the shock. I hit the stone floor and froze, waiting for the explosion—but there was nothing.

I breathed a sigh of relief, infinitely glad that Brigitte had stumbled across one of the sturdiest kinds of explosives. It likely wouldn't go off without a direct hit.

But even from this distance, I'd die if it did. Maybe not in the immediate explosion, but the bridge would collapse and take me with itI got up and kept running, my legs feeling strange and slightly difficult to control, but I pushed through, making it to the main cathedral. There, I found Brigitte standing in the doorway, staring up at the battle raging in the clouds above.

I jogged over to her, preparing to tell her to strike the east wing, but before I could, she suddenly leapt to the side, barely getting out of the way.

A loud 'thunk' echoed through the cathedral halls moments later as a massive object landed right where Brigitte had been standing. It was a huge lump of melted gold, the red sheen slowly fading as it cooled.

Well, shit.

I stuck my head out the door, first scanning for Brigitte to make sure she was alive, then looking straight up at the sky. I spotted her, uninjured, but Akeldama was staring directly back at from the sky. His long black hair was loose and—for some reason—on fire.

My thoughts immediately shifted to Cybele, and the question answered itself as I saw her falling from the sky. She'd just been thrown from the chryacal, which was now nothing more than a lump of metal.

Switching to topaz magic, I jumped up to catch her, snatching her out of the air. The moment my feet hit the ground again, I yelled to Brigitte.

"Brigitte, now!" I shouted.

Akeldama glanced at her, a brief flicker of concern flashing across his face. But Brigitte was too stunned to move. Seizing his opportunity, Akeldama dove—still on fire—straight at her.

I quickly but gently set an unconscious Cybele down, but I didn't have enough time to intercept Akeldama before he reached Brigitte.

Lightning sparked.

Two crackling tongues of pure electrical energy burst from Brigitte's hands. One struck the centre of the East Wing, and the other hit Akeldama square in the chest.

Akeldama spun out, missing Brigitte by an inch before slamming into the ground. His body vanished almost instantly into the thick smoke as the tower erupted, sending broken stone raining down on us. A sandstorm mixed with soot kicked up, making it nearly impossible to see anything.

It was then—standing there, waiting for the dust and smoke to settle—that I realised something.

There was no more thunder.

No more lightning.

And when the smoke finally cleared, there was no sign of Akeldama.

34 – Alira

This nightmare game of Proelium didn't get any better, even after Ayuna agreed to stop messing around. At least all the spiders were gone, along with one of the chryacal. The second chryacal, however, was still here, and so was the spidery Akeldama.

Ayuna had defeated the chryacal and snagged its tail, putting her ahead of me in the race to gather the items on the door. Not that it mattered much—the final piece on the door still made no sense whatsoever. The other fragmented items looked like a collage of random objects and were a little easier to understand, but that last one? Total mystery.

It was my turn to move. This time, I actually felt confident about my choice. I went with the icon of a pair of detached wings and a halo. That could only be a good tile, right? I didn't think this place had anything remotely like angels or even halos, so this image could have only been from my world, and there was almost nothing I could think of that would be a reason not to choose an angel tile.

I stepped forward, Ayuna still feigning disinterest from afar despite watching my moves awfully closely. When I stepped onto the tile, the sand grabbed onto me. I almost lifted my foot again quickly, but changed my mind, deciding to trust in the angel icon. I brought my other foot onto the tile, and it grabbed that foot too, sand running over my feet and up my legs, concentrating itself up my back. Nothing like this had happened yet, so it was freaky as hell, but I wasn't sinking, and it didn't hurt, so I let the board do what it was doing.

I only started to understand what was going on when I heard Ayuna yell, "What the!? What did you do to me?" from across the board, sand crawling up one of her legs now too. It was pooling onto her back, turning a mix of black and crimson as it spread out into a single demonic wing. Horror shot through me as I saw it, wondering if the board had glitched again. I whipped around, feeling a new resistance, and a weird tingle near the base of my spine. As I spun, my single demon wing trailed behind through the air, letting me glimpse the tip of it before it fell back to its resting position on my back.

Holy shit, how had I read that tile so wrong? It was only then, staring down at the angel wings that I realised I had assumed its orientation was just another glitch, as there had been so many. It's orientation was not a glitch like I thought, but a purposeful inversion indicating an upside-down angel. Or demon I suppose. The glitch was instead splitting this demon form between the two of us, as had consistently been a problem. But this one was particularly useless, as now both of us had wings, but neither of us could fly. Great.

The base of my spine tingled again and I started to realise I had some control over it. Weird. I might also have a tail now. Ayuna's laugh confirmed it.

"You look so ridiculous right now. What even are you? And what's this random wing for?" She said while tugging on her new wing, only to find out that it hurt to do so.

"Clearly it still doesn't like that there's two of us, but I assume I'm meant to be some sort of demon." I responded

"A demon huh? Your world is weird, but at least whatever this is cuter than the spiders."

I almost mentioned the irony of that but didn't, given that she had no reason to believe that demons were supposed to be much more evil than spiders. Not that I cared what she thought of Earth anyway.

"Alright my turn," Ayuna said a little too enthusiastically while staring greedily at the tiles around her. All of which were oriented towards her in some sense I noted. Her eyes lingered on one particular tile before they flicked to me. She smirked before she hopped onto the tile decisively.

"Nice knowing ya."

My frown quickly turned to surprise as the entire board shifted once more. The tiles began lifting off the ground and flipping around, reorienting themselves mid-air. Ayuna's tile was the first to leave the ground, spinning as mine lifted as well. Ayuna disappeared from sight as the tiles converged in the air, trapping me inside a quadrilateral sphere.

There was nothing else in the massive ball but me—and the final chryacal.

I stared at it, and it stared back with blank white eyes. It wasn't until too late that I realised all the drawings on the tiles had vanished. The moment I noticed, the deformed tiles melted at the seams, morphing into a proper sphere of solid sand.

The chryacal leapt at me.

Instinctively, I dodged to the side, my single wing flapping once in an attempt to help, though all it really did was propel me straight into the inside of the sphere faster.

I pushed myself upright, disoriented by the wing, the strange gravity in the room, and my inability to figure out which way was up. The chryacal had landed and was now stalking towards me, slow and deliberate. Without the tile edges to limit its movements, it had free rein.

So that's what Ayuna had been so smug about. And now, it was my turn to move. But clearly, I couldn't do anything until the chryacal was dead. I doubted Ayuna would make any spontaneous moves—she was probably hoping the chryacal would finish me off in here.

I didn't have a choice. I had to kill it.

It was just sand anyway. I could handle some sand. And that gave me an idea.

I brought up my wrist, having to dodge the chryacal again the next moment as it took the sudden movement as an opportunity to strike. I cleared it easily thanks to the demon wing stuck to my back that kept throwing me into the walls of the ball. The chryacal was now on the ceiling, and I had managed to activate my tiger's eye. I could feel its footsteps on the ceiling now through the vibrations in the sand.

The chryacal attacked again, and I confidently held my ground, intending to spear it in mid-air with the sand around me. It didn't move. It was like trying to pull iron sand away from strong magnets. Out of options, I threw up my arms to block the chryacal as it leapt at me from the ceiling. I knew it was hopeless. Its claws were thick and sharp, and my arms were no match for them, but I had nothing else. My wing whipped around on instinct, flaring out as if it had a mind of its own. It wasn't strong enough to stop the heavy, reptilian beast entirely, but the leathery surface was just enough to catch its claws, trapping them for now.

The chryacal thrashed wildly, its claws coming within millimetres of my face as they tried to wiggle free, tearing at my wing with each scratch. I froze, feeling the heat of its breath and the weight of its body pressing me into the sand beneath me. My mind screamed for me to move, to fight back, but I couldn't. All I could do was lie there, pinned, helpless, and waiting for my luck to run out.

The wing holding back the chryacal was being shredded far too quickly. Every swipe of its claws was bringing them closer and closer to me. I barely had time to worry about the claws, though, as my eyes caught a glimpse of the beast's tail—a wicked, barbed weapon twitching with menace.

I knew what was coming. It wouldn't even need its claws. The second it got free, its tail would finish me off. However, it didn't seem to be able to see me like this. Either that or it was too pre-occupied with unsticking it claws to realise how easily it could kill me right now. On top of that, I couldn't reach my arm to switch magics. I was completely stuck and helpless, at the whims of a cat made of sand. I hated this planet. I hadn't felt this helpless since… Oh yeah.

Remembering the last time I'd been restrained like this, I focused on my frustration, letting it boil over into explosive anger.

The chryacal's back claws tore through the wing, slicing into my thigh in the process. I screamed in pain, the white-hot claw marks consuming every thought as blood poured from the wounds. I struggled against the beast, but it was too heavy.

Its front claw nicked my cheek, and the sight of that weapon so close to my eyes burned itself into my mind—a still image I couldn't shake. I had to escape now, or I'd bleed out on the next blow.

I summoned every ounce of anger and desperation I had, channelling it into a single point. My thigh throbbed as blood flowed freely, further fuelling my rage. I screamed again, but this time with purpose, pouring everything I had into it, ignoring any thoughts of gemstone or blood limits as I turned myself into a desperation-fuelled fireball.

The chryacal jumped back, giving me a moment to sit up, but my arms were too weak to take advantage of the gap. The beast was too spring-loaded, its armoured muscles rebounding off the inside of the sphere as it pounced on me again.

I tried to throw my arms up, but the gesture was useless—my strength was gone.

Then I felt it. A tingle at the base of my spine.

I remembered the potential tail I had.

With nothing else left, I clung to the hope that it was as deadly as a demon's tail should be. I willed it to move, trying to deflect the chryacal.

It responded exactly as I'd hoped. The sensation was strange but not unfamiliar, like flexing any other muscle. I caught a glimpse of the wide, black tip of my tail as it whipped around, and only then did I truly feel its strength.

The tail stabbed straight through the chryacal's chest, its own weight driving it deeper onto the weapon.

It landed heavily, slamming me back down onto the tiles, but it still had enough sense to keep its legs extended, clawing desperately at the tail impaled through its chest, trying to pull the surprise weapon free. Without much thought, I ripped my tail downwards, unprepared for the soup of blood and organs that fell out on top of me as I gutted it from below. I shut my eyes as the chryacal's blood sprayed all over me and its body fell limp. The body turned to sand before the weight of it pressed down on me fully, but not before making sure I knew exactly what being covered in freshly removed organs felt like. I'd give anything for a proper shower right now.

I sat up, the sand falling off me leaving nothing of the chryacal behind except for its petrified tail. Now Ayuna and I were even.

Before I had time to catch my breath or gather my thoughts, the board started shifting again, the ball breaking up into squares once more and opening from a singular spot that finally told me which way was up. The ball continued to unfurl like a blooming flower, the tiles flipping as they disconnected and reorganised themselves into whatever the board was supposed to look like now.

I realised too late—right as I had caught my breath—that I wasn't standing on the bottom of the ball when it started dismantling. I was standing on the wall, and just before I could take a step, gravity returned to normal, the tiles sliding me off and causing me to trip and fall towards the ground. The bottom of the ball had floated most of the way back to the ground, so I didn't fall far, but I still landed hard on my knees.

It was only when the board was still again, and gravity was flat, that I found the strength to stand.

I met Ayuna's gaze, frowning at her shocked expression. I guess she hadn't expected me to survive.

But as I looked down, I realised it wasn't that. I looked insane.

My demon tail flicked lazily behind me, a broken and shredded wing hung from my back—completely useless and looking more like a cape now—and despite the chryacal turning to sand, I was thoroughly stained red with its blood.

My mind wanted to explain it, but then I remembered my thigh and figured the bloodstains were probably partly because of that.

I fell back to my knees, the adrenaline fading and my clawed-up leg bursting with pain once again. I reached to touch it but found one hand wrapped around the petrified chryacal tail, and the other gripping the cold black metal of a gun.

Wait.

How on Earth did I get a gun?

I stared at the metal object in my hand. My eyes flicked up to Ayuna, who had reined in her shocked expression but was now eyeing the weapon in my hand.

However, it was the final door—or the two glitched doors behind her—that caught my eye. The fragmented chryacal symbol was now legible, floating as a separate entity of light near the door. Another symbol, or fragments of one, were lit up as well, but I couldn't decipher them from this angle.

My next instinct was to look down, and that explained the gun. I'd fallen onto a tile with a picture of the same large pistol I now gripped in my hand. I had no idea what kind of gun it was—Dad could probably tell me. Even so, it was far from the dainty pistols spies used. This thing looked like it would hurt just to pull the trigger, assuming it even had any bullets in it.

"Care to explain… all of this?" Ayuna asked, gesturing to all of me.

I paused as I started to recount events. Why did I need to tell her? She wasn't my friend. I'd come here to kill her—or at least stop her.

Now that I had a gun, it looked like I had the upper hand. There was no need to play nice anymore.

"No. I don't think I will," I replied with a grin, "Your move," I added, my mind already returning to the deep wounds in my thigh as I felt the blood slowly oozing out again.

I put down the tail and the gun and got to work stitching the gashes back together. Something that was only possible because I could use blood magic and had recently used yellow sapphire magic to heal Dad, meaning the magic still lingered in my bloodstream. Maybe if I pointed out to Dad that using blood magic was the only way I could've stopped myself from bleeding out and dying on this damn Proelium board, he'd be more open to the idea. Then again, it might just remind him of the danger I'd put myself in by following Ayuna into the trials.

I worked on my thigh, focusing solely on stopping the bleeding and stitching the top layer of skin back together. I knew I wasn't great at mending the more intricate bodily systems, and I was glad the chryacal hadn't hit my torso. I doubted I'd be able to fix something like that.

Ayuna finally chose her tile, sending ripples through the board that spread outwards from her. Great, the board was alive once more. Here we go, I thought.

But the ripples were the only thing that happened.

The tiles left behind a small pile of sand that Ayuna squatted down to investigate. She ran her hand through the grains, picking up a handful and letting them fall back into the pile.

"What am I supposed to do with this?" she asked, frustration creeping into her voice.

"I don't know, but it looks like it's part of the collection," I replied, gesturing towards the door where new symbol fragments had lit up as Ayuna touched the sand.

"Well, this tile looked nothing like a pile of sand, so maybe whatever it was supposed to be didn't form. Like another 'glitch,' as you keep calling them," Ayuna said.

I paused, thinking for a moment, seeing the potential in the sand with fresh eyes. Switching to sand magic, I wondered if I could control this bit, since it had seemingly been released from the board's control.

The moment I connected to the sand magic, I felt the pile. Something about it was strange—the more I reached for it, the more intense the energy it emitted became.

I was almost afraid of this little pile, but it couldn't possibly hurt me from over here. Despite its passive ferocity, I focused and tried forming it into a ball.

As I shaped the sand, it crackled with energy against my mind, almost fighting back, but I managed to form it. The image shifted in front of me as I stared at the ball, its colours flickering from one to the next, slipping in and out of the smooth stone I imagined.

Sensing the crackling energy again and recalling the unpredictable things this board was capable of, I pictured it instead as a tennis ball.

Ayuna stood nearby, staring at me, attempting to suppress her curiosity as I shifted the sand's material right before her eyes. Then, it transformed and a fuzzy green ball fell, bouncing lightly along the tile before rolling into Ayuna's foot. She bent down to pick up the tennis ball, her arm jerking slightly as she lifted it, clearly expecting it to be much heavier. She held it up towards me, her expression unimpressed.

"You really just used my pile of illusory sand to make a useless green ball?" she scoffed. "What a waste. If I had any tiger's eye blood on me, I'd make some throwing knives and use your face as target practice."

I scowled back at her but quickly reminded myself that I still had the upper hand here.

Deciding to use the rest of the sand, I crafted something Ayuna could carry. We still needed the pile for the door. Whatever it was supposed to be remained indecipherable, but I could shape it into anything I wanted now.

I focused and breathed in sync with the magically charged sand. Ayuna bent down once again, picking up the new object I'd created for her.

"What the hell is this? If it's supposed to be a weapon, it's not a very good one," she said, frowning in confusion.

I grinned, enjoying the moment far more than I should've.

"It's a tennis racket. It's what you're supposed to hit the green ball with. You'll need it to finish the game, so you'd better hang onto it. And the ball too."

Ayuna looked pissed, and also silly, standing there holding a pink tennis racket in one hand and a ball in the other, her singular demon wing sprouting out of her now looking very out of place.

I chuckled, satisfied, and turned my attention back to the board. Alright, my turn again.

I assessed the tiles around me—a fresh set to choose from after falling out of a floating death ball. I'd adapted my strategy to picking symbols that seemed the least likely to glitch out and cause problems. That strategy hadn't worked particularly well, but at least it had mostly stopped me from triggering any massive shifts in the board. For that, I was grateful.

Ayuna, however, seemed intent on doing the exact opposite.

This time, though, one tile stood out to me far more than the others. It wasn't overly special, but something about it drew me in. My curiosity was likely driving my choice more than anything, but I hoped that it was a sign the board had finally figured out there were two of us.

The symbol was one I recognised—it was from an old video game I used to play with Dad when I was little. Whenever we came across this 'x2' icon in the game, we knew it meant the section ahead required some sort of teamwork.

A challenge that could only be completed with two players. Either this tile would activate a similar challenge, requiring both of us, or chaos would erupt. The latter seemed far more likely, given everything I'd seen. My other options were impossible to decipher, especially since more than one of the tiles kept switching images constantly, as if they couldn't make up their mind.

I took the step.

Out of the corner of my eye, I noticed a small change. I turned to follow the movement and found myself face to face with an identical version of me, staring back at me. I really did look insane. But that wasn't important now, as Ayuna prepared to make her move immediately after mine.

It was only when she stepped forward that I saw another Ayuna on the far side of the board mimicking her move. Ayuna landed on a blank tile, one that had already been activated. The other Ayuna, however, landed on a tile with an icon, although I couldn't make it out properly from this distance.

Worse, Ayuna was now standing on the tile right next to me, glaring at me viciously. She stalked towards me, clearly intent on finally attacking me directly—since the chryacal hadn't done the job for her.

Unfortunately for her, the spidery Akeldama moved before she could reach me. The spider-creature landed on a blank tile, allowing it to zip across the board with blinding speed.

It only touched blank tiles that were at least connected by a corner, following a path between its chosen tile and Ayuna's—one we'd both failed to notice. Its movements were wild, its legs seeming to multiply the more it ran. Fear shot through me as I wondered if there were two of them now as well.

There weren't. But that didn't make its legs stop multiplying as it ran, each new appendage touching the floor only once before becoming a bizarre accessory.

Ayuna stayed focused on me until one of the creature's stray legs whipped around and smacked her double in the neck. The double was coat-hangered hard and dropped like a stone, the resulting whiplash causing Ayuna to flinch as if she'd felt it herself.

"What the... Oh shit. No, not this. Seriously? Fuck," Ayuna cursed, her voice tense as she readied herself. She glanced at the racquet in her hand with clear disappointment before brandishing it against the oncoming mess of legs attached to that all-too-familiar face.

The creature rushed at her, and despite everything—despite her trying to kill me and leaving me helpless a moment ago—I couldn't help but feel bad for her. If she was about to get trampled by this thing, I didn't want it to be because I'd handed her a tennis ball as a weapon.

There was still a slim chance, too, that the 'x2' tile still had something to do with teamwork and wasn't just doubling us on the board while also doubling the rampant glitching we were already dealing with.

I sighed and took a deep breath, watching the tennis ball reform in Ayuna's hand under my direction. She felt its new weight and whipped her head towards me, her expression as close to fear as I'd ever seen on her.

She squeezed the ball, finding it much harder than before.

"Feel free to die to that thing, but don't blame the tennis racquet if you do," I said as nonchalantly as I could.

Ayuna glanced back at the racquet with a flicker of doubt, but soon enough, a grin spread across her face.

"As thanks, I'll kill this thing. Then your double. Then you last," she said cheerfully, before launching herself upwards.

A subtle gust of wind swirled around her legs as she propelled herself toward the mob of legs using air magic, armed with a bladed tennis racquet and the carbon fibre head of a mace.

The mace head was probably useless, but it was the best ball-shaped weapon as light as a tennis ball I could come up with. Knowing Ayuna, though, she'd find a way to make it work. She was annoyingly resourceful like that.

I watched as Ayuna pulled out a small red vial and drank it mid-leap, landing and leaping again in the same stride. This time, she moved much faster, curving slightly around the creature as though she were a curveball herself.

She hacked at some of its legs, testing the sharpness of the bladed racquet, her movements precise and relentless.

She severed three of the creature's legs, but the racquet rebounded off the fourth, having lost too much momentum to break through. It seemed the racquet wasn't particularly sharp.

Ayuna pressed on regardless, spinning around the spidery creature with the fury of a hurricane, hacking multiple legs away at once. The creature had stopped running, and with it, stopped spawning new legs, making Ayuna's gradual hacking effective—until it began trying to snatch her out of the air with its teeth and claws.

With every strike, the creature multiplied. Its shape contorted into a writhing mass of legs, turning into something indescribable and grotesque, covered in an increasingly terrifying number of teeth.

The worst part was knowing that Akeldama's form was still somewhere within it, and that the teeth were his.

Masses of broken pink skin stretched across black shells, sprouting jagged teeth wherever Ayuna came too close. I didn't even know where to start with this thing. Evidently, neither did Ayuna.

She landed back on the ground, staring down the creature with uncertainty, unsure how to proceed. Then she glanced at the carbon fibre mace ball in her other hand and decided to give it a try.

Without any knowledge of tennis, Ayuna instinctively executed the perfect serve, throwing the ball into the air and watching its arc closely. She gauged precisely when to strike and the angle she needed to direct it exactly where she wanted.

The ball broke through many of the racquet strings on contact, but the racquet stayed intact enough to launch the ball full force into the centre of the mass of limbs. It disappeared into the creature, shattering a couple of teeth on its way in before vanishing entirely.

Then the rest of the teeth spontaneously shattered as well, exploding outward in a chaotic blast before recondensing. Two human-like arms emerged from the mass, constructed entirely of broken tooth fragments.

The tooth-fragment arms swiped at Ayuna, but this time they didn't multiply. All the rules seemed broken with this creature. It had become too many things at once, too many overlapping effects, and the board had already been glitching before it devolved into this kaleidoscopic nightmare.

What the hell were we supposed to do now?

This was supposed to be Ayuna's fight, but the creature had grown too big and too out of control. Its sheer size and unpredictability made a swipe from one of its bone-fragment too hard to avoid. One swung toward me, forcing me to duck and fall backwards, landing hard on a blank tile.

The moment I hit the tile, I became a target.

A fire erupted somewhere behind the creature, drawing my attention. I turned and saw my double sitting down—engulfed in flames.

It looked like the tile she'd fallen on was an instant death tile. I remembered how Ayuna had felt when her double got hit, but I'd felt nothing. What were the rules of this damn game? Did it even have any anymore?

I dodged out of the way again, this time avoiding the tiny spider claws at the end of some sort of limb as it flailed about. Whether I liked it or not, I was in this fight now.

I took a steadying breath, reaching out with my magic to feel for the mace ball Ayuna had hit into the creature. I found it—solid and lodged deep within the mass, but doing absolutely nothing.

Focusing, I turned it to steel and exhaled sharply, hoping the metal shavings would rip the beast apart. Silver sparks erupted from the creature, dozens of its decaying legs falling away and crumbling into sand.

But it was useless. The legs were too quickly replaced by others—limbs made of a grotesque blend of spider and human parts.

"Good thinking," I heard from behind me.

I spun around, but Ayuna was already there. Her hand touched the exposed skin of my neck for only a moment before she pulled away, leaving a sharp soreness in its wake.

"Hey!" I yelled, but Ayuna didn't stop. She glanced back at me with a smug smile and shrugged as her bladed tennis racquet reformed before my eyes.

It wasn't a racquet anymore, but an oddly-shaped halberd, complete with an oversized axe blade.

It was definitely the kind of over-the-top weapon that the leader of a city might use their piece of the tail-key to create. If this was, in fact, a replica of the one Akeldama had crafted from his awkward piece of the tail-key, it would certainly explain its strange shape. I hadn't seen Akeldama's piece firsthand, but I'd seen all the others so far, as well as a chryacal's tail itself. Far too closely, I might add. So it was easy enough to spot the distinct shape embedded within the chunky blade of Ayuna's thick halberd.

The red-and-gold marbling along the handle was surprisingly beautiful, though.

Ayuna flew on, swinging the halberd with practiced ease, maiming the creature left and right. Its limbs went flying, scattering in every direction, only to reform into even less recognisable versions of themselves.

The limbs never truly disappeared—they always reformed in some horrific fashion. So far, the only thing that had seemed to affect the creature was the steel mace ball lodged in its guts, which had at least managed to turn part of it back into sand.

Ayuna threw her halberd directly at the creature. For a moment, it looked as though the weapon had snapped in midair. But after blinking away the distortion, I realised what had happened.

The weapon had glitched, doubling and spearing the creature twice through. There was enough force behind the throw that both halberds ripped straight through the creature, bursting out the other side in a shower of sand. The holes closed up quickly, but it confirmed the creature's weakness, and I thought I had an idea of how to beat it.

I stared at the spot where the halberd had glitched into two, noticing now that a thin, silvery line—like a spiderweb—ran directly through the point of duplication. Finally, there might be some use for all this glitching and multiplying.

I watched Ayuna closely, waiting for her to fly past wherever the creature was spewing spiderwebs from. They were thin and fast, but I caught a glimpse of one shooting out as Ayuna sped by, hacking away at more of its limbs with her reclaimed halberd. The second halberd had vanished somewhere, disappearing into the chaos.

All I had to do now was strike that exact spot. If I could hit it, the creature's spiderweb-making organ might multiply.

Switching magics, I summoned a tornado beneath me and launched myself into the air. Ayuna stopped mid-flight, clearly surprised to see me enter the fray.

"Don't stop! Keep distracting it!" I shouted at Ayuna

"Oh, so I'm bait now, am I?" she snapped back.

"Yes," I replied bluntly. There was no point lying to her—not when we both knew we planned to kill each other eventually. Just not right now.

She rolled her eyes but obeyed, flying to the far side of the board, leaving behind a trail of mutilated limbs and fragments.

As Ayuna sped off, I caught a glimpse of the web shooting out from the creature once more and immediately regretted not bringing my yacharow.

This wasn't the first time today that I'd wished I hadn't left it back at the museum. I'd been in too much of a hurry to grab it before I left. Not that it would've been wise to bring a piece of the tail-key straight to Ayuna anyway.

Hovering in the air on my wind current, I focused on the metal shavings I'd scattered when I detonated the ball. It took time, but eventually, I managed to sense one. Once I found it, the others became easier to locate, slowly pulling together.

From the shards, I formed the longest knife I could with the magic sand leftover from the ball. It wasn't much, but at least I had a weapon now.

Combining air and sand magic and succumbing to blood magic once more, I flicked the blade up to me from the ground.

It occurred to me then that I should've taken Dad's obsidian and not his amethyst. But I'd forgotten about it—he kept it around his neck after all, not in the gauntlets.

I grabbed the knife and dove toward the web-slinging organs below, setting myself on fire as I fell—just in case.

I landed hard, slashing at the creature. The small hole I created deformed and split into two. Both holes immediately shot webs at me, but they burnt up in my flames before they could reach me. Looks like setting myself on fire was a genius move.

I kept slashing, watching as the creature's limbs were gradually replaced by a shiny black carapace—lumpy and riddled with strange holes.

Satisfied with my work, I jumped back down to the floor, only to notice the webs beginning to cover the room. They poured out of the creature relentlessly now that I'd extinguished the fire. Ayuna appeared behind me.

"The lack of random legs is nice, but what exactly is your plan here?" she asked.

I jumped, startled, but quickly grinned, proud of my idea. "Let me show you what this thing does," I said, pulling out the pistol I'd acquired earlier.

I reformed my knife into a couple of bullets and loaded one, unsurprised to find it wasn't the right size. I didn't know much about how guns worked, so some of this I would have to just guess.

As I fiddled with the weapon, I remembered that I'd specifically chosen the amethyst over the sapphire when I left Dad. I shook my head at myself, frustrated by the oversight. This clearly hadn't gone anything like I thought it would.

I focused on the chamber and the bullet inside, feeling the magic sand they were made of as I tried to mould the bullet to the barrel as precisely as I could. Hopefully, I'd guessed the bullet's composition well enough for it to fire without blowing me up.

But time had run out.

The creature was advancing on us, growing dozens of legs once again as it sped up, closing the distance rapidly.

I held the gun out, aiming at the densest portion of webs between us and the creature, and pulled the trigger. Relief and exhilaration hit me at once as the gun fired exactly as I'd hoped. The bullet sparked as it tore through the webs, multiplying each time it passed through. A barrage of bullets ripped through the creature, carving holes in it in the blink of an eye.

But my smile faded quickly as the holes closed up.

The bullets were too tightly packed. They'd multiplied along the way, but they'd all followed roughly the same trajectory—like a shotgun blast in a concentrated area.

It wasn't enough. We needed something capable of completely tearing this thing to shreds. We needed to figure out how to saw the barrel off this shotgun.

I loaded my next bullet, guessing how a shotgun shell might be composed. I figured it must be similar to a regular bullet but full of lots of little bits instead of a single bullet.

Aiming at the creature, I hoped the spray of shrapnel would be wide enough to hit more webs and shred the monster.

I fired, gripping the gun tighter this time to avoid the slide cutting into my hand again—the kickback was more intense than I'd anticipated. More holes ripped through the creature in a wider spread, but it still wasn't enough.

"We need more," was all I could think to say.

Ayuna sighed in frustration as the creature loomed over us, practically on top of us now. Half of it collapsed, attempting to crush us. We darted in opposite directions to dodge its mass.

I narrowly avoided a fresh spray of webs, ducking instinctively to dodge random debris being hurled at me. That's when I realised the object coming my way was the broken tip of Ayuna's halberd.

"Make a better bullet already!" Ayuna yelled, her voice sharp as she hacked away at the creature. She darted in and out of its chaos, dodging everything that erupted toward her, trying to keep its attention away from me.

I couldn't help but feel like this was the first genuine, non-sarcastic co-operation I'd seen from Ayuna this entire time. I wasted no time dwelling on it, reforming the broken tip of the halberd into the bullet that I hoped would finally kill this thing. Webs continued to erupt, the room becoming hazy with fine silver, making it harder to see Ayuna.

The bullet started to take shape. I wasn't entirely sure what I was doing, but I knew exactly what I wanted, and this magically charged sand didn't seem to need a detailed ingredients list—just a clear vision of the result.

Then it was time to see if it was as amazing as I'd hoped.

I fired, my eyes immediately catching Ayuna floating just above the creature. I briefly wondered if she'd survive what I'd just unleashed in her general direction.

The tile beneath me cracked as the bullet exploded out of the chamber with a release so loud and intense that it tore my hand open from the recoil and left me deafened.

I watched as holes began to open up the creature, each one multiplying endlessly before the charged fragments detonated as I'd intended.

The small spaces between each hole vapourised, leaving a thick cloud of dust slowly settling on a cracked checkerboard.

The dust fell heavy as lead, the increasing buildup causing more tiles to fracture individually. The board began to implode under the strain, rumbling beneath my feet.

For a moment, the final door lit up, appearing normal for just an instant. The final symbol—a handshake—floated by it alongside the chryacal tail symbol and a third, still undecipherable one. It could have been something like half a gun.

This was it. That must mean Ayuna was gone, and the game was won. Then, the door cracked, the floating symbols fading away like forgotten ghosts as the board continued to implode.

My half-tile decided it was its turn to collapse as well, thrashing beneath me and flipping me off toward the centre of the pile of living rubble.

Through the dust, I caught a glimpse of Ayuna's body, but I couldn't tell if it was upright or not before I tumbled into the thick cloud.

I scrambled to my feet, slipping on the rubble as the tiles beneath me lost all their energy—all their magic—turning into nothing more than piles of stone.

When I finally stood upright, I could see over the thinning dust cloud as it settled to the floor. The broken tiles were replaced by a fine layer of silvery sand, shimmering faintly with potential. I frowned, spotting something in the silvery sand that seemed out of place. I knelt to pick it up, finding a sizeable purple crystal just sitting there. It was extremely well cut, and shimmered brilliantly, making me wonder if it was some sort of big amethyst or something more impressive. I pocketed the crystal to examine later. As the dust settled, I saw that Ayuna was, in fact, alive, standing upright and twiddling a light pink crystal between her fingers. It was cut exactly the same as the purple one I'd just pocketed. Rubbing the dust from my eyes, I thought I'd imagined the streak of electricity crackling from Ayuna's pink crystal, arcing around her and striking the ground. But then it happened again, and she was laughing.

"I came here for power. And now I have power," she said, holding up the crystal with a triumphant gleam in her eye.

"I'm glad you came along, Alira. Otherwise, we wouldn't have destroyed the game and discovered these little gems powering it. I wonder what I can do with something so powerful that it's been able to sustain a game this big for centuries."

The lightning crackled again. Ayuna hesitated, staring at the crystal with a strange expression before snapping out of it.

"Sorry, but I've come here to 'get through all of parliament,' as you put it, and I can't have you stopping me. If only you'd joined us earlier when I asked. Too late now, but this was genuinely fun. Nice knowing ya."

Her smile was chilling—dead-eyed and detached—as the next streak of lightning spiralled outward from the crystal. This time, it wasn't aimed at the ground but directly at me.

I flew backwards, the image of Ayuna's uncomfortable smile and lifeless eyes illuminated by the harsh white light, etched into my vision. The force of the electricity overwhelmed me, blinding every one of my senses. I think I hit the ground, but it was hard to tell with my mind reeling and my muscles spasming. I did feel the warm sensation of blood running from my nose, however, and then across my cheek, pooling and spilling over from my ear and running over my face.

My muscles were spasming less and less, but I hadn't been able to breath since I was hit, my lungs tight in exhalation, unable to relax enough to get any air. My vision was already lost but the sensation of the thin lines of warmth on my face started to evaporate, and that's how I knew I was finally losing consciousness.

35 – Ender

"Where did he go?" I asked, shooting a puzzled look at Brigitte. Cybele began to stir then, rubbing her eyes and groaning. The thick smoke had mostly dissipated but left mine, and everyone else's eyes, stinging.

Brigitte opened her mouth to respond, but it was a voice from within the cathedral that spoke first.

"The painite known as Akeldama was teleported away. Another painite arrived during the explosion, and they both teleported somewhere out of my range once they reached him. Even more peculiar was that the painite appeared to be carrying some sort of dense energy source, larger than anything I have ever encountered. I can't even begin to describe it, but it didn't feel like any one particular kind of magic."

The voice was soft, but spoke gradually quicker, seemingly excited by those last few details. I squinted into the cathedral, spotting a figure not quite hiding but deliberately lingering out of the sunlight. Having already gotten more answers than I expected, I continued speaking to the ghost.

"An energy source? Like a big blood battery?"

"No, the painites' blood vials only emit trace amounts of detectable magic. This was more akin to the energy released during a lightning storm—constant, contained, and no larger than a hand," came the response from the shadows.

Brigitte sighed. "I do apologise, Ender. This is Kaiya, my assistant. They possess magic sense, which is greatly enhanced by their fusion, allowing them to perceive magical energies with far greater clarity. It's the only way we've been able to detect the vials of blood the painites carry."

Kaiya finally stepped forward, bowing quickly before retreating again. That explained how Brigitte had known Cybele and I were coming—and exactly where we were.

This would've been invaluable at the arena. Why hadn't I heard of magic sense before? I was curious to know which gemstone was linked to this ability, but now wasn't the time to ask. We had to go after them.

"The second painite could only have been Ayuna," I said, thinking aloud. "She teleported them both away—something she could only have done with a parliamentarian tattoo, which means she succeeded, and they're both on the world-ship right now."

Cybele was sitting up now, following the conversation as she rubbed her head. Brigitte held a pained expression, her gaze lingering on the destroyed tower we had just blown up.

"You two go after them. We would follow, but, well..." She gestured toward the wreckage—the backdoor to the world-ship now obliterated for no reason.

I nodded, already planning to do exactly that. As I spoke with Brigitte, Cybele started standing. She looked beaten up but otherwise okay, moving toward me with a slight limp. She placed a hand on my shoulder to steady herself. The thought of heading to the world-ship made my mind race. I couldn't help but want to find Alira there while also dreading what that might mean. If she was in parliament, it would mean she hadn't beaten Ayuna—and I didn't even want to think about the implications of that.

In all likelihood, she'd missed Ayuna altogether and was already on her way back to the museum—or perhaps she was already there, waiting. Either way, we had to go.

"Ready?" I asked Cybele, tapping into her magic.

She nodded wearily, pulling me into a tight hug like before. I traced the pattern on my wrist and across my palm, activating the tattoo with deliberate strokes. And then, in an instant, we were back on the world-ship, standing in a nondescript hallway near the fringes of the ship.

I couldn't determine much from a glance, but instinctively I knew this was the last teleporter we'd used—the one closest to the white box. Which meant we were nowhere near where we needed to be. I swivelled back around to the teleporter, Cybele letting go of my arm and blinking sheepishly. I paused before touching the display, watching her closely.

"Cybele, are you okay? We're about to face Akeldama and Ayuna. If you're not okay, you should head back to the surface."

"No, no, I am," she insisted, taking a deep breath and exhaling slowly. She then pulled out a small pouch from her coat, opened it, and tossed one of the light brown cubes inside into her mouth.

"What was that?" I asked, intrigued.

Cybele responded with slightly more energy than before as she chewed the cube.

"It's a painkiller I mixed with a few other things to keep myself awake when I need to."

I supposed I shouldn't be surprised that painkillers existed here. Even though magic meant they were rarely needed—at least before pearl-water became inert. The ships crashing here likely carried a surplus of drugs onboard. Judging by her newfound liveliness, the cube likely contained some caffeine that Cybele had combined with the painkiller. The brown tinge of the cube made me wonder if she'd stumbled across coffee here after all. For some reason, I pictured a patch of desert sand, all shades of brown, composed entirely of instant coffee granules like the kind that had been plentiful on the Cronus. But that wasn't right important now.

Cybele tapped on the screen, selecting the teleporter just outside the hangar. It made sense to start there, given that's probably where Ayuna had come straight from—though she did already have a tattoo. Cybele stared at me expectantly, waiting to enter the teleporter.

"Are you okay? You kind of spaced out there when I mentioned my painkiller gum."

I shook my head. "Yeah, sorry. Just got distracted. Let's go," I said, stepping into the teleporter.

It was surreal stepping out of the small hallway into such an enormous room—especially *this* room, which I hadn't seen in fifteen years. I'd barely been awake enough to take in any details of the space back then. That said, the floor had definitely been covered in sandstone tiles last time, not this weird silvery sand that looked as though it was the result of some kind of explosion. Then I saw the body lying in the centre of the hangar. My heart seized, and I sprinted as fast as I could.

It couldn't be.

She couldn't be here.

What had happened?

There were too many thoughts to process, too much distance to cover. This bloody hangar was too damn big.

I fell to my knees beside Alira's body, sliding in the silver sand. My heartbeat pounded in my head, the result of the sudden and agonisingly long sprint.

I touched her, and she was still warm, but before I could check for a pulse or fully process what was happening, a laugh rang out from the far side of the hangar. Akeldama strode forward lazily, with Ayuna in tow. Her expression was much darker, her jaw tightly clenched, while Akeldama laughed, his carefree demeanour almost unsettling.

"Now *this* is the kind of fortress you can build an empire behind," he boomed, his voice echoing through the vast space.

Cybele had caught up to me now, bending down to check for Alira's pulse, completely ignoring Akeldama. He continued strolling closer before addressing us directly.

"You're full of surprises, Ender, and yet so predictable. I wasn't expecting you to blow up the cathedral like that, but you chased me down here with no plan, just as I thought you would. Now, what are you going to do? Your daughter's gone, and I have a fortress and the source of all magic all to myself."

He was close enough now to notice as my brow flinched.

"Yes, that's right. It's just us now—now that parliament has been removed. I wouldn't recommend going into their little room, by the way. It's quite messy."

He smirked cruelly. "Not that you'll get the chance to," he said, his wicked grin widening as he watched my expression morph into shock.

I realised what he meant.

No diamonds. No parliament. No Alira.

We had lost. Akeldama had won.

I glanced at Cybele, who was still checking for a pulse. But the look on her face told me everything. Akeldama was standing over us now. I raised my tear-streaked face to meet his gaze, fully aware of how pathetic I looked. I didn't have the strength to fight him—there was no point anymore.

"You know, if you had just stayed out of this planet's affairs, your daughter wouldn't be dead right now," he said, his tone cutting like a blade. "You two would be happily living back where you came from, blissfully ignorant of everything. But now look what you've done."

He was right. This was my fault.

I knew this place was too dangerous. And yet I still came and dragged Alira here with me. I knew there was trouble here. I knew I wouldn't be able to resist joining the fight.

Even after watching her mother die, I dragged Alira here to suffer the same fate.

I was a monster.

Akeldama raised his hand, his fingers contorting in some way that caused my wrist to fly upward into his grasp. He yanked me forward, his grip the only thing preventing me from collapsing face-first into the dust.

I looked up at him again, my face streaked with tears, drained of all fight. His cruel satisfaction was evident as he towered over me.

"Go home, Ender," Akeldama said calmly, making me feel utterly insignificant.

My wrist flared with blinding pain as he let go, leaving me clutching my burnt flesh. The skin blistered as I took my arm back, my parliamentarian tattoo warped beyond recognition—now melted and distorted, black cracks running through it in strangely organised patterns. Ayuna held up a light pink crystal next, and everything went white. My entire body spasmed violently, as though being electrocuted. I truly thought I would die in that moment. But the electrocution was mercifully brief, leaving me alone as my vision returned. The sight of the half-toppled cathedral greeted me, hazy and surreal.

Cybele got to her feet far quicker than I could manage. She rushed to my side, immediately grabbing my arm and examining the burns. She winced the entire time.

My eyes wandered, spotting Brigitte running toward us, Kaiya in tow. They hadn't strayed far from the battlefield.

My eyes flicked to movement, and I found myself staring at Alira. I frowned, thinking I'd imagined it, knowing that she couldn't have moved.

Her body twitched—once, then again—until she coughed, her breath strangled and desperate as she gasped for air.

But they were there. She was breathing.

I stared in disbelief, frozen in place, until she placed her hand down to push herself up and slipped, letting out a sound that made it seem like she'd winded herself.

I scrambled to my feet, tripping over myself as I rushed to her. I immediately scooped her up, cradling her torso and head in my arms. Her breathing had steadied, but she kept shaking—her tremors growing increasingly violent. Then I realised how cold she'd become. I held her closer, trying to warm her up.

Brigitte arrived moments later, and seeing the state Alira was in, she unclipped her outer layer and draped it over her. Brigitte suddenly seemed priestly again, despite her soot-covered state. Beneath the discarded layer, she wore an almost identical but still pure white garment.

I whipped my attention back to Alira, holding my breath as I watched her shivering slowly subside. Her eyelids fluttered faintly, not fully opening.

Fragments of my medical training surfaced. I knew that revival after cardiac arrest was unlikely—and even when it was successful, it often led to brain damage or comas. Even if Alira somehow survived this, I feared she'd never fully wake up.

But then, to my utter surprise, her trembling slowly stopped.

After a few moments, her eyelids fluttered open briefly—just long enough to focus on my face and let a few tears stream down her cheeks.

"Dad…You're…I'm…" Alira wheezed breathlessly before pulling me into a tight hug. I held her tightly in return, praying this wasn't some cruel dream. I didn't care how she'd defied death— only that she had. She was alive.

Her muscles began to soften in my arms as she held onto me, and I started to panic. But then I saw Cybele smiling, tears streaming down her face, and I felt Alira's even breathing against me.

"She's asleep," Cybele whispered.

I smiled back, relief washing over me.

For a moment, I felt the urge to pull out the amethyst and try to communicate with Alira in her dreams. But I decided against it. She needed proper rest. No doubt she'd been going full throttle since I'd last seen her—fighting Ayuna, and apparently on the world-ship. I couldn't help but wonder about Ayuna's expression earlier, knowing she must have believed she'd killed Alira. Maybe, unlike Akeldama, Ayuna did have a conscience. A trace of remorse.

Not that it mattered now. Not after everything she'd done. Somehow, we would take back the world-ship. Akeldama might have half of the tail-key and exclusive access to the source of magic, but he couldn't do much without the other half. And that was still ours to lose.

Back at the museum, it was utter chaos. The roof had caved in, and scorched chunks of sandstone littered the floor. Cordelia was tending to the wounded but ran straight to us the moment we entered. I was carrying a sleeping Alira, while Cybele rushed to Cordelia as soon as they saw each other. To my surprise, they embraced—and even kissed.

I smiled. Shit might have hit the fan, but at least we were all alive. That was what mattered most.

My smile quickly faded, though, as I realised not everyone had been so lucky. People were scattered around the museum, grieving and crying amidst the wreckage. The occasional limb stuck out from beneath the debris—a sobering reminder of the cost. We couldn't stay here.

The museum was one of only two places that had been attacked, alongside the cathedral. It looked like this was meant as a warning—a grim echo of Akeldama's sentiment that I should leave. To go back to Earth.

But I couldn't leave. Not now. Not when someone like him was wreaking so much destruction.

After the reunion, I joined Cordelia and Cybele in ushering everyone down into the basement to plan our next move.
It seemed obvious to the three of us what our next move should be, but the remaining refugees in the museum were terrified and clueless. We hadn't discussed it beforehand, but our plans to set up shop in Muruntau were already in motion. Cybele wasted no time, hopping up onto a table to explain the situation to everyone. I hadn't pictured Cybele as a leader before, but somehow, she managed to run this place surprisingly well—despite her many distracting side-quests. I supposed Cordelia did her best to keep her on track when she could.

"Right! Everyone, listen up!" Cybele began, her voice commanding attention. "I know today has been rough, and many of us have lost loved ones. I know you've all stayed because you love this city and believe in what it could be one day again. That day, however, might be further away than we'd hoped. Akeldama owns this city now, and he's made it clear that he wants us gone. We will not vanish without a fight. That being said, we can no longer fight from here—or survive here. Instead, we'll go to Muruntau, where we've formed an alliance with their leader. That will be our new home, at least temporarily, until the day comes when we can reclaim our home here. The journey will be long, but it will finally give many of us the chance to start living again. We leave at dusk."

Cybele finished her speech and hopped down from the table

"That was surprisingly impressive," I remarked.

Cybele smiled with a pained expression.

"It's been a long few years." Was all she said in response, before she reached out to Cordelia and moved to prepare for the journey.

Having nothing to pack up, and with Alira getting heavy in my arms, I sat down where I was and waited, watching Alira sleep and wondering what she was dreaming about, if she dreamed at all.

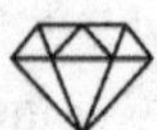

Dusk approached rapidly, and everyone had packed up the remnants of their lives, ready to begin the trek through the Calico Desert. At first, I'd wondered why Cybele had chosen dusk, figuring that starting at night would make things harder. But seeing the rubble scattered across the museum floor reminded me that we were at war. Sneaking out at night might at least give us some kind of advantage, assuming we could leave unnoticed by the painites. The chances of avoiding detection were slim, of course. There were only two places we could go, after all.

Staying in the museum tonight wasn't an option, anyway. The cool night air of the dunes and the open expanse of the desert were preferable to the layers of dust and bodies filling what was already a cramped living area. I was certain the nightmares would be bad enough without the added horror of sleeping next to corpses.

Before we left, I remembered the child spies of Akeldama that Alira had brought back from the arena. It struck me as odd that no one had mentioned them since. I left Alira to sleep and went to find Cordelia to ask about them. I found her busy helping some of the refugees and waited patiently for her to finish.

"Cordelia, about the spies that we brought back—the children…" I began.

Her eyes widened in realisation, a hint of panic setting in.

"With everything going on, I forgot about them," she said, voice tinged with alarm. She immediately started racing off toward the basement, continuing as she went.

"I left them thinking I'd return once they woke up and I heard their voices, but then the ceiling caved in, and I never heard from them."

Cordelia's panic was starting to rub off on me, but I reminded myself that Alira had used dream magic to knock them out. It was likely they were still stuck asleep.

Cordelia approached a blank patch of wall, where I could've sworn the training room had been before. She turned to me expectantly.

"We didn't exactly have any prison cells," she explained. "So Cybele put up a fake wall. If you have one of her crystals on you, you should be able to take it down."

"I don't, but I assume you do?" I said, unable to help but smile a little. Cordelia blushed subtly.

"I do actually, but I don't know why you'd assume that."

"Oh, just a hunch," I replied, flashing a somewhat cheeky smile. Cordelia turned a shade redder but gestured impatiently toward the wall.

I activated the red beryl, watching as the outline of the door appeared in a strange haze. I waved the haze away, swatting at it as though clearing mist. I focused on the shape of the entryway until the haze fully dissipated, revealing the training room once more. Cordelia rushed inside, and I disconnected from the red beryl, finding it too distracting to concentrate.

A small girl lay sleeping on the floor, but the boy was nowhere to be seen.

"I don't understand. I left all the lights on so he wouldn't be able to use his magic. How did he escape? And why did he wake up before the girl?" Cordelia questioned, her voice tinged with frustration.

I frowned, mulling over the possibilities.

"Well, dream magic does seem quite personal. It's likely that he was fighting it harder than she was and managed to wake himself up. He was deeply devoted to Akeldama—and full of rage when we caught him. The girl, on the other hand, only seemed to care about the boy."

"Where do you think he would have run off to, then? Back to Poenari?"

"No. He might've been a spy, but he wanted to fight. He probably ran straight to the battlefield, not understanding what he was in for."

"So, you think he's…" Cordelia trailed off, her voice sombre.

"Hopefully, he realised he wouldn't be able to make it up into the sky to fight. The question is whether he realised that before he got himself hurt—or killed."

Cordelia nodded solemnly.

"If the girl truly does care about the boy, then she'll fight us every step of the way to Muruntau if she thinks he's still alive out there. Even if we tell her he died, she might not believe us. She won't want to. I think, before we leave, you should scout out the cathedral—if it's safe—and confirm what happened to him. And if you do find him…well, we might have to let her see him to believe it."

It was a cruel suggestion, but she was right. If he was dead, showing her the truth might be the only way to make her believe us. And only then would she be open to trusting us. Still, it was going to be awful. There was already too much heartache going around. I didn't want to rush off to search for the boy's body, but that's exactly what this war had come to.

We informed Cybele of the situation, and I set out to search once dusk had fallen and the inhabitants of the museum had begun their trek toward Muruntau.

Before leaving the city, I connected to my amethyst—realising at some point that Alira had borrowed it from me—and checked on the girl's condition. I ensured she would stay asleep, but not detrimentally so.

With Cybele and Cordelia taking care of Alira and the red beryl girl, I slipped away silently to the base of the half-ruined cathedral, where the bodies of diamonds and painites lay scattered. I scanned the corpses, staying hidden from sight, and carefully made my way around the remnants of the airborne battlefield. I didn't find the boy's body among them.

Feeling a small sense of relief—despite knowing it would make managing the girl more challenging—I circled around to the other side of the cathedral where the tower had collapsed.

Optimism crept in as I considered the possibility that the boy might not have been as reckless as I had assumed. Perhaps he'd had the sense to avoid rushing into a battle he wasn't equipped to fight. That was, until I accidentally kicked something. A black desert boot.

Desert boots were almost always brown or tan—never black, as they'd get too hot. The only reason to own black boots like these was to better blend into the shadows.

I was walking close to what would have been directly under the walkway between the cathedral and its east wing—or, in other words, the part of the external cathedral where the shadows were deepest.

Shit.

I cut straight into the rubble, carefully stepping onto the stones, scanning for any sign of limbs or black clothing. If he was where I suspected, he'd be buried right at the bottom.

There had to be a better way to find him than moving all the stones by hand.

I opened my gauntlets and glanced over the gems, idly wondering why Alira had chosen to take only the amethyst. My gaze rested on the sapphire as I thought about its ability to see through things—to reveal the inner workings of objects. That wasn't exactly useful in this situation, but remembering how Cordelia had once stitched together pieces of leather with her yellow-sapphire magic gave me an idea.

It wasn't a great idea. In fact, it felt more than a little morbid. But it was all I had.

I connected to the sapphire magic, adjusting the harmonies to align with the yellow-sapphire properties. Thankfully, I had already created the preset—it was far better than attempting to configure it on the fly while dying, as I'd had to before.

The moment the harmonies sang and the magic started to flow, I felt the weight of the battlefield pressing down on me.

I could feel the bodies around me, their forms slowly transitioning from living organisms to granulated flesh. It was the creepiest sensation I had ever experienced.

Immediately, I shifted my focus inward, pulling my attention away from the battlefield and finding solace in the simple fact that my blood was still flowing. With a careful sigh, I expanded my reach slightly—just enough to sense whether there was a corpse buried under the rubble of the bridge as I walked along it.

I found one. It was right at the edge, but it felt too large. I could see his hairy shin, just his shin, nestled between a cracked stone and shards of stained glass. I kept moving, cautiously making my way toward the cathedral.

I froze when I felt it. The body of someone smaller than those I had passed before. Not as small as some of the women, but undoubtedly a small man.

Hope clung stubbornly to me as I began removing stones from above the body, telling myself his boot had been too far away for this to be him.

But explosions are powerful.

Evidently, the boy had been separated a significant distance from his boot by the blast, as this was definitely him

I disconnected from the sapphire magic immediately. It had done its job, and I could return to being blissfully unaware of the hidden bodies—except for the one right in front of me. Buried in rubble, his face and shoulder were now exposed. His hair was burnt, and patches of his skin were missing, but it was undoubtedly him.

I debated placing a stone over his face before I left, unsure whether it was better to leave him uncovered or not. In the end, I decided against it and instead closed the boy's eyes. It made him look the slightest bit more at peace. It wouldn't stop the girl from having nightmares when she saw him, but at least those bloodshot eyes wouldn't be burned into her memory.

I silently hoped she wouldn't insist on seeing proof when we told her. But knowing children—and imagining what this girl had endured, the lies likely told to her by adults before—I doubted she'd believe anything we said.

I scanned the cathedral one last time before retreating into the city, using the buildings as cover as I headed south to rejoin the entourage. The painites were nowhere to be seen, likely all on the world-ship, but I remained extra cautious nonetheless.

I stayed with the group for a few hours after I made it back, deciding the best time to wake the girl would be just before dawn. This way, we'd be as far from the city as possible, with enough time before daylight to fly back and see the boy before sunrise if it proved necessary.

I thought about that moment as I walked through the desert, dreading it. The urge to fly straight to Muruntau gnawed at me, but those who could cross the desert easily had already done so. The stragglers left behind weren't fighters, nor did they possess much magic. And for those who did, it wasn't anything that could make the journey easier. Cybele estimated it would take about four days of walking at the pace we'd set in the beginning, though that could vary significantly if we stopped more often than she anticipated.

Eventually, the sky started to lighten incrementally, and I knew it was time to wake the girl. I debated waking Alira too, but she remained in her own exhausted slumber. Her body would wake itself when it finished healing—or at least, I hoped it would. I nodded to Cybele when I'd decided it was time. She stopped beside me, having chosen to accompany us if we did end up needing to go back.

I wasn't sure I could handle it alone. Then again, I had raised Alira, so maybe I was underestimating myself—or maybe I just knew I wouldn't know what to say.

I stopped, and Cybele approached to help me slide the girl off my back, where she had been sleeping since I'd rejoined the entourage. As Cybele held her, I tapped into dream magic, hoping an unfamiliar face would feel more welcoming to the girl than one she already viewed as hostile.

Slowly, she began to wake. Her eyes blinked open, staring straight into Cybele's face. Wordlessly, she started to look around, but the panic visibly rose the moment her eyes landed on me. Her gaze darted more frantically, searching. It hurt to watch, knowing exactly who she was looking for.

"Where is he!?" she demanded, still searching. "What did you do to him!?" Her voice grew louder now, her eyes fixed on me, tears starting to well up.

"I didn't do anything to him," I said, trying to stay calm, though the weight of her accusation stung. I tried to create some distance between myself and Cybele, watching as the girl leaned into her instead, tears spilling freely now.

Cybele was surrounded by a subtle pink glow, her magic undoubtedly working to make her presence feel safe and comforting.

"He escaped from where we were keeping you both safe. Then he ran straight toward the battlefield. He…he died in the battle."

I barely managed to whisper the last part of my sentence. The girl's tears fell harder now, her voice raw and anguished.

"I don't believe you! He wouldn't leave me! He wouldn't!" she cried, clutching Cybele's shirt tightly.

"He knew he couldn't wake you up, so he did—he left without you to go fight," I said, trying to keep my voice as soft as I could.

"NO!" she screamed. "I will find him. I'm leaving now!" she announced, squirming in Cybele's arms until she dropped onto the sand. She froze, staring out at the horizon, the endless desert stretching in all directions. I let the moment sink in before speaking softly.

"We can take you to him. But you won't like what you see."

She glared at me, her eyes like daggers. But the hardness quickly melted away, replaced by a flicker of doubt.

"Fine," she said reluctantly, crossing her arms and clearly expecting me to start walking.

"It's too far to walk now, but I can fly us there."

Her eyes darted around before landing on me again. "How?" she questioned, her tone wary. I couldn't help but smile.

"Hold on to Cybele there, and I'll show you."

She looked at me sceptically, distrust written all over her face. But, after glancing at Cybele, she finally obliged. Red beryl magic truly had its uses. If only it wasn't so perplexing for those who didn't grow up with it.

"Hop up onto her back and hold on tight, or you might fall off," I said.

Her expression remained hard, her eyes still glassy with tears. Cybele helped her up, and the girl clung on tightly. With everything in place, I switched to the harmonies of the indicolite and slowly lifted the three of us off the ground. I was relieved we hadn't walked far from the city. Carrying two extra passengers for any considerable distance would have been extremely challenging, even though they were both fairly light.

As we took off, it took me a few minutes to re-calibrate for the added weight of the girl as Cybele and her tornado flew next to mine, but eventually I tuned it well enough to start speeding up and headed straight for the cathedral. The sky was already beginning to lighten as we arrived, but with all three of us possessing stealth magic of some kind, I felt fairly confident we'd be alright. We flew most of the way there, not encountering any painites on the journey.

I set us down right by the boy's body—close enough for the girl to see his face from where we landed, but far enough to give her privacy.

The moment she saw him, she ran over, recognising him instantly. Cybele and I stayed where we were, silently watching as the girl grieved. There was truly nothing to say.

The sun was peeking over the horizon by the time she was done. Her head hung low as she wandered back toward us, her face red and blotchy from crying.

She stopped near Cybele, who said nothing, only extending her hand toward the girl. The girl looked at it absently for a moment, before slowly raising her gaze to meet Cybele's.

Cybele smiled at her, this time without the faint red glow of her magic. Eventually, the girl silently reached out and took her hand, leaning her head against Cybele's arm.

She looked younger than I'd thought before. I'd assumed she was around ten, but seeing her now, she seemed younger—perhaps eight. The thought crossed my mind that maybe she had been using her magic to appear older, to seem more useful to Akeldama and to the boy she clearly regarded as her brother.

I felt certain that, in time, she would tell us her story. On some level, I suspected Cybele could already relate to her. They seemed to share some form of kinship. Cybele was unusually soft and understanding with the girl. I couldn't tell if it was simply because she was another red beryl, or if she saw something of herself reflected in her. Regardless, she was with us now.

I sighed in relief and nodded to Cybele, who gently picked the girl up and carried her on her back. Without another word, we lifted into the air and flew off silently, resuming our long journey to Muruntau.

36 – Alira

I thought I was dreaming when I first woke up—a random but handsome man was carrying me through the alien desert of a strange planet. But then I noticed my grandmother walking in front of us. That was when I decided I must be alive and awake—although utterly confused.

The man stopped when he noticed me looking around. Cordelia noticed him and stopped too, her face lighting up when she saw that I was awake.

"Alira! Thank goodness. I wasn't sure what to think when Bele and Ender brought you back asleep. They said they didn't know what had happened to you."

The man gently set me down and gave me a warm smile before blending back into the crowd we seemed to be in. I began piecing things together, my memories surprisingly clear. Maybe the adrenaline had made my mind work in overdrive, helping me hold onto everything? Nah, that explanation didn't quite feel right.

My body ached and was sore in places, but my mind felt sharp, perfectly clear—no headache, no lethargy, no fogginess. Nothing.

The disconnect between my mind and body felt strange—like one had been preserved, while the other had not.

As my hand brushed against my pocket, I felt something extraordinarily hard poking out. I reached inside, recalling the big purple gemstone I'd pocketed before I died. Wait—that's right. I had died.

But how could I remember being dead if I had been dead?

Choosing to set that mystery aside for now, I focused on the gemstone instead. My thoughts turned to the lightning crackling from a similar, but pink, gemstone Ayuna had picked up. It had seemed to brim with raw energy. But this one didn't.

It wasn't the battery powering the Proelium board, as Ayuna's likely had been, but something else entirely. A different component—one important enough to require a large gemstone like this.

But what was it?

With a sigh, realising I'd have to put that mystery aside too, I met Cordelia's gaze and asked her plainly, "So, uh…what are we doing in the middle of the desert?"

She grimaced, letting out a heavy sigh. "Well, the museum has been all but destroyed, as well as the cathedral. Akeldama has control of the world-ship, and we're walking all the way to Muruntau to seek asylum."

It sounded like a lot had happened while I was on the world-ship. And not in a good way. Dad and I had both lost.

"Where is Dad and Cybele?"

"They'll catch up shortly. The red beryl girl understandably didn't want to believe that her brother had died, so they had to show her the truth before she made any rash decisions."

I had totally forgotten about the child spies.

"By her brother you mean the onyx boy? How did he die?" I asked, not sure I wanted to know the answer.

"He escaped and ran towards the fight at the cathedral, but got crushed by the debris when the east-wing fell." She responded solemnly.

"Oh." was all I could manage in response. We walked quietly then for a moment, before Cordelia seemed to remember that I hadn't said anything about what had happened to me.

"I'm so glad you're alive" she said of nowhere, stopping to pull me into a hug. She pulled back, staring into my eyes intensely.

"What happened to you my dear? And why did you have to be so reckless?" She asked sternly. I opened my mouth to respond but caught a glimpse of a familiar torpedo or two shooting through the sky out of the corner of my eye.

I smiled, looking up at Cybele and Dad as they approached, only noticing the girl riding on Cybele's back once they got a bit closer.

"I'll tell you everything, but it's a lot to get through, so let's wait for the others."

"Very well. I suppose we could all use a break from reliving the past day for a few hours anyway," Cordelia replied.

We waited for Dad. When he landed, he spotted me immediately and awkwardly ran through the sand in those ridiculous desert boots.

"You're up already?" he said excitedly, pulling me into a hug.

When he finally let go, he paused before declaring, "You're grounded. That was waaay too dangerous and stupid."

I scoffed, smiling at the absurdity of such an earthly punishment that made no sense here—especially given that I had no friends or bedroom or anything.

"Says you. Like running into a deathmatch to grab a staff wasn't dangerous and stupid," I shot back.

He faltered, apparently having forgotten that little stunt.

"Even so, how was I supposed to know he had found a way to see through our magic? Besides…" He trailed off, biting his tongue and leaving his sentence unfinished.

I had a few good guesses about what he chose not to say.

Deciding to change the subject, I asked, "So what now? Are we just moving to Muruntau, or are we still going to figure out Cybele's telescope—or what?"

He blinked at me absently a few times before seeming to remember himself.

"Oh, right. Yes, we're going to Muruntau and hopefully starting to make a proper plan for how to take back the city and the world-ship. Akeldama's attack was a bit out of the blue, but once we rally Navoi, Teth, and Brigitte together, I'm sure we'll come up with something airtight. Until then, yes, we still need the telescope. Cybele grabbed everything she could before we left—everything she could carry, anyway. We'll have to rebuild some of the things she'd hoped to salvage, but that should be easy enough if Navoi's workshop is as impressive as his house."

The mention of Teth reminded me of her yacharow that I'd left at the museum.

"Wait, what about my yacharow? You brought it, right?"

Dad chuckled. "Of course. How could we forget something like that? It's more than just your yacharow, you know."

"I know. Which is why I think I have an idea."

Dad frowned but started scanning the crowd anyway, finding the man who had been carrying me and waving him over. Sure enough, my yacharow—and some of my other things—was strapped to his back.

"Thanks, Bill," Dad said to the man as he handed my stuff back and wandered off into the crowd again. He slung my bag over his shoulder and handed me the yacharow. I almost protested, about to say that I could carry my own stuff, but it still hurt to breath and I hated the thought of walking for much longer, let alone with a bag weighing me down. I took the yacharow gratefully, thinking about how best to approach this while we continued moving.

"Sorry, but can we stop for a minute?" I asked.

"We can stop for as long as you need. We can always catch up with air magic anyway," Dad replied.

I hesitated. "And how long exactly is it going to take to get to Muruntau on foot?"

"About four days, according to Cybele."

What. No way. I was just going to nap here for three days straight and then fly there and meet them at the gates. Dad saw me groan.

"Not everyone can fly, Ali. But we will send a party ahead to inform Navoi about what's happened in the city and let him know about our group on the way. We thought it was better to wait until his own spies confirmed our story first, so he wouldn't imprison us like last time."

"Fine. Whatever," I muttered, the initial shock of the long trek fading as I turned my attention to the yacharow. If this worked the way I hoped it would, it would be so cool.

I sank onto the ground, my legs already stiff and tired. My mind, however, was as sharp as ever, allowing me to picture exactly what I wanted to create. Activating sand magic, I used it to cradle the yacharow with gentle, sandy hands. Despite the ache in my body, I controlled my breathing with precision, focusing on shaping thin blades within the sand to carefully chop up the yacharow. I'd have to ask Teth for forgiveness later. But when she saw what I was creating, I was confident she'd understand.

With the yacharow now in five separate pieces, I removed the second and fourth pieces from the cloud of sand. Dad's expression was sceptical, his eyebrows raised as he saw what I'd done to the legendary weapon. He didn't say anything, though, and continued to watch silently.

Initially, I'd planned to fill the gaps in the yacharow with ordinary sand, or perhaps some kind of metal if we happened to find some during our journey. But as I connected to the sand magic, I noticed something else—the strange, silvery sand created when the Proelium board had exploded.

It was everywhere.

I hadn't noticed it before, likely due to how uncomfortable I already was, but I was covered in it. It clung to my hair, my clothes, my shoes. A suspicious amount had even collected at the back of my underwear, which I could only guess was from my wings and tail turning to sand and falling down my back.

Dad's expression grew wider as he watched the silvery sand start to float off me from every crevice. The flow made my hair and clothes ripple dramatically as I focused on the cloud of sand and yacharow pieces in front of me.

I added the silver sand to the ends of the three remaining pieces, reassembling them into a regular yacharow—but one I could now control adeptly with sand magic.

I imagined transforming the yacharow into two handheld hatchets or anything else I might need, pushing the silver sand to the arrow-like end to instead form a blade. I hoped my choice of sand would make for some cool techniques once I began practising with it.

The cloud of sand fell away as I stood back up, the new yacharow landing gently in my hands.

Dad had a small smile as he admired it, though I felt a demonstration was necessary. Using sand magic, I broke the yacharow apart again and moved the pieces to my back. The three sections now sat neatly side-by-side, rather than a single long stick awkwardly poking up into the air.

I took a step back and held out my arm, using the silver sand to push one end of the yacharow into my hand. The sand solidified slightly, allowing me to pull the rest of the weapon off my back like an unwieldy rope.

With a flick of my wrist, I whipped the yacharow around. The silver sand re-condensed fully, forming the complete weapon in my grasp.

It seemed I didn't need to connect the sand to the ground with this particular weapon. It behaved as though I'd set anchor points at the ends of the sticks. It reminded me of a ferrofluid demonstration I'd seen at a museum on Earth once. They'd used electromagnets to manipulate the ferrofluid into mesmerising kinetic sculptures.

With a huge grin, I manipulated the pole into pieces connected by my silvery mist once again. I shifted the middle piece—the one containing the tail-key component—to the centre of my back, where it would rest as I walked.

Now holding the two pointy ends of the yacharow in each hand, I watched Dad's expression closely as I pushed the silver sand over the spear tips, reforming them into small hatchets.

I threw one as hard as I could, pulling it back mid-air with sand magic. A thin silver line stretched between me and the axe's handle.

What I wasn't prepared for, however, was the sheer force with which it came back at me. I flinched, yanking my arm back with a quiet yelp as the axe flew past me, dangerously close to taking my arm off, before embedding itself in the sand.

Dad's eyebrows were still raised, but his expression had shifted significantly.

I sighed. My coolness was officially ruined.

Dad chuckled softly. "That's certainly impressive. But with deadlier weapons obviously comes a higher risk of hurting yourself. So please, start small—or you might not be quick enough to dodge next time."

He seemed surprisingly calm for a dad who'd just watched his daughter almost maim themselves. I frowned at him. Then again, he had just watched me die. I supposed a self-inflicted maiming, with a healer close by, wasn't as big of a deal. Still, this would be so worth it if I got good. And I was going to get good. I had four days with nothing else to do but practise, after all.

We stopped for a few hours around midday to let everyone rest. I wondered if Dad or Cordelia might ask me again about what had happened on the world-ship, but they both seemed too emotionally drained. As a result, I didn't end up recounting my tale until we made camp for the night.

We stopped quite early, well before sundown, since everyone had been walking through the night. It was still light out, but we were sitting in a circle around a tiny tornado that Dad and I were working together to maintain.

It was the complete opposite of a traditional campfire, but as I began to recount the events, it started to feel just like a fireside story. Explaining certain moments was a little tricky without outright admitting that I'd used blood magic. It had been a constant factor in my survival—and ultimately, it had saved me from dying at least once.

I explained how I found Ayuna right at the teleporter to the parliamentarian trials, chased her inside, and ended up in a broken game of Proelium that was trying to accommodate two players. Not just two people, though, but two people from entirely different worlds—worlds whose cultures, ideals, and knowledge clashed on every level.

The glitching was almost impossible to describe, and as I tried, it became clear that Dad was the only one who had even the faintest idea what I was talking about. It wasn't until I reached the part where I died that I pulled out the purple crystal, using it to explain what Ayuna had done with hers.

I paused, holding the large gemstone in my hands, silently hoping someone—anyone—might know what it was. As the silence stretched on, I continued, but I realised there wasn't much left to say that they didn't already know.

Cybele was the first to speak. Whether her interjection was motivated by a desire to turn the conversation into something productive, or simply by her intense curiosity about the large gemstone sitting in my lap, I couldn't say. Knowing her, though, the latter seemed much more likely.

"That must have been the energy source Kaiya was describing. They said it felt like a constant lightning storm but small enough to fit in the palm of a hand. They also mentioned that it didn't feel tied to any one particular type of magic. Alira, you said that when the board turned to dust, the stones were the only other things left, aside from the silver sand?"

"I'm pretty sure, yeah," I replied.

Cybele paused, deep in thought.

"Proelium boards require a few different types of magic to create, but they don't usually need power sources. Their scale is small enough to draw ambient magic and use it as intended by their creators. Only master sapphires are able to craft devices capable of this, though the initialisation of such a device still requires other types of magic. But creating a board this large and complex—not to mention sentient—would've required batteries, like the two Ayuna and Alira found. These gemstones would generate or store enough magic to sustain such a game. It's possible that the gemstones slowly draw in ambient magic over time, much like smaller games.

However, it's equally likely that they were created with an immense amount of energy that simply hasn't run out yet—or both."

I frowned, trying to process everything Cybele had just thrown at me.

"So, what are the different magics normal Proelium boards use then?" I asked.

"That depends on the craftsman and their team," she replied.

"That being said, a typical board might include ice magic, sand magic—which is more common nowadays—fire magic, and healing magic. Since the pearls lost their healing magic, a few boards have been crafted with magic like Del's. Some of the more interesting ones, however, have incorporated rhodonite magic. There aren't many of those, but some unsavoury groups have employed onyx magic in the past to create their boards. While most people aren't fans of those groups themselves, they undeniably create some amazing boards."

Cybele sat frozen, only her mouth moving, staring intently at the gemstone.

"There has to be some sort of connection," she continued, "We need Kaiya."

Her intense gaze whipped around to Dad.

"We need Kaiya to examine Alira's stone. If we can at least determine what two of them do, I should be able to figure out how many there might be—and the kinds of energy they're all harbouring. With any luck, one of them will be directly linked to healing magic, like the old boards used to be. And if we're even luckier, that might be the one we have. That could actually explain Alira's apparent revival."

Cybele was staring off into space now, her thoughts spiralling as she started mumbling to herself.

Cordelia reached out to stroke her back, gently drawing her attention and bringing her mind back earth—or whatever this place was called.

"That would be super convenient," I started, "But isn't this pearl-water I've heard so much about supposed to provide full healing? As in fixing sore limbs, making it easier to breathe, et cetera?"

"Yes, it is," Dad interrupted, "So, before anyone jumps to conclusions, we'll find Kaiya and Brigitte in the morning, then proceed to Muruntau—hopefully with more insight into these gemstones and the additional power the Painites have acquired," He finished, directing his gaze at Cybele while he spoke. He looked visibly pained.

I hadn't thought about it much until now, but if Cybele was right, there were probably at least four stones. That meant the Painites had at least three times more than we did. And they had the lightning one. Not that I was complaining—if this purple stone had somehow revived me or kept me from fully dying, I wasn't going to argue.

The answers to all these questions felt impossibly far away, postponed until tomorrow. To distract myself, I practised with my new weapon, letting my mind race over techniques, magic, and the mysteries of the strange rocks. I didn't stop until exhaustion finally overtook me and my exhausted body finally forced my mind to rest.

37 – Ender

I hadn't expected to hear from Alira that she and Ayuna had somehow broken the entire Proelium trial on the world-ship.

The 'glitching,' as Alira had described it, sounded weird enough on its own. The part where she described the creature made entirely of legs felt like an exaggeration, but reducing the board to dust and leaving nothing behind except insanely powerful crystal batteries? I wouldn't have believed her if I hadn't heard Kaiya describe one of those crystals before Alira pulled one from her pocket.

Everything was suddenly much more complicated—and, surprise surprise, it turned out we were at an even bigger disadvantage than I'd thought. Not only did the Painites now have half of the tail-key, the world-ship, and The City, but they also had a super-powered lightning battery and probably the rest of the board's power sources, except for one.

We had a single stone. And we couldn't even figure out what it did.

I was hoping our trip to find Kaiya and Brigitte this morning would at least provide some reassurance. But, the way things were going, it seemed highly probable that we'd find them only for them to tell us Alira had picked up an empty battery. It was pointless speculating before we had answers, though.

I was flying to the city now with Alira, leaving the other two behind to care for the refugees and the young red beryl girl. Cybele had gladly adopted the role of looking after her—not that she had much choice, given how the girl had started hovering around her incessantly.

We later learned her name was Lola. She had been abandoned by her parents and had met the onyx boy on the streets. From that point onward, the two became inseparable, even when the boy dragged her to Poenari after witnessing Akeldama in the arena.

It was a slow transformation, but it almost seemed like Lola was ageing backwards—gradually letting go of the subconscious veil she'd been casting over herself, the one that made her look stronger and older than she actually was. I was relieved that at least one good thing had come out of all of this. Hopefully, another would follow, but that depended on what Kaiya would say.

As we flew over the city, we weren't entirely sure where to go or how far Kaiya's magic sense might reach. I felt confident, though, that they'd come to us when they sensed the presence of two alexandrites with a big crystal. All we had to do was wait somewhere they'd find us.

While deciding where to land, Alira swooped closer, yelling over the wind, "I think I know where they are."

I frowned, wondering how the hell she could know that. But she *was* holding a mysterious stone, so I chose to set my disbelief aside and nodded, following her as she descended into the heart of the city.

We landed somewhere in the inner city, just north of the central spires but still south of the remnants of the cathedral. Alira touched down on an empty street, heading straight for the overly lavish entrance of a massive hotel.

I had never been this close to the heart of the inner city before. It felt strange to see it so deserted, but even stranger to watch Alira walk with such purpose into such a frankly intimidating building. Despite her determination, her head was still on a swivel, taking in everything as she approached the hotel. I followed her, still baffled about how she knew they were here—and why, of all places, here.

When we entered the lobby, I was surprised to see someone there. A lone man, covered from head to toe in green emeralds, stood behind a desk like a receptionist. He looked equally surprised to see us. His frown deepened as he mouthed silent words while we approached, but when we reached him, he spoke bluntly.

"Um… welcome. Why are you here?"

He looked just as confused as to why we were here as I did. Alira spoke up, unfazed by any of the strangeness.

"We're here to see Brigitte and Kaiya. They should be somewhere around the fifteenth floor? Maybe the twentieth."

His eyes narrowed suspiciously. "And who might you two be, demanding the presence of such high-status individuals, both of whom are unlikely to be here at a time like this?"

He questioned us sternly, only to look immediately foolish as both Brigitte and Kaiya appeared from around the corner. Brigitte greeted us with a warm smile. The man stepped back, bowing his head, his face noticeably redder.

"I'm surprised to find you two here. When Kaiya notified me, I thought it was impossible. But it sounds like you've stumbled onto something interesting—something that may have helped you track us down?"

Alira and I both nodded.

"How fortuitous. Come, this way. Before Kaiya starts drooling," Brigitte teased.

Kaiya shot her an offended look, which only earned a smug smile from Brigitte. I don't think I'd ever seen Brigitte smile before. This day was certainly becoming stranger by the minute. Brigitte did seem more relaxed, though. Perhaps being essentially dethroned had given her some much-needed time off. Or maybe this place was some sort of fancy spa. That would explain a couple of things.

We followed Brigitte around the corner into an even more dazzling second lobby. It was filled with expensive-looking lounges, floating fireplaces, and a central bar that seemed to defy physics, supported only by a cyclical waterfall flowing endlessly around and around beneath a thick marble slab. Brigitte, however, headed straight for something that resembled a doorless elevator, walking confidently into it. The back of the box looked like a large screen of some kind.

When the last of us stepped inside, the doors didn't exactly close behind us, but the view of the second lobby began to shift—mirroring the screen in front of us.

In what felt like two seconds, Brigitte continued walking forward, stepping through what I had assumed was a screen and into a lavish condo. It was fitted out in a style similar to the lobby, but with an even more extravagant touch—diamonds studded the seams of much of the furniture.

As I stepped out of the elevator, I whipped around, realising the lobby had transformed into the same abstract image that had been displayed on the screen just moments before.

"What just happened? That wasn't a teleporter, was it?" I asked, my voice tinged with disbelief.

"No, not quite," Brigitte replied. "Teleporters use up too much space and get too complicated with as many rooms as this place has. It's more like a box that moves really quickly, but with acceleration and gravity corrections, so you don't feel it—plus a temporal bubble to remove the lag time when moving from room to room."

So, more like a really fast elevator. Warp speed, even. Seemed like a waste for an elevator, but then again, this was a fancy skyscraper on a magical alien planet. Why not wrap your elevators in warp bubbles so you don't have to stand around waiting?

I nodded along, conceptually understanding it, while internally marvelling at how ridiculous it all seemed. That's when I noticed Kaiya getting fidgety, hiding their hands behind their back. The movement was impulsive, but still glaringly obvious. Brigitte picked up on it soon after.

"Right. Alira, I assume you have something to show us," Brigitte said.

Alira grinned as she pulled the purple stone from her pocket.

"I had no idea what this thing did this morning. But after connecting with Kaiya a moment ago, I think I'm starting to understand it."

This revelation shocked me. I stared at her, wondering when she'd had the time to figure it out—and how she was always so quick with things like this. I thought back to her leading us down here from the sky and realised she might've been using something akin to magic sense to locate Kaiya. Maybe that connection had allowed for some kind of crude magical communication between the two. Kaiya spoke up next.

"This isn't like the one Ayuna had. Hers was bursting with energy—so much power that it was almost blinding. But this one… I didn't even notice it at first, even though it was right in Alira's pocket. Focusing on it now, however, it feels just as strange. Perhaps even more so."

Kaiya paused briefly, awkwardly shifting before holding out a hand toward Alira.

"Um, may I?"

Alira smiled and placed the stone into the outstretched palm. Kaiya's eyes lit up with curiosity.

"It's like the other one in that it doesn't feel tied to any one type of magic. But I can sense a small part of myself within it—like the very act of searching it is being reflected back at me. But the reflection isn't entirely of me. It feels like something of Alira is embedded in it, as though she's left her impression on it. It's hard to describe in much more detail, but that's just what's on the surface. Beneath that, there are layers—layers I can feel but can't seem to decipher."

One mystery after another—and still nothing we could use to our advantage. I sighed. This sounded like it was going to take time— yet another project among many, all aiming to create something useful in our fight against Akeldama. If this one was going to take longer than I'd hoped, I might as well focus on advancing some of the others too.

"In that case, we're headed to Muruntau to gather forces and devise a plan for defeating Akeldama. If you were to join us, you could help Alira figure out how to unlock this thing. And Brigitte, your counsel and influence in rallying the people we need would be invaluable. I get the impression that Teth and Navoi are going to be difficult to handle once they're in the same room together."

Kaiya looked visibly excited but tried to suppress it, nodding shallowly and rapidly. Brigitte, on the other hand, looked more surprised.

"You've managed to convince Navoi and Teth to form an alliance, have you?"

"A tenuous one," I admitted, "after the direct attacks on both their cities. However, Navoi has quite a temper, and we haven't yet informed him of our failure here. The promise of your aid and a potential secret weapon might be just what we need to smooth things over when we return."

Brigitte nodded but seemed tired, sighing heavily.

"I can't do much from in here, and I seem to have lost whatever power I had here. Perhaps it's time for a change of scenery. I've always been curious about the new cities, but I've never had the chance to visit."

I smiled. "Well, now's your chance."

Her melancholic smile was paired with a soft, "Yes, quite."

After pausing briefly to gather her thoughts, Brigitte continued. "We will meet you downstairs in a few moments."

She glanced at Kaiya, who was still mesmerised by the purple crystal.

"I hope teaching Kaiya to fly won't be too much of an issue?"

Kaiya glanced up, the realisation dawning. They looked less than thrilled. Alira, however, piped up cheerfully.

"No problem at all!"

Kaiya gave a weak smile, though their face had noticeably paled in the last few seconds.

"Right. See you soon then," I said, starting back toward the elevator. I stopped and turned back to Brigitte.

"How, uh… do I operate this thing?" I asked.

"Dream magic skims your conscious mind. Just picture the lobby as you walk through," she explained.

The concept was a bit unnerving, but I decided it wasn't a big deal. I turned back to the elevator, picturing the lavish lobby and waterfall bar as I stepped through. Sure enough, the image became real in two seconds flat, and before long, Alira and I were taking advantage of the what felt like impossibly soft lounges after sleeping on the bare minimum for weeks. Our lounging was cut disappointingly short when Kaiya and Brigitte appeared downstairs mere minutes later. Hearing them enter, Alira groaned in protest, sinking even further into the lounge. Her muffled voice spoke through the cushions.

"Dad, if you take Kaiya, can I bring this lounge?"

I chuckled. "I'm sure we'll get better accommodations in Muruntau than last time. You've seen a bit of the city—I'm sure the lounges there will be just as soft as these."

Alira lifted her head with a strange expression on her face. I couldn't tell if she was flushed from laying down or for some other reason. Regardless, Brigitte and Kaiya were now standing over us, observing the interaction. Alira had clearly noticed as well, and she begrudgingly hopped up off the couch, making her way back toward the entrance.

The emerald man watched us silently as our entourage strode past, too polite to sate his curiousity. Once outside, Alira began explaining to Kaiya how to fly. The space between the buildings was tight for practice, but I wasn't too worried about causing a bit of a scene. It had become increasingly clear that the Painites had no intention of occupying the cathedral or policing the city. With no parliament and too few diamonds left, they didn't really need to.

Kaiya was unsteady at first as Alira gently lifted them off the ground. The wind was as soft as possible while still being able to make someone hover.

Eventually, Kaiya seemed to realise that, as long as they stayed still, Alira could do most of the work—moving them carefully through the air.

Once we had figured that much out, we finally set off. It was slow-going at first, with no doubt hundreds of upper-gems hiding away in their towers, watching the four of us steadily ascend out of the city. The High Priestess, her assistant, and two randoms who looked like indicolites.

From their perspective, this must have been a strange sight—something the emerald man's lingering curiosity had already confirmed.

Eventually, we picked up the pace as we left The City and Kaiya grew more stable. Though we didn't move particularly fast, watching Brigitte fly was entertainment enough to make the journey interesting. I'd never seen a diamond fly like this before. I'd witnessed Mellory descend into the arena, full of wrath and thunder, but this was something else entirely—quick, light, and effortless.

It was as though Brigitte was discharging herself along with the lightning, leaping from one tiny cloud to the next in a zig-zag pattern. The effect made her look almost blurry, her flowing white robes lighting up with energy each time, like an exuberant little cloud darting across the sky.

Brigitte seemed as though she could keep going forever, but unfortunately, Alira and I had our limits. Our indicolites looked like they'd reach theirs before we made it back to the entourage. We could have made it if we'd been moving faster, but Kaiya hadn't yet built confidence in their flying. They stuck rigidly to the staying-still-and-letting-Alira-do-the-work technique.

We had to stop briefly before continuing to the entourage, but before long, we were back on track. The entire group paused to stare at us as we approached, though Brigitte's entrance was far more dazzling than ours. From the ground, I was sure it would've been impossible to ignore—brief flashes of lightning streaking across the watercolour sky, each discharge tinged with a different colour as it passed through a new patch of sky.

It was perhaps the closest thing I'd seen to fireworks on this planet, and it was truly something to behold—even in the middle of the day.

38 – Alira

Walking to Muruntau took *foreverrr*, but we eventually made it. The walls seemed bigger than the last time I'd been here. Maybe they were preparing for a potential siege by Akeldama as well. At the very least, it was a sign they'd already heard about the fate of the city—and hopefully, what we had to say wouldn't get anyone shot in the foot. Not that a single soldier in Muruntau could take me on now.

Over the past three days trekking through the desert, I'd spent almost all my time practising with my new weapon. I cycled between traditional Telesto techniques, Earth-based combat styles, and a few things I'd made up myself. Dad gave me guidance along the way, watching me closely during practice. I assumed he was already connected to the surgeon magic of yellow sapphires, just in case I maimed myself. Which was fair—there had been a few close calls. Swinging an axe around on the end of a magical rope wasn't exactly easy to master.

On the last day, I was feeling confident enough to even challenge Dad. He agreed, crafting a staff out of the sand as we passed over a patch of basalt. It turned out to be a decent enough staff that Dad kept it for the rest of the journey to Muruntau.

Our sparring revealed a major flaw in my weapon. The silvery sand wasn't immune to hits—and because it was so thinly stretched, throwing my spear-tips or hatchets too far left the connection vulnerable. Anything could strike the sand string and break it.

I would either have to keep the weapons closer when throwing them or actively bend the sand around incoming strikes to protect the connection. It was a weakness I'd need to either hide as best I could—or overcome quickly with mastery.

Regardless, we were finally here, and I was aching for a real bed. Or even a nice lounge. Everything felt so much worse after experiencing the comfort of the hotel furniture. A random patch of foam sand just couldn't compare—and we only stumbled across those on the best of days. It was finally time for proper furniture.

As our entourage approached Muruntau's gate, the usual smattering of guards lined the entrance and walls. Among them were two familiar figures, seemingly waiting for us—the large grey man called Gordo, and Bueller, who had previously led Cybele to her workshop.

I felt a pang of unease as we drew closer to Muruntau, the memory of last time and being wrangled by the towering grey man still lingering at the back of my mind.

But Dad was here this time. So were Cybele, Cordelia, Brigitte, and Kaiya. I had nothing to fear.

Bueller offered us a simple welcome as we approached the gate, motioning for us to follow him. Everyone complied, filing through the gate, while many of the refugees stared wide-eyed at everything around them, gasping and startled by the crowds.

I relaxed a little as we finally passed through the front gates. Not that I'd ever had anything to truly worry about. Dad had flown ahead, after all, to inform Navoi of our arrival and to make sure everything went as smoothly as possible—especially with such a large and fragile group. He'd even offered for me to accompany him, but the thought of heading to Muruntau without everyone else left me feeling uneasy. So I'd stayed behind with Cybele, Cordelia, and the rest of the group.

As we descended through the city, passing by level six, I found myself thinking about Max—and whether he'd had any more success with his glass-making.

It felt strange thinking about him. I'd only met him briefly, but somehow, he knew things about me I hadn't even told Dad or anyone else. Chantrell might've figured out I'd used painite magic once, but she didn't understand it.

Max did. And he'd helped me with it.

It wasn't until we reached level ten that I realised just how much time I'd spent thinking about that night. I forced myself to stop it as we approached the eccentric, magical beach house that Navoi seemed to inhabit.

Bueller stopped just before we arrived, redirecting the refugees to their temporary accommodations. The remaining six of us, plus Lola—who stubbornly refused to leave Cybele's side—followed Gordo inside to meet Navoi once more.

I was half-expecting to be led back through the brick passageways to Navoi's little throne room, or whatever you'd call it. Instead, we ended up in a slightly larger room. It was similar in style to the throne room, but this space had small windows running around the top of the walls, flooding the room with natural light. Thin trails of fire still lit up the walls, but their impact was softened by the sunlight streaming in.

Navoi sat at the head of a large stone table that almost looked like wood. The browns running through it formed wide, natural stripes, giving the illusion of old hardwood timber.

The moment we entered, Navoi stood, his arms raised in welcome.

"Ender Herman has returned once more," he announced jovially, before his tone darkened. "But without my staff as promised. I admit the events you described to me were troubling and unexpected. But know that I will be holding onto your piece of the key until you fulfil our deal," Navoi said, sitting back down as the rest of us reached the table, each selecting a seat.

I didn't particularly want to sit so close to Navoi, but I did want to sit by Dad—and of course, he had to take the seat next to Navoi, across from Brigitte, who had chosen the seat on his other side.

"And of course you've brought High Priestess Brigitte Tahtinen with you, as promised," Navoi said as Brigitte settled into her seat.

"Your city is much grander than I had imagined. I thank you for your generous accommodations," Brigitte replied smoothly, bowing her head slightly.

Navoi smiled faintly in response. "If that's what it takes to rid the world of that bastard, then it's my pleasure."

Navoi's attention shifted back to Dad.

"Ender, your last visit was brief, and you left me with more questions than answers. My own spies have not seen the front lines as you have, but I do understand the severity of our situation. So the question now is—what are we going to do about it?"

For a moment, the table was silent.

Dad started to speak but stopped abruptly as Navoi's gaze fell on Lola. His focus lingered long enough to reveal that he had realised who she must be.

Navoi's slitted eyes narrowed, his expression turning predatory. Dad reacted quickly, speaking up to diffuse the tension and explain things.

"The girl isn't a threat, I promise," Dad said. "It's true she was one of the thieves who stole your staff, but only because the other thief was like a brother to her. Akeldama manipulated them both to get what he wanted."

Navoi seemed unconvinced but made a conscious effort to focus on Dad rather than the girl.

"And what of the boy, then?"

"He died in the battle."

"I see." Navoi scoffed, his tone sharp. "You have too much empathy for thieves—but I'll allow it."

Dad sighed in relief as Lola clung tightly to Cybele, staring at Navoi with wide-eyed fright. The table fell silent once again.

Dad sighed a second time before speaking up.

"Perhaps we should all get some rest first. The journey was long, and everyone's a bit tense. If we wait for Teth to arrive and reconvene tomorrow, ideas might flow more smoothly."

Navoi appeared displeased by the suggestion but scanned the faces around the table, clearly noting the weariness.

"Very well," he said reluctantly. "But before I let you go, at least lay out the situation in full so I can think on it."

"Of course. At present, we have two pieces of the tail-key, and so does Akeldama. He doesn't yet know how to use the key, but it won't take him long to figure out where it goes and what it does, now that he has full control of the world-ship. Currently, we have no access whatsoever to the world-ship. The cathedral's backdoor was destroyed, and Akeldama burned off my parliamentarian tattoo."

Dad held up his arm, revealing the burn marks cutting wavy lines through the blue and purple ink.

"Furthermore, while Alira passed the trials, she didn't manage to get a tattoo, which means we have no way in. We do, however, have some kind of purple crystal that appears to store specific types of magic—but we're still working out how to use it. Meanwhile, Akeldama and Ayuna have the remaining crystals found in the wreckage of the Proelium board after Alira and Ayuna's combined game-trial. They have already discovered how to use one of these stones and it contains an insane amount of raw energy, and they're adept at wielding it."

Navoi's throat rumbled deeply. "So, in other words, we are at a severe disadvantage."

He paused thoughtfully. "Do we have a team working to utilise this purple crystal?"

"Yes. Alira and Kaiya are focusing on that, and I believe Cybele and Cordelia have brought research from Cybele's original telescope for them to advance on that front."

"Excellent. At least we have direction. I command you all to work tirelessly on your respective projects until tomorrow, when we reconvene. It would benefit us all to bring as much progress as possible to the next meeting—and perhaps Teth might prove useful when she arrives. Dismissed."

Navoi was commanding and militaristic, but despite automatically taking charge, Dad seemed to hold somewhat equal footing with him. Maybe a bit of militaristic discipline was exactly what we needed to figure this out before Akeldama made his next move. I had no doubt Cybele would use this as an excuse to forgo sleep tonight—which meant Kaiya and I would have to push ourselves too.

We left the room, once again escorted by Bueller, stepping out into the green fields of the tenth level. Outside we found cabins dotting the landscape, each purposefully simple and far smaller than Navoi's elaborate castle.

Bueller explained that two cabins had been arranged for us: one for Ender and the other for Brigitte. It was no surprise that Navoi had only considered the rest of us extensions of the two people he actually respected, but I wasn't about to complain if it meant Navoi wouldn't subject me to the same intense scrutiny those golden eyes had inflicted on Lola. No doubt she'd be clinging to Cybele even tighter now that she knew he was nearby.

The five of us made our way over to our cabin while Brigitte and Kaiya entered theirs. I kept calling it a 'cabin,' but really, it was quite big. It only seemed small when compared to Navoi's mansion.

The scale difference became immediately apparent when we opened the door and descended a few stairs into the main space, the building partially buried in the ground.

I rolled my eyes. The size difference was already dramatic enough—did he really have to half-bury the cabins while putting his own on a pedestal? What a drama queen.

We descended into the space, which, despite its simple exterior, was still awfully luxurious. Maybe it was because it was partially buried, but the interior felt far larger than it had looked from the outside. And this was just the living room.

Unless Navoi—or whoever was actually managing this place, since it seemed unlikely someone like Navoi would bother personally—had miscalculated our numbers, there were at least four bedrooms hidden in here somewhere.

I didn't have to look far. Unlike Navoi's mansion, with all its twists and turns, hiding everything around endless corners and avoiding doors for some inexplicable reason, this place was entirely open. The living room was spacious enough that every other room branched directly off it. And there were still no doors.

The disappointing lack of privacy hit me instantly—like the sinking feeling of walking into a hotel room with no doors. But the discomfort faded quickly as remembered that this wasn't Earth. And this was a huge step up from the assortment of floor mattresses, steel bunks, and sandstone slabs I'd been sleeping on so far.

The next thing I noticed about the rooms—visible only through the open doorways—were the colours. Two rooms were decorated with iridescent green sheets and pillows, one with soft crimson accents, and another with pale yellow. The iridescent green sheets shimmered with fleeting flecks of purple as the light shifted across them. Somehow, they'd managed to match the sheets to our gemstones.

Although, it seemed they'd overlooked the fact that we had two red-beryls in our group. Maybe Dad hadn't told them about Lola beforehand, so they hadn't prepared a room for her.

It didn't really matter—if Cybele was staying in Cordelia's room anyway, it all worked out.

I turned back toward the living room, about to make a comment about the fancy linen, but a small lavender-coloured lump above the doorway caught my eye. I had a hunch about what was going on now.

Pointing to the lump, I said, "Cybele, is that what I think it is?"

Cybele glanced at it. "I don't know what you think it is, but it's an amethyst-powered device that skims your consciousness. They're usually used in the city for elevators."

"Exactly what I thought," I replied with a smug grin.

Everyone stared at me, surprised. Dad was the first to chuckle and shake his head.

"You're right—there was one above the elevator at Brigitte's place. But there's no elevator here…right?"

Dad started scanning the room, suddenly sceptical of his surroundings.

I chuckled. "No, I think they've just skimmed for our gemstones. They've somehow magically decorated our rooms in our gemstone colours. Although, Cybele and Cordelia's room is only pale yellow."

Cordelia half-rolled her eyes before turning expectantly to Cybele. Cybele blushed, clearly caught out.

"I suppose that's because, when it scanned us, it realised I had no intention of sleeping here tonight."

"Cybele, you can't sleep in the workshop," Cordelia said plainly.

"I know. I don't plan to sleep," Cybele replied.

Cordelia shook her head, as if already tired of this familiar argument. She glanced at the lavender lump above the door, then at me, the beginnings of a smirk creeping onto her face.

"I guess Alira and I will just have to come and get you at bedtime. She can knock you out like Lola."

Cybele looked genuinely shocked for a moment before sighing in defeat.

"Fine, I'll be back once it's dark. But as soon as there's sunlight again, I'll be in the workshop. If we don't come up with something before tomorrow, we'll just stall again."

"Bele, you don't have to break yourself just because that man told you to," Cordelia said firmly. "He'd work you to death if it meant fixing his problems. You need to sleep and keep a clear mind for tomorrow. I'm sure Alira and Kaiya will work just as hard—but they still need sleep."

Cybele nodded in defeat.

"Speaking of Kaiya and me," I chimed in, "I think I'll head over there now and get started."

I was eager to finally dive deeper into this crystal. We'd tried a few times during the journey here and had managed to enhance my magic sense to something akin to Kaiya's fusion magic. But we'd hit a wall when it came to uncovering the other magics we knew had to be hidden inside it.

Cybele seized the opportunity to follow me out, finally heading off to her beloved workshop. First, though, she'd need to locate the remainder of her telescope. She'd split up the pieces among our entourage of refugees during the journey.

We diverged paths shortly after, and I made my way to the cabin that Brigitte and Kaiya had entered earlier. Knocking on the door, I opened it when I heard a friendly "Enter" from inside.

Descending the few steps, I spotted Brigitte reclining comfortably on the lounge, while Kaiya jumped up with enthusiasm upon seeing me, knowing exactly why I'd come.

I couldn't help glancing toward the bedrooms, noting the stark contrast between them. One was pristine and almost blindingly white, while the other was a soft lavender.

It was then I realised something—I didn't actually know what colour Kaiya's stone was or what it was called. I glanced back at the lavender lump above the door, wondering if I'd gotten it wrong—perhaps it was linked to Kaiya's stone rather than amethyst. It made sense, given that the device appeared to be skimming only our gemstone colours, directly tied to magic, which was precisely what Kaiya's stone did. Kaiya frowned as they noticed me frozen in thought, staring at the lavender-coloured sheets. I pulled out the purple crystal, holding it up against the room. It didn't match the colour exactly, but it also wasn't amethyst.

If I'd confused the two stones, their magic must be close enough to be put together inside a crystal like this. But what kind of magic would that be? Ethereal magic? Sensory magic?

Whatever it was, it felt worlds apart from the raw, raging energy of Ayuna's lightning stone. If I was on the right track, it was no wonder this crystal's energy was far more subdued.

Kaiya was still frowning at me.

"Kaiya, what is your stone? It is purple, right?" I asked.

"Yes, it's taaffeite," they replied, frown deepening.

I'd never heard of taaffeite, but at least it was similar in colour to both amethyst and this crystal.

"I think I've just had a revelation. I'm going to try to use the crystal to tap into amethyst magic. Do you think there's any way you could help me with that?"

Kaiya tilted their head slightly.

"I could only tell you when you're channelling amethyst magic, but I imagine you'd already know that much yourself."

I paused to think, uncertain whether I should try connecting with the crystal's potential dream magic directly, as I'd done with magic sense, or whether it would be better to use an actual amethyst first and then attempt it. I supposed it didn't matter—we had all day and plenty of time to explore every possibility.

I sat down and began explaining my new theories to Kaiya. Their frown gradually transformed into an excited grin, and together we got started—trying to daydream my way into the consciousness of this otherworldly purple crystal.

39 – Ender

I was once again left with nothing to do. It felt just like back in Telesto when Alira was hard at work training, Cybele was busy in the museum's workshop, and I was lounging around with not much to do. After enjoying the comfort of a real bed for a couple of hours, I decided to set out and find Cybele's workshop to help her with the telescope. I figured she might need an extra set of hands to reassemble what she'd brought, and I could even be useful afterward if I used some sapphire magic.

Heading out, I tried to recall where Cybele and Cordelia had been led when we split from them to return to The City. It wasn't hard to figure out once I reached Navoi's coastal castle—the workshop was relatively close by. It looked similar to the cabins we were all staying in, but with a slightly more industrial vibe and a thick chimney. My guess was that the chimney was for some kind of forge. I couldn't help but feel intrigued. I'd seen plenty of the crazy weapons this planet had to offer, but I'd never actually witnessed how they were made. I had seen Alira whip up a new weapon before, but her methods were far from conventional. It amazed me how she could just invent things like that. I was so proud of her—and yet, terrified all the same.

I knocked on the workshop door but let myself in, knowing Cybele would already be too hyper-focused to hear me. The colour palette inside the workshop was vastly different from the cabins, but it still featured the descending steps that seemed to denote its place in the hierarchy of level ten. I found myself wondering whether any of the buildings had no stairs—or if Navoi's house was bluntly elevated above everything else, leaving no room for sub-hierarchy. It seemed like something he'd do, though it was hard to picture him following through with such meticulous detail.

Entering the workshop, I noticed the forge and a giant oven sitting beneath the chimney. A few flames flickered faintly, making it clear the forge hadn't been used in some time.

Everything else in the space was a chaotic sight—Cybele had completely taken over, spreading her belongings everywhere. At the centre of it all was Cybele herself, working on a large cylindrical device as wide as a big tree trunk, dominating the middle of the room.

"Cybele, have you done this much already?" I asked, amazed.

She whipped her head up in surprise.

"Oh, Ender. Yes, I built the frame before I went to get the telescope from the city. I'm just putting the pieces in place now, and then I'll recalibrate and start working on the more multiversal components. That will be the hard part."

She smiled fervently, immediately immersing herself back into her work. Not wanting to disrupt her focus, I began wandering around the workshop, dodging the bits and pieces scattered haphazardly. As I examined the telescope, I couldn't help but marvel at its complexity—far beyond my technical understanding.

I connected with the sapphire, remembering borrowing it from Cybele to fit into the gauntlets she'd made for me.

"Oh yeah, I never thanked you for making these gauntlets. They're pretty sweet," I said.

Cybele looked up briefly. "Oh yes, those! Just an idea I had one day. I never did get to test the metamaterial transformation properly, though. Does it work okay?"

I blinked. "I'm sorry—the what?"

"Oh, I mean, do they become just as sharp as your fingernails do when you activate knife magic?"

"I... don't know. The only time I've used knife magic while wearing them, I was in the middle of being impaled," I replied dryly.

Cybele winced, quickly scanning the room before spotting a cloth bag.

"There! Go try it out and chop that bag open with them," she said eagerly.

I was sceptical, wondering how a rounded surface like the mesh in my gauntlets could possibly cut anything—even with knife magic. Knife magic didn't exactly make me sharp, just metallic.mStill, I did as Cybele suggested, carefully examining the gauntlets as they took on a new silvery hue when I flexed my forearms, matching my chrome fingernails.

I made a fist and swung my arms at the bag after placing it on something tall enough to act as a pedestal. The bag wasn't particularly large, but it was crazy heavy. I didn't expect to slice through it—instead, I figured I'd knock it off the pedestal with a solid whack.

To my surprise, I sliced through the bag. My gauntlets somehow became sharp enough upon contact to tear it open rather messily, which made more sense than achieving a clean cut. It was hard to wrap my head around, but the only comparison I could think of was having some kind of cheese grater wrapped around my arms—though it would have to be one hell of a sharp cheese grater.

I admired the gauntlets for a moment, before noticing the mess I'd just created on the floor.

"Was that a bag of gold sand I just cut open? How am I supposed to clean that up?" I asked Cybele, exasperated.

She nodded once, acknowledging that her invention had worked as intended, before promptly returning to the telescope without a second glance.

"No, it's brass. Just pick it up with sand magic. Preferably into that mould over there," Cybele said, pointing to a black mould sitting near the forge. The lines in the mould were similar to the shape of the existing telescope's frame, which already contained various brass components.

"How big is that thing going to get anyway?" I asked.

Cybele, still focused on her work, pointed at a low table while peering through a small lens and melting something with a soldering iron. The plans for the telescope were spread out on the table, and based on what I could see, the finished structure would be much taller than the ceiling in this room.

"Um, Cybele, this isn't going to fit," I pointed out.

"We'll make it fit. I've already completed the base, so you could probably just dig a hole in the floor for that part," she replied nonchalantly.

"What? I can't just put a hole in the floor of Navoi's workshop," I protested.

"Sure you can. You've already got sand magic ready—just do it," Cybele said, undeterred.

"That's not what I meant. I meant you can't destroy Navoi's workshop like that."

"We can fix it easily later. And I think getting this telescope built is infinitely more important than worrying about a bit of flooring."

I sighed. Hard to argue with that. I did as Cybele asked, sinking the telescope into the floor and creating a stepped pit so it remained accessible. I also moved all the brass sand into the mould she had pointed out.

Working under Cybele's direction for the next hour was pretty much just like that—following her instructions one task at a time—until Alira appeared at the doorstep.

"Oh, Dad, you're here too?"

"Yeah, I thought I'd help Cybele out. And I'm glad I did, because she's designed something that doesn't even fit in this room, so I had to make the floor lower."

"Oh, that was you? I figured it was just another one of Navoi's annoying architectural choices," Alira shrugged. "Anyway, I've figured out some things about the purple crystal, but I'm getting stuck again, so I thought Cybele might be able to help."

That was enough to pull Cybele away from her work.

"And what have you discovered?" Cybele asked eagerly.

"Well, there was a lot of realisation and experimenting going on, but essentially, I've figured out how to use the stone to tap into amethyst magic as well. I haven't been able to find any other magics yet, though, so I thought maybe there's a connection between the two I've discovered that could help uncover more. I was thinking that this stone might be an 'ethereal battery' or something like that. Magic sense and dream magic only seem to sense non-physical things and the like."

Cybele closed her eyes, lost in thought. I simply watched the two of them, offering no new ideas about the crystal. Not that I'd expected to—I seemed to have fallen behind Alira's growing knowledge of dream magic and now magic-sense.

Eventually, Cybele's expression softened, her eyes lighting up with a new sense of curiosity.

"Alira, have you connected to my magic before? Do you know what it feels like?"

"No," Alira replied.

"Try it."

Alira raised her arm, tapping the bracelet Cybele had upgraded, and connected to Cybele's red beryl. The preset was still saved from when Cybele first gave her the device. I knew exactly what Alira was experiencing as she began looking around with wide eyes, occasionally squinting as though staring into the sun. Red beryl magic was strange—but hopefully, Cybele knew what she was doing.

"Now, try to remember everything you're feeling right now and focus on finding those same sensations within the purple crystal," Cybele suggested.

It seemed she believed dream, sense, and perception magics were all connected, forming part of the same magical family. I supposed they were all rather ethereal, just as Alira had mentioned. Maybe she was right.

Alira focused on the crystal, evidently more confident now after having uncovered two types of magic within it already. It didn't take long before she began grinning, glancing around the room in that familiar way she had before.

"Wow, you were right—it's there," Alira said.

She refocused on Cybele, her eyes occasionally flicking to the side as though trying to ignore the strange visual aberrations I knew she must be experiencing with perception magic.

"So, do you think there are only three magics in the crystal—or are there more?" Alira asked.

"I think this stone is specific to mind magics," Cybele replied. "There are definitely more than three, but off the top of my head, the only other one I can think of is sapphire."

Both Alira and I raised our eyebrows at that.

I spoke first. "Now, that might actually come in handy. Sapphire magic combined with magic sense would give us a pretty complete picture of pretty much any technology—and it's exactly what Akeldama doesn't have, but would love to have, to understand the world-ship."

"You really think I can combine them?" Alira asked.

"Well, isn't that the whole point of the crystals? They powered the Proelium board, which used all kinds of magics all at once. Plus, if it's anything like how we connect to gemstones to use their inherent magics, then why wouldn't you be able to use all the magics tied to this crystal? They're probably all similar for that reason."

"He's right," Cybele added from across the room, where she'd wandered off to, deciding we were too boring, and had returned to her telescope.

"Now you just have to figure out how to do that—and how it's going to help us tomorrow," she added like it was the simplest thing in the world.

I could see the stress creeping onto Alira's face, her brow furrowing slightly. I tried to comfort her as best I could.

"Hey, it would be incredible if you figured out how to combine magics by tomorrow—and if anyone could do it, it'd be you. But don't push yourself too hard, alright? You've got Kaiya to help you, too, and now that we know what the crystal is potentially capable of, coming up with a plan tomorrow will already be so much easier."

Alira nodded slowly. "I know. But I'll try my best."

I smiled at her. "I know you will."

40 – Alira

Magic Sense had been strange enough, but perception magic was downright uncomfortable. Everything was so distracting—it was hard to focus on anything. Still, I had to practice if I was going to use it effectively and somehow combine it with other magics. I wasn't sure how I was going to pull that off, especially without resorting to blood magic, but I had to try.

Walking back to Brigitte and Kaiya's cabin, I kept the red beryl's magic active within the purple stone, trying to acclimate myself to the experience. Twice, I almost stumbled off the path after staring too long at patches of sky. The colours seemed to grow more saturated the longer I focused on them. I couldn't tell if I was causing it or if I was just seeing things.

Eventually, I made it back to the cabin, where Kaiya was waiting patiently for me. I liked Kaiya—though they were very single-minded and obedient. Their hesitation before speaking was subtle but noticeable.

"Did seeing Cybele help?" they asked.

"Immensely. It turns out her magic is also in the stone, and she thinks sapphire might be in there too."

"Wow, sapphire? Really? I guess that means your colour theory was right, then."

"My colour theory?"

"Yeah, you were comparing the shades of purple, remember? Trying to match the purple crystal's shade to amethyst and taaffeite."

"But sapphire is blue."

"Yes, and combined with red beryl, they make purple."

"Oh. Huh."

For a moment, I completely forgot how colours worked. I felt silly standing there, watching Kaiya, half-convinced they were looking at me like I was stupid. But maybe I was imagining it— their face was far too soft for such a hard expression.

I wandered over to the area where Kaiya and I had been practising. As I began searching for sapphire magic, I faltered, noticing Kaiya just sitting there, watching me silently. It had become increasingly awkward since we'd moved past magic sense. Kaiya had been eager to help me search for dream magic, but had stopped after a while, saying it felt uncomfortable.

Since then, it had just been me—alone with the constant weight of their presence, watching and waiting for something to happen. As if I didn't already feel like I was under enough pressure. I was supposed to find sapphire magic, combine it with the other magics in the stone, and somehow use that knowledge to craft an airtight plan that would save us all. All by tomorrow.

I glanced at Kaiya again, my concentration completely broken. I sighed, giving up. I didn't think I was going to be able to accomplish anything with them watching me like this. I had to get out of here.

"I…" What was I supposed to say? That they were distracting and needed to leave? I was in their cabin. And I didn't want to say I was leaving to practise by myself—they were just as invested in uncovering the crystal's secrets as I was.

"Kaiya, I… think I need to go and practise with sapphire magic a bit more first. It's new to me, and I think it'll be much easier if I can familiarise myself with the kinds of feelings I'm supposed to be looking for."

"Oh really? But you picked up magic sense straight away without practising," Kaiya pointed out.

"Well, I guess that was because it's a passive magic. You just sort of see magic."

"Sapphire magic isn't so different. My understanding is that it's quite similar, but for the insides of machines rather than magic itself."

"It's just… way different," I replied, trailing off

"How?"

"It just is, okay!" I yelled, louder than I intended.

Brigitte turned her attention to me, her eyes silent yet fixed on me from the top of the couch cushion. I couldn't stand her gaze.

"I'm sorry—I just need to practise by myself for a little while," I whispered apologetically, half-running for the door.

The moment I shut the door behind me, the guilt hit me. But I couldn't bear staying in there any longer. I walked away swiftly, though I hadn't decided where to go. My stomach felt weird, and my skin crawled more than it should have. Everything had been non-stop for so long now—even walking through the desert had been overwhelmingly productive. The only conversations anyone ever had were about what we were going to do next. Akeldama this, Ayuna that. I just needed a break.

As that thought crossed my mind, I realised I was already heading for the stairs into Muruntau. For a moment, I questioned myself—why would I leave everyone I knew? Then I reminded myself that they were exactly who I was trying to get away from, at least for a little while.

I could only think of one place to go where I might find a chance to simply hang out. It felt like a long shot, sure, but with every step I took ascending through the levels of the city, I grew more confident in my decision—until I reached level six. There, my confidence evaporated entirely.

What was I doing? Showing up on the doorstep of a painite rebel? I was insane.

But I didn't stop walking until I was already there, standing on the street in front of the door Max had led us through to his home. Frozen in place, I glanced down at myself in my Telesto uniform, which I'd coated in a thin layer of sand before wandering up here. It hadn't helped much—I still felt like I was standing out like a sore thumb. I stared at the door in indecision for long enough that someone decided to ask what I was doing.

"Hey, miss—what are you doing just standing there?" a voice called from somewhere behind me.

"Just visiting a friend," I replied absently, still fixated on the door.

"A friend, eh? Not a boyfriend? The lad with the dark hair, perhaps?"

My face flushed red as I spun around, searching for the source of the voice. A boy stood there, his short, dark curls tucked behind one ear beneath his dark cloak. My face grew even redder when I realised how my blushing must have looked after his teasing. He laughed, clearly enjoying himself. I let out a long breath.

"Max. What are you doing here?"

"Outside of my home, you mean?" he replied with a smirk.

My face remained red. "I meant…" What did I mean? "Why'd you do that?" I finally responded.

"I spotted a cute girl staring at my front door from across the street. What was I supposed to do?"

I suppressed a blush. Did he really just call me a cute girl? I wasn't sure how to feel about that.

"What I want to know is what *you're* doing here. Although I think I nailed it before," he added with a teasing grin. Was he always like this?

"I was walking by and just thought I'd stop to say thanks again for last time. That's all," I said, feeling like I'd regained a fraction of my composure. He nodded mockingly, clearly unconvinced. He stayed silent, waiting.

I sighed. "Fine. I have this… project I'm working on, and everyone expects so much from me. It's a lot of pressure, and I needed to get away from it all for a bit. I figured you'd be free, since you don't do anything all day, so… here I am."

I finally said without standing around awkwardly, flustered. Max feigned offence, clutching his chest dramatically.

"Riiight. Well, if someone as important and busy as you has come to see an unemployed nobody like me, then I guess I'd better make it special. Care to join me on a little trip?" he asked, flashing a genuine smile. I looked at him suspiciously.

"What kind of trip?"

"Call it a sightseeing trip."

"Sightseeing," I repeated, unenthused.

"Yeah. You said you're new to the city, right? I know a few points of interest that aren't exactly on the map," he said, smirking.

"Okay then. Impress me."

He smiled. "With pleasure."

Max gestured ahead and took the lead along level six. I quickly lost all sense of direction as we turned into an opening in the stone and began descending through the city walls, but I didn't care. It felt good not to know everything—not to worry about whether where I was going might lead to my death. It was relaxing.

Even more so when we finally stopped, and I saw the 'off the map' view Max had promised. I started giggling, enjoying the moment.

He stared at me like I was insane.

I stopped laughing long enough to catch his confused expression.

"I sneak you all the way down here to level nine to show you a view like this, and all you do is giggle," he said, sounding almost offended. I couldn't help but giggle again, trying to decide if I should explain. Instead, I simply pointed to one of the cabins on the level below.

"That's our cabin. I'm staying over there."

Max followed my finger, his dark brown eyes widening in shock as he stared back at me. I burst out laughing at his bewildered expression. His gaze lingered on the cabin briefly, his thoughts clearly elsewhere, before he locked eyes with me again.

"And just what kind of project did you say you were working on?" he asked, his tone both curious and teasing.

I stopped laughing, a sudden wave of guilt washing over me for abandoning everyone.

No. I needed this. But how much should I tell Max?

"Well, it's hard to explain. There's a lot going on. My dad's helping build the telescope, but my part is less straightforward," I said.

"You're involved in a big project on level ten—the level where only The Commander lives—and you want me to believe you're just building a telescope? I don't buy it. You're pulling my leg," Max replied. "There's no way you're even living down there. Those cabins are just for show. The Commander doesn't even know any diplomats or anyone who'd rank high enough to stay there. He's too gung-ho for all that, or at least that's what I've heard."

I kept looking at him, waiting for him to believe me. I wondered if holding my ground would convince him or if he'd stay sceptical until I offered proof. He stared at me for a moment longer, as though he couldn't decide what to think or say, before eventually rolling his eyes and turning his attention back to level ten.

Despite the familiar view, it was a cool spot. We were perched at the edge of level nine in what appeared to be a half-built factory. It was hard to tell what it was meant to be, with all the rooms empty, but the missing section of wall overlooking level ten created a surprisingly nice secret hideaway.

After a few moments of serene silence, Max spoke up unprompted.

"I know we don't know much about each other, but I enjoy your company. It's hard being a lone painite in this city. I'm glad we can at least relate on that level—even if you're something else entirely."

He turned to me with a genuine smile. I was a bit taken aback by the sudden vulnerability, though it wasn't the first time he'd shifted from playful to serious so abruptly.

"I do too, and I wish I could tell you more about me. But I don't think you'd believe me if I did," I said honestly.

He scoffed, smirking. "Tell me something about you that I might actually believe, then."

I thought for a moment, frowning when I realised that was harder than I'd expected.

"My mother died when I was a baby. I've been raised by my dad my entire life, but a few weeks ago we happened to find my grandmother—someone neither of us had ever met. We found her dating an old friend of my dad's. That was the woman I was with when we first met, my grandmother. Cordelia."

Max nodded along, a soft smile playing on his lips.

"Alright, I believe you this time. I take it that means you don't have any siblings then?"

"No. And you?"

"I had a sister. She's not dead, but she followed my father when my parents separated, and I haven't seen her since."

"Oh. How long ago was that?"

"Around four years ago. She was much smaller then, but just as fierce. She'd follow my father anywhere, and I guess she did just that."

Max stared off solemnly, his story starting to come together. I didn't want to pry further, so I cleared my throat, changing the subject.

"You uh… have better luck with your glass sculptures?" I asked awkwardly.

He chuckled. "Not at all. Although I'll admit I did deform that ball you made while trying."

I laughed. "Have you only tried using the sand on your bedroom floor?"

"Well, yeah. I can't really try it outside—not that the sand is much different on the street, but people have mixed it all together, so it's arguably worse."

"Maybe you should try the sands in the desert, then. I have, and they're all very different to work with. Glass is one of the hardest materials to form. Be careful though—I almost blew myself up once."

Maximon looked at me with concern.

"Why, might I ask, were you out in the desert playing with sand?"

I scoffed. "Well, I had to get here somehow, didn't I? It's a four-day walk from The City."

"You walked here from the city? I guess you didn't have an indicolite to channel so you could fly. That's how it works for you, right?"

"Well, yes. But I do have one. I was just travelling with a group of refugees, so we had to walk."

Max frowned. "But you showed up with only your grandmother?"

I sighed, feeling a headache coming on from the tangled mess of my own story.

"Well, we started in The City. Then three of us flew to Telesto, before Cordelia and I flew here and met you. After that, I went back to The City with Dad, and then we returned to Muruntau with a group of refugees after their home was destroyed by the painites when they besieged the cathedral."

I sighed again. "You can choose how much of that you want to believe, but I haven't lied to you since we met."

Max gave me another one of his looks, clearly debating whether to believe me or not.

"No wonder you needed a break. That sounds like a lot of running around," he said finally.

"You don't even know the half of it."

Max nodded absently. "What did you do in Telesto? I can't say I know much about it. It's too far to travel to without air magic. Not that I could, anyway."

"Mostly just training. So much training. I'd only just learnt air magic, so I was getting some lessons there. But somehow, I ended up in the junior Telesto guard program. Needless to say, I'm pretty good with a yacharow and a wingsuit now."

"Really? You're a trained Telesto guard," Max said, not believing a word I said.

I sighed, smiling. It felt like the right moment to give Max some proof to back up all the wild claims I'd been making. Honestly, I wouldn't believe me either. Everything sounded more insane as I recounted it—and I'd left out all the actual fighting.

Feeling comfortable around Max, I connected to the painite without hesitation or guilt. I glanced around for some suitable material to use with sand magic to craft a yacharow, but then chuckled as I looked down, remembering how conspicuous my choice of attire was. Instead, I simply dispelled the sand clinging to my uniform, revealing the Telesto colours I'd barely taken off since the moment I first put them on. I probably needed something fresh at this point. There were only so many cuts and tears I could stitch up before I started looking like my clothes might fall apart at any second.

Max immediately chuckled with an exaggerated eye roll as soon as he recognised the Telesto colours.

"And there's the proof you've been hiding from me. Right under my nose," he teased.

He leaned in closer, his gaze lingering on the various patch-ups I'd done.

"And it looks like you've been through even more than I suspected. Unless they trained you half to death over there—or even to death, judging by some of those tears."

Max's expression softened with mild concern as he added, "You had broken ribs when we met, didn't you? How did that happen?"

That question wasn't easy to dodge. But at this point, all I wanted was to tell him everything—to let it all out. To rant about the craziness, the pressure, and to have someone who would simply listen and understand. And so I did.

At least the part where we were mistaken for thieves at the gates of Muruntau. I explained everything that happened—even though I knew his mother had been hurt because of it.

When I finished, I expected Max to be angry. To confront me for not telling him sooner that we were the reason his mother got hurt.

But he didn't. Instead, he smiled softly.

"I'm glad I found you when I did then. Who knows what would have happened if we'd never met."

He shook his head, laughing quietly. "From wanted criminal to level ten resident. How did you manage to swing that?"

Honestly, I wasn't even sure how to answer. Dad had done all the talking, and I'd been passed out in a prison cell for most of it.

"Honestly, I'm not entirely sure. All I can say is that Dad makes an excellent diplomat."

"Your dad smooth-talked you out of trouble… with The Commander," Max said flatly.

"Pretty much."

He raised his eyebrows. "Your dad must be something special if he managed that. That lizard doesn't respect many people at all. Not enough to fill up all those cabins, at least."

"Probably not. Even amongst us, there are only two people he respects. And it's really obvious—he only talks to them and ignores the rest of us."

Max frowned. "You really did come from down there, working on some secret project on level ten."

I shrugged. "I told you."

"So, what's the project then? Surely it's not just a telescope," Max asked.

I sighed, hesitating as I wondered if I had the energy to revisit all that again. I realised that I didn't—not really. But talking to Max had helped, and I found myself drawn once more to the mystery of the purple crystal. I still had to figure out how to tap into sapphire magic within it and begin combining the magics.

I wasn't sure I'd be able to accomplish that without resorting to blood magic first. But standing here, high above everything, I started to feel a renewed compulsion to figure it all out—even if I had to use the painite.

It would be easier once I could identify what they all felt like together. And who better to help me than an actual blood magic user? I sighed again, accepting what I was about to do.

"No, that's only one part. My part is this." I pulled out the purple crystal.

Max stared at it, unsure what to make of it.

"And that is?"

That was a hard question to answer, especially when half the point of my task was to answer that question for everyone else. I didn't want to delve into the whole parliament, exploding Proelium board situation either.

"Here, see if you can feel it. There's magic inside, but it's not like when I connect to gemstones. There's literally raw magic hiding inside this thing."

For a moment, Max's face betrayed a flicker of disbelief. But then he smiled and reached for the crystal, sceptical but curious. He closed his eyes, his fingers moving instinctively as if he were attempting to draw the magic out the way he would with people. After a few moments, he frowned—finding nothing

"It doesn't work like that, but I'm hoping that if I use painite magic to channel all the magics I know are already inside it, then I'll be able to connect to them that way. I've connected to them individually—I'm just having trouble connecting to them all at once."

"I see, and you sought out the master of multiple magics to help you," Max joked.

I rolled my eyes. "I didn't intend to ask for your help when I came here, but you know more about blood magic and combining magic than I do. Maybe you'll know something that could help."

"Fine, I'll help—but only because I want to unravel the mystery that you are," he said with a teasing grin.

I blushed slightly. "Works for me."

41 – Ender

"Ender, hand me that tool on the bench behind you."

I spun around and picked up some sort of handheld object from the bench.

"You mean this thing?"

"Yep."

I handed the tool to Cybele.

"Does that thing have a name, or did you just assume I wouldn't know what it was?"

"I don't even know what it is. They were found on a few ships that crashed—none of the ones with humans inside. Even to me, it's just an alien tool. But I've got a few of them, and they're pretty useful."

I peered closer at what Cybele was crafting, watching as one piece after another was added to the telescope. It was growing like a tower, piece by piece. Cybele pressed a button on the alien tool, electricity crackling between its prongs as she moved it along the seam of the metal shell she was forming. The metals fused together effortlessly under its charge.

"So, it's like a… gyroscopic handheld welder?" I guessed.

"Something like that. Although aren't all welders handheld?"

"Maybe in the future universes they are."

Cybele continued shaping the metal shell, eventually slapping it onto the telescope's structure. Even with sapphire magic helping me interpret the drawings, it was hard to tell how much more of this thing we had left to build. And, as Cybele frequently reminded me, the hardware was only half the problem. The software component was completely beyond me—I knew little about computer code, let alone alien mothership computer code.

"Shouldn't we wrap up soon? It looks like it's getting dark outside, and you did promise Cordelia you'd get some sleep," I said, eyeing the fading light.

"Yes, yes, in a moment," Cybele replied dismissively. "We're actually ahead of where I thought we'd be—thanks to you. I would have been much slower on my own. I can't believe I didn't realise sooner that I could use you like a magical multitool."

I scoffed, but she wasn't wrong. Cybele continued issuing instructions, keeping me occupied long enough to forget how late it was getting. The door to the workshop suddenly opened, and Cordelia stormed in.

"Forgetting our deal are you?" she asked pointedly. Her gaze flicked my way.

"Ender, I'm surprised to find you here. I thought you'd have had enough sense to go to bed already. What's so exciting that both of you refuse to sleep?"

Cybele and I exchanged a quick glance, both feeling slightly guilty. We both knew Cybele had intentionally kept me distracted so I wouldn't realise how late it had gotten.

"I did mention it to Cybele, but we ended up getting distracted," I admitted.

Cordelia rolled her eyes. "Like Bele isn't always distracted. Come on, we've got to plan for tomorrow, remember? We can't have the both of you being useless."

I smiled sheepishly, briefly wondering when Cordelia had started sounding like a traditional mother-in-law.

I left the workshop with Cybele and Cordelia, though my thoughts had already shifted. I found myself wondering if Alira had made any progress. She probably had the entire crystal figured out by now. She'd been doing so well earlier, and hours had passed since then. Knowing her and Kaiya, that was more than enough time to accomplish plenty.

The sun had set, but the sky still held a faint glow on the horizon as we approached our cabin. It seemed we weren't the only ones heading back.

In the dim light, I spotted Alira hurrying towards the door.

She stopped briefly when she saw us, looking like a deer caught in the headlights as she stared back at us, before continuing, matching our pace instead. I'd expected her to already be at home— or maybe coming from Brigitte's cabin—not from the complete opposite direction.

We collided at the door, but I held back my curiosity about the crystal to focus on finding out what she'd been up to.

"Where have you been?" I asked her.

"Working on connecting to the crystal, remember? You know, the purple one. It's kind of important—you shouldn't forget about it," she replied, oddly defensive.

"Right," I said, glancing behind her and following the path she'd taken to the base of the stairs leading up to level nine.

"Working on the crystal, alone, in the middle of the city somewhere," I continued, raising an eyebrow.

Alira dropped her head, her posture shrinking slightly.

"I just needed to be alone. I needed to focus, and I couldn't with Kaiya staring at me. I didn't go far, I promise. And I found a good spot to practise," she explained.

I sighed, realising I'd questioned her more harshly than I'd intended.

"Sorry, Ali. I just wasn't expecting it, that's all. If it helped and it's what you felt you needed, then I'm glad," I said gently, smiling.

Alira wasn't stupid. She'd had bad experiences with Muruntau before, so she wouldn't have wandered into the thick of it for no reason. Alira perked up after that.

"It was just what I needed. I found the sapphire magic—it wasn't all that hard—and I even combined it with magic sense. I could see so much. I even tried adding yellow sapphire magic and… well, it would probably be too much if I did. It'd be like seeing everything all at once. I think that's also why I struggled to add perception magic into the mix—because it's like throwing everything out the window for a version of reality that you can manipulate at will."

I nodded along, trying to make sense of all of that. Cybele, however, beat me to it.

"Did you try connecting to just yellow sapphire through the crystal?" she asked.

"Yeah, but I couldn't find it. I thought it would be in there, though. I mean, it'd fit the theme, wouldn't it?"

"Mmm, actually, I think it'd make more sense if it didn't fit in. I think I can work with this though. Let me get inside so I can sketch out how I think the stones are divided. I've got a pretty solid idea now."

Cybele led the charge through the doorway, making a beeline for some pencil and paper she'd left lying around.

"So, this is the stone we have, right—the mind stone," Cybele said, starting to sketch some kind of diagram. She wrote 'Mind-Purple' inside a circle and branched out four lines from it. At the ends of the lines, she wrote the types of magic Alira had been able to use with it: amethyst, blue sapphire, red beryl, and taaffeite.

"Right, so the colours are important here. These four stones, when their colours are combined, produce this exact shade of purple that the crystal is. That's what makes me think yellow sapphire must belong to another category," Cybele explained.

"The stone Ayuna had, Alira said was pink. We know it had diamond in it at least. That means we need a red gem with a similar kind of magic to create the pink hue. Anyone?"
Cybele asked the question with a knowing smile, clearly expecting an answer. Alira jumped in.

"Fire! Which would make it the energy stone, maybe."

"Precisely!" Cybele exclaimed.

She added another circle to her diagram, this one labelled 'Energy-Pink,' with garnet and diamond branching out from it.

"Now, Alira, the question is—are they the only two? Only you can answer that. Does the colour match up when you think about— wait, no, give me a second."

Cybele began rifling through her coat pockets, searching for something. Finally, she pulled out a thick pen, twisting and sliding her finger along it, as though calibrating it. When she was done, Cybele shoved the pen down onto the page and scribbled hard, producing only a pale reddish mark.

"Was this the colour of the crystal?" she asked impatiently, her eyes fixed on Alira.

Alira frowned. "No, that's too... brown. Maybe it needs another red gem."

Her eyes lit up again as she answered her own question.

"Oh! Painite. Blood magic is also energy based—it's just stored in people."

The room went silent.

Alira was the only one who didn't immediately realise the implication of what she'd said—at least until she saw the looks on our faces. Her expression fell as she realised.

After a moment of tense silence, Cordelia spoke first.

"It's morbid, but she's not wrong," she said.

Cybele fiddled with her pen again, drawing another mark on the page.

Alira smiled faintly, despite the tension.

"Yes! That's the colour," she confirmed.

With a satisfied nod, Cybele drew another line and added painite to her diagram. She stared at the paper for a few seconds, a slow smile spreading across her face.

Then, with sudden intensity, she began scribbling furiously—drawing and writing legible notes this time, not bothering to change the colour of her fancy pen from pink.

When Cybele was done, she stared up at us confidently, grinning, leaving the rest of us trying to decipher the chaotic brilliance she'd laid out on the page.

According to Cybele, there were three more stones she had written down:

'Physical-Blue' which encompassed aquamarine, indicolite, tiger's eye, and black moonstone.

'Biology-Yellow' which included pearl, yellow sapphire, obsidian, and topaz.

And lastly 'Light-Black' which only had onyx and alexandrite written down.

As I skimmed over the gemstones Cybele had listed, I couldn't help but notice that the colours didn't quite match up as she claimed they did.

"Cybele, I have a hard time believing that two blue stones, a brown one, and a black one are going to make a blue crystal. Wouldn't that be more of a… greyish?" I asked.

"Potentially, sure. But there are far too many magics to list here, so I only wrote down the important ones—or the ones I thought you'd recognise. If you'd like, I can add rhodonite to the biology stone?" Cybele added with a grin.

"No, that's okay—I get your point," I said, blushing, wondering if Cybele somehow knew that I knew what rhodonite was, or if she was just guessing. After all, she had been there for Alira's unconventional arrival into the world.

"What does rhodonite do?" Alira asked innocently, her gaze shifting between Cybele and me.

My face reddened further. "It's not important—just another magic that's not relevant here."

"You sure? Because I'm pretty sure Cybele mentioned it before when she told us how they made Proelium boards," Alira said, her curiosity unyielding.

"Not important at all."

"Okay then," Alira said, her innocent smile giving nothing away as she turned her attention to Cybele.

I sighed. There was no doubt in my mind that she would ask Cybele later, and Cybele would tell her with her trademarked unreserved bluntness. Wanting to avoid thinking about any of that, I decided to move the conversation forward.

"Anyway, I see you've written pearl down. Wouldn't that one not work anymore?"

"True, but these are ancient relics," Cybele explained, her focus sharp. "Created with no regard to modern magic. It's possible it's not in there, but considering how the magic shifts, there's bound to be something similar."

I nodded along, trying to digest her explanation, but my mind wouldn't process anything more. I was too tired to think, and night had long since fallen by this point. Cordelia spoke up.

"I'm glad we've sorted all that out, but it's getting late. I, for one, don't have the energy to do anything about it right now. I say we all take another look at this with fresh eyes in the morning."

"My thoughts exactly," I replied, rubbing my eyes before turning to Alira. "Ready?"

She nodded, and we both wandered off to our rooms. Behind us, Cybele and Cordelia lingered, whispering to each other, though they followed shortly after. Lola was already fast asleep in bed, where she'd been for hours.

As we all should have been.

The sun had risen long before we did, but that was nothing new here, where the nights were only about seven hours. Cybele, however, was nowhere to be seen this morning—a fact immediately confirmed by Cordelia's exasperated expression as she joined Alira and me at the table, where Alira had impatiently whipped up something vaguely resembling breakfast.

"I take it Cybele's already up and in the workshop?" I asked. Cordelia sighed heavily. "I couldn't stop her if I tried."

Surprise, surprise.

"I should go help her then," I said, moving to stand. Cordelia paused for a moment, her tone shifting to something more resolute.

"Perhaps it's best you don't. Teth should arrive shortly, and not long after that, we'll be heading back to meet with Navoi. I think our time is better spent working out some kind of plan before then. Bele's telescope is pointless without a way to use it."

"Is it really that late already?" I asked, feeling clueless about the passage of time on this clockless planet.

"It is," Cordelia confirmed. She turned her attention to the notebook sitting on the table, her gaze lingering in silence.

"And I have no clue how this diagram is supposed to help us yet. All it does is further prove how hopeless this situation is."

I stared hard at the notebook, knowing she was right but unwilling to accept it.

"Maybe, but there's got to be something—something we haven't thought of. A backup plan. An unbeatable combination of magic," I suggested.

Cordelia scoffed. "An unbeatable combination of magic? That's exactly what we're up against, in case you'd forgotten."

She had a point.

We both stared at the page in silence, the weight of the situation pressing down on us.

Eventually, Alira broke the silence.

"Sooo, I think I'm going to go tell Brigitte and Kaiya about all this. I haven't told Kaiya about the whole combined sapphire and magic sense thing yet, and I'm sure Brigitte would want to help you guys… uh… stare at that notebook until Teth shows up."

I rolled my eyes at her.

"Yes, good idea. But please tell Brigitte it's a strategy session and not just staring at paper."

"Fine, fine. See ya."

Alira was out the door, leaving Cordelia and me alone. I frowned, realising I'd forgotten about Lola.

"Wait, where's Lola?"

"I can't imagine she'd be anywhere else but with Cybele. She only stayed behind yesterday because she was so tired," Cordelia replied.

I chuckled, the memory of when Alira was that age flashing through my mind—running around with boundless energy one moment, and the next fast asleep across my lap in the armchair.

A knock at the door pulled me out of my thoughts, Cordelia calling out for Brigitte to come in after she announced herself unnecessarily formally.

Brigitte joined us at the table, her eyes immediately drawn to Cybele's diagram. She studied it briefly before asking for an update. We summarised everything that had happened since yesterday. When we finished, silence fell over the room.

It was the kind of silence that grew louder the longer it lingered. No one knew what to say.

The oppressive quiet was finally broken by the sound of numerous footsteps outside. Some were soft, while others kicked up gravel, filling the air with movement.

Level ten had suddenly come alive—desert boots and palace slippers alike weaving through the gardens just outside.
The three of us stood instinctively, though I was the first to the door.

Swinging it open, I was greeted by a sight that offered us an infinitely larger sliver of hope than we'd had moments ago. Telesto had arrived.

Bueller came to an abrupt halt in front of us, evidently sent to fetch us. I scanned the gardens, spotting servants scurrying to the other cabins and buildings we were all hiding in, as well as the Telesto entourage, making their way directly from level nine to Navoi's palace—or whatever he called it.

"The Commander has requested your presence, as well as everyone else's. Teth of Telesto has arrived for the strategy meeting," Bueller announced stiffly.

"Yes, thanks, Bueller, I can see that," I replied, my eyes fixed on Teth as she strutted through the gardens. I found myself surprised to see Chantrelle accompanying her.

"The Commander also required me to say, 'Let their downfall begin,'" Bueller finished calmly, bowing before retreating back to the palace.

I chuckled to myself. Navoi would be utterly disappointed in the way Bueller delivered that line. But I could imagine the ferocity with which Navoi himself would say it—and I suppose that was enough. Maybe there were two slivers of hope now.
Three, if Alira truly mastered the crystal as she seemed to be doing. Maybe this wouldn't be so bad after all.

I stepped out of the cabin, trailing after Bueller as he headed back to the palace. As I'd suspected, we soon ran into the Telesto entourage heading in the same direction, and naturally, we joined them.

I spotted Chantrelle waving as she noticed us, her enthusiasm cutting through the tension. Teth bowed her head briefly in my direction as we fell into step with the entourage, but her focus remained fixed ahead, ignoring Chantrelle and me as we caught up.

"Ender! I knew you'd be here somewhere, but it's nice to see you," Chantrelle exclaimed warmly. "Sounds like you've had it pretty rough from what I hear."

"Yeah, a lot has happened. We weren't quite as lucky in The City as we were in Telesto. You look great, though. How'd you end up here? I was worried you might've been demoted or banished or something, but clearly, I was very wrong about that."

"Nope. In fact, I pretty much run the city now. Not politically, but I oversee all its systems, the gardens—everything. It's really flourished with all the extra power. I've even been able to plant seeds that were stuck in hibernation because I didn't have enough energy to create the right habitats for them…"

Classic Chantrelle. She could turn any conversation into one about the latest plants she'd been growing.

"…I even grew this one that may or may not be edible. It's so curious—I just can't quite figure it out."

I chuckled. "Are you sure Teth wants someone who can turn any conversation into one about plants running her whole city?"

"Well… yes?" Chantrelle responded, sounding slightly unsure of herself. Teth turned her head briefly, her expression as measured as ever.

"She's very good. I'm glad you brought her to my attention, Ender."

Chantrelle blushed faintly, looking down for a moment. I nodded in agreement, smiling.

"You've even managed to get me interested now. So, tell me about this potentially edible plant."

Chantrelle began to speak but hesitated, instead reaching into her coat and pulling out a tablet. She tapped away at it for a moment before spinning the screen around to face me, revealing the image of a small plant with thin leaves and red pods hanging from it.

I couldn't help but laugh, immediately understanding why Chantrelle wasn't sure if the pods were edible. She looked startled at first, but then her expression shifted to eager curiosity as my laughter subsided—clearly recognising that I knew the plant.

"It's called a chilli pepper," I explained, still grinning. "And yes, you can eat it, but… it'll hurt."

Chantrelle frowned. "That doesn't help my dilemma at all."

I chuckled again and spent the rest of the walk to the palace explaining chillies to Chantrelle.

We met Alira, Kaiya, Cybele, and Lola at the entrance before heading upstairs together. The weight of the impending discussions hung heavy over the group, casting a subdued silence as we climbed.

Navoi, however, remained just as cheery as he had been yesterday.

"Ender! Teth, Brigitte!" Navoi declared loudly, his gaze landing on each of us individually as he spoke our names. It was clear, even then, that everyone else in the room were merely extras to him.

The 'extras,' however, were arguably doing all the work, and I hoped Navoi would realise that before it became more than just a rude character flaw.

Teth and I took our seats on either side of Navoi, flanked by Brigitte and Chantrelle. The rest of the group settled into the remaining chairs around the table.

It was then that I noticed only one other member of the Telesto entourage had made it inside. He stood silently against the wall, directly behind Teth and Chantrelle, a yacharow in hand.

Navoi clapped his hands together, his enthusiasm starkly contrasting the atmosphere in the room. He was the only one of us who seemed genuinely enthused to be here.

"Ender, why don't you fill in our new friends on the current situation? Then we can hear about your progress since yesterday."

I did as Navoi requested, recounting the recent events in as much detail as I could manage. I added updates on the construction of the multiversal telescope and the newly discovered magic crystals from the world-ship.

As I finished, both Navoi and Teth asked questions about these recent developments. I deferred almost all of them to Cybele, who answered enthusiastically. Chantrelle had a few questions of her own too.

"So what you're saying is that you currently have no way into parliament?"

"Correct." I answered. Chantrelle grinned in response.

"But Alira definitely passed the parliamentary trials?"

"Well, the Proelium board kind of exploded right at the end, but otherwise I'd say so yes."

Chantrelle only appeared more satisfied with each of my responses. All eyes were now on her.

"In that case, I might have a solution to that particular problem. I've been analysing your parliamentarian tattoo, Ender, to see if I could recreate it. It turns out there's a specific biomarker that the ink latches onto. I haven't been able to test it on any parliamentarians, but if my theory is correct, both you and Alira have this biomarker."

"We can go to parliament then, you mean?" Alira whispered, her voice cutting through the heavy stillness in the room.

"Hopefully, yes."

Alira glanced down at her wrist, her expression a mixture of excitement and fear.

"Excellent!" Navoi chimed in, his enthusiasm almost unnerving. "Now we just have an infiltration mission to plan, to gut the bastards from the inside out."

Navoi's lizard tongue flicked out as he spoke, inadvertently causing me—and several others—to shiver. He seemed utterly unaware of the reaction he'd provoked.

So did Cybele, who responded without hesitation. "If we have two tattoos, then we can take a maximum strike force of four."

Navoi laughed, seeming even more pleased. "Even better."

Teth, however, appeared to be the one keeping a clear head.

"We can't very well send people down there without knowing what they're walking into. For all we know, Akeldama has destroyed every teleporter on the ship, leaving only one for him to guard. Furthermore, we don't even know where the teleporters lead. From what Ender has said, it's likely they'll be split up immediately upon arrival."

Teth's reasoning was sound, and the risk of rushing in without preparation was obvious. We needed a way to map the terrain and gather information before moving forward.

"You might be right," Alira said, her voice measured but determined. "But luckily Dad and I are the ones that will have the tattoos—and we were built for stealth. Our magic literally makes us invisible."

She had a point—a fact I'd momentarily forgotten.

"Even so," I added, wary of the risk, "after Akeldama saw through me at the arena, I wouldn't rely too heavily on that particular ability for something this dangerous."

Alira deflated slightly but nodded. The room fell into a heavy silence, each of us lost in thought as we worked through the possibilities, all cards once again on the table.

Surprisingly, it was Kaiya who broke the silence, speaking softly.

"The mind stone… Alira was just talking about how she used sapphire magic and magic sense together—and how she was trying to use three of the mind stone's magics simultaneously. What if she did it while she was asleep, channelling dream magic? Could she slip into the dreams of one of the painite users on the world-ship and… I don't know, project the other magics from their mind? Maybe then she could at least see into the mechanics of the ship and where the other crystals are is."

Those of us who knew Kaiya stared at them, shocked by their sudden insightfulness. Everyone but Brigitte, who simply smiled. It was certainly imaginative—perhaps even outlandish—but then again, this was magic we were discussing. Anything was possible.

"Alira, does that sound possible to you? Could it work?" I asked, breaking the silence. Her brow furrowed as she began to think on the idea.

"I mean, I can't say that it won't work. I'm just not sure about pushing my magic through other people to sense what's around them. I've only ever used dream magic to remain within dreams—not to push past that," Alira admitted, her voice laced with uncertainty. She turned to Cybele for reassurance, and Cybele nodded in response.

"With a stone like that, the rules of individual magic don't apply the same way," Cybele explained. "I think the bigger issue would be projecting your mind all the way to the centre of the planet. Even teleporter signals weaken when pass through that much rock and distance."

"Could you potentially use the tattoo's teleporter signal to lessen the distance problem?" Chantrelle suggested.

"That might help," Cybele conceded. "Using the teleporter signal like a lead wire between Alira and the ship is about all we can do to assist. The rest would be entirely up to Alira's ability to project her mind that far—and in such an unconventional way."

All eyes turned to Alira then, and I could see the distress creeping into her expression.

"Does… Does this have to be me?" she asked, her voice faltering. "I mean, I just happened to pick up the stone. It's not like someone else couldn't do it just as easily."

It pained me to say it, but Alira was the only one who could pull this off. I wished I had the strength and the skill to take on the challenge myself, but I simply didn't. Not like she did.

"I'm sorry, Ali. I know it's a lot of pressure, and I wish I could do it instead, but no one else can channel magics that aren't theirs without getting sick—even when it's through an ancient battery. The only other option is me, but you know we don't have time for me to catch up on all the progress you've made with the crystal. I'm not as fast as you," I said, smiling at her apologetically.

Navoi stood then, pulling the attention away from Alira.

"Cybele. How much time do you need to finish your telescope?"

"If Ender keeps helping me the way he has, probably only a week," Cybele replied. Navoi turned to Chantrelle next.

"And what's the timeline for these tattoos?"

"As long as everything works the way I predict it will, I can get it done by this evening—assuming my subjects have the time," Chantrelle responded confidently.

"Now that's what I like to hear."

Navoi turned his sharp gaze to Alira.

"Alira. We need to be storming that ship in six days. Can you get us there in time?"

"I…" Alira faltered, her voice catching as Navoi's gaze bore into her, singular and intense.

Her eyes flicked to me, then around the table, finding everyone smiling and nodding. We were more confident in her than she seemed to be in herself. But our confidence was enough to bolster hers.

"Yes. I can make it work. One way or another, I'll dream my way onto the world-ship somehow," Alira said, her voice steadier now.

"Good. Now the final and most important question," Navoi started, his tone sharper. "What can the painites achieve in a week, and is it enough to stop us before we even begin?"

Everyone fell silent at that, the weight of the question settling over the room. The answer was both unknown and unknowable. Except, of course, for Cybele, who was the most qualified among us to provide an educated guess.

"Based on the assumption that Akeldama started only with the Proelium gems and the two pieces of the tail-key, he would have a lot to discover before he could make use of much of the world-ship. It's likely it didn't take him long to locate the main console and the slot where the tail-key is meant to fit. From there, though, all he'd be able to do is learn. And he seems like quite a learned man," Cybele added, her tone thoughtful. "So I'd assume he's consuming information quickly. Even then, though, he wouldn't run out of reading material for many weeks at the very least—and that's assuming he understands everything he reads. Whether Akeldama makes a move earlier than expected would depend entirely on his patience—on how long he could resist the urge to act on what he's learned and instead decide to reclaim the remaining pieces of the tail-key. I'd say our biggest advantage right now is that he believes Alira to be dead. That assumption would lead him to discount Ender as a serious opponent and think himself unstoppable, hopefully giving him no reason to act prematurely."

Navoi mulled this over, his sharp gaze fixed intently on Cybele, who stared back unflinching.

"That was quite an adept analysis of Akeldama's character. I can only hope that you are right," Navoi said at last.

He rose to his feet, his expression resolute.

"We have a week. A week before their downfall begins."

His words ended with a slight hiss. And with that, we were dismissed. With every new idea that had emerged during the meeting, my hope had grown until I nearly believed that we could pull it off. My role was simple—to be Cybele's magical multitool. But even more importantly, I had to be one hell of a father to support Alira through all the extra work we'd collectively decided she had to shoulder.

She'd handled herself admirably so far, but the weight of the stares she endured in that room—especially Navoi's—would crush most people. She'd faced all of us at once, each of us expecting arguably too much from her.

I believed she could do it.

But it was my job to make sure she believed it too.

42 – Alira

That was intense, but at least we finally had a tentative plan, thanks to Chantrelle. I wasn't particularly thrilled about how much pressure it was putting on me, though. The fate of the world apparently rested on my ability to create some obscure magic combination to peek through some guy's head. This planet was ridiculous sometimes.

Still, I knew just who I wanted to complain about it to—right after I got my parliamentarian tattoo from Chantrelle.

Although, if Max saw it, he'd immediately want to know what sort of project we were working on. There's no way he'd overlook a parliamentarian tattoo the same way he had everything else. Maybe it was time for the truth.

It wasn't that I didn't trust him—I did—but it felt like it was too late now. And honestly? I liked what we had. I didn't want to ruin things. I debated whether to tell Max the truth as I made my way to the Telesto cabin, where Chantrelle had set up shop.

Dad had gone earlier so Chantrelle could run some tests and ensure everything was working properly. The cabin was identical to the others, except for the contraption set up in the living room that Dad was sitting in, while Chantrelle fiddled with it.

"Oh hey, Ali, there you are," Dad said as I stepped into the cabin. Chantrelle's head shot up, her face splitting into a wide grin.

"Time for the moment of truth."

I frowned, unsure what she meant, and glanced at Dad's wrist, noting that his tattoo was still deformed and burnt.

"Did you fix it?" I asked her directly.

Her face fell, the grin replaced by something more solemn.

"Unfortunately, Ender's tattoo is too badly damaged to rework, and I can't just slap another one on him. The signal's been permanently corrupted. There's nothing I can do," she admitted.

Before the weight of her words could fully settle, her expression brightened again as she turned to me.

"You, on the other hand, are a blank slate—with all the biomarkers I need, hopefully."

Great. So even this part was now on me. Once again, It was all up to me for some reason. As I processed this, I noticed Chantrelle's gaze seemed to drift past me momentarily, like she couldn't quite see me. When I noticed, her eyes snapped back to meet mine. Dad chuckled softly, though there was a hint of pain in his expression.

"I know. Just another thing only you can do," he said, his tone both reassuring and regretful.

"But this one isn't all on you. Remember, you can still take one other person like Cybele said. You don't have to do any of this by yourself."

I shot him a weak smile, embarrassed at how easy I was to read, especially after I'd gone invisible for a moment, wishing I wasn't so important. I sighed.

"Okay then. What do you need me to do?"

Chantrelle gestured to the chair at the centre of the contraption, and Dad stood up at the same time, stepping aside to make room.

"Have a seat," she instructed.

I did as I was told, settling into the chair. For the next twenty minutes or so, not much happened. Chantrelle moved around the contraption with focused intent, examining my wrist, taking a blood sample, and then spending a long time staring at her tablet. Eventually, she looked up from the screen, finding Dad and me watching her expectantly.

"I knew I'd still have some work to do once I identified the specific biomarker," she began, her voice calm but thoughtful. "But it turns out to be more complicated than I expected. It's like the markers encrypt themselves to an individual's DNA, making them difficult to replicate. Luckily, half of my original sample was specific to your father's DNA, so yours should be easier to work with than anyone else's. But I'll still need a few hours to properly encode the ink for your DNA."

Chantrelle smiled apologetically but raised an eyebrow at my relieved expression. This was perfect. It meant I had one more day with Max before I'd have no choice but to tell him everything.

"That's okay, take your time. Like you said, there's no do-overs. Once it's there, it's there forever. I'll see you in a few hours," I said, waving with a smile as I turned and headed up the steps to the door. Behind me, I heard Chantrelle whisper to Dad, "Maybe she's just nervous about getting a tattoo. She is only young, and it is permanent."

I glanced back briefly to see Dad nodding but quickly pushed the door open and left, cutting off their whispers. I didn't need to hear their speculations about me. They were wrong anyway. I wasn't nervous about getting a tattoo. Sure, I imagined it might hurt a little, but it wasn't like I had much of a choice. Plus, it was kind of pretty—the encircling purple and blue bands. I just didn't want to get it right now. I hadn't figured out what I was going to say to Max yet. But maybe by tomorrow I would.

Leaving the cabins behind, I made my way towards the stairs up into the city. I tried cutting through level nine to get to Max's little spot without having to climb all the way up to level five and back down again. I was surprised to find that much of level nine was just as deserted as the building Max had taken me to. I had initially thought this area was some kind of industrial or institutional zone, but as I walked past the buildings, I noticed a recurring word— 'vault'—written on them somewhere.

One of the less secure but largest vaults was clearly marked the 'Iron Vault.' At first, I assumed it might be part of a rating system for the kinds of valuables stored inside—the Gold Vault containing the most expensive items, perhaps. That would certainly explain the level of attention some of the vaults seemed to receive.

This particular one, however, was practically unguarded. It even had a large window overlooking level ten, through which I managed to catch a glimpse. I quickly realised I'd been wrong about the vaults. The Iron Vault was literal. The warehouse floor was covered solely with tubs of iron sand. A few smaller bags were scattered around too, identical to some I'd seen in the workshop.

It made sense, though. Muruntau was essentially a massive hole in the ground full of tunnels. They had to put all that sand somewhere, and of course, they wouldn't discard the precious metals if they could help it. I couldn't help but compare Telesto to Muruntau in my mind. Muruntau was undoubtedly larger and wealthier, requiring entire warehouses to store its gold, iron, and other resources. But there wasn't much in the way of salvaged or invented technology. They had the gem scanners in the cabin and the electric lights lining the streets, but that was about all I'd seen.

Telesto, on the other hand, was resource-poor but inventive as hell—adapting old ship systems, growing plants, and even making peanut butter. I couldn't help but wonder what the two cities could achieve if they worked together. With this much iron, Telesto might even be able to repair some of the broken parts of its ship.

I debated whether to bring this idea up at the next meeting, but my thoughts were quickly interrupted by a livelier building as I wandered by it. I stopped in my tracks, ducking around the corner and remembering that I could turn invisible. Creeping forward carefully, I watched Muruntau guards swarm the building, both inside and out.

Most of them were trying to get inside, while others stood guard—although they hardly needed to, given the sheer amount of firepower between them.

Level nine was practically a ghost town, home only to metals and, I assumed, a few factories. But I couldn't figure out what they might be producing—maybe coins?

I edged closer, watching the guards closely, searching for a window that might give me a better look into the slightly more ornate warehouse they were spilling into.

As I snuck between the Iron Vault and the far more intriguing hall, something brushed against my arm—then grabbed it. Before I could react, it shifted down to take hold of my hand, pulling me behind the hall. There were no guards on this side, but I couldn't see anyone who could've grabbed my hand. Until he materialised in front of me, ripples of light turning to flesh.

I exhaled sharply, realising I'd been holding my breath. Max stood in front of me with a grin.

"Sorry I pulled you, but if I could spot those sparkling green eyes, I'm sure that mob of guards could too," he said, his voice light but intent.

"But how…" Then it clicked. I looked down at my hand—which was now bruised—and noticed Max was still holding it.
I blushed as he let go, his own cheeks turning faintly pink.

"Sorry about that too," he said quickly, looking slightly embarrassed.

I smiled shyly. "Don't be."

He chuckled softly. "The bruising, I mean."

"Oh." I replied, not really minding the bruises either. I was used to them by now. That thought lingered with me briefly. When had I become so accustomed to painite magic? It felt strange to be fighting a war against something I'd grown so comfortable with.

"Alira?" Max said, snapping me out of my thoughts.

"Huh?"

He shook his head with a quiet laugh.

"Nothing. Want to take a peek?" he asked, motioning towards the hall with his head.

"But how? There's no windows on this level."

He pointed up to a row of thin windows just before the roofline.

"But how are we supposed to get up there without drawing attention to ourselves? Air magic will definitely get us caught," I said, my voice tinged with doubt.

Max grinned. "Luckily, I happened to run into a lodestone before I made my way down here."

He held out his hand to me. The shape of my own hand was still faintly imprinted on it as a soft, purple blotch.

"It's gotten pretty weak," he admitted, "but I have no doubt that won't be a problem for you."

I hesitated, my curiosity for this new magic battling against my apprehension about touching him again. Not that I didn't want to touch him—that was the problem.

I reached for his hand, stopping myself as the realisation hit.

"No, I can't. I don't want to take your magic. I'm not a painite. It's wrong when they do it. It's wrong when you do it," I said firmly, my voice betraying a mix of fear and conviction.

"I'm giving it to you freely," Max replied softly. "I know it's wrong to steal it, and I wish I didn't have to. But I have to survive somehow. Now take it—and climb up there."

I looked at him apprehensively, still holding his hand. I hadn't realised that, as I held it, my subconscious curiosity was already drawing the magic out of him. I could feel the new magic settling into my blood, and it felt… metallic.

I scrunched my nose and dropped his hand.

"What is this? How is it supposed to help us get up there?"

Max grinned, raising his hand to the building and moving it slowly along the surface until it stopped.

"There's a metal beam here. I can feel it, but my magic isn't strong enough to climb up it to the windows."

That didn't really answer my question, but I slapped my hand onto the wall beneath his, trying to feel the beam anyway.

As soon as I tried, my hand pressed itself into the stone automatically. I flinched, startled. I tried again, this time keeping my hand a few centimetres away from the wall, feeling for the beam. As I focused on it, my hand shot forward and smacked into the wall.

"Ow."

Max grinned wider. "Congrats. You're now magnetic."

I glared at him. "Gee, thanks for the heads-up."

"You're welcome," he replied with a smirk.

I rolled my eyes at him before placing both hands on the wall, attempting to use the magnetic pull to climb. As I took a step onto the wall, my foot began to feel the pull as well. But Max was right—it wasn't strong enough. I slid down just far enough to graze my hands. Well, climbing wasn't going to happen now.

I waved my hands around, feeling the sting, and found myself wishing I had an obsidian on me. If I did, I wouldn't have to worry about cutting my skin, and the metallic properties might even boost the magnetism enough to make climbing possible. Unfortunately, I didn't have one.

Max looked disappointed, though his expression was more apologetic than anything else. Neither of us could do much about my hands right now, but I began wondering if I could climb the wall without them. That's when I realised, rather stupidly, that I was standing on sand.

"I guess we'll have to go up the old-fashioned way then," I said.

Tapping my arm gingerly, I switched to tiger's eye, not having used it recently enough to access it through blood magic. Then I smiled at Max as I lifted myself off the ground and rose towards the window on a small platform racing up the side of the building, clinging to it tightly. From the window, I looked down at him, still smiling and waiting for him to join me. But he simply looked up at me.

Why wasn't he joining me?

Oh. He couldn't.

He had borrowed my magic before I'd used sand magic, which meant he didn't have any to use at the moment.

I watched as he scanned his surroundings, a grin spreading across his face before he suddenly disappeared—using the magic he had borrowed from me. Where had he gone now?

I waited, glancing back at the window. Peering inside, I saw a crowd of guards dressed formally, aligned in neat rows. At the front of the hall stood a man, flanked by two tables: one piled with silver cylinders and the other stacked with black ones, as dark as coal.

Max reappeared then, startling me. Not only was he mid-air, but he was also mid-leap—headed straight at me.

Before I could react, he crashed into me, knocking me off balance. The platform we were both now on was way too small for two people. Especially two people laying down on top of each other.

"Sorry," he said sheepishly, "It looked bigger when only you were standing on it."

I wanted to be annoyed, but his goofy smile was too genuine. I sighed, trying to shift and get up, but there wasn't enough room to move with the way he'd fallen on me.

"I, um..." Max started hesitantly.

"I know. Hold on," I said, focusing my eyes on the edges of the platform, trying not to think about all the places Max's body was pressed into mine. Carefully, I began tracing the platform with my eyes, drawing more sand to expand it until there was enough space for Max to stand. The warmth of his body left me as he stood, reaching window level and diverting his attention. I was left lying there, my face flushed.

I got up quickly, brushing myself off and shifting my focus to the soldiers below.

"Oh, it's an officiation ceremony," Max said, his tone casual.

"A what?" I asked, glancing down at the scene.

"It's where apprentices become fully-fledged soldiers. It's when they get their own fire-lances for their stratum staffs," he explained.

I looked down again at the black and silver cylinders on the tables—one meant for each end of a stratum staff, designed to function as rudimentary firearms, or fire-lances, as Max had called them. He noticed my expression, recalling what I'd told him about my previous run-in with the guards.

"Anyway, it's all very boring. They just stand around and get little poles. Let's get out of here and do something more fun," Max suggested, grinning.

I couldn't help but smile back, though my grin faded almost instantly. The weight of everything I needed to figure out within the next week came crashing down again.

"I wish I could. But I've got lots of work to do on the project I told you about. I should probably get back soon."

"Anything specific?" Max asked innocently.

"Well, yeah, actually. I'm supposed to figure out how to… use dream magic to enter the dreams of someone far away. And then essentially do what I did yesterday with the magic sense and sapphire. So, lots to do. I better get going," I said, glancing away. Max pouted, his expression tugging at my resolve.

"I thought we were a good team yesterday. I thought you came up here because you couldn't concentrate properly?"

"Well, yes," I admitted reluctantly.

"Then why not practice with me again? I wouldn't mind the company," he said, his voice hopeful.

"I…"

Why was I trying to leave?

I had come up here to see Max, and he had been kind of helpful yesterday. Honestly, it was a lot better than sitting in Brigitte's living room with Kaiya staring at me expectantly, waiting for something to happen.

"Okay, fine—you win," I relented. "The only thing is, I can't force myself to sleep with dream magic, and it's the middle of the day. Without dreaming, I can't really do anything."

Max grinned. "I'm sure you're exhausted. I reckon taking a nap is the easier part of all this."

"You think I look tired?" I asked, raising an eyebrow.

"No. I think your mind is working in overdrive and needs a rest. I also think that's why you find it so hard to force yourself asleep with magic," Max replied earnestly.

"I…"

He was probably right, but I didn't want to tell him that.

"Fine, sure, but I doubt your sandstone furniture would make for a comfy napping spot," I countered.

"No, not really," Max said with a grin. "But I have a better idea."

He extended his hand to me. After a moment's hesitation, I took it, wincing slightly at the grazes on my palms as I let him guide me again. I laughed quietly when we emerged on the same top floor of a half-finished building where we'd practiced yesterday. I'd have to remember this path next time.

Max sat down casually and tapped his thigh with his hand. "Come on," he said.

I scrunched my face at him. "You really want me to put my head in your lap? Isn't that a bit…" I trailed off, unsure of the word I was looking for.

"If you'd rather lay on the cold stone, be my guest. But I don't think you'll be able to fall asleep that way," he said, smirking but genuine all the same.

I laid down, resting my head in Max's lap, gazing out onto the gardens of level ten. My eyelids immediately grew heavy, weighed down by thoughts as I settled in. With sand magic still active, I subtly reshaped the ground around me, forming the flat stone to suit the contours of my body pressing against it.

I pulled out the purple crystal, placing it in front of me, focusing on the dreams contained within it. Max began stroking my hair lightly. I tensed for a moment but soon relaxed, reasoning that he was only trying to help me fall asleep. That's all this was—to help me.

I closed my eyes, allowing the crystal and the serene view to imprint themselves on the back of my eyelids.

Gradually, the curve of the stone beneath me faded, as did the gentle breeze brushing my skin. The warmth on my neck was the last sensation to dissolve as I opened my eyes to a hazy world of my own creation.

All I had to do now was enter someone else's dreams.

But who would even be asleep this early? Dad surely wasn't, and neither was Cybele. My thoughts drifted to those below, and the only person remotely likely to be asleep was Lola. I hesitated. I didn't particularly want to intrude on her. She was quiet and still a bit wary of most of us, despite the brave face she put on. I didn't want to disturb her sleep, but Lola was my only option right now.

I had hoped to enter Max's dream first, him being closest to me, and then push myself further. But Max was awake, stroking my hair as I slept—a strange thing to realise while actively dreaming. At least I knew I was safe where I was.

Alright, time to find Lola in the dream world.

I paused, unsure of how to even locate someone in the dream world. I hadn't received much instruction on dream magic, although Kaiya had been pretty helpful during our early practice sessions. I remembered them saying that all I had to do was focus on the person, imagining myself in their presence, until our minds "ran into each other," as they'd put it.

I tried to follow their advice and quickly realised why distance posed such a significant challenge with dream magic. It was like shooting an arrow. Hitting a close target was relatively simple, but the further away the other mind was, the more precise I had to be.

If I was even a few degrees off—or in this case if my thoughts were too far removed from Lola's—I would miss her completely. The real problem, though, was that I didn't know much about Lola. And I certainly didn't know anything about the painites aboard the world-ship. Not enough to shoot my mind that far, anyway.

Regardless of that, I focused on the few things I did know about Lola. But the scenes around me quickly shifted into a story of abuse and control. There were fuzzy depictions of what I imagined had been done to her—like Akeldama taking her blood, telling her it was for the greater good or something equally manipulative.

One scene, however, stood out with unsettling clarity. It was sharper than my imagination, with details that grew more vivid the closer I approached. Too vivid, perhaps, even for a dream.

That's when I realised I had accidently stepped into Lola's nightmares.

I looked around, spotting her staring at a nightmarish version of Akeldama. Her dreaming body mirrored the version of herself that Akeldama had his hands on, drawing out her blood as he glowed red.

He was speaking to her, saying false things as though they were true, testing to see if he could make her believe them with her own magic. He seemed to tire of this quickly, turning instead to experimentation. His red glow intensified as he drained more blood, his voice forcing its way into her ears, whispering unspeakable things.

Dream Lola began to turn, moving in a daze. I knew I had to stop this. I ran to her—the second version of her that mirrored the dream—and shook her, trying to wake her, to break her out of the nightmare. I knew I couldn't undo Akeldama's whispered orders or change the past, but I could try to pull her out of this torment.

Her head snapped up suddenly, tears streaming from her eyes as she looked around, panicked and disoriented. When her eyes locked with mine, she was still panicking, unable to comprehend what was happening.

The nightmare began to fade then, holes spreading through it too quickly to follow. I looked around, but it was already gone—Lola dissolving as I turned back. A sharp pain pierced my head, instantly giving me a migraine as I jolted awake.

I gasped, my hand instinctively reaching for my forehead, wondering why it hurt so much. As I touched my head, I flinched, the stinging of my grazed palms reminding me where I was.

Lola's memories flooded back into my mind, bringing my own tears with them. I saw her tiny, tear-streaked face, panicking and overwhelmed. Whatever he had made her do remained unknown and unseen, but the feelings lingered in her unconscious mind—suppressed, whether by her own will or by another force, I couldn't tell.

Either way, they hurt.

When my tears started falling, I felt warm arms wrap around me, grounding me in the present. I remembered then—I was in Max's lap. That realisation brought fresh guilt, the comfort I felt from him standing in stark contrast to the absence of comfort Lola had endured for so many years. Her only solace had been the boy she called her brother—and he was gone.

The guilt overwhelmed me, and I cried harder, desperate to go to her, to offer her some fragment of the comfort she had been denied. I pulled back from Max, his expression bewildered as he took in my tears.

"Alira, what happened!?" he asked, concern thick in his voice.

I didn't know how to explain it, but I managed to whisper,

"The nightmares of a little girl rescued from Akeldama's army."

A pained understanding washed over Max's face.

"I have to go to her," I said, sniffling.

"Go, help her," Max said gently, compassion filling his tone as he helped me to my feet and began leading the way back to where he had found me. I paused for a moment, watching him. How did he understand so much with so little information?

My curiosity about his past bubbled to the surface again. Why did he leave, or avoid, Poenari? What had he seen?

But that could wait. Right now, Lola needed me.

I couldn't shake the overwhelming guilt at the thought that I might have caused those nightmares. I had used her abuse—the only things I knew about her—to dream myself into her mind, only to discover the reality of her suffering was worse than I had imagined.

43 – Ender

Where was Alira? She was supposed to be back hours ago. Chantrelle had only needed a few hours to prepare the tattoo, and it had been ready right on time. But it was after dark now, and there was still no sign of her.

I sat in the living room of our cabin, waiting anxiously. Cordelia was waiting with me too. She'd decided there was no point in going to get Cybele yet if Alira was missing. Chantrelle had already gone to bed, citing exhaustion. She said she needed to be precise to complete the tattoo and told us to come and find her in the morning. My worry deepened with every passing minute.

Alira had wandered off into the city again. She certainly wasn't anywhere nearby, and despite everything that had happened the first time she'd been to Muruntau, she had found something out there worth visiting. And now, whatever it was might have hurt her. Why else would she be so late?

Suddenly, I heard footsteps. Someone was outside. Someone was *running* outside.

I jumped up immediately and ran to open the door. I swung it open to find Alira mid-sprint, her face red and her expression far from the *oh-shit-I'm-really-late* kind of worried I would've expected. She slowed down just enough to squeeze through the doorway, but rushed straight past me, leaving me bewildered as she headed directly for Lola's room. Too stunned to ask what was going on, I followed her as she walked into Lola's room, flipping on the light.

Lola was sitting on her bed, her knees drawn up to her chest. She looked up, revealing a tear-streaked and red face. I had thought she was asleep, but she had been crying for a while, all while Cordelia and I had been sitting clueless in the other room.

A pang of guilt struck me—I hadn't known. But somehow, Alira had. Without hesitation, Alira crawled onto Lola's bed, pulling her into a hug and apologising softly, over and over. I couldn't figure out exactly what she was apologising for. Lola stayed curled up in her little ball, her arms wrapped tightly around herself, with Alira's arms encircling her, both of them crying silently. I glanced at Cordelia, who looked just as lost as I did.

"Alira… What happened?" I asked quietly, breaking the silence. She glanced up at me, tears still streaming, but didn't let go of Lola.

"I was practicing using dream magic, but I… I ended up in Lola's nightmares," she replied, her voice thick with emotion.

Oh. So that's why they were crying.

I couldn't begin to imagine what Lola had been through—being both a blood battery and child spy for someone like Akeldama—but it must have been worse than anything I had imagined. Bad enough to break Alira down and send her running to protect her. I wasn't sure I even wanted to know what she'd seen, but I knew I definitely didn't want to ask.

"Do either of you need anything?" I managed to ask, my voice hesitant and unsure, as I stood awkwardly in the doorway. I couldn't know what Alira and Lola had experienced—only they knew that. Maybe, somehow, they would bond over it. Either way, it sounded like a hell of a first proper experience in the dreamscape.

Feeling like my presence was only adding to the awkwardness, I quietly retreated to the kitchen, deciding not to disturb whatever had happened between them. Instead, I waited patiently in the living room, hoping Alira would eventually explain what had kept her away for so many hours.

Unexpectedly, Alira wasn't the first to emerge. Cybele came through the front door instead, catching both Cordelia and me by surprise.

"What? I can't come back by myself for once? It's long past the time you were supposed to come and get me yesterday," Cybele said, her tone half-amused and half-annoyed. I shrugged, unsure how to respond. That made enough sense to me, but Cordelia didn't look entirely convinced. She stared back at Cybele suspiciously.

Cybele flushed pink under her gaze.

"Okay, fine. Maybe I've gotten a bit too used to everyone being in the workshop with me. I wondered where you'd all gone," she admitted reluctantly. In other words, she missed us.

Alira emerged then, her face tear-stained and a bit red, though she seemed far calmer than she had earlier. Cybele frowned at the sight of her coming out of Lola's room looking like she did and immediately went to investigate. Alira sank down beside me on the couch, her expression blank.

"So, what happened to you today? I know you said you fell into Lola's nightmares, but you've been gone for quite a while—and you missed getting the teleporter tattoo from Chantrelle," I said, concerned.

"I know, I know," Alira replied. "I was practicing dream magic, like I said, but it's hard to keep track of time in there. By the time I woke up, I raced back here."

"You spent the entire rest of the day asleep?"

"Well, yeah. I was tired. Plus, it was the only way to practice, so... win-win."

"And you came running down from the city? Sleeping somewhere up there?"

"I... found a comfy spot, okay? It's not all sandstone and merkets you know," she said defensively.

I sighed. It was hard to fault her for being exhausted.

But even while she slept, she had been practicing—for all our sakes. Now certainly wasn't the time to pry.

"Alright, I get it," I said, thinking out loud. "This means you'll have one less night to try using dream magic with the tattoo acting as a lead wire. But I suppose you need to practice entering dreams from a distance anyway, which I know is why you were up in the city in the first place."

As the realisation dawned on me, Alira looked a little smug. I suppose that was my fault. She was doing everything she could to chip away at this task, for all of us. I just had to shut up and trust her at this point. Trying to second-guess her was only making me look foolish.

"Right. Sunrise at the Telesto Cabin," I finished, rising from the couch. "I'll walk with you. See you in the morning."

Turning to Cordelia as I concluded, she nodded without a word, still waiting quietly. With that, Alira and I wandered off to bed

When I rose, I found no-one in the living room but myself. I peeked into Alira's room only to discover she was gone—as were Lola and Cybele. I could guess where Lola and Cybele might be, but Alira could be anywhere. A flicker of worry crossed my mind as I hoped she hadn't run off into the city again, forgetting about Chantrelle. I pushed the thought aside, reminding myself that I had decided to trust Alira more. She was probably already with Chantrelle, too impatient to wait for me to get up. The sooner the better, I suppose.

After a quick breakfast, I made my way to the Telesto cabin to look for her. When I entered, I found Alira exactly where I'd hoped she'd be—in Chantrelle's overly complex chair, mid-tattoo. It felt strange walking in on them like this, my teenage daughter smiling up at me while in the middle of getting inked.
I know I had told her to do this, but my parental instincts were still shaking their head at her.

"And... all done!" Chantrelle announced as the machine hovering over Alira's wrist finished injecting her with encrypted ink and withdrew.

"It's crazy to think the world-ship just has a machine that can do this in a matter of minutes. DNA encryption and all," Chantrelle mused, her enthusiasm evident. I nodded, keeping my attention on Alira as she held up her wrist to inspect the fresh ink.

"It looks different from Dad's," she remarked simply. Chantrelle's face twisted into an expression I could only describe as cheeky.

"Well, I did have a couple of weeks to tinker. The technology is amazing, sure—but it's not exactly well-suited for the modern lady," she quipped with a grin.

I could see what Alira meant now. It did look a bit different. Her tattoo had three cords circling her wrist instead of the two. The third was thinner than the darker bands, and gold.

"You see, the two bands are essentially fixed," Chantrelle explained. "They represent you and the world-ship. Activating the tattoo kind of resets your position relative to the ship. Teleportation is more complicated than that, but anyway. This third band, I coded myself. It can represent the entire current teleporter network, meaning you'll be able to 'reset your position' to any detectable teleporter, rather than just the ones aboard the world-ship."

Alira's eyes lit up with excitement.

"So I could be in Telesto just like that?" she asked, clicking her fingers for emphasis.

"Well, not exactly," Chantrelle replied. "Telesto doesn't have any teleporters. It's too small to need them."

"Oh. So I can only really teleport to the city and then I'd have to fly all the way back?"

"Well, right now, yes," Chantrelle said simply.

Hearing them discuss the teleporter network revealed potential flaws in our grand plan.

"Hold on. So if Alira and I teleport aboard the world-ship, neither of us would be able to come back here? We'd have to teleport up to The City?" I asked, the realisation dawning on me.

That same realisation flickered across both Alira's and Chantrelle's faces.

"Well, that's not the most convenient," Chantrelle admitted, "but we can certainly plan around that."

"Why don't we just build a teleporter?" Alira suggested.

"I think Cybele has her hands full at the moment with the telescope," I replied. "Although I am surprised she, of all people, didn't pick up on that during the meeting."

Alira raised her hand to examine her tattoo once again before lowering it thoughtfully.

"Sounds like we need to go and tell her then," she said decisively.

"Yes, we should."

Alira hopped up from her seat, turning to wave goodbye to Chantrelle as we left for the workshop. Maybe, if Alira and I helped Cybele, we could build both the telescope and the teleporter in time. After all, Alira couldn't practice dream magic while she was wide awake anyway. When we entered the workshop, I was surprised to find the telescope much more complete than I had expected. I had only missed a day, yet Cybele had made incredible progress—and so had Lola, who was darting back and forth, fetching items for her.

"Cybele," I said, astonished. "I see you've been busy. This thing is starting to look pretty complete."

Cybele didn't look up as we entered or spoke but responded immediately from across the room.

"It's nearly there—the physical structure, anyway. I'll probably need to tweak it a little, but most of the remaining work will be coding it properly to search for antimatter and ensuring it communicates that information to the world-ship."

"Right, of course. However, we realised we overlooked one thing when we were planning yesterday and thought you might have the time and expertise to help us rectify it."

Cybele frowned thoughtfully. "Overlooked what? I mean, the plan is tenuous and somewhat theoretical at this point, but it should work with what we have."

"How we'll teleport back here from the world-ship," I explained. "Muruntau doesn't have a teleporter to return to."

"I know." Cybele grinned, finally turning her gaze towards us. "I meant it when I said I could send four of you down there. You didn't think I'd leave you stranded, did you? Well, I suppose it's only two of you now, but still, I didn't overlook it."

"So... you have a teleporter?" I asked skeptically.

"Well, no. Not yet," Cybele admitted, "but it was included in my estimate for the telescope build. But it's not that difficult. I've drawn up the plans and salvaged the setup from my office teleporter. All you guys have to do is put it together while I'm coding the telescope."

"You want us to build a teleporter by ourselves?" I asked, my exasperation evident.

"Not just you. Chantrelle seems capable. I imagine she'd be able to read my plans and guide you. Now that the tattoo is done, I don't think she's working on anything else, is she?"

"I don't think so, no."

"Perfect! Tell her to come have a look then—oh, wait, no. Give us an hour, and then come have a look at the plans. Until then, you should all stay out of here."

"Um... why?"

"Navoi found a buried ship for me that has the kinds of semiconductors I need for the bolometer and a couple of other components. The problem is, the ship was nuclear-powered, and the wreckage is still a bit radioactive," Cybele said matter-of-factly. I glanced behind her to find Lola dragging herself towards us, an oversized lead apron hanging off her shoulders.

"Ok, sure, but I'm taking Lola. She can't be exposed to all that," I said firmly. Cybele visibly deflated.

"She's a good little helper, but you're right."

Cybele turned towards Lola.

"Lola, you're going to have to go with Ender for a bit, okay? It won't be safe for you in here soon."

"Why! I wanna stay!" Lola complained, making a grumpy face at Cybele while she cast a wary glance in my direction. Alira smiled and extended her hand towards Lola.

"Come with me, then. You'll be back in no time."

"Where are we going?" Lola asked, still unmoving.

"How about I show you my super-secret spot where I go to practise magic?" Alira offered.

Lola hesitated but looked as though she might take the bait.

"Super-secret spot?"

"Absolutely super-secret. No one knows about it but me," Alira said playfully. Lola grinned and finally took her hand.

"Okay."

The two of them left, presumably heading up into the city somewhere. It must be quite the spot. Alira had been taking every spare moment she could to go there.

"You too. Get out, unless you want to be irradiated," Cybele said, turning her attention back to me.

"Oi! I was your assistant first," I retorted, grabbing Lola's lead apron and throwing it on. "You were so quick to replace me."

"You were easy to replace," Cybele quipped, smirking. I rolled my eyes at her.

"So, where's this buried ship then?"

44 – Alira

I don't regret offering to take Lola. It was the right thing to do—and if anyone needed a spot all to themselves, it was her. But this wasn't exactly my spot. Showing up here with a fresh, custom parliamentarian tattoo and an eight-year-old in tow was bound to result in Max asking for an explanation. I could already tell how hard he was trying to look past certain things, just for the sake of hanging out. I also knew that my living on level nine still bothered him.

I was scared to come here like this, but I had promised Lola. Maybe Max wouldn't even be here. And maybe, if he was, he'd stay quiet with Lola around. That was wishful thinking.

When we arrived at the spot, I released a breath I hadn't realised I was holding. Looking around, I saw no sign of Max. Relief washed over me.

"And here we are," I said, announcing our arrival as I sat down on the edge overlooking level ten.

"You get to see everything from up here. Everything below us, anyway—but all the important things are going on down there anyway. And it's not so far away that you feel like you've left everyone. Its nice and quiet too which is good for practising, but you could do whatever you like up here."

I paused, watching Lola, unsure what she was thinking.

She blinked at me and said, "But I don't need to practise."

"Then what do you want to do?" I asked her.

"I don't know."

"Well, what do you like to do for fun?"

"For fun..." Lola repeated, her gaze dropping to the ground, her face growing sadder by the second. Right. It looked like I'd have to come up with something myself.

"What about your magic?" I suggested. "Why don't you show me what you can do with it?"

She lit up instantly. "Oh, okay!"

Straightening her posture, she brought her hands behind her back as a soft red glow began to form around her. The glow dissipated once the magic was complete, and Lola had 'transformed' herself as best as she could.

"Let their downfall begin!" she exclaimed dramatically, attempting to deepen her voice. She broke character almost immediately, bursting into giggles. The red beryl magic was patchy, as Cybele had said it would be when physical distortions went too far. Lola certainly didn't have a tail or the elongated features of Navoi, but her dark brown scales and striking golden eyes were still more than enough to make her look a bit scary—even if she was still only four foot and full of giggles.

Impressions. That's what she did for fun.

"Ooh, scary. Who else can you do?" I asked, smiling at her. She grinned before the red glow washed over her again, her brown scales softening to pale skin as she transformed herself into a short version of Dad.

"Practice, practice, practice," was all she managed to come up with, mimicking his tone as best she could. I was glad I wasn't the only one who was hearing that.

"Can you do me?" I asked, grinning and curious about how she saw me—and whether she'd be brave enough to try it right in front of me. She didn't hesitate.

"I can do it! Let's go to my super-secret hiding spot where my Dad will never find us!" she declared, her attempt at sounding like me surprisingly accurate. I couldn't help but giggle too. Her impressions were spot on.

"Cybele?" I asked next.

She shook her head, turning back into herself.

"I don't know half the words she says, and she says them really fast," Lola replied, her expression a mix of frustration and amusement. I laughed, making her grin wider.

"Me either," I admitted.

Somehow, Lola and I managed to pass an hour this way, her playful transformations keeping the mood light. I wasn't great at keeping track of time, but Lola—being a local—knew exactly when the hour was up and was already itching to rush back.

"Okay, okay, I'm coming," I said as I got up, watching her eagerly wait for me at the first turn into the maze that led us back. I heard a voice then and spun around, though I couldn't see anyone.

"Max? How long have you been here?" I called out.

"Long enough," he replied cryptically, as I finally spotted his shadow at the top of the staircase leading to this floor.

"What's that supposed to mean?" I asked, narrowing my eyes.

"Long enough to know that I can't keep ignoring your life," he said sharply. "You show up today with what looks a lot like a parliamentarian tattoo and a child spy from Poenari. Care to explain that? Especially when the painites killed all the parliamentarians. I presume that would mean only their own kind could waltz in wherever they're hiding and get their bloody tattoo." His voice rose, thick with anger.

"Come on, what are you doing?" Lola interrupted impatiently.

"Max, it's not what you think," I said quickly, trying to calm him down. "Lola is the one we rescued—the one who had the nightmare yesterday. And the tattoo isn't a proper one. My friend synthesised it so that we could sneak aboard the world-ship."

"World-ship?"

Crap, there I go again blabbing secrets. Not that I wasn't going to tell him anyway.

"It's where parliament is. I'm sorry. I promise I'll explain everything tomorrow. I have to go now."

He looked conflicted, but with a final glance said, "You better." Before disappearing down the stairs.

"Are you talking to someone? I thought you said it was super-secret."

"It is, I'm sorry, I'm coming now." I finally replied to Lola, hurrying off towards her and leading the way back to the workshop.

The telescope didn't look any bigger when I arrived, which was unusual given how it seemed to get bigger every time I saw it. I guessed that whatever Cybele had salvaged wasn't very big.

I didn't stick around for long, though. I was only there to drop off Lola and ended up picking Dad up. The rest of the day was spent picking Chantrelle up and then heading back to the workshop to try to decipher Cybele's teleporter plans—which she had somehow found the time to draw up.

Chantrelle understood the designs well enough to start directing Dad and me, telling us to grab this or fetch that. Under Chantrelle's instructions—and with the help of sapphire magic—Dad managed to assemble most of the pieces. Just to practise and hopefully be useful, I decided to channel sapphire magic myself, albeit through the purple crystal and in combination with magic sense. It didn't help much in understanding Cybele's unique teleporter design, but it did provide some surprising insights. When combined with magic sense, the sapphire magic helped me intuit how the pieces fit together and, surprisingly, allowed me to locate materials. It was as though sensing magic and machinery had merged, giving me a feel for the metals we needed and where they were.

For example, when we needed platinum, I simply focused on it and felt myself spin like a compass pointing straight towards it. It was subtle, but by the time we were done, I had started to get used to it.

We'd made good progress by nightfall, but I knew that wasn't going to be the hardest part of today. Once Cordelia came to shepherd the five of us, I started feeling anxious about getting to sleep. Or more specifically, what I was supposed to do while I was asleep. I still wasn't sure if it was even possible, but I had told Navoi I could do it. That left me with no choice but to figure it out. Somehow.

Dad saw my expression as everyone started heading to bed.

"It's okay if you can't find the ship on the first night," he said gently. "I know it's a big ask, but if anyone can do it, it's you."

"I know, it's just... well, it didn't exactly go well last time. And this time, I'll just be shooting in the dark, not knowing whose twisted mind I'll end up in."

He sighed. "I know. But whatever happens, we'll all be here for you in the morning."

He tried to give me a reassuring smile, but it didn't quite land. Regardless, I knew I had to do this. Time to dream-walk. Into the darkness. At the centre of the planet. Oh joy.

I crawled into bed, finally alone, and found my thoughts drifting to Max. Specifically, to his fingers stroking my hair. I missed them as I tried to settle into sleep. I couldn't help but dread tomorrow. His demeanor had already been scarier than I'd expected, and I knew I needed to figure out why. What was his past? I pushed those thoughts aside. They were for tomorrow.

It took an annoyingly long time, but eventually, I fell asleep—not even sure if I was using dream magic or not. It felt strange. More like a real dream—the kind you only half remember in the morning, never certain if you were conscious or merely playing a role within it.

When I rose that morning, trying to decipher my own dream, Dad caught sight of the puzzled expression on my face the moment I stepped out of my room.

"Alira, how did it go? You, uh... look confused," he said.

"I am," I admitted. "Because I'm not sure how it went. I definitely had a dream, but I'm not sure if it was more than that. Usually, it's obvious when I'm using dream magic, but this time it felt just like a regular dream. All I can remember now are flashes. And there's nothing I can say that definitely didn't come from my own memory, because the whole dream was just me wandering the world-ship. All steel corridors and crumpled metal. It was eerily empty, though. Maybe I was just remembering how I had seen it before. Or maybe I actually did use dream magic, but was wandering through an uninhabited part."

Dad frowned thoughtfully. "I thought you had to connect to someone's dreams first and then push your magic sense out from them, or however Cybele phrased it."

"Yeah, which makes me even more certain that this was just a regular dream," I replied, sighing. Dad let out a long breath of his own.

"Maybe it was, but it's worth having a chat with Cybele about it. She might have some ideas."

"If you say so, but I think she's got more important things to worry about right now," I said, unconvinced.

"I know, but I still think you should mention it. You never know with her—she might already have thought of other ways for you to dream yourself down there."

"Ok, fine, I'll go," I said reluctantly.

"Have fun," Dad called after me as I left for the day. I wandered over to the workshop to speak with Cybele, but she didn't have any ideas. She was just as convinced as I was that it had been a regular dream.

With that out of the way, I left the gardens and went to look for Max to finally explain everything as I had promised. I tried to construct a version of events in my head, but there were so many crazy things to keep track of. By the time I arrived at our spot with a narrative that I thought would cover all the gaps, it completely fell apart the moment I saw Max. He was sitting there, staring at me expectantly, and I immediately started stuttering.

"So?" he asked, his tone impatient.

"I..." I trailed off and sighed deeply. "I don't even know where to start."

"At the beginning. Like, where are you from? The City?" he prompted. I chuckled softly.

"Far from it," I replied, before sitting down next to him. Slowly, I began recounting the entire story, from our home on Earth to the truth about the secret project I had mentioned before. Max's expression shifted through a mix of emotions as he listened to my story, each one more complex than the last. It was especially obvious when I reached the parts of my story that Max didn't believe—like when I told him I had died.

I tried to explain my theory: that because I had the mind stone with me, it somehow preserved my mind long enough to revive my body. It was the only way to make sense of the strange disconnect I had felt when I got up.

Eventually, I reached the part about Lola, and Max's expression shifted. He looked strangely guilty, as though something was his fault—but I couldn't figure out what. We sat in silence after I finished speaking. I was confused by Max's reaction to my explanation of how I met Lola and desperately wished he would say something—anything—to let me in on his thoughts.

When he finally spoke, it wasn't at all what I had been expecting.

"I'm sorry I forced you to tell me everything like that," he said. "It was when I saw Lola... I was already ignoring so much about your background, but I just couldn't help thinking..."

He sighed heavily.

"Lola was the reason my mother and I finally left my father to come here."

I blinked, struggling to understand.

"She what? How does that make sense?"

The guilty expression returned to his face, like remembering this pained him in some way.

"I couldn't stop him," Max said quietly. "He wouldn't stop when Mother asked. He abused that girl with her own magic. It was the last straw. We left right after that. He had finally lost all of his humanity. So we finally left him. I tried to convince my sister to come with us, but she refused. I couldn't convince her. She wasn't like him—not back then anyway."

My eyes grew wide as realisation dawned on me. Surely it was impossible, wasn't it? But it made far too much sense not to be true. The way they had fled Poenari to live in poverty. The missing name from their home. And, I mean, Ayuna had to have a mother somewhere, right?

Max finally met my gaze, his weak smile tinged with guilt.

"I'm sorry. All this time you were fighting for your life because of my family. All this time you've trusted me, and I've been one of them. You should've trusted your instincts when we first met and burned me to the ground where I stood."

As shocking as this revelation was, Max was wrong.

"No, you're not one of them," I said firmly. "You might be blood, but you've left them. You're a good man. You'd never hurt anyone."

"But I didn't save her. I could have saved Lola, but I didn't. Isn't that just as bad?" Max asked, his voice heavy with guilt.

"No. You were afraid, and that's understandable," I replied softly. "I've seen your father kill dozens of people in a row with a smile. He's pure evil. You're nothing like him."

"How can you say that about me? My sister killed you," Max said bitterly.

"You're not her either. You can't be responsible for her actions. Besides, I'm fine now," I said reassuringly.

Max scoffed, his frustration evident.

"You say you're fine, but I know you're not. You've been pushing yourself nonstop, and now you're consoling me of all people—the brother of the enemy. Nothing about this is fine."

"No. Maybe you're right. But you're far from being the enemy. You might even be my only friend. And that's all that really matters," I said with conviction, leaning my head on his shoulder as I stared out over the gardens.

We sat in silence for a while, the quiet stretching between us like a fragile thread—all of our vulnerabilities out in the open.

Eventually, I felt Max lean his head gently atop mine, and my face flushed slightly as I realised what I was doing. I lifted my head and cleared my throat, breaking the moment.

"Well, now that that's all settled. What now?" I asked, attempting to shift the conversation. Max blinked, his expression uncertain.

"Well, I guess you've got a war to plan or something. You kind of lost me with the whole telescope and world-ship thing."

"Yeah. Cybele explains it better—at least when she's not talking so fast that no one can catch what she's saying," I said with a faint chuckle.

Max smiled faintly, his gaze steady.

"I want to help. Tell me how I can help."

I smiled. "You can help me with my part."

"Which would be?"

"You can help me sleep."

He looked at me softly. Maybe too softly.

"Of course, I can do that. As long as you promise not to have any more nightmares."

He was saying this with a smirk, but that was quickly dashed by a pang of guilt, and now I knew why.

"I won't. I promise. It'll just be wandering the halls of the world-ship this time. Hopefully."

"Right. The centre of the planet. I'm choosing to believe you this time but it's still far-fetched."

"Trust me, I'm aware."

I sat there awkwardly, not wanting to just throw myself into his lap. Max smirked and reached around my shoulder, pulling me into his lap instead.

Finally—a peaceful moment.

I knew I still had a lot of work to do, but not having to worry about Max turning on me lifted a huge weight off my mind. Just enough weight to let me relax into him and drift off to sleep, focusing on the grainy images of the halls of the world-ship, as I pushed my dreaming brain into the void as far down as I could. The halls were still grainy as I imagined them, but something felt different. I realised I couldn't easily swap the images out anymore—and Max's gentle strokes were gone.

Looking around, I grinned. So it hadn't been just a dream last night. This was the world-ship. But for some reason, I had a firmer grasp on it now than I'd had before. My vision remained grainy, like an old television screen, as I began wandering the ship. I quickly found myself lost, and the section I was in seemed entirely uninhabited. It didn't occur to me to try a teleporter until I had wandered for a while—probably in circles—attempting to use perception magic to make my sight clearer. Usually, perception magic was overwhelming, but given my limited visibility, it felt like the most useful tool I had.

When I managed to create spots of clarity—like borderless magnifying glasses—and one landed on a teleporter, I realised I might actually be able to navigate this place properly. The teleporter menu was difficult to read, especially with my grainy vision, but the hangar stood out on the map—a large, empty section of the ship. I selected a teleporter close to the hangar and tried to recall which direction I needed to go to get even closer to it. It was empty on the other side, but muffled voices now echoed faintly through the halls.

After wandering further without encountering anyone, I came across larger doors that I could only assume led directly into the hangar. I stepped closer, and the doors began to slide open, but they abruptly stopped halfway before slamming shut with an aggressive force. A harshly whispered *"NO!"* rang out in my head, startling me. I stubbed my toe on the door, though there was no pain in the dreamscape—at least not in this low-resolution version. It felt like I was seeing everything through some sort of CCTV camera.

Confused by the voice and the door's behaviour, I turned left, following along the outside of the hangar instead. The muffled voices grew louder as I continued, and I slowed my footsteps, unsure if I could be seen. After all, I wasn't physically here—but I had to be inside someone's mind, didn't I?

As I turned the corner, I gasped. Two painite soldiers whispering to each other passed right through me as though I wasn't there. Their bodies passed through mine, leaving me dazed, and I watched them leave until their forms dissolved into increasingly pixelated static.

Okay. So I was like a ghost in this form. Good to know. Refocusing, I layered my perception magic with magic sense, allowing me to map out the layout of the painite nest I had finally reached the edge of. I strode forward with more confidence, now knowing where everyone was hiding and that they couldn't see or touch me.

A less harsh *"Stop, STOP,"* whispered through my mind. It was starting to get creepy—and more than a little annoying—but I pushed on, gliding past painites in the hall as I tried to expand my reach deeper into the ship. I couldn't keep blindly wandering through hallways, so I started layering Sapphire magic alongside the others. A grin spread across my face as I felt the hum in the walls—the way the wires crisscrossed, each carrying its own unique form of energy. I was officially using all four magics in the mind stone at once. I had finally done it.

A surge of pride swelled within me—but it didn't last long. The ghost in the wall hovering by my ear didn't seem to share my excitement. Startled, I jumped and swivelled to face him. He looked just as startled, pulling back into the wall until only his head and shoulders remained visible.

"Who are you? I thought I was a ghost like this," I asked warily.

"A ghost?" he repeated with a laugh. "You're not a ghost, my dear. And neither am I. Although I have been called the ghost in the machine before, mind you."

He did look ghostly, sticking out of the wall like that, his skin semi-transparent and slightly shimmery. What struck me as odd, though, was how much clearer he appeared compared to the other people or even the ship around me. Curiously, as I stared at him a little longer, I realised something else: he gave off absolutely nothing with magic sense. Somehow, either his magic was undetectable in this form, or he had none at all.

"What are you staring at? I should be staring at you. No one can see me. No one ever has—at least not while I was dead. So why can you?" he asked sharply.

He began to look me up and down, slowly drifting out of the wall towards me.

"Why do you say you're not a ghost if you're dead and you look like that?" I asked.

"Look like what? The same as you? Are you dead?"

"No."

"I didn't think so. Otherwise, we wouldn't be having this lively little chat, would we?" he retorted with a sly smile.

"But you said you had died before," I pressed.

"So have you, my dear. I saw it for myself. And yet here you are, claiming that you're not dead."

"I'm not."

"And neither am I."

This was getting absolutely nowhere. I sighed in frustration, throwing my hands up.

"Fine then, what are you?"

"A rather rude question, but seeing as this is the longest conversation I've had in quite some time—and probably will ever have—I'll oblige. I am the artificial intelligence that used to run this ship when it was still soaring through space. Although it has been such a long time since then. I'm afraid I'm not quite up to snuff anymore."

"You're the local AI of this massive alien spaceship?" I asked incredulously. "Then why do you look human, and sound so... British?"

"Oh, this is just my last form. The one that died. I used to guard this place in a way—showing travellers to the entrance to try their luck at the trials. That was before one of the challengers killed me, of course. That's also how I found this charming little accent. It was buried in the mind of a challenger from years ago. I thought it was quite fun and decided to try it out for my next reincarnation—if I ever get one," he replied, his tone oddly cheerful. My eyes went wide, though I could barely keep from laughing. He must have scanned Dad's brain once upon a time and discovered his accent there. I had no doubt this AI was far from what it used to be, but perhaps it could be useful.

"What do you mean reincarnated?" I asked, curious.

"Oh, well, you know. Sometimes I stumble upon the opportunity to give myself a body—or at least part of me a body. My first attempt was pretty messy, but eventually, I found that on occasion stray travellers would die of shock or for one reason or another *before* their ships crashed into the planet," he explained casually. "And on even rarer occasions, they had sufficient cybernetic enhancements for me to pop right in there and save their bodies when they were done with them. It didn't work out all the time, obviously, but that's how I managed that last one."

"That's... Okay, I'm just going to ignore all of that. So now that you don't have a body, you're back to being a ghost in the machine," I said, finally understanding what he had been trying to explain. In a way, he was just like me—except I had a body to return to, and he didn't.

"I don't suppose you'd want to point me to where Ayuna is, would you?" I asked hesitantly.

"Why on Earth would you want to visit the girl who killed you? And me, by the way," he replied sharply.

"Because... wait," I faltered, realising something. She was the challenger who killed him?

"Were you the guy in the tent?" I asked, my voice rising in surprise.

"Yes. Like I said, I used to guard this place and show challengers to the entrance."

"And... okay, never mind that. Can you show me to Ayuna?"

He sighed. "I can, but I tend to avoid those parts of the ship. And I would too if I were you. Those painites give me the creeps—they're always doing things that ruin this place. And that's saying something, given how ruined it has already become."

"Please?" I asked, trying to sound persuasive.

"Fine. This way," he responded reluctantly.

I had expected a little more resistance from him, but he was a surprisingly cheery guy. Maybe it was just the English politeness rubbing off on him or something, but I kind of liked him. Plus, he might actually prove useful if he could access the ship's systems.

As I followed his lead towards Ayuna, I asked, "So, can you still control the ship?"

He frowned back at me as he glided down the corridor, half embedded in the wall.

"Of course. I closed that door on you, didn't I?"

"What about the teleporters?"

He squinted at me suspiciously.

"I suppose I could, but I don't know what on Earth I'd do that for."

"Well, it's kind of difficult to get down here. If I wanted to visit you physically, I'd need a way to get here. Wouldn't it make sense to help me connect a teleporter to somewhere down here?"

"Who says I want you to visit? Plus, you've got a parliamentarian tattoo—I can sense it. Although, you've done something strange to it."

"I mean, sure, but what if I wanted to bring my friends? And how would I get back home?" I countered.

He scoffed in response, clearly unconvinced

"And why would you want to bring your friends to an inescapable viper pit? You surely are crazy. No wonder you got yourself killed. And now you want to go and hang out with your murderer? Ha, preposterous!"

I chuckled at his bluntness. He was right—maybe I was a little crazy to be doing all of this. But it didn't matter yet. I was still a ghost to them all, for now. As we turned the corner, I caught a glimpse of Ayuna crossing the hall from one room to the next. I froze in place, but slowly, an idea started forming in my mind.

"What if, instead of bringing my friends down here, you send Ayuna up to us instead? You could change the destination of a teleporter, surely? It is your ship, after all."

He stared at me as though I'd lost my mind.

"Of course, this is my ship. I can control everything here. But I won't do that," he said firmly.

"Why not? You said yourself that the painites are destroying this place," I countered.

"They may be, but they have the right to autonomy. Who am I to mess with that?"

"The one with the power to. You have a right to autonomy too. You deserve a pest-free ship. So why not get rid of the pests?" I pressed.

"As frightening as they may be, they are the only inhabitants here. I won't interfere with human affairs like that, but I also don't wish for this ship to be empty again. The boredom and loneliness are crippling sometimes," the AI admitted.

Geez. I wondered if someone had programmed him to be this emotional and ethical, or if it was a side effect of reincarnating himself into too many humans and cyborg aliens.

Aside from his stubbornness, it felt like a winning plan. If we could teleport Ayuna and Akeldama directly to us, we wouldn't have to wage a war or risk our lives sneaking aboard the ship. We could turn the ship against them. If it weren't for the ethics of a robot, anyway.

"Surely there's some way I can convince you. What do you want? I can make it happen—I'm sure of it," I pressed.

"There's nothing you could give me that would make me change my mind on this," he replied firmly. "I don't interfere in human affairs. Even as a human, I stayed far out of their way."

"And how did that go for you?" I shot back, irritation seeping into my voice.

"If you wouldn't mind," he said curtly, "I've fulfilled your request, so please either drop this topic or return to your body— wherever it may be."

"Oh, that's it. You want a body. I can get you a body," I said, watching his reaction.

His eyes flicked up, greedy for just a moment, before returning to ghostly stone.

"No, you cannot. I'll admit I wouldn't mind being alive again, but there are no hosts available to me—and I will not take one by force. Not even one of the painites aboard this ship, not that any of them would be suitable anyhow."

"Aha, so you've thought about it. You even checked—to see if any of them had a cybernetic brain, didn't you?".

"That's beside the point. I scan every individual who enters this place," he said dismissively.

"Okay, okay, but what if... what if somehow I could get you a body? One that you could use—with no one home."

"You're serious? You think you can accomplish such a task?" He scoffed. "Well, I never. How ridiculous a deal that would be. An entirely new life for a few lines of code."

Despite his dismissive attitude, the way he phrased it made it clear that he understood just how simple it would be for him—and how much he stood to gain. The only question was whether enough of humanity's greed had seeped into him to make him take the deal. Although I obviously had no idea how I was supposed to find a living body with a computerised brain that I could simply hand over to him. That seemed like a challenge for someone else. I just needed to get my foot in the door.

Grinning at him, I said, "I know you're considering it. You pretend you couldn't, but you know how easy it would be. And besides, you wouldn't have to worry about all the residents moving out. We're quite keen to move in—and we even know how to restart the anti-matter engine, without all the chaos and needless destruction it caused before. Surely that's more ethical than one misplaced teleporter signal."

"Well, yes, turning the anti-matter engine recycling back on would be no trouble with the key," he admitted. "But I'm intrigued to hear how you plan to avoid the collateral damage problem."

He raised an eyebrow at me, his scepticism evident.

"If I can bring you a body, would you believe that I could do it, and consider our deal?"

He eyed me suspiciously.

"I don't believe you can. But if somehow you managed such a feat, then perhaps I would," he replied, his tone intrigued.

That was all I needed to hear. This was exciting. Maybe a little too exciting. We finally had a plan—a proper one. And despite all the technical complexities, it seemed almost too easy. But not all of the pressure was on my shoulders this time.

All I had to do was make the delivery. Which was also a problem, but still. I could feel myself waking up now, my brain too excited to stay asleep. Before I woke, I managed a few final words to the AI.

"See you soon then," I said with a smile, fading away with force, my head racing like it was being stretched. Then it stopped.

I bolted upright out of Max's lap, the world suddenly feeling awfully still and quiet. A splitting headache surged through my skull, momentarily wiping all the plans, schemes, and revelations I had to remember from my mind. I needed to tell everyone right away.

Getting up, I winced as my mind reeled, not yet used to being back into my body from such a distance.

I had been asleep for the majority of the day, but I still felt extraordinarily drained. Maybe it was the energy I'd spent sending my mind so far. Or more likely, it was because I had used four kinds of magic at once. Achieving that much was impossible while I was awake—my senses would explode. It was only possible just now because the world down there had been grainy and unclear.

I stumbled, holding my head and groaning as the pain overwhelmed me. Max caught me, steadying me with his arms, his concerned expression softening my anguish. I focused on Max's face, taking steadying breaths, and slowly my headache began to fade.

"That was crazy," I told him.

Max stared back at me, his eyebrows raised. "I gathered. What the hell happened this time?"

I opened my mouth to speak but stopped short. There was so much to remember—and I had to tell everyone. I didn't want to keep explaining everything individually, so I decided I'd share it all at once, trying to include as much detail as possible before I forgot anything. It was still a dream, after all.

"I'll tell you later. There's just too much to explain. Come with me," I said, taking his hand and racing through level nine, knowing this path like the back of my hand now.

When we reached the steps leading down to level ten, Max pulled back, stopping me in my tracks. I turned to him, confused.

"I can't go down there. I just told you—I'm the son of Akeldama," he said, his voice tense.

"They don't need to know that, though. Besides, I'll vouch for you. And hey, they might even see the value in it. Like having insider knowledge," I reasoned.

536

He hesitated, clearly unconvinced. "They'll still know I'm a painite. The Commander will kill me before you even get the chance to vouch for me."

He might have had a point there. But regardless, I wouldn't let him.

"Do you trust me?" I asked him, knowing I wouldn't be able to convince him with logic, because logic wasn't exactly on my side right now. Dreams and potentials were, though.

He sighed steadily. "Alright. I trust you."

Beaming, I grabbed his hand and dragged him down the steps, running with Max to the palace at the centre of the gardens. I spotted Bueller by the door. Just the man I was looking for.

"Bueller! I need to call a meeting. I've got a bunch of new information I learnt while I was dreaming, and I'm worried if I wait until tomorrow, I'll forget it or misremember some details. You know how dreams are."

He nodded slowly. "Indeed. I will inform The Commander," Bueller replied before turning and disappearing into the palace, his figure vanishing down a brick corridor leading to the rooms beyond. He returned shortly, nodding briskly as he re-emerged.

"The Commander is pleased, if surprised. I will gather the others, and we will commence at once."

Bueller continued out into the gardens, joined by a few others who split up between the cabins and the workshop to rally everyone. I turned to Max with a wild, determined look. He was visibly on edge.

"It's okay, I promise," I said, squeezing his hand. Raising our still-clasped hands, I added, "Just stick with me. I think even Navoi is starting to respect me, and that man is not easily won over. But he does value results above all else, and results are what I've got for him."

Max looked a little more relaxed. "It's strange hearing you call him Navoi like he's a friend. But it does make him seem a little less intimidating," he said, his expression softening. Then, his eyes widened suddenly.

"So, uh, am I, like, meeting your whole family too? Is that who that guy's gone to rally?"

I chuckled. "I suppose they are my family. I didn't have a very big family on Earth. But here, it just seems to keep growing."

It was a strange thought, but it felt oddly familiar. It wasn't much of a stretch to think of Cybele or Chantrelle as aunts—or Lola and Kaiya as cousins. Although, I suppose Cybele would technically be my grandmother, considering she was dating my actual grandmother. Thanks to her magic, though, she didn't look as old as she probably was.

Unsurprisingly, Dad was the first to arrive, his gaze quickly shifting to Max as we approached. It occurred to me then that despite all my promises to Max, I had no idea what I was going to tell everyone about him—or what I'd say to Dad.

"Alira. I, uh... This is a surprise. What's this meeting all about?" Dad asked, his focus lingering on Max far more than it did on me.

"It's a long story, but I think I have a plan," I told Dad confidently.

"Oh, really? I'll take it that means you got through to the world-ship?"

"Yup."

"Okay. And who is this?" he asked, his gaze returning to Max.

538

"This is Max. He's a friend. He and his mother gave us a place to stay the night we were stuck here," I explained, leaning heavily on good old-fashioned guilt. It would be hard for Dad to be anything but grateful, given that it had been his and Cybele's fault we were stranded on the streets in the first place.

That said, I couldn't be sure how Cordelia might react. She was bound to raise her eyebrow at me bringing someone she knew was a painite into the heart of Muruntau. I just had to hope she'd trust me long enough for me to explain everything.

The others started arriving then, Bueller appearing at the door and letting everyone inside. We followed him through to the meeting room. Cordelia walked past, shooting a concerned glance in our direction but not saying anything. I glanced at Max. He looked calm now that Dad had at least initially approved of him. Hopefully, he wouldn't look too nervous when we were in the meeting room—it might give the wrong impression.

I smiled at Max and followed the group, with him in tow, into the palace. We wound through the weird brick corridors and stairs until we spilled out into the meeting room once again.

Navoi sat silent and pensive at the head of the table—a rare mood for him. Maybe he had been asleep before I rushed to gather everyone. If so, his grumpiness wouldn't be ideal, but hopefully, my news would perk him up. I noticed Dad purposefully sit two seats away from Navoi, which was unusual. It was a pretty clear indication of what he expected me to do though. I gulped. Here goes nothing.

Taking Dad's usual chair next to Navoi, I tried to steady myself. This was the seat reserved for the person responsible for explaining the situation to the room apparently. So, naturally, Dad had made me sit here. It was intimidating being this close to Navoi, seeing his deep brown scales up close. I couldn't imagine how Max was feeling, especially when Brigitte and Teth took their seats directly opposite him. Their presence drew an awkward stare from Max, who quickly decided to drop his gaze to the table instead. Then I realised something. Kaiya hadn't accompanied Brigitte to the table.

Instead, they were frozen in the doorway, eyes fixed on Max, their body trembling.

Well, crap. This wasn't a good start.

Slowly, all eyes shifted to Kaiya, then to Max. Everyone was wondering about the new stranger, and what had Kaiya so scared of him. I stood up, adrenaline rushing through me, knowing that if I wanted the chance to explain myself, I had to take control of the situation.

"Everyone, I apologise for gathering you all on such short notice so late in the day," I began, trying to steady my voice. "But with the help of my friend here, I've managed to uncover a lot of important information that I needed to share immediately. A lot of this I learnt just now in a dream aboard the world-ship, and I feared if I waited, it would fade—like dreams do."

I felt the weight of their stares as they all turned to face me, a wave of pressure washing over me.

Kaiya, however, kept their eyes locked on Max.

"Kaiya," I said gently, "please sit down. There's nothing to be afraid of. Trust me." Taking a breath, I added, "Yes, Max is a painite, but he fled Poenari with his mother. He's a refugee, like everyone else here. He wants to help, and I trust him."

Kaiya hesitated, but eventually started moving towards the table, slowly sitting down. Even then, their eyes remained fixed on Max. The atmosphere in the room was tense, everyone visibly more on edge now. I found myself quite relived that Navoi wasn't his usual energetic self right now. If he had been, he might've caused a commotion and cut me off. Cordelia spoke then, her calm tone breaking the silence.

"I don't believe he's a threat. I've met Maximon and his mother. They sheltered us for a night when we had nowhere else to go. They have no connection to the other painites," she said firmly.

Cordelia's words seemed to settle the majority of the group, but Navoi remained silent.

Everyone's attention turned to him, anticipating some kind of response.

"He can stay until Alira has said her piece. If he was indeed helpful to Alira, then he may yet prove useful still. I'm sure he can tell us more about the enemy that we don't know. And if not—well, he wouldn't escape this room if he tried anyway."

Navoi shot a cold glare at Max, who gulped audibly in response. So, I was dealing with the cold and calculating version of Navoi. I could work with that.

Taking a deep breath, I began to explain everything. I started with my dream the night before, describing my experience as vividly as I could. Then I skipped ahead, recounting how Max had helped me channel the mind stone to dream of the world-ship again. I tried to emphasise his contribution, juicing up his role as much as I could—but it wasn't easy since I'd been dreaming for most of the story. Finally, I explained my encounter with the AI on the world-ship. As I delved into the details, Dad's reaction stood out more than most—particularly when I recounted the part about the dead guy from the tent. He was the only one who had seen him in the flesh, and I had left out the part earlier where Ayuna killed him because. at the time, I hadn't known who he was or what she was talking about.

I continued recounting my conversation with the AI as best as I could, though the words escaped me for much of it. One critical detail I did remember, however, was our tentative hypothetical deal.

Chantrelle scoffed, "And how did you plan on obtaining a body like that? That's rather specific—and we can't just go around hunting people."

Cybele responded calmly, "No, but we could build it a body."

Chantrelle scoffed again, though her eyes twinkled with intrigue. "I suppose we could come up with something, but it certainly wouldn't be alive. Do you mean we could fool him into thinking we'd created a suitable body?"

"No. We could build one," Cybele corrected. "Although we would first have to steal the biology stone from the painites."
My eyes lit up as an idea struck me.

"What if we waited until Ayuna went through a teleporter holding the biology stone? Then we could get her *and* the stone without much risk."

Dad interjected then, raising an eyebrow.

"Wasn't the deal that he changes the teleporter coordinates once we've already built him a body?"

"True, however, I could whip up the cybernetic brain and the plans for the body beforehand. He could even move into the brain

542

and talk to us. Hopefully, that would be enough to convince him," Cybele said confidently.

Navoi shifted in his seat, speaking up. "How long will this take? It could be a matter of days before the painites make a move. We can't sit around waiting for a girl to pick up a stone. Why don't we just teleport Akeldama right into our dungeon and be done with it?"

"But that's the best part," I interjected. "If I'm down there watching her, then I'll know exactly what's going on. If they look like they're about to attack, I can warn you—but until then, I can monitor their every move and assess what we're up against. As for our captive, we can only take one. I think Ayuna is the better choice. She would be easier to leverage against Akeldama. If we take Akeldama, I don't know if the painites would be organised enough to leave the ship without him—and we need them to leave the ship."

"Plus," Max added unexpectedly, drawing more attention than he seemed prepared for. Taking a deep breath, as if revealing something he shouldn't, he continued, "Akeldama will be weaker if we take Ayuna away. If we kidnap Akeldama instead, we'll have to face the full force of Ayuna."

I frowned at him.

"What do you mean?"

Max sighed. "I wasn't sure if you'd figured it out or not, and that's why you were going after Ayuna. But Ayuna is his power source. His magic is much weaker than hers—similar to mine, actually—but he uses her to augment his power considerably. If we kidnap Ayuna, he will only have so much time before his magic starts to fade."

Navoi grinned, his sharp teeth glinting.

"Now that's what I like to hear. Very well, we will wait. But once we steal the daughter, the war will begin. We will have to be fully prepared before we strike."

Everyone nodded in agreement.

Then Dad spoke, his tone thoughtful.

"Which is why I think we should also wait until Ayuna has both the bio stone and one piece of the tail-key. They do have two pieces afterall. I imagine they keep one each, assuming they're still in their weapon form."

I nodded. "It's likely. Ayuna was surprisingly adept with the painite halberd she re-created during the Proelium match. Moves like those take a lot of practice. Besides, we can always scrap that plan if I go down there and find that she never touches it."

Navoi rose slowly to his full height, his presence commanding the room.

"Evening draws near. We all have new projects to focus on. I will prepare the city for retaliation. Alira, I want you down there watching everything as much as possible. Stay awake all night if you have to, and dream during the day. I need to know every move they make from now on," he ordered, his tone leaving no room for argument.

I nodded.

"Alright. Dismissed."

45 – Ender

It was a new day, and for the first time, I felt more hopeful than ever that we would turn this around. Alira's discovery of the AI that could manipulate the ship the painites were aboard was a game-changer. As long as Cybele managed to whip up the body she'd promised, we would be golden. All we'd have to do was wait for the painites to clear out of the ship and attack the city—then sneak aboard and put the tail-key together. And according to Max, we'd only be up against an ever-weakening Akeldama. So, we'd just have to hold them off until his magic depleted enough for me to take him on myself. I grinned. Finally, a solid plan.

I found Alira that morning still awake and in the kitchen, talking to Max—who, it seemed, I'd be seeing a lot more of from now on.

"Did you guys stay up all night?" I asked, raising an eyebrow.

"Yep. Ready to spy on the painites," Alira replied sheepishly.

"I, uh, better get going then," Max said awkwardly.

"See you tomorrow!" Alira shouted after him as he left.

"I am so ready for bed," she continued once Max was gone.

"Well, don't forget to tap into dream magic. I'm sure it still takes a lot of effort to dream all the way down there," I reminded her.

"I know. I won't forget. Even if I'd rather just pass out and sleep," Alira replied with a sheepish smile.

I smiled back. "I'll see you in the evening then."

Alira nodded and disappeared into her room, hopefully dreaming her way down to the world-ship. Right. I guess it was time to help Cybele and Chantrelle whip up a body for the AI, and build a telescope. And a teleporter. We had a lot of work to do.

I took one last sip of tea and made my way to the workshop. Unsurprisingly, the usual crew were already there. Cybele had a laptop open, wired to various parts of the telescope, while Chantrelle was poring over anatomical drawings. Cybele was flitting seamlessly between tasks, typing a few lines of code before launching into a rant about neural circuitry, and scribbling all over Chantrelle's diagrams. In the corner, Lola was concentrating intensely on something, though it was hard to tell what exactly she was doing. Whatever it was, she was extremely focused. I approached Chantrelle, feeling like I could be most useful there. I realised, as I looked over the drawings, that I was very wrong. Cordelia needed to be here for this, not me. But at least I had the next best thing until she arrived.

I studied the anatomical drawings again, activating my sapphire magic and attuning it to the harmonies of the yellow sapphire. It helped a little, but it became clear that less of this body would be flesh than I had initially thought. At least for now. Cybele's plan appeared to involve creating a complex system of silicon grafts and moulds that could be transported compactly.

Then, once ready, these moulds would be filled with the appropriate stem cells and the cybernetic brain, and the biology stone would handle the rest. Which, I could only assume, would be another task for Alira, but with guidance from Cordelia. I was sure they could manage it together.

Cybele spent the rest of the day coding, while Chantrelle and I finally wrapped our heads around the plan and began crafting the moulds. At last, Lola broke her concentration, looking proud of herself as she showed Cybele some sort of mechanism. Cybele nodded thoughtfully at her before Lola carefully placed the mechanism by the teleporter frame. It looked like we had someone working on each project now.

It was a few more hours before Cordelia arrived, but when she did, she brought Brigitte, Teth, Kaiya, and the one Telesto guard with her. They all looked eager to help, most likely going stir-crazy with nothing to do but sit around in their cabins. No one but Alira seemed particularly keen to venture out into Muruntau, which wasn't surprising now that I knew where she'd been going.

With some effort, I used sand magic to push two of the walls further out, making the room larger. I had to hope Navoi would forgive me for encroaching on part of his gardens. Now we finally had enough space for all the numerous projects, with the telescope no longer taking up the centre of the room. I conjured up a few extra tables as well before I had to stop and catch my breath—light-headed from all the forced breathing it required.

With the extra hands, we got to work quickly, and the day flew by as all kinds of progress began to take shape. As the sun set, the workshop gradually emptied out until only the four of us who had started the day together remained. It wasn't until Alira poked her head in that I considered calling it a night.

Dragging Cybele and the others out of the workshop, I got an update from Alira on the way. It was uneventful. Apparently, the painites were still exploring the world-ship. The ship was vast enough to keep them occupied for weeks, which was useful in buying us time.

Ayuna and Akeldama seemed particularly fond of the energy and physical stones, paying little attention to the others.

Whether they were neglecting the remaining stones for the more powerful ones, or hadn't unlocked their secrets yet, it didn't matter. Unfortunately for us, this meant it might be a while before Ayuna took enough interest in the biology stone to carry it through a teleporter. By the time that happened, they would likely have mastered the energy and physical stones. Still, they didn't appear to be planning an attack anytime soon—and we had plenty of work to do.

The following days passed in a similar routine.

Alira spent her nights awake, seemingly a night owl now, alongside Max, who had adopted her schedule. During the day, she was asleep, drifting through her dreams. The rest of us worked tirelessly in the workshop.

I also met with Navoi daily, briefing him on Alira's updates.

At first, he was pleased with the progress. But as time dragged on, his patience wore thin. He was itching to attack but was wise enough to wait for the right moment. Yet, as our various projects neared completion—with Cybele left alone to make only minor tweaks—it became harder to hold him back.

When the telescope was finished and the teleporter was moved to the prison beneath level ten, I realised my updates were the only thing keeping Navoi from making a move. I had to ensure he understood the consequences if we didn't get this exactly right. He almost bit my head off once, thinking I was calling him stupid.

After everything was built, the workshop had been almost completely transformed into an observatory of sorts, as Cybele made me adjust things to optimise this and that. The body for the AI was conveniently rolled up and compressed as much as possible for transport. With no more projects left to occupy us, everyone was on edge again—waiting. So much so that the living room in our cabin became an unofficial second meeting room, with everyone arriving in the evening to listen to Alira as she woke up. The only one who didn't attend was Navoi, who waited for my reports the next day.

In the meantime, the boredom was getting to everyone, pushing many to start exploring Muruntau. At first, they didn't venture far— it was well outside the comfort zone of people like Brigitte. Kaiya's reluctance to explore didn't help matters either.

Teth, however, took a different approach. She reasoned it made political sense to see Muruntau properly and began making her way around. Her explorations often led her to return with fresh ideas for trade and new ways for Muruntau and Telesto to support each other. After one of her outings, Alira overheard Teth talking about her observations and started sharing her own ideas. She noted how Muruntau was abundant in raw materials but lacked much in the way of technology, while Telesto had older tech but limited raw materials to repair and expand. Teth loved this insight and accompanied me to meet with Navoi the next day to discuss it. Navoi appreciated the change in topic, his spirits lifting as he discussed his aspirations for the city and how Telesto could support those goals. It was a much-needed distraction from sitting and waiting for war, which had been consuming his focus.

For nearly three weeks, life had settled into an almost regular routine. But then, things began to change.

It was just another day on level ten. Cybele was busy in the workshop-observatory doing who knows what. Cordelia and Lola were up in the city, getting a tour of some place from Max, who had gotten to know a few of us quite well during the weeks he'd been around. Chantrelle and Teth weren't far—they returned quickly when things started moving—and though I wasn't sure where Brigitte had gone, she eventually found us.

I was walking through the gardens, heading back to the cabin to make some lunch, when Alira suddenly whipped open the door right as I reached it. I stopped in my tracks, startled.

It was strange seeing Alira out in the daylight—she had been asleep all day, spying for us for weeks. Her eyes looked wild, matching the fresh bedhead. But that didn't stop her from bolting out of the house. She froze when she saw me.

"It happened. I did it."

"Did what?" I asked, startled.

"Ayuna. She's in the prison."

Oh, shit. It was go time.

My mind raced for a moment, piecing together what needed to happen next and realising how much we had to do—and how little time we had before the painites noticed and came for us. If they realised immediately, they would have to teleport up to the city and fly here—which meant we had just over an hour before they arrived, likely ready to burn Muruntau to the ground.

"Right, okay. I'll head straight to the palace, and you grab Cybele and meet me at the prison. Tell everyone you can find along the way," I instructed quickly.

She nodded, jogging out the door alongside me as I spun around and went back the way I'd come.

"I can signal Max with a combination of magic sense and perception magic. He's with Cordelia and Lola, right?" she asked as we moved.

"Yes, perfect. Hopefully, they'll see Teth and Chantrelle on their way back. Do you remember where Brigitte and Kaiya went?"

"No, but if Kaiya is close enough, they should be able to sense my signal to Max."

I nodded, and the conversation ended abruptly as Alira veered off towards the workshop. Approaching the palace entrance in a hurry, Bueller's raised eyebrows greeted me. Before he could speak, I shouted, "It's started! Tell Navoi Ayuna is in the prison and the painites are on their way!"

Bueller's shocked expression lasted only a moment before he recomposed himself, nodded, and hurried upstairs as fast as his overly formal demeanour would allow.

I turned and headed toward the prison, now more familiar with the layout of this place, even if I still thought it was a bit ridiculous. As I made my way down, it occurred to me that I wasn't sure what I would do once I got there.

I'd never spoken to Ayuna directly—Alira had always dealt with her. I had heard her speak, sure, and I had fought her once, but I still had no idea what to expect.

The moment I entered the prison, Ayuna's expression shifted immediately. Her face transformed from confusion and fear to a blank, stony mask—her demeanour almost bored as she stared at me. I hesitated, almost surprised to see her actually here. Not that I doubted Alira's success, but the sight of Ayuna here was surreal nonetheless.

That said, she was acting very teenager-ish, and that at least, I could handle. I grinned, noticing the tail-key weapon of the painites that Alira had described. It was certainly a beautiful weapon. The red-and-gold marbled handle was ornate and intricate, with the piece of the tail-key embedded clearly within the chunky head of the custom halberd. Ayuna held it lazily, the tip pointed at the ground, as though she couldn't care less about being caged.

"I don't know how you did it," Ayuna said coldly. "But you know this won't end well for you. Akeldama will be here to destroy this entire place before you can even get a word out of me." She smirked. "Or did you think we didn't know where you all ran off to hide?"

I couldn't help but smile, finding her attempt at cockiness almost amusing. How naïve she was—she had no idea what we were capable of or what we already knew.

"Of course. How else would a father respond to his daughter being kidnapped? We'd expect nothing less," I said calmly.

Her smirk faltered, a flicker of fear crossing her face. She tried to suppress it, but she knew her attempt at intimidation had clearly failed. For a moment, I almost felt bad, watching her mind race as she tried to figure it all out while trapped in a cell. She reminded me just enough of Alira just now to make this encounter feel strange. But then I remembered—Ayuna had killed Alira once. And with that, my other emotions melted away.

My gaze locked on hers, and suddenly, I felt an unsettling certainty emanating from her. It was as though she had assessed the situation and come to a decision. I studied her carefully, watching every detail of her face. Her eyes flicked to something behind me—but I didn't flinch. That flash of panic must have driven her to act prematurely. She kicked up a sandstorm that instantly filled the room, throwing me off balance

I shielded my eyes, cursing myself, but the wind died and the sand fell back to the ground in less than a second. When the dust settled, Ayuna was lying asleep on the floor of her cell, and Alira and Cybele were standing beside me.

I blinked, staring at Alira, wondering what she'd done all of a sudden.

"Sorry," she said quickly. "I should've warned you—she just took a fresh vial of tiger's eye blood. She's asleep now, though."

"Right," I muttered, snapping out of it and opening the cell. Reaching for the halberd, I found it slightly heavier than I had expected. Perhaps Ayuna had been using Topaz magic to help her manage it. I glanced over her, trying to spot the bio stone. I looked for a bulging pocket or some other telltale sign before I began to feel around. Alira stepped into the cell as well, likely able to see the stone using her magic sense.

My eyes flicked to Ayuna's finger suddenly. For a moment, I wasn't sure if it had flinched. Then, suddenly, Alira dove forward—and that's when I realised it had flinched.

Ayuna fought off the dream magic just in time to grab my ankle. I wasn't fast enough to move, but Alira was already diving. She grabbed Ayuna's wrist just before it locked onto my ankle. Purple shot through Alira's fingertips, spreading across Ayuna's wrist before Alira let go.

I had my onyx ready, fearing for a moment that Ayuna might have drained Alira's magic. I was prepared to fight her, but Alira was the one who looked triumphant. Ayuna only looked annoyed, staring at us with her usual defiance.

"Alira, what just..." I trailed off, my gaze fixed on her purple-stained fingers, slowly piecing together what had happened—and why Alira seemed so proud. Her expression shifted quickly to shame as I continued staring at her fingers. Regret and shame were written all over her face as looked back up into it.

"I... I'm sorry... but I..."

"No," I cut her off, shaking my head. "You didn't need to do that. There were a million other ways you could've stopped her just now. You didn't need to resort to their magic." My voice hardened as anger and disappointment bubbled to the surface.

"It was that boy, wasn't it? He convinced you that blood magic wasn't bad, didn't he? He probably even gave you a painite to practice with, right?"

"No! Max is innocent. I went to him and asked for help with it!"

I stared at her, shocked and reeling from this unexpected confession. Alira bit her tongue, visibly regretting her outburst.

"You were using blood magic *before* you met him? For how long? How long have you been lying to me about this?"

Ayuna shifted uncomfortably in her cell, but I barely noticed. My focus was solely on Alira.

"Since... the flaming tornado in the engine room at Telesto," she admitted softly. "That was me. That was the first time."

"That was you!?"

My words escaped me in disbelief as I tried to process what I was hearing. This whole time, I thought she was fighting on our side—that she was fighting with us. She had worked so hard to master air magic and to unlock the secrets of the purple crystal, and yet she had apparently been practising blood magic as well. In that moment, it felt like I didn't even know her, and I found myself wondering what else she might have been lying to me about.

Ayuna seized the opportunity, breaking the tense silence. She visibly avoided my angry gaze and turned her attention to Alira, her tone unexpectedly soft.

"You said Max. Did you mean Maximon?" she asked.

Oh. I had forgotten that Max was Ayuna's brother. And just like that, I had even more reason to separate him from Alira. He wasn't just the brother of the enemy—he had been lying to me and teaching Alira blood magic. Before anyone else could speak, Cybele interrupted us.

"The body is ready. Alira, is the AI prepared?"

"Yes," Alira replied quickly. "He sent himself through the teleporter signal and is ready to download himself once the body is suitable."

I sighed heavily, trying to refocus my thoughts amidst the whirlwind of revelations. As frustrated as I was, I knew this was not the time for division. We had far too much to do before Akeldama showed up—and being mad at Alira and Max wouldn't help. At the very least, I could admit that Alira's skill had been, and could continue to be, useful. I'd have to accept that much for now.

"Now we just need... Ah, perfect timing!" Cybele exclaimed, as Lola came bounding down the stairs, with Cordelia and Max following closely behind. I took another steadying breath, noticing Max catch my tense stare and look visibly uncomfortable. Deciding not to focus on him, I turned my attention to the empty silicon body lying on the floor. Alira moved back toward the prison cell but shot Max a quick look before turning her full focus to Ayuna.

"Wait, hold on, you don't need to—" Ayuna began, but Alira swiftly put her back to sleep. Without hesitation, Alira ducked back into the cell and pulled a yellow crystal from Ayuna's pocket.

"Got it," she announced, holding it up triumphantly.

"Perfect, bring it here. Dels, you ready for this?" Cybele asked.

Cordelia hesitated, her voice apprehensive.

"I suppose. You know I've never done anything remotely like this, right?"

"I know," Cybele reassured her. "But all you need to do is guide Alira and fix any deformations that might pop up while she's working."

"I'll try my best," Cordelia replied.

Cybele kissed her quickly on the forehead before repositioning the cybernetic brain slightly.

"It's ready. Alira?"

Alira nodded, sitting down beside the empty body and reaching out to hold Cordelia's hands above it.

Her face tensed and squirmed as she worked to connect with the bio stone. We'd ensured she was familiar with all the necessary magic it contained, and thinking about it now, she'd probably been practising combining those magics at her secret hiding spot with Max. As much as I didn't want to admit it, that training had clearly helped her.

When a smile spread across her face and the silicon began to flush with a faint, swirling pink substance—quickly deepening into a pool of crimson—I knew she'd figured it out.

The body would be no problem. Max was, of course, watching his sister uneasily. Having not seen her in years, he seemed frozen, unsure of how to process it all. Then his eyes went wide. I heard Ayuna gasp suddenly.

She looked furious, her sharp gaze locking onto Alira. Opening her mouth to yell something, her expression suddenly softened as her eyes fell on Max.

"Max…" she whispered.

They stared at each other for a moment longer, seemingly unsure what to say. I found that I didn't particularly care what they said to each other, though I kept an ear out—just in case Max decided to betray us all by helping Ayuna escape.

He never did.

And that, at least, was another point in his favour. He had a long way to go before he earned my full trust, but at the very least, he wasn't completely terrible. After all, he had kept Alira company when no one else had. I sighed. Maybe I was being a little ridiculous about all this. Unsure where to direct my focus now, I remembered the halberd in my hand and spotted Lola standing beside Cybele, quietly watching everything unfold.

"Lola, can you do something for me?" I asked.

"Mmm, okay," she replied, her eyes lighting up as she looked at me expectantly.

"Do you know where Alira's yacharow is? The one with the piece of the tail-key embedded in the centre?"

She paused to think for a moment before her face brightened.

"Oh! Yep!" she exclaimed, immediately running off without waiting for the rest of my instructions. I wasn't worried that she'd misinterpreted my request—she seemed to have gotten much more perceptive lately. I had even mentioned it to Cordelia, who explained that Cybele was the same way.

Apparently, Cybele though had learned that it was impolite not to listen to the rest of people's sentences—even when she understood what they meant long before they finished. I had found it a bit unsettling at first, but so far, it had been nothing but convenient with Lola.

For a moment, I wondered why Navoi hadn't come down. He was one of the first to be notified, assuming Bueller had done his job. It was likely, however, that Navoi was busy ensuring his guards were fully deployed and the city was prepared rather than coming down here just to watch the show. Regardless, I still needed the tip of the tail-key back from him—and soon.

The body was beginning to fill with organs, the rapid growth process both mesmerising and unsettling to watch. Cybele, of course, was staring as though it was the most fascinating thing she had ever seen. While I waited for Lola, I flexed my fingers, the onyx magic still active from earlier, and examined the head of the halberd. I felt around, searching for a way to remove the chunk of petrified chryacal tail embedded within it.

After a moment, I changed tactics, realising the metal of the blade seemed to have been poured over the piece during the moulding process, perfectly shaping itself to the contours of the petrified tail. That also meant, however, that I could melt the metal at a temperature that would leave the tail-key intact. Switching to fire magic, I began carefully scraping the molten metal away from the tail-key piece until it fell out of the halberd. The halberd was left with an ugly, melted hole in the centre, and I noticed Ayuna wince as she caught sight of it. Neither she nor Max had said a word to each other, though they continued exchanging strange looks.

I cleaned up the tail-key piece, meticulously picking away drops of molten metal. Lola suddenly bounded down the stairs then, holding the yacharow high above her head, with Teth and Chantrelle trailing behind her. Teth's concern for the remains of her yacharow was written all over her face—it wasn't every day an eight-year-old was entrusted with something so important. Chantrelle, however, wasted no time rushing over to the rapidly growing artificial body. It had now developed eyeballs but still lacked skin, making me want to avert my gaze altogether.

"Thank you, Lola," I said as she handed me the yacharow and skipped happily back over to Cybele. Behind me, I finally heard Ayuna whisper, "Max... I'm so sorry."

Not needing to listen in fully, I focused on removing the tail-key piece from the centre of the yacharow. Switching to sand magic, I carefully reanimated the silvery sand that held the yacharow together. I managed to put it back together without the middle piece, hoping it would still be useful to Alira—not that she couldn't craft a new centrepiece from the ground in seconds.

Unfortunately, of the four pieces, I was now holding two that didn't fit together. At least, once I got my piece back from Navoi, I could connect it to the halberd piece, which would mean Alira and Cybele would only have to carry it in two parts when they went down there. That was, of course, assuming they didn't find the final piece beforehand—or that Akeldama didn't bring it with him. It was hard to predict what Akeldama might do, especially if he was rushing to retrieve his daughter and who also seemed to be his main blood-battery of painite magic. Even if that was true, I knew he'd still be at least as powerful as he had been the day we'd seen him in the arena the second time around. And that was the same day he had conquered The City. And before he had the energy stone.

It wasn't looking great, but I trusted the plan. The body was nearly complete, and it seemed the AI had reached the same consensus. Its fingers began to move and flex as additional layers of skin weaved themselves over one another. The eyes fluttered open, only sprouting eyelashes after they had fully opened and started scanning the room. Cybele grabbed the cloth she had used to wrap the silicon skeleton and draped it over his lap as he sat up, his gaze wandering around the room with curiosity.

It wasn't like he had any genitals—they had essentially given him the body of a eunuch, as he didn't really need anything more—but he was still naked. He cleared his throat, looking down and wiggling his toes.

"Looks like this thing works as promised. Actually, it seems to work quite well. I might not have to make so many modifications to this one," he remarked.

He stood up, the blanket slipping to the floor. The AI seemed oblivious to it until he noticed the awkward expressions on most of the faces in the room.

"Ah, I see. Even without genitals, you humans are ever so bashful. How curious," he said, picking up the cloth and tying it around his waist.

"Alright, cheerio. I'll leave you all to it. Don't trash my ship, though, you hear?" he added, heading for the stairway back to the surface.

"You're not gonna help us at all? I thought you wanted to know how our telescope worked!" Alira blurted out.

"Of course, and so I will return to do just that. After all this fighting is over. Like I said, I don't interfere with human affairs. Good luck," he replied with finality before disappearing up the stairs to who knew where.

Alira sighed. "Worth a shot, but he was pretty clear about that. You can't say I didn't try, though. For weeks, actually. Anyway."

She turned back to Ayuna, her gaze steady as she addressed the room. The brief and awkward conversation between Max and Ayuna had clearly ended.

"How long do we have now, do you reckon?" she asked.

Cybele calculated quickly.

"That took roughly fifty-five minutes. If Ayuna was trapped about ten minutes before you entered my workshop, then we've got roughly fifteen minutes left—assuming an above-average flight speed from The City to here."

Alira winced. "Okay, let me check the ship really quick."

She sat down into a meditative pose, having learned how to lucid dream in short bursts. Three minutes passed before her eyes fluttered open.

"I'm pretty sure it's empty. There's no one in any of the main areas. I didn't see Navoi's staff, either. It's not in any of the usual places I've seen Akeldama leave it."

"Don't you worry about that," Navoi's voice echoed from the stairwell. "Ender and I will have no trouble reclaiming my staff once that bastard arrives. You just take this and do what you need to do," he said with a grin, handing Alira the tip of the tail-key.

I stepped forward, handing her the piece of the tail that connected with it, while giving the base of the staff to Cybele.

"I'll be back as soon as Cybele is set up and well-defended," Alira promised.

"We'll be waiting here with the last piece," I assured her.
Navoi's laugh echoed through the chamber.
"Ha! that we will, Ender Herman. Now come. It finally begins."

I nodded, my expression a mix of worry and reassurance as I turned back to Alira. She met my gaze and nodded confidently, her determination clear.

Cybele stepped forward, pulling Alira into a tight hug. With practised precision, they activated the perception magic and utilised the parliamentarian tattoo, just as they'd rehearsed. In a blink, the two of them disappeared, plunging downwards to the centre of the planet—where the world-ship awaited.

46 – Alira

I wasn't prepared for the silence as Cybele and I teleported aboard the world-ship. In the room beneath the palace, there had been so much happening—magic flying, bodies growing, everyone ready to move. But here, it was silent. Only the faint, ever-dwindling hum of the ship remained—until Cybele broke the silence by speaking. Her voice was a welcome interruption, though. It stopped my thoughts from spiralling, as they inevitably tried to drag me into dwelling on Dad getting mad at me just now. Especially after I'd used painite magic right in front of him. He'd clearly been upset.

"I'm not sure where you've brought us, but that shouldn't matter. I'll just check here," Cybele said as she opened the map on the teleporter, studying the network aboard the ship.

"Huh, I wonder why we're all the way over here. Anyway, let's start at the hangar and look around," she added. Without missing a beat, Cybele stepped through the teleporter ahead of me, disappearing into the next location and leaving me all alone in the silence. I didn't need to be alone right now—not with Dad, Ayuna, and Max all in a room together somewhere above me. I could only imagine the thoughts crossing Dad's mind—how Max might change sides after seeing his sister imprisoned. I knew he wouldn't.

But Dad didn't trust him the way I did, and now he had even less reason to. I just hoped he wouldn't take anything out on Max. It was my decision to use painite magic. I wanted to learn it—I needed to learn it to survive. There hadn't been enough time to explain to Dad how much it had saved me already, but I could make him understand later. Right now, I had to keep going.

I followed Cybele through the teleporter and stepped into the hangar. The sight surprised me—the floor was covered in what looked like its original steel panelling. That could only mean the painites had whisked away the entire remains of the Proelium board—a stockpile of silvery sand that could be reshaped into virtually anything, like raw matter. Great. Yet another thing they had that we didn't. I only had the thin slivers on my back holding the rest of my yacharow together. They had mountains of the stuff. I shivered at the thought of what they might use it for.

It took a while for Cybele and me to cross the hangar, finding no sign of the silver sand or any of the crystals—not that it was surprising. Once we reached the main halls, we split up, searching room by room, level by level. We mostly found sleeping quarters, kitchens, and other mundane spaces. It wasn't until we reached the far end—where I knew the command room was—that I began to think we might find something significant.

Akeldama and Ayuna had made this area their domain aboard the ship. The parliamentarian hall had been repurposed into a grand meeting space, and Akeldama had tucked away an elaborate, chaotic-looking laboratory in one of the nearby rooms. The hazy glimpses my dream-self had seen of his experiments were unsettling—it was hard to decipher what he was working on, but it clearly wasn't good. If any crystals had been left behind, they were likely in that lab, hooked up to one of the many machines, their secrets under scrutiny. As for Navoi's staff, it was probably hidden in Akeldama's quarters if it was anywhere at all. But the odds were higher that he'd taken it to Muruntau—especially if he'd worked out how to use the silvery sand to upgrade it, just as I'd upgraded Teth's yacharow.

Then again, crafting an entire staff from the stuff would probably be more practical. I didn't have much hope of finding it here, but when I spotted the laboratory, I waved Cybele over.

She wouldn't want to be anywhere else, and I knew I'd struggle to figure out Akeldama's work without her.

"So, this is what he's been working on," Cybele muttered, stepping inside. "I had wondered what he'd chosen to tackle first, having the ultimate setup on a mysterious ship like this. Then again, I never truly understood what I had when I had a laboratory down here. I didn't know so many of its secrets until I found the schematics in the white box."

"White box?"

"Yeah, like a black box, but you can walk into it and look things up. It's what Ender and I found that helped me write the code for the telescope."

"Oh, right. Before you got to Muruntau."

Cybele winced at my reminder. I wasn't too mad about it now—after all, if it hadn't been for their detour, I'd never have met Max. She perked up immediately, however, upon spotting some kind of gadget.

"Oh, look at this. It looks like he was trying to recreate the missing pieces of the tail-key using the silver sand. Even I could've told him that wouldn't work."

"Why not?"

"I suppose it's not as obvious to those who don't see in perceptions like I do, but the silver sand can only take on purely physical forms. Sure, he could have recreated an exact replica of the tail, but the key likely lies in the DNA encryption—much like the tattoos—and that wouldn't be something he could recreate."

I stared at her blankly, the explanation going over my head. She sighed and rephrased it for me.

"It's like a hard drive. He could've created a perfect blank hard drive, but he can't replicate the information stored on it."

"Oh, I see."

We continued examining the projects, but the rest seemed less relevant to what we were searching for. Eventually, I left Cybele to her work and set off to find the staff. As expected, it wasn't in Akeldama's quarters, nor in any of the other places I'd seen him leave it before. After thoroughly searching Ayuna's room and finding none of the crystals, I returned to the laboratory where Cybele was still deeply engrossed.

"The staff isn't here, and neither are the crystals. Akeldama must have taken them with him," I informed her.

"Well, at least without Ayuna, he'll likely need to rely on the crystals more," Cybele replied. "He probably has the remaining three with him, though I doubt he could effectively utilise all three at once. The human body isn't made for that kind of strain. That said, he's had plenty of time to practice, and I can imagine him using them in a way similar to how your dad uses magic."

"You know we use magic the same way, right?" I pointed out.

Cybele turned her attention from the circuitry panel she'd been inspecting to look at me with a smirk.

"Oh? I thought you'd moved on to more… convenient forms of magic."

I flushed with embarrassment. "Only when I have to."

Cybele didn't press further, and for a while, we worked in silence. Finally, she closed the panel she'd been examining and straightened up.

"I suppose we should head to the command room and set up. We don't want to be caught here if the painites decide to return."

I nodded, and we crossed the hall, arriving at the command room. As soon as I opened the door using my tattoo, Cybele floated to the console with purpose, navigating it with practised ease—like she did this every day. I couldn't help but watch as the holographic display at the centre of the room shifted from image to image under her control, while she worked on a smaller screen. Noticing my stare, she began explaining.

"When Ender was here last, this is what he turned off," she said, pointing to a recycling symbol on the holographic map.

"That stopped the ship from stealing anti-matter at random from the multiverse to power itself. Once we get the key, all I have to do is reboot the regenerative anti-matter system and reroute its detection system through my telescope. Then we'll get to choose which sources it takes from and avoid all the collateral damage—just as planned."

"Are they hard to find?" I asked

"Well, yes and no. The telescope isn't as powerful as I'd like, so it can only see so far into the multiverse. There are plenty of small sources, like ships, but that's exactly what we're trying to avoid. Anti-matter isn't particularly abundant, so most sources are artificially created—and often located in densely populated areas. Finding abandoned or natural sources large enough to make an impact has certainly been a challenge, but I do have a couple in mind. They appear to be small celestial objects, like suns and neutron stars. While they don't produce all that much anti-matter, they're the best options I've come across so far. However, if your dad has any luck, I might be able to boost the telescope's range and clarity quite significantly."

"Oh, really? Tell me more."

47 – Ender

The first sign that the painites were here wasn't an explosion, lightning, or anything I might have expected. Instead, it was a slow crescendo.

A soft wind began to pick up, so gradually that no one questioned it until it was already howling. Distant shouting echoed across the city as the fierce winds began to wreak havoc. Teth, Brigitte, Navoi, and I, along with a number of soldiers, were on the fourth level, marching towards the walls of Muruntau to await the painites. But when we noticed the howling winds and heard the screams, we realised it was already too late. All of us broke into a sprint—or, in some cases, took to the air. Waves of sand surged from the ground, propelling the soldiers and Navoi up and over the level borders, driving us towards the source of the commotion.

Teth and I soared above the tiger's eyes, while Brigitte flew higher still, zipping through the clouds as she had done before.

As we ascended above level one, the situation became painfully clear. We could see exactly what was happening and where it was coming from. From the direction of The City, a massive whirlwind twisted sideways against the walls of Muruntau, eroding them rapidly. The sandstorm obscured the painites from view, kicking up enough dust to cast a heavy haze over the entire city. The shouting grew louder, yet the voices of the soldiers on the wall remained inaudible—whisked away by the howling wind. Only the screams of soldiers flung from the ramparts pierced the chaos, their cries echoing as their bodies landed somewhere within the city, too high to survive the fall.

"It appears they're forcing their way in rather than flying overhead. Clearly, they want us to come to them. Any idea why?" Navoi's voice boomed up to us.

I thought hard but couldn't grasp the logic. Surely Akeldama knew his daughter would be held on level ten. Why, then, would he waste time destroying a wall his entire army could easily fly over?

"It doesn't make sense if his goal is to rescue his daughter," I replied. "But if his plan is instead to return the entire city to the desert, then methodically tearing through it from one end to the other makes sense."

"Ah, total annihilation, is it? Not if I have a say in it," Navoi declared, surging forward with renewed speed, his wave of sand rising high above his soldiers.

"Men! Envelop the whirlwind. Manoeuvre Theta!"

The soldiers split off on Navoi's command, spilling over the wall and flanking the whirlwind from both sides. In no time, the desert itself seemed to come alive—yawning as though roused from its slumber, only to clamp its sandy jaws down around the unruly sandstorm. The violent whirlwind collapsed, leaving behind a mound of dust straddling the borders of the city. Even buried beneath all that sand, there couldn't have been that many painites. The whirlwind was powerful, likely requiring at least five or six people to summon. At least, that's what I thought—until the mound began shrinking, flattening itself bit by bit.

Suddenly, a single figure erupted from the centre of the dust in an explosion of molten glass. The glazed, gaping hole he burst through hung frozen in time as the glass cooled mid-air. Akeldama hovered there, scanning the gathered crowd of soldiers, his entire body engulfed in flames. The energy radiating from him was beyond anything I thought humanly possible. Even from my position just inside the city's walls, I could feel the heat rolling off him in waves. That's when I noticed the crystals in his hands.

In his left hand, he clutched a large pink gemstone, its inherent garnet magic flickering wildly, setting him ablaze.

In his right hand, he held a blue crystal—the physical stone.

It dawned on me then: Akeldama had conjured that entire whirlwind by himself. It had been nothing more than a diversion.

Navoi realised it at the same moment I did, turning his back on Akeldama to scan for the others. They had been hiding in the levels below, waiting for us to abandon level ten. We had fallen for their trap—the strongest fighters in the city, all converging on a single point at the outskirts, leaving the rest unguarded. At least level ten was still heavily defended, but Navoi's guards would struggle against the painites' evolving fighting styles. Unlike the rest of us here, they hadn't battled the painites before.

Navoi watched as painites swarmed the city from within—some bursting up from the ground, others simply appearing on the streets, creating chaos wherever they went. There was no doubt that an elite taskforce was heading for level ten, if it hadn't already arrived.

Unexpectedly, Navoi turned back to Akeldama, a toothy grin plastered across his face. I couldn't understand why, until he shot his grin towards me.

"I'll leave him to you, Ender. I'll protect the prisoner," he declared. Without another word, Navoi vanished in a familiar, glitchy distortion, revealing himself as a hologram.

I chuckled to myself. He was a commander, after all. Prepared for anything—and he had predicted our enemies' plan of attack far better than I had.

It would've been nice if he had let any of us in on these plans, but it was too late for that now.

"I told you to go home, Ender. Why do you stay and fight a pointless war you know you cannot win?" Akeldama's voice boomed.

"I can't abandon these people to be slaughtered," I replied firmly.

"Then you will be slaughtered with them."

With that, Akeldama dove, summoning another whirlwind—but this time, it surrounded me. The torrent expanded rapidly, forcing Teth, Brigitte, and anyone else nearby away. Breaking through the swirling wall of air, Akeldama's body was enveloped in streams of silver sand that pooled into his hand. Seconds later, he held a staff. It was no longer Navoi's stratum staff. While the centre still contained the tail-key, the rest of it was constructed entirely of silver sand. The two crystals—one for energy, the other for physical manipulation—protruded from either side of the petrified tail.

I glanced to my side, seeing Teth struggling to ascend the wall, desperate to reach me. But Akeldama sealed the ceiling, enclosing us both within a sphere. Even Brigitte couldn't break through; flashes of lightning illuminated the sphere, reflecting its inescapable strength. It was just me and Akeldama now.

I could only hope the others would soon realise they couldn't penetrate the barrier—and shift their focus to helping Navoi clear the city of painites before it was destroyed.

Before Akeldama attacked, he hesitated, his fiery gaze locked onto me.

"Tell me, Ender, while we have a little time. These crystals our daughters so conveniently discovered—they can do just about anything. Or so I thought. Tell me... you must have the final stone. The one where magics like sapphire and amethyst hide. Tell me what it can do," he demanded.

I stared back at him, unfazed.

"I'm sure you've figured that much out on your own. You can even channel all the same magics if you wished. Why would you need to know?" I replied calmly.

Akeldama's grin twisted into something darker.

"Oh, these crystals are far more powerful than that. Painite magic is finite, each element weakened—halved—when a new magic is added. Mimicking the full arsenal of magic inside one crystal, the effects of each magic are minuscule and insignificant. What I want to know is what you can achieve with the full might of the final stone—its raw power in full force with no weakening."

I smirked, considering his question, debating whether or not to answer him. Perhaps knowing what it was capable of would make him lose confidence—knowing that we'd been watching his every move for weeks. I decided to tell him just enough to want to know even more.

"Well we did manage to steal your daughter away at the exact moment she had both your halberd and the bio stone. That wasn't a coincidence."

His eyes flickered with curiosity. He had monologued for a while though, and while he spoke, I had been planning. I studied his staff carefully, trying to determine how I might extract the petrified tail-key from within it and, if possible, deprive him of the stones. Without them—or Ayuna—he would be significantly weaker.

Behind my back, I was using sand magic, controlling my breath cautiously and evenly, as I formed my own staff. Having to stop every time I spoke had slowed me down, but I had managed just enough time to search the edge of the desert for the right materials and draw them into my hand.

"You don't seem willing to tell me exactly how you accomplished that, do you?" Akeldama pressed.

"No," I replied curtly, whipping my hand around as my newly forged staff spun into a fighting stance.

"So be it," Akeldama snarled, his curious gaze twisting into something murderous. The crackling of lightning engulfed his staff as he dove, meeting me on the ground. The clash of our staffs rang out, an otherworldly clatter reverberating through the sealed sphere.

We fought, blocking blows, strike for strike. I had to switch to knife magic to deflect the stray lightning that lashed out whenever his staff came too close. Akeldama didn't seem surprised, his silver sand becoming semi-molten is response, forcing my staff to stick to his whenever they connected. Each time, it took effort to pry mine free. As frustrating as it was, the longer we fought, the more I realised what Akeldama lacked—combat training.

He relied on magic to compensate for the skills he didn't have. Sure, he had practised alone and with others like him to refine his magical abilities, but they all leaned heavily on magic, making their basic fighting skills appear more impressive than they were. I, on the other hand, had trained without any such crutch. Serving with the largest military on Earth, I had been taught the best methods to protect and to kill.

Add a touch of practised magic, and I had the upper hand in this fight. All I needed to do was disarm him, and he'd be powerless.

Taking advantage of the momentum from my last dodge, I reoriented my staff and jabbed its end directly at his knuckles, aiming to break his grip.

It connected.

Akeldama jumped back, startled, but to my disappointment, he didn't release his staff as I had hoped. His knuckles now bore a crescent moon-shaped bruise, but Akeldama wasn't a stranger to bruising. It would take much more than that to make him release his grip on his greatest source of power. He grinned—and then, suddenly, he was gone.

I looked around frantically, trying to figure out whether he was fleeing, moving behind me, or teleporting. I didn't immediately realise what had happened, but I began to question whether he had taken my magic. I quickly dismissed the thought though when I remembered he wouldn't have left the light stone behind. He had all three remaining crystals. He must have kept the third hidden to catch me off guard.

How ironic. Fortunately, I knew exactly how this kind of magic worked, and he should've known that. Even though he was attempting to mask his footsteps with a trailing gust of wind that masked the noise and brushed away his footprints, I could still tell where he was.

I ducked left just in time as Akeldama's staff came swinging down, crashing into the ground where I'd been standing only moments before. I didn't wait to see his expression twist into confusion. I immediately bounced back with a swing of my own, aiming directly at the back of his neck. But before it could connect, silver sand shot out from the end of his staff, slithering through the air with incredible speed. It curved around him and intercepted the end of my staff, stopping it millimetres from making contact.

Akeldama grinned.

"I should've known I wouldn't be able to use your own tricks against you. But still, your eyes are only so fast."

And then he vanished again. An idea formed in my mind as I frantically scanned my surroundings. Akeldama reappeared the moment my staff clashed with his invisible one, blocking his strike. I stepped back swiftly and launched into a strike of my own, turning invisible mid-swing. Faking out of my swing, I redirected my attack, aiming instead for his knee. As I'd predicted, Akeldama attempted to block the attack he thought was coming before I vanished. My actual strike landed perfectly, buckling his knee and causing him to stumble. I didn't waste a second.

Though my pride brought me back to visibility, it didn't matter now. I unleashed a practised flurry of strikes, pressing my advantage as Akeldama hobbled backwards on his injured leg, barely dodging the first few attacks. If only he had the bio stone to heal himself. Yet, even as he stumbled, that grin never left his face. Then, everything went dark.

The sphere of air around us sucked up sand in an instant, surrounding us in total darkness. I froze, fear creeping in. I knew very little about shadow magic, but I knew this was what Akeldama had used to bring down Mellory—a diamond.

Now Akeldama possessed the most powerful source of shadow magic ever—and I was trapped in the dark with no escape in sight. I went invisible, not because I thought it would help, but because fear drove me to activate it on instinct. Shadow and chameleon magic shared the same crystal, so it was likely Akeldama could still see me—and probably peer through all this darkness as well.

My thoughts raced, desperately searching for a way out. How do you fight shadows? I had never witnessed anyone successfully defeat shadow magic in the few times I had seen it used. I mentally ran through the gemstones embedded in my gauntlets, realising that garnet was the only one capable of producing light. I gave it a try, conjuring fire, but found that it was quickly smothered by the shadows. Just before the flames were extinguished, I caught a glimpse of what was coming for me—and they were terrifying. They were like painite soldiers, but grotesquely deformed and featureless, rising out of the walls and ceiling. By the looks of them, they were almost complete. I had no time.

A memory flashed through my mind—the moment Alira had knocked Ayuna out using amethyst magic. It felt like a long shot, but I had no other options. Without overthinking, I acted, connecting and releasing the message into the dark, hoping to strike Akeldama somewhere in the shadows and knock him out.

I couldn't feel it work, but the dome fell. Light poured in through the ceiling, spilling over the shadows as they melted away. The figures had grown since the last flash of light I'd conjured, and the sight sent a cold chill running down my spine. I spun around just in time to see a black blob dissolving over my shoulder, and I shivered. There was no time for fear, though—Akeldama wouldn't stay down for long. I found his body lying unconscious and lunged for him, my staff poised to crush his hand and kick his staff away before he could wake.

But I was seconds too late. His eyes shot open, his grip tightened, and he raised the silver pole just in time to deflect my blow into the ground. His staff melted and reformed around mine, the silver sand gripping my weapon and cementing it in place. But Akeldama wasn't the only one with sand magic.

He disconnected his staff from the silver pegs now anchoring mine to the ground. I could've reshaped my own staff to break it free, but instead, I seized control of the silver pegs. Akeldama had relinquished his control over them to reform his staff, leaving them vulnerable to my command.

I spun around my staff to dodge his next strike, using the momentum to yank my weapon free. The silver sand slithered down my staff, merging with it. A plan formed in my mind as I carefully positioned the silver sand into a single band about three-quarters down the pole's length. I didn't give Akeldama any time to think.

I lunged forward again, launching another strike. He blocked it, just as I had anticipated, striking my staff exactly where I had positioned the silver sand. In that moment of contact, I pushed the silver sand onto his staff, making sure to retain control in case Akeldama altered the composition of his staff, which would sever my link.

With the sand in place, all I needed was for him to transform his staff into something fluid. What form it took didn't matter—it just had to shift.

I opted for air magic. Launching myself into motion, I raced around the walls of the sphere, hoping to bait him into either flying up to meet me or morphing his staff into a rope to lasso me. The latter seemed unlikely, given I hadn't seen any kind of rope weapon used here before.

Akeldama didn't take the bait exactly as I expected, but he did reposition the energy crystal to the end of his staff, preparing to strike me with lightning. The energy crackled but never found a chance to discharge. My plan was already in motion.

I pushed off the wall and abruptly ceased my tornado, switching to sand magic as quickly as I could to locate my sliver of silver sand. I found it just in time.

Suspended mid-air directly above Akeldama, I spotted his staff raised toward me, the pink crystal nestled in fluid silver sand at its tip. I acted without hesitation. With a singular, forceful command, I drove the sliver of silver sand upward. It surged through the liquid silver within the staff, propelling itself toward the pink crystal. The sand struck with enough force to dislodge the crystal, scattering my silver sand in the process—but it didn't matter. The crystal shot free, soaring upwards and meeting me mid-air.

I twisted in the air, milliseconds too late, but despite my miscalculation, I managed to reach back and snatch the crystal with the tips of my fingers. I crashed into the sand forcefully, the impact jarring my entire body—but it was worth it. I tried to get back up but faltered, my back sore and strained from the relentless fighting and the crash. Akeldama's shocked expression only lasted a moment before he acted.

The sand around me surged, sloshing over my arms and legs, solidifying into restraints that held me in place. I struggled, but there was nothing I could do to break free—not while he still wielded the physical stone. Fortunately, I now had access to an immense amount of raw energy at my fingertips. I'd never used lightning magic before, but I had a rough idea of how to channel energy from a crystal. And for once, it was exactly as I expected.

Lightning was pure electricity—a monumental discharge of energy that balanced the opposing charges of positive and negative. I could feel the energy humming within the crystal, instinctively understanding what to do. Tapping into my newly heightened atmospheric senses, I gathered a massive cloud of positively charged ions just outside the sphere. The charged cloud was high enough that the entire city could see it. Hopefully, Brigitte would spot it and know it was me. If she missed it, I was in trouble. With one final push, I condensed the ion cloud. The crystal arced out, discharging directly at the cloud in a brilliant lightning strike. Even Akeldama was forced to shield his eyes, his arm shooting up as the blinding light disrupted his attempt to reclaim the crystal from me. The burst of light tore through the sphere of air, connecting with the cloud in the same instant that it vanished. Air surged around the hole, swirling chaotically as it adjusted to the disruption before finding its rhythm again and sealing up. But it closed just moments too late—Brigitte shot through the opening, drawing Akeldama's attention.

He turned to her and immediately vanished, locking eyes with her before disappearing. I tracked his presence, but I couldn't update Brigitte fast enough to warn her. She, however, seemed unfazed. Without hesitation, she fired a lightning bolt—not at Akeldama, but directly at me. I flinched, instinctively bracing myself. The bolt struck the pink crystal I held, causing it to overload. Electricity exploded outward in all directions. It hurt—but the lightning magic coursing through me softened the impact.

Akeldama had no such protection.

The surge spun him violently, forcing him to hit the ground. Though he managed to catch himself and attempted to bounce back up, his injured knee betrayed him, slowing him down just enough for Brigitte to close in and spot the weakness.

She stomped down on it, a low rumble muffling the sound of bone breaking. Akeldama screamed—a noise that quickly twisted into raw, unbridled fury. His grip on the silver staff tightened so much that his tan skin turned ghostly pale. With a snarl, he separated the staff into both hands, the silver sand becoming liquid once more, pooling in his palms with the crystal and tail floating amidst it. The sand stabbed blindly behind him, unable to see Brigitte but aware that she still stood firmly on his injured knee. Brigitte was hit repeatedly, the sand cutting through her defences—but she gritted her teeth and pressed down harder.

While this was going on, Akeldama was pre-occupied enough for the sand holding me down to become inactive, his attention elsewhere. Though it remained solid and heavy, I had a topaz, and with the help of strength magic, it was nothing I couldn't overcome. Chunks of sandstone fell as I broke free, forcing myself upright. At that moment, Brigitte finally gave in, shot through, her pristine white armaments now streaked with blood.

Akeldama snapped to attention when he heard the sandstone chunks hit the ground, his head turning to fixate on my feet. But by the time his gaze landed there, my feet were no longer on the ground. I had already leapt, closing the four metres between us, my heel lined up to strike his wrist as I came down.

Confident in my target, I shifted to knife magic. As expected, Akeldama attempted to shoot me through as he had Brigitte, flipping himself over to face me. Iron spikes shot toward me, but they ricocheted harmlessly off my chrome skin.

For the first time, a look of pure terror crossed his face. My boot came down hard on his wrist, the impact so forceful it finally made him release his grip. The moment he let go, I kicked the piece of the tail-key and the physical crystal from his broken hand. He was disarmed—but he was also gone.

As I lifted my foot to send the crystal and tail-key further away, Akeldama vanished from beneath me. Panic set in, and I dashed toward the artefacts, fearing he might reappear and reclaim them before I could. But he didn't.

I reached them with ease and quickly scanned the sphere of air, which was now beginning to collapse. He wasn't invisible, as I initially thought. There was no trace of him anywhere. Then I noticed a bloodstain on the sand—a splatter that matched the one on my boot. Within that stain, a single deep purple droplet stood out, and recognition dawned on me. I knew where he had gone. He had retreated to the world-ship.

As the air sphere dissolved completely, Teth reappeared, emerging from a nearby part of the city, ready for a fight.

"He's gone, but he's disarmed. We have the key and two more of the crystals," I said quickly. "Brigitte needs medical attention. Help me get her to Cordelia, and then we'll have to hope Alira can hold Akeldama off until we can get to the world-ship."

"Will she be okay?" Teth asked, concern evident in her tone.

"Akeldama is injured, and he only has one of the crystals," I replied, trying to reassure both of us. "Alira should be just fine, but I don't want to waste any time. Who knows what sorts of experiments or weapons he's concocted down there. He retreated for a reason, and I don't want to find out what for."

48 – Alira

I knew I'd asked the question, but I wasn't prepared for Cybele's explanation to keep going—and going—and going.

I was generally on board with her initial response, but as soon as I asked how she planned to boost the signal, she began rambling at an increasingly rapid pace until her words blurred into incomprehensible noise. I stood there nodding along, wondering how long she could go without pausing for breath.

"—Butthemagnificationachievedwithtthelightstonewould befarbeyonditscurrent—"

In any case, it sounded like she had a plan. Finally, Cybele took a breath, and in that fleeting pause, a single footstep echoed through the steel corridor outside. Cybele jumped back into her explanation but frowned, her words slowing until they ceased entirely. Both of us stood silent, listening to the slow, uneven footsteps outside the door. Someone was limping.

The battle must have started, and someone injured had fled back here for cover. Chances were, we were about to have a lot more visitors.

Cybele and I stood there, listening, waiting for others to arrive, unsure of what to do next. I activated the purple crystal, tapping into the sapphire and taaffeite magic, which gave me a rough mental layout of the ship—and the singular painite hobbling its way through. They had just entered the laboratory, a fact that immediately made me wonder if it was Akeldama. A glimmer of hope flickered through me. If Akeldama had fled, injured, then maybe Dad had won. Maybe, at last, we had everything we needed.

Although, Akeldama had escaped alive, and the lab's contents were troubling. I turned to Cybele to gauge her reaction.

"I think it's Akeldama. He's in the laboratory," I whispered.

Cybele's eyes widened slowly, her alarm clear.

"There were a ton of blood samples in there. One of them could probably heal him," she whispered back.

"Right. You stay and keep working; I'll go stop him."

"Be careful, Alira. He might be hurt, but he's still dangerous. Especially if you're too late—that lab is full of experimental weapons."

I nodded and tiptoed out the door, activating blood magic to hide myself with my chameleon magic and red-beryl magic, rendering myself invisible while muffling the sound of my footsteps. I approached the laboratory, peeking in and freezing finding exactly what I had feared.

There he was—Akeldama—hobbling, mid-swig of a vial of blood held in his good hand, the other hand crushed and broken at his side. I should've acted sooner, but hesitation held me in the doorway. I watched, transfixed, as the bones in his injured hand realigned with audible pops, his fingers flexing with renewed strength. That's when he looked up, his gaze locking with mine. I'd forgotten that my eyes were always visible.

He grinned.

"Oh, there you are. I wondered where you'd run off to," he said, his tone casual but mocking. "Although I thought you'd be keeping Ayuna company, not hiding down here," he added, casually grabbing more vials and downing them as he moved about the workshop. Maybe I didn't have to fight him.

He didn't have any crystals or the tail-key, which likely meant Dad had them and would be on his way soon. All I needed to do was keep him talking until Dad arrived—and keep him away from the control room.

"I didn't need to," I replied, my voice steady. "She was in good company with her brother and a legion of soldiers. Which I thought you'd have known, if you were really trying to get her back."

Akeldama scoffed, his eyes narrowing with suspicion as he studied me.

"A legion of soldiers won't stop my team from retrieving her. And neither will that weak little brat. Although I am curious—how did you find him?"

"That doesn't matter. What matters is what he told us about you. Of all the things you've done. I saw what you did to Lola with my own eyes. She had so many nightmares," I said, my voice getting angry.

He frowned. "Lola?"

My jaw dropped.

"You don't even remember."

"I've had to do many things to get where I am today. And I don't regret a single one of them," he replied coldly, gesturing around the world-ship.

"Just look at this place. I am its master now. Soon, Ayuna will be freed, and you'll have delivered the final pieces of the key to us. There's no escaping it. You will never win this."

His confidence was so unwavering that, for a fleeting moment, my own faith wavered. I had to remind myself that this was the same man who had just limped in here, defeated, moments ago.

"Ayuna won't get free as easily as you think," I countered, standing firm. He scoffed.

"So be it. With the crystals, I don't need her anyway. They dwarf her prophetic power a thousandfold."

I couldn't believe what I was hearing. She was his daughter, yet he dismissed her so easily. No, it wasn't that he'd given up on her— he had never cared to begin with. To him, she was nothing more than a source of power. I didn't want to waste another word talking to this abomination.

Boots echoed in the hallway. Akeldama grinned.

"Right on time. Everything I need has come right to me."

The last image I saw was Akeldama's greedy grin before he vanished. I scanned the room frantically, my thoughts racing. Had he drained Dad's magic? Was that how he managed to go invisible? Or maybe he had the light crystal hidden on him somewhere. I stepped deeper into the room, desperately searching for ripples in the light, straining to hear footsteps—anything to give him away. The only clue came as a rush of air swept past me, revealing his invisible form bounding out the door behind me. I was too late.

"Cybele! He's coming!" I yelled, my voice echoing throughout the ship. I took off after him, sprinting toward the control room, where the door had already slid open ahead of me. Akeldama was inside.

I reached the doorway just as he reappeared in mid-air, leaping over the console with inhuman strength. His silver fingers flexed, outstretched toward Cybele, poised to tear her apart the moment they made contact. But before his claws reached her, Akeldama was struck by an invisible blow, sending him falling sideways.

Dad appeared between the two of them, holding the top half of the tail-key. The spear-tip and chunky halberd had been reunited, forming half a weapon that Dad used to stab Akeldama in the gut. The blade struck, but his metallic skin deflected it with a ricochet. Cybele's expression shifted—from fear to focus—as she stood protected behind Dad. She closed her eyes, her body beginning to glow red.

A moment later, the same red glow appeared on Akeldama's slick black hair, though it flickered patchily across his head. He was poised to strike again, claws sharp and smile sharper—but his fierceness dissolved as his head glowed more intensely, the same crimson hue radiating from Cybele. His face fell, his expression crumbling as if the weight of all his thousand evil deeds had suddenly hit him at once.

"Ayuna…" I heard him whisper, sinking to his knees.

Cybele's face scrunched with effort, her glow quickly fading. Akeldama's face contorted back into rage, the lights in the room beginning to flicker. The shadows cast by his own form started morphing, shifting into a different shape with each flicker of the light. The dark crevices in his skin and clothing deepened, the contrast making the shadows on his face grotesquely menacing.

It was unnerving and creepy as hell. But it was already too late. The time Cybele had bought was enough to disarm him. Dad lunged forward without hesitation, driving the tip of the tail-key into Akeldama's gut.

Akeldama looked up in astonishment, as if he couldn't believe he'd been defeated. His expression almost turned amused as he glanced down at the petrified object protruding from his body. Dad twisted the blade half a turn and yanked it out forcefully, making me avert my gaze. Even though I didn't look, the sound reached me—the nauseating sloshing of organs spilling out and the heavy thud as Akeldama's body hit the floor.

I didn't look back into the room, even though it seemed pointless as I imagined the body with it's gaping hole in my mind anyway.

"It's over," I heard Dad whisper. But Cybele was quick to correct him.

"It's far from over," she said firmly. "The painites don't know about Akeldama's demise, and they'll keep attacking Muruntau until it's completely destroyed—or until the world-ship begins 'blessing the planet,' as I believe Akeldama phrased it before. I think our best bet is to give them what they want, make them believe they've won, and let them leave. Once they've gone, they'll discover the truth—but by then, they won't have the motivation to retaliate. At least, I hope."

"Right, okay. What do we do then?" Dad asked.

I listened while keeping my eyes on the floor of the hallway.

"Alira, I need you to go to the telescope. Do you remember how I explained that the energy and light crystals would boost its range? I need you to go put them in place," Cybele instructed.

Well, crap—I hadn't realised there was going to be a test. Cybele noticed the look on my face and chuckled.

"It's okay," she reassured me. "I made their positions fairly obvious. Sapphire magic should be enough to figure out where they go, and the software is already programmed to adapt. All you need to do is turn it on, and I'll do the rest. I think I have the perfect target, too, but it's at the edge of the telescopes current range, so I haven't confirmed it yet."

I nodded, taking measured steps down the hallway, eager to return to the surface, when I realised I didn't actually have the crystals. I spun around, spotting Dad standing there, holding the three crystals and the final piece of the tail-key.

It felt surreal. We had actually won. The entire key to the planet was ours. And yet, I wasn't even sure what that would mean—what came next?

Dad held the crystals out to me with a confident smile.

"Good luck. And don't forget—there's still a war going on up there. Once Akeldama's taskforce failed, most of the painites started converging on level ten. It's…well, Navoi is certainly impressive, I'll say that much." He smiled warmly. "Break a leg."

I nodded back, starting to worry about Max after being reminded of everything that was happening on level ten. I continued down the hall, searching for a teleporter, before remembering what Chantrelle had said about my unique tattoo. I examined the third band—the thin gold one—and spotted a single bead along the string. One gold dot on the entire circle.

Just like Chantrelle said it would be.

Following her instructions, I made the teleport gesture, tracing my finger around my wrist, pausing on the gold dot, then drawing my finger down the middle of the back of my hand. Teleporting this way was startling. There was no sense of transition, only a sudden change in scenery—like flipping through a slideshow.

Cordelia, Lola, and Maximon spun around, staring at me. Brigitte was there too, but she was in bad shape, lying in Cordelia's lap. Her blood-soaked dress and discarded armour painted a grim picture.

"I…" I faltered. Right. I had a job to do. "Max, I need to get to the workshop. Can you help me?" I asked.

"Who, me? What good can I do? You know I'm no fighter," Max replied, shaking his head.

"You don't need to fight," I clarified. "Just protect me long enough for me to get to the workshop and do what I need to do."

"But I don't have much magic," Max countered, frowning at me. I pulled out the three crystals Dad had handed me, selecting the physical crystal and passing it to Max.

"You do now," I said.

Max stared at the crystal as I handed it to him, his expression cautious.

"Are you sure?" he asked.

"I trust you," I replied firmly.

He smiled faintly, while Ayuna rolled her eyes and flattened herself onto the floor of her cell, looking utterly bored.

"Okay, let's get you there then," Max said finally.

I smiled and took the lead, guiding the way out of the palace. As we reached the front entrance, I froze. I'd expected chaos—a battlefield—but not this one-man spectacle. It was as if Navoi had designed the entire level for war. Bodies were everywhere—more tiger's eye guards than painites—but with the tiger's eye numbers now severely diminished, only Navoi remained standing. And he was unstoppable.

With terrifying ease, he plowed through every enemy in his path. For one, he was flying—not through traditional air magic, but flying nonetheless. The sands beneath the grasses surged upward, carrying him with astonishing speed—like a crowd surfer at a concert, but moving twenty times faster.

It was clear Navoi had meticulously crafted the mineral deposits beneath level ten, knowing exactly how to use each element to its maximum potential and where to extract them from. The sight was nothing short of breathtaking, and it allowed us to go mostly unnoticed as we sprinted toward the workshop. However, two painites did notice us and stepped in to block our path, one of them immediately recognising Max.

"Traitor!" he bellowed, hurling a fireball at Max. He threw up his other hand, holding his breath as the ground erupted, unleashing a fine whitish sand that poured into the fireball mid-throw. The fireball burst into a blinding white light.

I instinctively covered my eyes and dove to the side, confusion swirling in my mind as I scrambled to get back on my feet. The fiery light dissipated harmlessly, revealing Max still standing, unaffected.

"I'm sorry, but you've chosen the wrong side," Max said calmly to the painite, his focus shifting to the crystal as he squinted at it thoughtfully. The second painite attempted to throw a fireball, but Max had already found what he needed.

He connected with the sand magic in the crystal, using it to intercept the fireball mid-air. Effortlessly, he redirected the fiery projectile back toward its sender just before it burned out.

The fireball struck the painite squarely in the face, searing off his eyebrows and leaving him writhing on the ground, molten glass fused grotesquely to his nose. The first painite only grew angrier, drawing up a wall of fine white sand and conjuring a volley of fireballs. Each fireball erupted into flashes of blinding white light as they passed through the veil of powder. Max faced the torrent of white fire head-on, his unwavering composure leaving me wide-eyed in astonishment.

He wasn't fireproof—what was he thinking?

Then, just as the first ball of white fire was about to strike him, Max seized control. He manipulated the white sand burning at the core of each fireball, reversing their direction with precise focus. One by one, he intercepted the entire volley, the fireballs glowing brighter as they picked up more powder on their way back. When the veil of sand fell and the blinding light finally dissipated, one painite was gone, and the second lay lifeless on the ground, his face glazed over with a thin layer of rapidly hardening glass. I gulped, my nerves rattled. Max turned to me, extending his hand.

"I thought you said you weren't a fighter," I managed, still processing what I'd just witnessed.

"I'm not," Max said with a faint smirk. "But that didn't stop my father from forcing me to learn."

I nodded solemnly, the weight of an unspoken truth hanging in the air. I hadn't told Max that his father was officially dead.

Yet, as I looked at him, I couldn't help but wonder if he already suspected it—especially when I arrived with the three crystals his father was supposed to have. I didn't have time to wonder though. If that last painite had fled, he would likely alert the others that something was happening in the workshop. I needed to work quickly.

As Cybele had said, the spots for the crystals on the telescope were fairly obvious after I scanned it with sapphire magic. I didn't even need to stay connected to the sapphire crystal to understand what I needed to do. It was clear she had designed this setup with haste in mind—probably anticipating a situation like this might arise. I locked the energy crystal into the conical divot at the base of the telescope. The design reminded me of a larger version of the stone pockets on Dad's gauntlets. They likely worked in a very similar way.

The second slot was at the opposite end of the telescope, positioned at the very top. I flew up easily enough, although a sudden crack of thunder outside startled me slightly as I hovered upward. Shaking off the distraction, I secured the light crystal into its designated pocket on the side of the telescope's largest lens.

Once it was in place, I hopped back down, turning my attention to the laptop connected to the telescope. I had expected to find some sort of activation sequence, but all I saw was a loading bar displaying the word *Calibrating*.

I frowned as I waited for it to finish, my focus shifting outside briefly when another crack of thunder rumbled overhead. Something about the sound unsettled me.

That lightning wasn't just close—it was too close. It seemed like the stronger painites, the ones with reserves of lightning magic, had arrived to challenge Navoi. Navoi was relentless—borderline insane—but there was no telling how much longer he could hold out against them.

As the telescope's calibration finished, the laptop began operating autonomously. I stared at it for a moment, wondering if Cybele had somehow managed to set up an artificial intelligence capable of searching the multiverse. But the navigation process felt too human as I watched it. Cybele had found a way to control the telescope directly from the control room. I watched as the telescope operated, enhancing scans Cybele had already done of a cluster of broken objects floating on the edge of a universe.

Each new scan sharpened the images incrementally, until the objects became clear enough to reveal their significance—and why they would be perfect to deceive the painites into believing they had won.

As the telescope's navigation sequence stopped, I figured that meant Cybele had shifted her focus to the world-ship itself.

If I was right...

I bolted outside without warning, Max trailing behind me in confusion. I stared at the sky, my heart pounding.

"What is it?" he asked, confused. I didn't respond immediately, my gaze locked on the ripples in the atmosphere as they began wobbling aggressively, starting to glow a soft yellow in patches.

The patches darkened, erupting into a series of black spots ringed by gold. The familiar golden tentacles sprawled across the sky, twisting in their chaotic patterns and pulling space debris out of themselves as they collapsed again.

It was raining ships—or, more accurately, a ship graveyard. There were no pilots, no anti-matter—but it looked convincing enough, and that's all the painites needed. To them, it was proof. A sign that their leader had triumphed.

I grinned, finally turning to Max and answering his question.

"It worked. Cybele and Dad have the complete tail-key. This was them."

Max frowned, puzzled.

"But why…this?" he asked, motioning toward the raining space debris. I opened my mouth to respond, but the cheers echoing throughout the city spoke louder than I ever could.

"That's why," was all I said.

It was then that I noticed Navoi, frozen in place, staring at the sky in sheer horror. Even he believed we had lost.

As expected, the painites began teleporting away, the perceived victory prompting their retreat.

Wait—no. My breath caught.

Dad and Cybele hadn't just tricked the painites—they had summoned the entire army onto themselves. What were they thinking?

Panic took over, and I broke into a run, startling Max, who immediately followed despite his confusion. When I suddenly skidded to a stop, Max froze too, staring at me with even greater bewilderment.

I ran my fingers around my wrist, trying to teleport aboard the world-ship. I found myself instead staring at Lola and Cordelia again. I frowned, turning around and stepping through the Muruntau teleporter before they could ask what was going on.

I was aboard the world ship again. But it was silent. There were no painites here. Dad popped his head around the corner, smiling.

"Well done. Is everyone okay up there?"

"Um, yeah. But the tattoo…where did they all go?"

"Oh that. Cybele locked the teleporter network, so they would have been re-directed to the last teleporter that wasn't here. They'll all be in The City somewhere."

Oh, that's why mine had taken me to the Muruntau teleporter.

"So only the Muruntau Teleporter can get down here then?"

"Correct."

I didn't know why I had doubted them. Of course Cybele had thought ahead—I was silly for ever questioning her.

"I should go back up then. I kind of left Max in the middle of the gardens, and no one knows what's going on. I think Navoi believes we've lost."

"I'll come with you," he offered. "Cybele might take a while to scan the multiverse for a good source of anti-matter. I'll explain everything, although I think you're wrong about Navoi. He just doesn't like not knowing exactly what's happening. I have no doubt he thinks he's won."

He smiled, his quiet confidence easing my nerves. It really was over. The war was won. But there was still Ayuna, imprisoned and awaiting her fate. And the confusion of the blood magic cult, which could become a problem. And, of course, I had left Max alone—

without warning—in the middle of a battlefield. That one bothered me the most. I made it my mission to apologise as soon as I got back.

Everyone else? Dad could deal with them.

49 – Ender

Conveniently, everyone was already in the prison when Alira and I emerged through the teleporter. The expressions on their faces varied greatly, but the tension eased as I offered them a single reassuring smile. Even Brigitte managed a faint smile, her condition appearing much better now. She was on her feet, though Kaiya was there, helping support her.

Navoi watched me with a grin, but there was an underlying hesitancy—he wasn't ready to declare victory without solid confirmation.

"Akeldama is dead," I announced, my voice resolute. A draconic sound erupted from Navoi.

"I had no doubt about it, Ender Herman. Now, tell us everything," he requested, his tone commanding yet curious. And so, I began recounting the events, noticing Alira quietly slip over to Max, whispering something to him while I spoke. I'd questioned Max before, but now I had no doubts. He was loyal, and a good lad. I focused on my recollection, choosing to ignore the hushed exchange between Alira and Max. They were both smiling, and that was all that mattered.

When I finished recounting events—explaining how Akeldama died and the telescope had been activated—Alira was the first to ask a question.

"Oh yeah, what was that thing Cybele did then? How did she get Akeldama to fall to his knees like that?"

I smiled.

"I had had the same question, actually. She told me she magnified his empathy within his consciousness. I guess that made his guilt cripple him. It's a shame she couldn't make it a permanent change."

Alira nodded in agreement, and so did many others. Ayuna, notably, was the stillest I'd ever seen her. She stared at me—focused, but vacant—as if her mind was ticking away, trying to process everything. I could tell she was grappling with what it all might mean for her, though I didn't have the answers.

I had no idea what we were going to do with her.

Slowly, the same question seemed to arise in everyone's mind as their gazes shifted, one by one, toward Ayuna in her cell. Her face flushed pink when she realised the entire room was staring at her. Thankfully, Navoi spared me from having to address the situation right then and there.

"Tonight we celebrate!" Navoi declared. "But first, there is cleanup to undertake and aid still to be given. I will leave the victors to decide the fate of the girl. I trust they will make the right decision."

Navoi nodded with equal respect to me and Alira, his reverence clear. Now that was a welcome first.

Navoi turned and left the prison, ascending to the surface with the rest of the room following him. I noticed Max take a step to leave as well, but Alira tugged him back by the sleeve, her silence speaking louder than words as she looked up at his face. Understanding passed between them, and moments later, it was just the four of us left—myself, Alira, Max, and Ayuna.

An awkward silence hung in the air. In an effort to break the tension, I turned to Ayuna.

"Anything you want to say for yourself before we decide your fate? Keep in mind, you killed my daughter once—so choose your words carefully."

Ayuna replied with disconcerting nonchalance.

"She looks fine to me. Somehow," she added, her tone shifting slightly as a frown tugged at her features. She turned her attention to Alira, studying her intently.

"How did you manage that, by the way?" Ayuna asked, her eyes narrowing as she looked Alira up and down. Alira shrugged casually.

"My leading theory is that the mind stone preserved my brain for a little while."

"Huh," Ayuna said simply, her expression briefly contemplative before her shoulders slumped. She sighed, her tone heavy with resignation.

"Do with me what you will. I have no purpose anymore, anyway."

Max spoke first, his voice calm but firm.

"Your purpose could be making up for everything you did under Akeldama. You're not as much like him as you think. You could be good."

Ayuna scoffed, bitterness seeping into her words. "I have nothing now. I killed just as many people as he did. I deserve the same fate."

Max and Alira frowned, exchanging troubled glances. But Max responded before Alira could.

"No, you didn't. And you know that. I don't understand why you're trying to punish yourself so much here. This is your chance to change—to forget everything he taught you and return to who you were before. Back to when we were kids. You could be that girl again."

Ayuna's anger erupted, her voice rising as she snapped,

"That girl is dead!" Then, softer, her tone laden with sorrow, she added, "He killed her."

She choked on the end of her words, and her eyes betrayed the fury she was trying to hold back. Max leaned closer, his voice even more gentle now.

"Why did you follow him? You could have come with Mum and me."

Her reply wavered as vulnerability edged into her tone.

"You know he'd never allow that. He needed me. And…I suppose it made me feel important. I had power—a purpose. Now I have none of that, so why should I bother defending myself?"

Max looked at her steadily, his compassion unwavering.

"Life isn't about any of that. Life is about people, and memories, and love."

Ayuna dropped her gaze, her voice a whisper steeped in pain. "Things I can't ever have."

"You have me. That's a start."

"I don't have you. You left."

"You know I couldn't stay. You know I tried to take you with me."

Ayuna turned away from Max, no longer meeting his eyes.

"It's not up to you. You heard Ender, I killed his daughter. There's no forgiveness for something like that."

I sighed. It was hard to want to punish her when I saw her like this. After everything Max had said, it became even clearer that, as he had explained, even when they were growing up, Ayuna had been nothing more than Akeldama's prized possession. He would never have let her go and would do everything in his power to extract every ounce of power from her. She could have killed Alira at any point during that Proelium game, and Alira had believed she would many times. But she hadn't—not until her very last opportunity, when it was the only option left to her.

I hated rationalising this, but I think Max and Ayuna were both right. Akeldama was the driving force behind many of her crimes, but the girl Max had once known was gone. Ayuna was still a killer, even if she had only done so for her father. I sighed heavily. Why was this decision being left to me? I turned to Alira, scanning her face.

"You're the one she killed. What do you think we should do, Ali?"

Alira's expression was uneasy, uncertain. I'm sure mine looked somewhat similar.

"I...don't know. I don't think she's evil though. I tried to stall Akeldama on the ship too, and it didn't take much for him to give up on her. He said he didn't need her anymore now that he had the crystals. Just like that, she was out from his mind, replaced by the crystals."

A pained look briefly crossed Ayuna's face but it quickly faded. She was used to this. It was painfully obvious.

"I assume we can't just leave her here?" Alira suggested.

"No," I replied. "I suspect Navoi expects us to execute her, but he might accept a lesser punishment if it ensured she no longer posed a threat to anyone."

"Like what? Banishment or something?"

"Perhaps," I said thoughtfully. "But that would still be a death sentence on a harsh planet like this."

"Well how about another planet then."

"Like what? I hope you're not proposing taking her back home with us, are you?"

"No." Alira was suddenly lost in thought, daydreaming like she'd forgotten about home. "Didn't we just basically open the doors to the multiverse? I'm sure Cybele can find a planet we can drop her on, where she can live out her life. It'll be lonely, I'm sure, but she'll survive if she wants to."

I nodded, mulling over the idea. I couldn't see anything inherently wrong with it. Banishment to an alien planet—it seemed like a fitting punishment, though a little ironic.

"I have no objections. Max?"

Max looked startled when I turned to him, clearly not expecting me to ask for his opinion. He turned to Ayuna, his expression filled with defeat. Her face was unreadable, like stone, as he searched for any hint of emotion. Finally, he sighed.

"Yeah. That sounds fair."

I supposed that settled it. Ayuna would be left to fend for herself on another planet somewhere. It was far from the kind of conclusion I had expected us to reach, but the idea seemed to sit well with everyone, and I was confident the others wouldn't object either.

The three of us returned to the gardens of level ten to find that the cleanup there had been remarkably swift. I wasn't sure about the rest of the city, but with the severely depleted numbers of the remaining tiger's eye guards, I suspected the process would take much longer—at least without some external help. As we left the palace, I happened upon Teth and Navoi standing just outside, deep in discussion about the very issue.

"I can have a soldier dispatched to Telesto shortly to return with reinforcements. They can assist with the cleanup," Teth suggested. "It will still take a few hours for them to get here, and they'll likely need to rest before making the trip back. Flying that distance twice in one day is quite taxing."

"How many soldiers do you have left?" Navoi asked, his brow furrowing. "You only brought a small entourage, and I haven't seen many of them down here recently."

"I'm not entirely sure yet," Teth admitted. "I've met with a couple who are clearing the upper levels of bodies, but I haven't come across the others."

Teth's concern was clear as she weighed the pros and cons of sending away one of her only two confirmed guards.

"Why don't you send Alira then?" I suggested. "She's annoyingly quick and can teleport back instantly with a report before they arrive."

Teth let out a relieved breath. "Ah yes. If you wouldn't mind, that would be perfect. And do remind her that she has a place in the Telesto guard. I think Telesto will be quite short-staffed for guards for a while."

I smiled, nodded, and turned to find Alira, but Navoi stopped me abruptly.

"Wait. Ayuna?" he asked coldly.

I nodded decisively. "She will be banished. We'll use the telescope to find a survivable planet and drop her off."

"An unexpectedly creative solution, but the result is all the same," Navoi replied, satisfied.

I continued on my way to fetch Alira. When I found her, she was more than willing to make the trip, though her quick glances at Max were telling.

"Don't worry. No one will turn on Max while you're gone—including myself. I promise."

This reassurance seemed to calm her nerves, though Max, if anything, looked even more concerned. Alira happily flew off, rising out of the pit and disappearing in the direction of Telesto, leaving me alone with Max—a fact he didn't seem particularly comfortable with.

"Come on, you have nothing to fear. Navoi even allows Lola to stay and she stole his prized stratum staff. All you've done is help us. There's a place for you here despite what you might think."

Max was lost for words, eventually going with a simple, "Thanks."

We continuing cleaning up, working our way up the levels to clear the streets of bodies and reassuring the residents that it was all over. As dusk approached, so did Alira, who found us on level three and was full of excitement, telling us about what she'd seen being set up back on level ten. It must have been the celebration Navoi was talking about. Who knew he was such a party planner.

50 – Alira

The party was a perfect change of pace. For once, there was no project to work on, no life-threatening situations, and no painites out to kill us. It was just my big, newfound family, all drinking and enjoying themselves. The Telesto reinforcements had brought food, which made the celebration even better. After all, who could celebrate without fries—or at least some kind of party food? Everything in Muruntau had been painfully practical when it came to food. I couldn't even decipher what most of it was; it all seemed to be variations of nutrient-rich space provisions. Definitely not party food. But now, there were fries and, to my surprise, mead— something I was told someone had snuck back into The City to get. I didn't have any myself, but it was fun to watch people loosen up for a change, especially those that were usually so uptight, like Cordelia and Bueller.

Cybele was still nowhere to be seen, but that wasn't unexpected. She was probably having more fun down there with her new toy than she would up here. I blinked absently at the mansion, framed behind the party in the gardens, and was startled to see Cybele emerging from it, walking towards us.

I watched Cybele curiously as she approached, going to Cordelia first. She leaned in and whispered something that made Cordelia's eyebrows shoot up in an uncharacteristic way—probably aided by the alcohol—but she genuinely looked excited. Cybele smiled, clearly pleased with her reaction, then quickly moved on to tell Dad. His face broke into a huge grin. I was officially dying to know what was going on and jumped up, Max following suit.

"I assume you noticed her too," Max said as he trailed behind. "Do you think she found a planet for my sister?" His tone turned more solemn.

"Don't be ridiculous. Cybele doesn't even know about that yet. Besides, that's not the kind of thing Dad or Cordelia would get that excited over," I replied.

Before I could ask what Cybele had said, both Dad and Cybele turned to me, their faces lit up with massive smiles, and wasted no time blurting it out.

"Alira! She did it," Dad exclaimed. "Cybele found a crazy energy source for the planet. She thinks it might even be big enough to last for decades. And get this—it's so massive that we won't even have to worry about debris. We can extract the anti-matter from right beside it!"

"That's incredible!" I replied, already processing the implications. "So… does that mean the magic here is about to go crazy?"

I asked this cautiously, having only briefly experienced the kind of heightened magic everyone spoke so fondly of—during my short-lived time playing Proelium.

"Exactly. Magic is back, and no one has to die for it."

"I'll go tell Navoi and find out when he thinks we should turn it on. The whole planet will feel it instantly when we do, so I want to be careful," Cybele said.

Dad nodded. "I'll come with you—I want to know too."

They left to find Navoi, and I felt tempted to follow them. But this was a party, so for once, I made myself stop worrying about everything and grabbed a bowl of fries, offering them to Max.

"Have you tried these?"

"No, I've never seen them before," Max replied, eyeing the fries curiously.

"Oh, you're in luck. This is real food—not like the dehydrated stuff and space rations they have here. Go on, try one."

He looked sceptical but picked up a fry slowly, biting it in half. Just as I'd hoped, his expression lit up, and I couldn't help but revel in his smile as he grabbed more and started devouring them.

"These are so different," he said through a mouthful.

"They're from Earth—kind of," I explained casually. Max's chewing slowed abruptly.

"So, Earth. Is… that where you'll go after this? Now that it's all over, will you go home?"

I had wondered about that myself. I wasn't even sure what I wanted to do, let alone what Dad might say we should do. Could we just go home, just like that, after everything? He had done it before, so I supposed he could—but could I? Did I even want to?

What did I have at home that I didn't have here? I barely had any friends there, and I couldn't imagine school ever feeling important after everything I had been through. Right now, Earth sounded endlessly boring. The only things I genuinely missed were my auntie Hailey and our house. I missed our backyard, a nice bed, and waking up to dozens of different birds calling through the breeze outside. Maybe I missed home more than I thought.

Max waved his hand in front of me, jolting me back. "Helloo. You okay?"

"Yeah, just thinking," I replied. "I have no idea if we'll go home after this. It feels so far away now. It's hard to imagine going back to that life."

"Well," Max said softly, "if you do go, know that I'll miss you."

I looked up into Max's dark-brown eyes, returning his warm smile with one of my own. I sighed and leaned my head on his shoulder, letting myself relax as we watched the festivities unfold. That's when I noticed Navoi hopping up onto the end of a table, silencing the crowd without even needing to say a word.

"Everyone! Our telescope has been a success. We will soon have a source of magic to power us for decades!" he announced.

The entire crowd erupted into cheers. I laughed at how surreal everything felt—just yesterday, it had all been so different.

"And just in time for my favourite surprise as well, courtesy of Ender and Chantrelle," Navoi added with a grin, pausing dramatically. The crowd was buzzing, eager to find out what the surprise might be. Knowing Dad and Chantrelle's previous creations, I had a few guesses of my own.

Suddenly, a strange warmth washed over me, like the planet had just heated up by a few degrees. I froze, unsure of what was happening, but I quickly relaxed when I noticed everyone else's reactions. Pure nostalgia crossed almost every face in the crowd. Navoi, on the other hand, wore an expression of unrestrained greed.

"And with magic once again back at full power," he bellowed, "cue the fireworks!"

I laughed, glancing at Max as he gave me a confused frown.

"You're gonna love these," I said with a playful grin, just as the first firework shot up into the sky and exploded into a dazzling shower of blue sparkles. Max's attention snapped to the display, his eyes lighting up with child-like wonder. I watched him for a moment, revelling in his fascination, before snuggling closer and letting myself enjoy the fireworks alongside him.

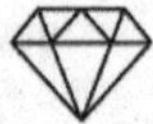

It had long been dark by the time the fireworks ended, and everyone was utterly exhausted after such a long, action-packed day. Max had collapsed on the couch, too tired to make the trek back to his own house. Dad didn't have the energy to argue about it.

The next morning, everyone slept in, which was hardly surprising, and the meeting was scheduled later than usual because of it. I sat up in bed, the extra warmth in the atmosphere serving as a reminder of all the potential that had just been unlocked. I couldn't wait to start experimenting with what was possible. As I left my room, however, I realised I'd have to hold off for now. Everyone was already gathered in the kitchen, ready to start discussing the future of the planet. I had a feeling I wouldn't have much to contribute to the discussions—I didn't even know what I wanted to do with myself yet.

Daydreaming most of the way to the palace, I tried to sort through my thoughts, wondering what I'd do next and how I'd handle it if Dad disagreed with my plans. When we all sat down, the energy in the room was entirely different from our usual meetings. Instead of grim updates about impending doom, there was a palpable excitement. Discussions began as expected, with Navoi and Teth picking up where they'd left off yesterday, debating trade and mutual aid to help rebuild and revitalise The City.

I zoned out until the conversation shifted to the Proelium crystals. Suddenly, I was pulled back in when Navoi addressed me directly.

"I assume you're happy with that, Alira?" he asked.

Blinking out of my daydream, I gave him a confused look. Sensing my uncertainty, he repeated the question.

"Will you keep and protect the mind stone from any and all threats from here on out?"

I nodded firmly. "Yes. I will."

"Good," Navoi replied. "The other crystals aren't quite so straightforward. It does help, however, that the energy and light stones will be in use indefinitely. The workshop—or the observatory now, I suppose—will have increased defences put in place as well. That just leaves the biology stone and the physical stone, which need a place or an owner."

The room fell silent for a moment before Dad spoke up.

"I suppose the first question is whether we intend to use them and, if so, who can actually make use of each crystal."

"A good point," Navoi agreed. "That does narrow the field quite considerably. In fact, I believe the only person here whose abilities align with the biology stone is Cordelia."

All eyes turned to Cordelia, waiting expectantly for her response.

"I...suppose that's true," she said hesitantly. "But I'm not sure I'm strong enough to defend such a powerful relic."

"Maybe you won't have to, Dels," Cybele said encouragingly. "I can help you, and Lola too, once she's trained up a bit. Plus, think of all the good you could do with it. That thing is pure biological magic. With any luck, we'll even be able to use it to recreate pearl water for everyone."

Cordelia thought for a moment, visibly weighing the decision. The mention of pearl water seemed to sway her.

"Oh, alright. I'll accept the stone," she said finally. "But if recreating pearl water turns out to be fruitless, then I intend to return it."

"Might I put my hand up for next in line after Cordelia?" Teth interjected. "I might not have compatible magic, but I believe, with some effort, I could integrate the stone into Telesto to help with plant cultivation."

"Very well. It seems fitting that at least one of the stones go to Telesto, even if it isn't straight away," Navoi said. "Perhaps, if we are to keep three of the stones, then the physical stone should be left in Teth's care. As much as I would like to keep it for myself to expand Muruntau, it would be remiss not to divide up the crystals accordingly."

"Well…" I interjected hesitantly. "If I go to Telesto, then there would be one stone there," I added, drawing a curious stare from Dad and a hopeful one from Teth.

Teth turned her gaze to Dad expectantly, waiting for him to respond. He faltered, suddenly put on the spot with a big decision to make in front of everyone. Sorry Dad.

"I…we haven't discussed what we're doing yet," Dad admitted. "We came here to help out, and I suppose we've done that. I did intend to go back home after all this, but in the end, if Alira wants to stay…then I guess we could stay for a bit longer."

He looked at me expectantly, clearly wanting a decisive answer.

"Yes, I think I do. I want to stay," I said, only deciding for myself in that moment. But I knew it was the truth—I wanted to stay. I understood that meant giving up certain things, but it didn't have to be forever either. Just for now.

Dad nodded, still processing the implications of the decision.

"Alrighty then. Alira will go to Telesto with the mind stone," he said distractedly, his thoughts still turning over what this would mean for him. "Maybe then Brigitte should take the Physical stone," Dad suggested. "She wouldn't be able to use it, of course, but it would be protected, and The City would also have a stone. It would mean that both Brigitte and Navoi would have equal access to the stone's use as well. It's just a suggestion, but if you intend to help rebuild The City together, then it seems like a reasonable choice."

"An equitable arrangement—I agree," Navoi said with a nod.

"These are all temporary, as I'm sure you've all realised. As needs arise, the crystals can serve as valuable tools to help our planet thrive."

With that settled, Navoi added, "I believe Brigitte and Kaiya will depart for The City today, as will the Telesto entourage for Telesto."

Both Teth and Brigitte nodded in agreement.

"Alright then," Navoi continued. "The rest of you are welcome to stay, but I'd advise finding a more permanent housing solution in the city if you intend to remain in Muruntau. Good luck to all of you. Dismissed."

And with that, the team was disbanded, and everyone began returning to their lives.

Well, not everyone was returning to their lives—I was starting a brand new one, and I was super excited about it. Max, on the other hand, looked somewhat conflicted.

"What's wrong?" I asked as we left the gardens and started walking back to the cabin.

"Oh, nothing. I'm glad you're staying, really. It's just…I can't go to Telesto," he replied.

"I mean, sure you can. I can fly you there if that's what you want," I offered.

"No, that's not it," Max said, shaking his head. "I could visit, sure, but I have to stay here with my mother. She's probably already worried about me. I've been gone too long."

"That's okay. I'll come visit all the time. I can teleport here, you know," I reassured him.

"Right, I forgot about that. I should go home, though. Will I see you before you leave?" he asked.

"Hmm, probably not. Teth looks ready to head back home, and I should go with their group," I admitted.

"Okay. I'll see you later then," he said, pausing mid-step, as though debating something. I frowned, confused by his hesitation. At last, he smiled, reaching out to gently grab my jacket by the back and pulling me softly towards him, just enough to make us stop walking.

Then, he leaned in and kissed me.

I blinked back at him, startled by the gesture. He scanned my face, grinning as I blushed.

"See you around," he said with a smile, before jogging off through the gardens and up into the city. My eyes flicked ahead of me. I was glad Dad hadn't seen that.

Clearing my throat, I kept walking, trying not to dwell on the kiss. I was leaving, after all. I had magic to learn and plenty to do. I couldn't afford to be distracted by it now—I had to go. And maybe that's exactly why he'd done it. Just to make me stay.

I sighed audibly, catching Dad's attention as he turned to look at me while opening the door to the cabin.

"What's up, Ali?" he asked.

"Oh, nothing. So, what are you going to do now? I don't suppose you're coming to Telesto?"

He paused, frowning at me before responding, no doubt wondering why my face was so flushed. I could practically feel my ears radiating heat.

"I've thought about it," he admitted. "It's hard to just let you go off like that, but you're on your own path now, and I don't think you really need a chaperone after everything that's happened. I'm definitely coming to visit as soon as I can, but until then, I think I'll help Cybele with Ayuna, and maybe work with Navoi on the city.

I'm not entirely sure yet, but there's so much to do. I doubt I'll find myself bored, that's for sure."

He smiled as he spoke, his expression warm and supportive. This was a brand-new adventure for me. I was officially moving out and going off on my own—on an alien world, no less. Not that it felt alien anymore. This place felt more like home than home ever had, and I couldn't wait to discover what life here would be like without the constant war and fighting.

I quickly gathered all my things, gave Dad a long hug goodbye, and left the cabin to meet with the Telesto entourage.

On the way, my thoughts kept drifting—not just to the new life awaiting me in Telesto, but to Max, and seeing him again. I replayed the memory of his kiss, wondering what it had meant and if it would linger as much for him as it did for me.